THRE

Volume 2:

Sew You Want to be a Hero

by Andrew Seiple

Cover by Amelia Parris

Edited by Beth Lyons

WARNING: Contains Profanity and Violence, and a Creepy Villain who likes Tentacles too much.

ISBN: 0692073205
ISBN-13: 978-0692073209

DEDICATION

With thanks to my online readers. Your feedback was invaluable!

CONTENTS

*****	Prologue	1
Chapter 1	Getting Your Bearings	5
Chapter 2	Raccoon Rumpus Time	23
Chapter 3	A Paw Full of Undead	44
Chapter 4	For a Few Undead More	58
Chapter 5	The Bear, the Vamp, and the Catlady	73
Cecelia's Quest 1	A Hard Day's Knight	92
Chapter 6	Born Again	105
Chapter 7	Career Planning	123
Chapter 8	Ogre Battle	138
Cecelia's Quest 2	Bad Comfort	150
Chapter 9	Mediocre Old Ones	165
Chapter 10	The Shadow Under Outsmouth	178
Chapter 11	Unsafe Sects	191
Cecelia's Quest 3	First Engagement	207
Cecelia's Quest 4	The Fall of Outsmouth	217
Cecelia's Quest 5	Winning Hearts and Minds	233
Chapter 12	The Daemon's Deadly Dance	245
Chapter 13	And Yet She Persisted	253
Daemon's Quest	The Woman She Needs to be	261
King's Quest	Torment	265
*****	Epilogue	269

ACKNOWLEDGEMENTS

With thanks to Neven Iliev, for writing an inspiring story, and demonstrating how gamelit could enhance a work, rather than distract from it.

PROLOGUE

Once upon a time, there was a teddy bear.

He befriended a little girl, and went on adventures with her. She was his whole world, and he felt safe and loved in her arms.

Then one day her father came and took her away from all childish things, and the little bear was left behind.

But he was no ordinary teddy bear. He was powered and strengthened by magic, and the many adventures he'd had with the little girl and her friends. It took years, but he got free of the trap that held him.

He pulled himself together, and made a voice from strings and things, and then he spoke the word **"Status."**

And this is what he saw.

Name: Threadbare

Age: 5

Jobs:

Greater Toy Golem Level 9

Bear Level 8

Ruler Level 4

Scout Level 3

Tailor Level 8

Model Level 2

Necromancer Level 1

Duelist Level 1

Animator Level 1

Enchanter Level 1

Golemist Level 1

Smith Level 1

Attributes

Strength: 79	Constitution: 83	
Intelligence: 58	Wisdom: 89	
Dexterity: 41	Agility: 51	
Charisma: 56	Willpower: 47	
Perception: 57	Luck: 53	

Pools

Hit Points: 216(236)
Sanity: 147(167)
Stamina: 102(122)
Moxie: 103(123)
Fortune: 110(130)

Defenses

Armor: 34
Mental Fortitude: 24
Endurance: 44
Cool: 20
Fate: 9

Generic Skills

Brawling - Level 20 (21)
Climb - Level 6
Clubs and Maces - Level 9
Dagger - Level 9
Dodge - Level 2
Fishing - Level 1
Ride - Level 7
Stealth - Level 3
Swim - Level 2

Greater Toy Golem Skills

Adorable - Level 15
Gift of Sapience - Level NA
Golem Body - Level 20
Innocent Embrace - Level 8
Magic Resistance -Level 4

Bear Skills

Animalistic Interface - NA
Claw Swipes - 16
Forage - 7
Growl - 1
Hibernate - 37
Scents and Sensibility - 10
Stubborn - 7
Toughness - 12

Ruler Skills

Emboldening Speech - Level 1
Identify Subject - Level 1
Noblesse Oblige - Level 1
Royal Request - Level 1
Simple Decree - Level 1

Scout Skills
Camouflage - Level 1
Firestarter - Level 1
Keen Eye - Level 1
Sturdy Back - Level 5
Wind's Whisper - Level 1

Tailor Skills
Tailoring - Level 36
Clean and Press - Level 1
Adjust Outfit - Level 1

Model Skills
Dietary Restriction - Level 10 (+20 to all pools)
Fascination - Level 2
Flex - Level 1
Self-Esteem - Level 1
Work it Baby - Level 2

Necromancer Skills
Assess Corpse - Level 1
Command the Dead - Level 1
Soulstone - Level 1
Speak With Dead -Level 1
Zombies - Level 1

Duelist Skills
Challenge - Level 1
Dazzling Entrance - Level 1
Fancy Flourish - Level 1
Guard Stance - Level 1
Weapon Specialist - Level 1 (Brawling +1)

Animator Skills
Animus - Level 1
Command Animus - Level 1
Creator's Guardians - Level 1
Eye for Detail - Level 1
Mend - Level 1

Enchanter Skills

Appraise - Level 1
Glowgleam - Level 1
Harden - Level 1
Soften - Level 1
Spellstore - Level 1

Golemist Skills
Command Golem - Level 1
Golem Animus - Level 1
Invite Golem - Level 1
Toy Golem - Level 1

Smith Skills
Refine Ore - Level 1

Equipment

Inventory
Tailoring supplies

Quests
Save Celia

But even though he could talk now, and even though he had many skills, he knew he could not save his little girl alone. And so the little teddy bear went looking for help...

CHAPTER 1: GETTING YOUR BEARINGS

The mountains shivered at the caress of spring. Warm winds blew from the west, peeling away the snow, sending the ice shuddering down the lower parts of the hills, and freeing the trees from their long slumber. Hardy mountain pines stood as solemn vanguards, as leaves and shoots started to stir below them, tasting sunlight, and finding it good.

And below the peaks, on the downslope of a gentle rise, a single teddy bear waddled through the woods, carrying a bundle of tools and cloth in his arms. His name was Threadbare, and he was on a mission.

But after only a few hundred yards, he realized something pretty important;

These woods were really dangerous, and he would probably need his arms free to deal with whatever trouble came.

So Threadbare turned back, and found his way to a pile of timber and rubble. From the outside it didn't look like much... the remnants of a house, fallen to fire, as a few weathered and charred beams attested. The beams poked loose from stones that had once been a foundation. A wrecked shed nearby, half-buried in an avalanche, seemed an exclamation point and lonely witness to what had once been a stately manor.

At least, that's what a bard might say. But the bear wasn't a bard. He was a hell of a lot of other things, but not a bard.

Crouching low, and worming his way through a muddy tunnel that twisted under the foundation, he found himself again in the crawlspace that had been his unwilling home for the last few years. Five years it had been, broken by hibernation, and the torturous act of worming his way from the ruins. Five years it had taken to get free. It was here he'd lost his family, and here he'd sworn to get them back.

But that was a very big thing, and very big things are made up of very small steps. And right now, the first step was to make himself a harness or something to carry his tailoring tools in.

Threadbare needed those tools, needed them badly. He had magical means of healing himself, but magic could run out. The spell he knew to heal himself worked from a resource called sanity, and generally the less you had of it, the worse your focus and judgment got.

So he dug around in the darkness, until he found the part of his creator's apron that remained. And for lack of any better ideas, he sat down and sewed an apron of his own.

It was harder than he thought, and it took a couple of tries, but perseverance paid off.

DEX +1
Your tailoring skill is now level 37!

He watched the words roll past with long familiarity, by now. They came up whenever he did something well enough to improve himself. They did that for everyone.

Slipping on his apron, not quite a twin to his creator's own thanks to the proportionate size of the tools to his body, he put the scissors into the back sheath he'd made for them, and nodded. This would do.

You have equipped an Apprentice Tailor's Apron!

Oh, nice! Maybe he could get more leather, to make a spare?

Then he caught a glimpse of cloth under his creator's apron, sunken in. Old wormtrails led into it, and Threadbare looked away.

His creator was dead, these five years. Threadbare had lost what was essentially his father, even if they'd never spoken a word to each other. Not that the little bear could talk back then.

"But I can talk now," he said, in his small, soft voice, and paused as an idea grabbed his mind and wouldn't let go.

Didn't he have a spell for this?

"Status," he said, and nodded in satisfaction. Why yes, yes he did! **"Speak with Dead,"** he chanted, and the air seemed to shift, shift and dance. Everything seemed to go stark monotone, the light got brighter and the shadows turned solid black. "Caradon? Are you there?" he asked.

Nothing. And he noticed he hadn't skilled up from it. Thinking carefully, it seemed to him that maybe this spell wouldn't get better unless you actually talked to dead people with it.

Strange, that Caradon wasn't here, though. Where else would he be? Maybe he'd passed on to wherever dead spirits go.

"Status," the bear said again, and looked at his sanity. It had cost five to cast speak with dead. He was about to turn and leave, when another thought struck him;

How did he regain sanity?

Previously, he'd regained it by leveling up, he thought. But that took time and a lot of work. From what he'd seen of other people, and by hearing his little girl's friends talk, it came back naturally, faster if you had something to drink. But he didn't need to eat or drink or sleep, so...

This was going to be important. He sat down and looked at his status screen, calling it up again whenever it started to fade away. After a few minutes the lighting returned to normal, as speak with dead faded. And after about ten minutes or so, he watched his sanity recover by a point.

Slow. Very slow, but he wouldn't run himself dry and have no way to recover it. That was good. Presumably moxie and endurance worked the same way. He could test those in the field.

Since it was easy to regain, he decided it was time to do the other thing he'd thought of, on his aborted walk into the woods. Threadbare bent low to the ground, and sniffed carefully around the little hollow in what was left of the basement.

Your Scents and Sensibility Skill is now level 11!

Odors filled his nose. Dankness, rot, his own scent... and an odd one. Sandalwood, he would have called it, if he knew the name for it. He had no way of knowing the proper terms, but he knew he'd recognize it again if he smelled it.

Threadbare had been trapped down here with the only other one of his kind in existence that he knew of. She'd dug them free, and been kidnapped for her troubles. But the things that had taken her weren't highly malicious, as far as he knew, so odds were pretty good she was still alive. Well, as alive as little toy golems were, anyway.

Threadbare thought he knew where he could find her, but it would be much, much easier to do so if he had her scent. And now he thought he did.

He waited hopefully, but no attributes rose. His wisdom was pretty high already, it'd take a few more good common sense ideas to raise it, he supposed.

Just before he was about to go out, his nose caught one more thing... the familiar smell of the laundry soap that Celia and her father, Caradon, used to do the wash with. It was a good smell, and one that reminded him of good times, so he hunted around until he found a few pinches of the spilled soap powder and tucked it into an apron pocket. If he got glum he could wash with it later, and it might make him feel better.

Outside the hole, he got the odor of the things that had taken her. He'd never gotten close enough to smell them before, and they were pretty distinctive. Also pretty rank by human standards. Which was good, because the smell was old, old enough he lost the scent trail a few yards away from the foundation.

Well, that was fine. He had something to check on first before he went trying to mount a rescue mission, anyway.

Threadbare started off into the woods again, checking his sanity one last time... and realizing, with his very good wisdom, that he had an opportunity, here.

If sanity and all the other pools for his abilities came back over time, then he could practice abilities as he walked, simple stuff to get their ranks up. He could activate something low cost, then wait until his pools refilled, then activate them again. It seemed simple and easy enough, and he *did* have a whole lot of stuff that was really far behind, due to his old speech impediments.

WIS +1

Okay, that settled it! That was a good idea, now it was time to put it into practice.

"**Status,**" he said again, and considered his options.

Threadbare had a ton of weird jobs, spread all over the metaphorical chart, mainly due to accepting every job unlock that had come his way. So thankfully, he had an easy time picking out stuff that sounded neat and wouldn't slow him down too much.

The things he settled on were Flex, which was a simple model trick that used stamina; Self-esteem, a similar model trick that used moxie; and Animus, which he well remembered. His little girl had used it quite a lot, back before times got bad, and it was a spell that used sanity. He eyed his fortune pool, but unless he was missing something, he didn't have anything that used fortune. Maybe he'd find something later.

In the meantime, three was pretty good to start with.

So Threadbare took the scissors out of their sheath, put them on the ground, and said "**Animus,**" laying a paw on them.

Golden light blossomed!

Your Animus skill is now level 2!

The scissors twisted on the ground, opening and closing mindlessly.

"Invite Scissors," Threadbare said. Nothing happened.

What was he missing?

Oh, right. "**Form Party,**" he intoned.

You have created a party!

You are now the party leader, and can access the party screen!

"**Invite Scissors,**" Threadbare said.

Scissors_1 has joined your party!

Your Creator's Guardians skill is now level 2!

Threadbare started walking. Now if the skill description was right, he should be able to mentally command the scissors. He called them to follow.

They tried. To their credit, they tried, squirming and clacking across the ground awkwardly. But they didn't have limbs, or anything else good for walking or even crawling.

No wonder Celia used plush toys, Threadbare thought, and bowed his head at the memory. Good times then. Good times gone.

Good times back again someday, if he had any say in the matter! Threadbare scooped up the scissors and sheathed them again. Okay, so they were useless as animi, but they were still good to practice his skill with.

Speaking of practicing...

"Flex," he commanded, and instantly felt confined, like his insides were bigger than his outsides. Threadbare squirmed, trying to get sorted... and unwittingly went into a brawny pose, legs wide, little arms out to each side and popping tiny biceps. *Almost,* he thought, *but not quite,* and twisted at the waist, flexing his back too, feeling the stuffing form into muscles there as well.

Your Flex skill is now level 2!

Wow, that felt weird. But a check of his status screen showed that it had buffed his armor and endurance by one. *Well worth the price of discomfort,* he thought.

That left one thing to try.

"Self-Esteem," he whispered—

—and instantly felt a bit more confident.

Your Self-Esteem skill is now level 2!

Threadbare checked his status again, and smiled to see that it worked much like flex had, only buffing his cool and mental fortitude instead.

He could smile now, he just realized. Having a flexible mouth opened up so many possibilities.

If he'd been a bit less innocent and more worldly, that thought would have probably sent his mind into some rather bawdy places. But he was a golem, and didn't have any particular urges that way anyway, so the connection went unmade. Which was probably for the best, all things considered.

Threadbare waddled off into the woods once more.

With his compatriot, the inestimable Missus Fluffbear missing, the next logical step was to get help. Although chances were slim, his little girl's friends had told her to rendezvous at Oblivion Point when she'd saved her Caradon. Well, her Daddy was dead and a lot of time had passed, but maybe they were still up there? The place had fish to eat, and everything. It was... possible...

Not really likely, but possible.

Threadbare retraced the path he'd taken five years ago, finding it overgrown, barely what Mordecai, his old scout master would call a deer trail. But he was small, and his hide was now thick enough that the underbrush didn't bother him much. He was getting a little muddy, but he knew a trick for that too. Tailors had a skill that let them instantly clean things like wayward teddy bears, and since he was a wayward teddy bear he was happy to have access to it.

Threadbare meandered over the hills, actually scrambling in a few places. Before, Celia had been carrying him. Now he had to manage on his own. But he was much stronger and more competent now, and he managed. The exertion cost him a couple of stamina, and gained him two levels of the climb skill, along with three agility boosts. And along the way he cast his spell and used his buffs whenever his stamina, moxie, and sanity got back to full. The skills slowly rose, as did his intelligence by a point, after one successful casting of animus.

Finally, he stopped to pause at the jutting boulder high up on the second cliffside, which overlooked the route he'd taken. He didn't need to rest, not really, but Celia and Mordecai and he had rested here the first time, and he liked the view.

It was night now, but the moon was out, and he could see relatively fine. He debated using his glow gleam spell, but... well, common sense said that was a bad thing. He was a tough bear, but he was a small bear, and the light would be seen a long way away. Better to run dark for now.

As he settled on the rock, his nose twitched. Scents and Sensibility fired up, and he smelled a strong scent. Some animal had marked this spot. Something big. Something familiar, though he couldn't quite put his finger on how he knew it.

Your Scents and Sensibility skill is now level 12!

It wasn't too old, which made up his mind. He'd been planning to shelter here for the night, but if a large creature had marked this territory, that was a bad idea. Threadbare glanced up at the full moon, and the cold stars above. So long as he stayed to the ridges, he thought, he should be able to see fine.

He'd be better off sticking to the ridges anyway. The big tree was next, and that should be easy enough to spot from high up, and then there was the little hollow where the raccants had lived. If they were still there, he wanted to stay out of that hollow anyway. At least until he'd gotten help.

It took longer to navigate through the darkness. He flexed, self-esteemed, and animated his way across the high hills, taking well into the morning to do it. Little legs didn't go as fast as he had with Celia, but he didn't stop to rest or even feel a lot of fatigue thanks to his golem/bear fueled endurance.

Not long into his walk, he cast animus, and did the invite again, and got the following messages;

Your Animus skill is maxed! Level up your animator job to increase this skill.

Your Creator's Guardians skill is maxed! Level up your animator job to increase this skill.

He checked his status. Those skills were only at level five. Curious, he stopped for his regular dose of flexing and self-esteem.

Your Flex skill is now level 6!

Your Self-esteem skill is now level 6!

Those weren't maxed. Why was that?

No, wait, his model job was higher level than animator. That was it. The higher your job level, the higher your skills could go.

Well, that was fine. If he did more animator stuff, maybe actually used the spells when they mattered, then he'd raise his animator level. From what he could recall of his relatively short life, (the conscious parts of it anyway,) he usually got levels after he survived really lethal situations, or killed enemy monsters. Maybe that was what he needed to do?

He waited hopefully, but neither his intelligence nor his wisdom leveled up. The little bear sighed. It was so hard having high stats in that area, finally. He couldn't just use them as a guide to figure out what to do. But then, he'd gotten a whole lot more reflective ever since his early days, so maybe high wisdom was a blessing there, at least.

Clearly, to be the most efficient at surviving the stuff coming his way, he'd want to have his skills leveled up before he hit trouble. So when he was moving around and not in clear and present danger, he should be practicing something he could gain skills at for every pool that had it.

"Status," he whispered into the night, and took another look to find something else that used sanity.

Well, being a bear (of sorts) had worked out great for him so far, hadn't it? He didn't think he would have survived if he didn't have the bear job. So he decided to fire up Scents and Sensibility, and see how that went.

"Scents and Sensibility," he whispered. And again the world of advanced odors opened up to him. But he didn't level the skill.

Threadbare walked, peering into the night, freezing every time he heard noise that seemed like it was approaching, keeping an eye out. He needn't have worried. Though he didn't know it, the area he was in was prime hunting grounds for Screaming Eagles, which had gotten more numerous since their main predator moved out of the region. Since Screaming Eagles were daytime hunters, the night actually saved him a ton of trouble. (As did the fact he actually had an average luck score, rather than the sucking mess of horrible karma that had been following him around for his early days.)

He did level stealth up twice, and once he came upon something that fled from him, that he never got a good look at. When he went to investigate where it had been, he smelled deer.

Your Scents and Sensibility skill is now level 13!

Okay, that made sense. Just casting it wasn't enough to level it, you had to smell stuff with it to increase the skill.

He found the big tree, peering at through the moonlight, remembering the branches. Remembering the honey he'd dug out of the hive there, and been unable to eat.

The little bear considered. He had a mouth now... and he also had dietary restrictions, and no idea if honey was unhealthy or not. If it was, it'd blow his dietary restriction skill away.

Man, being a model was tough.

He got his bearings, checked his course, climbed a tree for good measure so he could sight the course he wanted to follow...

AGL +1

Your Climb skill is now level 9!

...and found the peak he needed. Not far from what looked like a mass of campfires.

Threadbare would have blinked if he could have. There were people out here?

He got closer, keeping his Scents and Sensibility up, keeping to the thicker parts of cover. It took an hour, but his stealth crawled up two more points as groups of chattering things crashed through the underbrush ignoring him, and his Scents and Sensibility picked up a familiar smell.

These had to be raccants.

Your Scents and Sensibility skill is now level 14!

He didn't know why they had campfires now. But it looked like there were a lot more of them than the last time he'd been here.

Threadbare got just close enough to see the sharp fence of pointy sticks they'd made around the area in front of the old mine entrance, and the collection of patchwork tents around several fires, then he slunk back into the shadows, heading for high ground once more. There were at least a dozen raccants out, masked in wood and carrying clubs. Nothing he wanted to face right now.

He took it slow, gained another stealth level when a patrol nearly caught him, and managed to get out of their patrol radius without being detected.

You are now a level 4 Scout!

AGL+3

PER+3

WIS+3

Awesome! Come to think of it, scout skills like keen eye and camouflage would have probably been really helpful in that situation. He resolved to try them next time.

Finally, he came to the mountain cliff that led up to Oblivion Point. No Celia to help him this time, and it was pretty steep... "**Status**," he declared. Maybe there was something to help with this.

No, not really. Nothing that buffed climb or agility. But flexing would help endurance, which would keep him from getting tired. He flexed, and for the first time in a while, he didn't level it. It stayed at nine.

He decided that he had enough stamina to experiment, flexed again, and there it went.

Your Flex skill is now level 10!

Maybe the higher up you got in a skill, the more usages it took to level it?

INT +1

Yeah, that was it! It made sense, he supposed. Otherwise it'd be trivial to hole up somewhere and exercise your skills repeatedly until they maxed out. That sounded thoroughly boring, and he had stuff to do anyway, so it was kind of a relief to know he didn't have to do that. And you couldn't, anyway, not for all of them because things like Scents and Sensibility and Speak with Dead required stuff around to practice with.

Threadbare thought he might be getting the hang of how things worked. All it had taken was the loss of everyone and everything he ever held dear, forcing him into isolation in the wilderness, surrounded by hostile and uncaring monsters, and—

—the little toy sat down with a bump, as events caught up to him. The flex buff faded and expired, as he put his head in his paws and just sat there for a time. The stuffing behind his eyes hurt, and he knew that if he could have, he would have been crying. But he couldn't. Button eyes didn't cry. Instead he opened his mouth and sobbed, little rasping gasps.

He really, really missed Celia.

He wanted to go home.

But he had neither Celia nor home anymore, and after a while after the pressure left he stopped sobbing and stood back up. He flexed again, restored his self-esteem, which made him feel a bit better, and started climbing up the cliff.

AGL +1
Your Climb skill is now level 10!
Your Climb skill is now level 11!
Your Climb skill is now level 12!
Occasionally he'd slide down, or lose his grip and tumble downslope a bit, but he was very strong now compared to his size, so stopping his fall wasn't a big deal. He just caught ahold of the ground and pushed, until he slowed, and then it was back to climbing.

But during the climb, Threabare completely forgot about his buffs. Which was a pity, because otherwise his nose would have told him that he was going straight into the lair of the region's biggest predator.

The sky brightened as he reached the top, moon sunk below the mountains. Dawn soon, he knew. The bear hauled himself up over the cliff, got to the little plateau, and there was the curtain of blackness, dividing the mountain peak in half. There was the little pond... no so little now, swelled with the first of the season's snowmelt, and roiling with silvery fish. And there was the stand of pine trees, where Celia had sheltered and they'd built a small fire.

But no sign of either of the half-orc brothers. If they'd ever made it here, they were long gone.

Threadbare's heart sank, and the terrible despair that had struck him down at the bottom of the cliff came rushing back. He staggered to the trees, calling out as he went, "Jarrik? Garon? Bak'shaz?"

But his little voice fell into silence. The snow crunched underfoot, warm and... yellow?

Yes, there was a patch of yellow snow. Someone had peed here!
"Scents and Sensibility!"
Predator stink filled his nose, the same predator that had marked the rock. Big and deadly, and familiar, and...

Oh. Oh!

For the first time since he'd arrived, hope, that fragile thing with wings soared in his chest. He looked at the sky.

It had been so long. Would he remember Threadbare?

The little bear got to work, brushing snow away until he found the old firepit. Damp wood, pine wood went into a pile, and the little bear pointed at it.
"Firestarter."
Your Firestarter skill is now level 2!
A tiny spark leaped out, and the wood smoldered, but nothing happened.

No! He would NOT be denied!
"Firestarter! Firestarter! Firestarter!"

That did it. Around skill level four, the wood caught. Threadbare kept a few pointy pieces of wood aside. Then he glanced over at the pond, shucked off his apron, and stomped toward it with bearly determination. **"Forage,"** he said, leveling the skill up, and wading into the school of newly-born salmon.

Twenty minutes and one dexterity boost later, the sky was light, so light, and he knew the sun was just behind the eastern mountains. He eyed his eight fish, and decided they'd have to do. He tossed them over by the fire, and stuck them on the skewers, then put them over the flames. It took some fiddling, but soon he had them cooking.

You have unlocked the cook job!
Would you like to be a cook at this time? y/n?

No, that was pretty silly, he decided. The words went away, and he breathed a sigh of relief. What use was cooking to something that didn't eat?

Besides, he wasn't trying to cook them. He was just trying to get the smell into the air.

"Clean and Press," he decided, tapping his noggin. And instantly the fish blood and guts and grime and mud and dirt from traveling whisked away from him. He put on his apron again, buckled it, turned around—

—and there it was, looming over him in the predawn light. Twice as tall as he was, black as pitch, with suspicious yellow eyes fixated on Threadbare. A pair of high, pointed ears poked out from its skull.

Though Threadbare had no word for it, humans would call this beast a bobcat.

And while every instinct shouted at the bobcat to chase the little creature away from its good-smelling dinner, to assert dominance and steal its food, the big feline hesitated.

Because something about this little thing seemed familiar.

It leaned in, animalistic instincts activating its own Scents and Sensibility, and it sniffed the teddy bear. It sniffed him carefully...

...until it came to the apron pocket that Threadbare had tucked soap powder into.

And its eyes opened wide, as a rumbling purr burst from its chest!

He had not ALWAYS been a bobcat, after all, and he too had lost his home, his home that smelled of soap powder and hoomins and polished wood and comfortable napping spots in the sun and warm places in winter and that little toy bear—

It WAS the little toy bear!

"Pulsivar," said Threadbare, hugging the big cat, and then Pulsivar was purring and licking the little bear over and over again, and rolling around on the ground and purring and getting up and running in circles in pure joy.

CHA +1

LUCK +1

Well, Pulsivar celebrated for a little while, anyway. As much time as he could give the matter. Those fish smelled delicious and you had to have priorities, after all.

Threadbare watched happily as Pulsivar gobbled up the catch, even helping remove them from the skewers so the black bobcat could properly enjoy breakfast. Afterwards it simply flopped down next to the fire, half-on top of Threadbare, grooming him for all he was worth.

By befriending a wild beast you have unlocked the Tamer job!

You cannot become a Tamer at this time. Seek out your guild to change jobs.

The words faded as Threadbare laughed for the first time, tiny little giggles completely lost against the massive feline's purr. It didn't matter. Not one bit, because though everything wasn't right with the world, this, right now, made everything a bit better.

And though there was a lot to do, though so much bad had happened and he still needed to go and save everyone else he could, Threadbare sighed and relaxed against the warm, purring lump of fur and muscle that was his first foe, and first ally, and just enjoyed being cuddled again.

For now, this was enough.

And it was enough for Pulsivar, too.

Threadbare wanted to stay that way forever, but as the hours rolled by, his mind turned toward the next person he had to find.

A certain small bear...

*****

Raccants had a number of advantages over their base species. Raccoons were mostly nocturnal, and avoided doing anything in the day if they could help it. But raccants were a bit more flexible, and had more energy on the whole, thanks to a good endurance bump from their upgraded job. They could operate in the day or night or both, so long as they got some sleep at SOME point.

Which was a good thing, since the creature they knew as the Black Death mostly came out at night. Mostly. Over the last year, as it had started preying upon them, the fuzzy ring-tailed garbage hoarders had been forced to make a somewhat-fortified camp outside of their lair. To any passing human it would have looked like a teeny, half-hearted, randomly-built fence around a few kids tents. To the raccants it was their castle, their bastion to defend to the last, a masterpiece and triumph of engineering that would make any humans who saw it fall in love with it and adopt them all out of respect for their ingenuity!

Not that there were many humans around anymore. At all. Which sucked, and made for some hard winters. And a lot less interesting trash. They'd been forced to forage further and further afield because of that, with mixed results.

But the simple truth of the matter was that between the fortifications, the fires, and the noisy patrols they sent out at night to walk around the perimeter, the Black Death had only picked off a few of them over the winter. So it was working, and they were proud of it.

Which was why it was a bit of a shock when a small brown teddy bear fell from an overhanging tree branch, straight into the middle of camp, into the smoldering coals of the campfire. Hurriedly he got up and patted the embers away from him.

It was a good thing he had an apron. The sturdy little garment kept coals from his soft belly, otherwise he might have caught on fire right then and there.

A few of the raccants appreciated the craftsmanship, even as they reached for weapons.

Your Work It Baby skill is now level 3!

Threadbare tried a smile. He had been trying to get to the pole of the nearest tent to slide down it, but the end result was the same. This whole effort was because he wanted to try talking to the funny creatures, first. They were only about two or three times his size, and perhaps he could sort out things without a misunderstanding.

"Hello," he said, in his soft, quiet voice. With an air cavity about the size of a pair of grapes to work with, it was barely audible, even to the relatively good hearing of the raccants. "I'm looking for Missus Fluffbear. She's like me but black, and this big." He put his hand at about his waist. Or where his waist would be if he had one.

This was kind of exciting, he'd never been able to talk things out before! The raccants gathered around him, poking at him curiously with clubs. He pushed one away before it could rap him on the ear. "Please can you give her back?"

The largest of the raccants, one with a pair of stars made out of wet and dirty wood on his shoulders, tied there by uneven strings, swaggered up to him and chattered something that Threadbare completely failed to understand.

"I'm sorry. I don't speak that."

The raccant leaned over, grabbed his apron, and examined it. His wooden mask, which looked like a fat-cheeked blunt-nosed fuzzy thing, read "HMSTR," and it was very close to Threadbare's face.

"Yes, that is my apron."

The raccant plucked the scissors out of their sheath, and started picking out the other tools and items, handing them back to his subordinates. Threadbare, with a strength that surprised the big raccant, yanked his apron back and smoothed it.

"No," the little bear said.

Instantly the raccants closed ranks, pointing with sharp sticks and brandishing clubs. Threadbare shook his head.

Well, he'd tried.

The big raccant brought his club bashing down on the tiny bear—

—and blinked behind his mask as a crimson '1' rolled up from Threadbare's noggin.

Threadbare hauled back and punched the raccant in the mask, sending him staggering back, as a red '18' rose into the air.

Your Brawling skill is now level 21!
Your Weapon Specialization skill is now level 2!

And then the rest of the raccants, thoroughly spooked by the little creature, and aggravated at the intrusion, piled in on the teddy bear.

They might as well have been attacking a wall. Threadbare had flexed before he went up the tree, and between the buff and his thickened hide and stuffing, their clubs and spears did little. Still, there were many of them, and they had decent hit points, so his own counterattacks weren't thinning the numbers by much. And every now and then, one of them would get lucky and crit, and sneak anywhere from five to fifteen points of damage through.

Finally Threadbare accepted that he was going to have to play for keeps… especially when he saw a black from materialize out of nowhere, leaping over the fence and moving up to the back of the group he was fighting. These raccants were dead, Threadbare knew. He might as well get some practice in before they went down.

And the next time he got a chance to fight back, he went for a swipe instead of a punch.

The raccant fell back, staring at its slashed arm, and the '26' oozing out of it. The bear had claws!

Your Claw Swipes skill is now level 17!
Your Weapon Specialization skill is now level 3!
Your Weapon Specialization skill is now level 4!
Your Weapon Specialization skill is now level 5!
Your Brawling skill is now level 22!
Critical Hit!

DEX +1
LUCK +1
The claw swipes helped, but it was still a slog. But as Threadbare struggled, Pulsivar went to work. The big cat took down three of them one by one, swift, silent pounces that ended in blood and corpses. Finally, the remaining raccants noticed, and the second they did, they panicked!

The Black Death was upon them!

This was far too much. Raccants didn't have much in the way of moxie to begin with, and caught between a bear and a dark face, they broke like twigs and ran in all directions, scrambling over, around, or in some cases THROUGH their shoddily-prepared fence.

Threadbare nodded. Pulsivar, however, wasn't done. He started to bound off after one fleeing varmint, paused as another one stumbled, and fell behind—

"No," said Threadbare, walking up to him and putting his paws on the big black bobcat's chest.

CHA +1
Pulsivar paused, eyes narrowed, then sat down nonchalantly, and gave his fur a few good licks. Proper grooming was important before a meal. And during a meal. And sometimes after.

Threadbare smiled in relief, and petted Pulsivar. And smiled even wider, when his experience from the fight and comforting his friend rolled a long-awaited pair of jobs into their next level.

You are now a level 10 Toy Golem!
All Attributes +2!
You have learned the Bodyguard skill!
Your Bodyguard skill is now level 1!
You are now a level 3 Model!
AGL+3
CHA+3
PER+3
Checking Dietary Restrictions time counter...
Your Dietary Restrictions skill is now level 15!
Buff adjusted accordingly!

Threadbare watched the words flash by, then breathed a sigh of relief. As interesting and invigorating as all that had been, he couldn't pause now. He was in unknown territory, and the best scout he'd ever met had taught him that you don't waste time in unknown territory. He needed to repair, regroup, and renew his search for his missing friend. **"Mend,"** he whispered.

You have mended Threadbare!

You have been healed for 5 points!
Your Mend skill is now level 2!

Wow, that was pretty pathetic. He tried it a few more times, skilling up to level 5 and getting an int boost before he was fully repaired. He'd caught a few of critical hits back there. Small crits, but crits nonetheless. At least the amount he mended himself by varied, and it even broke double digits a few times.

At the end of his healing, he got another notice;

You are now a level 2 animator!
DEX+3
INT+3
WILL+3

He shook his head. Why was he leveling so much? Compared to the things he'd been through, that had barely been trouble.

But then Threadbare stopped and thought about it. There had been a good dozen raccants in the camp, and they'd all jumped him at once, fighting well together despite their relative weakness. He hadn't dropped any of them, really, Pulsivar had done most of the work toward the end of the fight. Yeah, if that had gone on a few more minutes they would have battered him down, or put him in a bad spot. Threadbare had some stuff that he could try if things got desperate, but... well, he had no idea how most of it would work.

As far as leveling up went, he thought that what was happening was that he was getting experience in the jobs that he used to get through each particular fight or tough spot. Golem, now, that was understandable. It had been a long time since he leveled golem, and since he'd done that he'd been hurt the worst he'd ever been, and only survived years by dint of being what he was. Model? Well, his apron had made a positive first impression and he'd been talking a lot at them. So social skills helped level him there. And he had flex and self-esteem going, though it was hard to tell if those counted as well. Duelist had probably gotten a little bit. And bear as well, though that hadn't leveled. Animator made sense because he was doing some actual healing with actual consequences using the animator skill, mend. And it was low level so a few spells and the animating practice he'd done to date were enough to bring the overall job to level two.

And here he was woolgathering again! In an unsafe location, too. He turned to Pulsivar, ready to get him rolling—

—only to find the cat messily devouring the choice bits of one of the raccant corpses.

Oh. Well, uh, they'd be here a little while then.

So instead Threadbare gathered up the trampled and muddy supplies that the raccants had taken from him, used Clean and Press on them, (skilling up twice,) and put them back in his pockets. The scissors were last, and they didn't need cleaning, thankfully.

Then he paused and looked around.

The raccants that had fled into the woods were long gone. Whether they'd be back or not, he couldn't say. But the mine entrance loomed, and that was where they'd have Missus Fluffbear, if indeed they had her at all.

Threadbare was pretty good at taking hits, but unless Pulsivar's new form had gotten a lot sturdier, then the big cat wasn't. And in that mine, in tight quarters, the big cat would have a harder time using his mobility and sneakiness.

"Party Screen," Threadbare whispered again, checking out the cat's hit points. Still One hundred and forty-five. He was level twenty one, and he had only a little better than half Threadbare's hit points. Given how nasty things could get, the little bear didn't want to risk his friend's death.

They needed something to stack the odds.

Well, he was a necromancer, wasn't he? And there were corpses a-plenty around, with probably some spirits he'd just made? That was how it worked, right?

So Threadbare reached out and poked one of the dead raccants. **"Zombies,"** the little bear whispered.

Your Zombies skill is now level 2!

The corpse got up, groaning—

—and died as Pulsivar pounced it, ripping it open.

"Um," Threadbare said. "No, it is okay, see? **Zombies.**"

Your Zombies skill is now level 3!

Another corpse risen, and another corpse put down as the cat bit it and shook until things snapped.

Okay. That wouldn't work. Pulsivar didn't understand the whole undead thing. Come to think of it, neither did Threadbare, not completely. Maybe he'd practice it later, when the cat was out hunting or something. Though Pulsivar showed no inclination to leave Threadbare's side, not since the morning. Finally the bear had just invited him to his party, and to his surprise, had instantly been joined. Threadbare wasn't sure how, since he was pretty sure the big cat couldn't read.

(He had no way of knowing that Pulsivar had found the secret to make the annoying words go away years ago, just like Threadbare had.)

The cat, proud of itself for taking care of the renewed threat, which had obviously just been a couple of the stupid prey playing dead, groomed himself smugly.

Stuck, Threadbare looked around the campsite. Fortunately, he found something suitable in short order. The head raccant in charge of the camp had his own throne in one of the tents. In actuality, most humans would have taken a look and recognized that it was a salvaged high chair, for babies to eat from.

But it had legs, and it was wood, and by golly it would do.

"**Animus,**" Threadbare breathed as he touched it. "**Invite Chair.**"

Your Animus skill is now level 6!

Your Creator's Guardians skill is now level 6!

Oddly enough, the tug from the casting was a little more draining than usual. Threadbare checked his status screen, and sure enough, he was down fifteen points instead of ten. Maybe because the high chair was big, bigger than him and made of wood?

Then, on his status screen, he saw his new bodyguard skill, and opened up its help prompt.

Oh, perfect!

BODYGUARD

Level: 10 Cost: 25 Sta Duration: 1 minute per toy golem level

Name a target party member when activating this skill. For the duration, you have a chance of intercepting each attack aimed at them, so long as you remain within two yards of them. Multiple attackers or overwhelming amounts of strikes may reduce the effectiveness of this defense.

Feeling a lot better, Threadbare marched out of the tent. The chair followed, creaking and rocking as its legs stumped along. He was a little worried as they approached Pulsivar and the cat glanced up…

…then went back to grooming. He'd been an animator's pet, after all, and would have been a familiar if Caradon hadn't stopped leveling the Wizard job years ago. Chairs could move, so what? That was just a thing that happened.

"**Bodyguard Pulsivar,**" Threadbare said, and toddled toward the cave, his high chair following behind.

Your Bodyguard skill is now level 2!

After a few minutes, Pulsivar followed. That little bear was being stupid again. Looks like it was up to the only adult around here to take charge of things.

Five steps into the mine, The darkness rose around them. Threadbare moved on cautiously, ready to cast a spell—

—and everything shifted.

CHAPTER 2: RACCOON RUMPUS TIME

Abruptly they were in a curving stone cave well lit with candles, and stolen lanterns. There was music playing from somewhere down the bend. Odd and thumping, it bore no resemblance to anything Threadbare had ever heard before. But then, he barely knew of music. Just a few songs that Celia would sing now and again… but thinking of that made his chest hurt, and he pushed it away because he had bigger concerns.

"We're in a dungeon," Threadbare told Pulsivar.

Pulsivar's eyes flicked back and forth, as his tail lashed. Everything had suddenly changed, and he didn't like that much. He liked the music even less, and a low growl rumbled out of his throat. Not a sanity-damaging one, thankfully.

"I know," Threadbare tried to tell him, but his little voice was lost in the music.

Okay, that was a problem. He'd experiment later, and try to fix that. But for now? He'd try to find his lost companion. So he set off again, and grudgingly, Pulsivar followed.

They came to the first cross corridor. Threadbare turned the corner—

—and was promptly jumped by a jumbled mass of junk and garbage.

The thing smacked him with a tendril made of rope and old tools, clocking him for '5' and knocking him against the wall. Surprised, he lashed back—

—and then Pulsivar leaped on it.

It was made of pretty sturdy stuff, and still had some fight in it after that, but Threadbare helped tear it to bits while the high chair slowly kicked it, sending up '1's and '2's with its piddly attacks.

The little bear thought that maybe there was something hiding under

23

the junk, but no, nothing was under there. The mob of trash had moved on its own and just slunk up and whacked him a good one.

Threadbare did find a few coins. A bunch of brown grungy ones and a couple of silvers. Garon had used those, Threadbare remembered. Maybe he could give them to Garon if he ever found the half-orc again? He tucked them into his apron pockets.

Two more trash mobs, a handful of coins, and a surprised raccant guard later, the tunnels opened up. Threadbare gazed upon a large cave, with multiple seats and benches made from stalagmites, free-standing and in rows. Ropes and chains of lanterns hung from the ceiling, flashing with odd colors, and at least three dozen raccants sat on them or jumped up and down, dancing to the music.

Garbage piled high around the cavern shook to the beat, piles of trash and even cans of the stuff shaking as the beat thumped on. Occasionally a can would boil over, and a new trash mob would rattle out, then head toward one of the corridors leading out of the cavern.

And up on stage, was a Raccant wearing a pair of baggy black pants, a gold chain, and some odd contraption over his eyes that Threadbare had never seen before. Though for once that wasn't due to his ignorance. After all, very few people in Cylvania would have recognized a pair of sunglasses.

That Raccant was dancing his heart out up there, jerking spasmodically...

...up until the point he stopped, and the music stopped with him.

The strange figure pointed at Threadbare.

As one, the audience turned to behold the tiny teddy, and as one they rose, irate that their song had been disrupted. Wooden masks in the shape of every domestic animal glared at Threadbare, who looked to Pulsivar for reassurance—

—and found the cat gone.

Well. Shoot.

The trash mobs, at least, left him alone. The raccant mob didn't.

At first, it wasn't so bad. His buffed armor was good enough to reduce most of the damage to minimal amounts, and the high chair, though not as sturdy, rocked back and forth and gave as good as it got. But just as Threadbare thought he was getting ahead, the figure up on stage started dancing again, and the music jumped with him.

It was a heartening song, a song that fired the blood and strengthened the arm...

...and it wasn't helping Threadbare one bit.

His enemies, on the other hand, drew strength from it! Their attacks turned from '0's and '1's to '3's and '4's, and to his horror, the little bear saw his high chair minion take a solid hit and collapse.

But maybe it was still salvageable? He lunged for it, opening his mouth to cast as he did. **"Animus—"**

—and his hand collided with a raccant's mask.

Your Animus skill is now level 7!

The mask shivered and twisted, sliding so the eyeholes moved away from its wearers eyes, and the raccant backed off, clawing at it frantically. He stumbled back into two more of the mob, who left off attacking and shoved him away, trying to stay out of reach as he panicked and lashed out.

Huh!

Well, why not?

Three more points of the animus skill, a point of dexterity, and six more castings later, Threadbare was down a fair amount of sanity, but half the mob was in disarray, and the other half was trying to stop them from trampling each other.

And finally Pulsivar made an entrance, slinking in from the side and starting to pick off the stragglers. One by one they fell, and Threadbare smiled as he popped his own claws. He'd found a weakness, now to capitalize on it!

Your Claw Swipes skill is now level 18!

DEX +1

Finally it was done, and they stood among the piles of dead concertgoers. Not one had fled, but this was a dungeon, so Threadbare didn't find it odd. Monsters worked this way, in dungeons.

The figure on stage was not happy, not in the slightest. The angry raccant chattered, and the music switched again, a high set of pipes joining a beat that started and stopped, started and stopped.

Threadbare didn't like it one bit. He darted over to Pulsivar. **"Bodyguard!"**

Your Bodyguard skill is now level 3!

Then he remembered his own plight, and the torn bits that were even now leaking stuffing. Not much, but enough to crimp his style. **"Mend! Mend! Mend!"**

He ignored the skill up messages from it, and ran to the high chair, slapping it with one paw. **"Mend! Animus!"**

But no sooner had it risen again, then everything stopped.

Then in a flash, the raccant was there, bashing the high chair to bits with a heavy hammer that he'd pulled out of literally nowhere.

He'd stopped because it was hammer time, and broken it down, just like that.

Threadbare popped claws and laid into him— or tried to, anyway.

The bard could dodge like nobody's business, thanks to his Raccant Touch This skill.

And for the first time in this fight, Threadbare started to worry.

Your Toughness skill is now level 13!

+2 Max HP

That hammer hit hard. Pulsivar came arrowing in on the side, got in a good swipe, but the bard was made of sturdier stuff, and he returned the favor—

—as Threadbare suddenly found himself pulled a few feet over, just in time to take the hammer hit instead of Pulsivar.

Your Bodyguard skill is now level 4!

Your Toughness skill is now level 14!

+2 Max HP

The fight went on for a bit, and Threadbare switched from trying to shred the guy to just trying to survive, letting Pulsivar do the real work. Fortunately that was a good strategy, and in the end, after three dodge skill ups and two more bodyguard skill ups later, the raccant fell, glasses shattering. Threadbare sagged into Pulsivar, hugging his wounds away with what remained of his sanity.

You have healed Pulsivar for 80 points!

Your Innocent Embrace skill is now level 9!

He was gambling here…

…a gamble that paid off, as the words appeared again, and he felt his reserves refill.

You are now a level 9 Bear!

CON+5

STR+5

WIS+5

Armor+3

Endurance+3

Mental Fortitude+3

You are now a level 3 Animator!

DEX+3

INT+3

WILL+3

Whew. Okay.

Digging through the remnants of the raccant, he found that somehow the creature's hammer had disappeared, but the gold chain and the baggy pants remained. The black pants almost sparkled, some kind of glitter worked into the material. They were too big for him—

—but he had a trick for that, now didn't he?

"Adjust Outfit."
Your Adjust Outfit skill is now level 2!
He took a sniff of them.
Wooooo, nope.
Your Scents and Sensibility skill is now level 15!
"Clean and Press!"
Your Clean and Press skill is now level 4!
They fit nicely, adjusted by magic to teddy bear size. Oddly enough, they only had one pocket in them, and it was really deep. Bigger on the inside than it should be, judging from the outside. But when he tried to put some of his coins in there, the pocket sealed up. It unsealed when he moved his paw away. Weird, he'd mess with that later.

Draping the gold chain around his neck, he picked the largest tunnel that didn't look like it went back the way they'd come, threw another couple of mends on himself, and stomped forward. Pulsivar followed, relieved that the noisy music was now gone.

Six more trash mobs, and a small group of raccants later, Threadbare's nose twitched at a T-junction in the cave. He took a sniff... and smelled sandalwood.

Missus Fluffbear! He hurried to the right, completely ignoring the sign on the wall.

BEWAR THE BEARSERKER

In his haste, Threadbare missed the tripwire. His little legs hit it, and his disproportionate strength snapped it like thread.

WHAM!

The floor under him fell away as the trapdoor opened, and the bear plummeted.

Pulsivar, just as surprised as Threadbare, stared, then readied to jump... and gave a frustrated howl, as the trapdoor slammed shut in the big cat's face.

Smooth, greased rock slid by under Threadbare's pants, which flapped in the wind of his passing. He flailed for a grip, found nothing, and spilled to the ground as the slide leveled out and opened up into a wide space.

More stalagmite benches surrounded the edges of the cavern, with chicken wire between the cheering raccants occupying them and the pit below. The pit Threadbare was now lying in. He stood up, brushing himself off, and looking around. The slide behind him sealed as soon as he looked at it, a stone door slamming shut as its counterweight tripped. He walked over and poked the stone door desperately, fearing for

Pulsivar.

Your Adorable skill is now level 16!

Your Work it Baby skill is now level 4!

Then a ratcheting metal noise came from behind, and Threadbare turned, slowly. The scent of sandalwood filled his nose, and for a minute his heart leaped…

…until he saw what was emerging from the darkness under the rising portcullis.

Four times his size, with pitch black fur, and bright-red button eyes, the plush toy was a walking behemoth. It bore a full-sized lumberjack's axe in both paws, and the weight of it strained the teddy bear's seams, revealing wisps of stuffing spilling out from stretched thread.

And worst of all, he recognized it.

"Fiyt! Fiyt! Fiyt!" Chanted the raccants above, and the giant-sized Missus Fluffbear roared, headbutted the wall next to her three or four times, sending up red '20s', then turned to glare at him.

Threadbare looked upon the twisted form of the one he'd come to save, and despaired.

But only for about a second, and no more. There was murder in his enraged comrade's button eyes, and he needed to do something about that. **"Command Golem! Stop and stand down."**

It was the first time he'd ever used that skill, but he was pretty sure the letters that followed made no sense at all.

Invalid target!

What? Why?

Then she was charging, and her axe caught him with a sideswing, knocking him off the rounded side of the pit, to tumble several yards away in the arena. He shook his head as a red '21' rolled up from his wound. Suddenly all that time leveling flex seemed time well spent.

"Command Golem! Missus Fluffbear stop!"

Invalid target!

Okay, something was going on here. But the enraged black teddy bear was charging for him again. Threadbare dove to the side…. But got clipped anyway, as she kicked him, this time with claws roughly about four times the size of his own.

Twelve hit points and a short trip later, Threadbare stood back up again. He needed time to think this over and she wasn't going to give it to him. But fortunately he was much, much stronger for his size, and much, much more nimble than he had any right to be. Not gymnast class, not anywhere near that yet, but far more than most. He ran and jumped, catching the bottom of the chicken wire lining and boosted himself up, out of her reach.

Your Climb skill is now level 13!

Instantly the crowd started booing him, and throwing nuts, bits of moldy bread, and the other snacks they'd been eating. Threadbare ignored them and looked down at the growling, murderous creature swiping the air underneath him with heavy, sweeping strokes. She didn't look like she was in a mood to talk, so that was out. Was there another way to sort this out?

He had a lot of stuff that he could apply, here, but did he have anything useful?

"Status."

Why yes, yes he did. At the very least, it couldn't hurt anything.

"Eye for Detail."

Your Eye for Detail skill is now level 2!

And as her status opened up, he twitched in surprise.

He hadn't been able to check her back in the ruins of his home, not while they spent all that time in that darkened basement, but he was pretty sure that what he was seeing didn't match what she should have. According to this, her name was "The Bearserker," her race was Construct, and her job was Optional Midboss. She was a fifth level midboss. No toy golem or bear jobs to be seen, and that just wasn't right.

Aside from that, her stats were surprisingly anemic. Everything was in strength and hit points. She hit hard, for her level, and had an okay Axes and Choppas skill, but her defenses were shabby. Not much sanity. Not much moxie or fortune. Decent endurance and about four hundred hit points, but this didn't line up with what he knew of her at all.

Fuzzy hands poked at his paws, and he turned to see the nearest group of raccants pushing at him through the chicken wire, trying to shove him back into the pit. They wanted to see stuffing, dammit!

Threadbare tried to climb away from him, but there were a lot of onlookers, and one of his paws was forced free. Only a matter of time for the other, he knew.

But that was fine. A great weight had been lifted from him. This wasn't Missus Fluffbear, couldn't be her. It just looked like her, somehow. He didn't know what was going on here, but he did know this;

He was free to beat the stuffing out of this misshapen mockery of his friend with impunity.

And he had a hitherto unused toolset to use to do so that was just ducky for the occasion.

"Guard Stance! Challenge Bearserker!"

Your Guard Stance Skill is now level 2!

Your Challenge Skill is now level 2!

Instantly the strength drained from his limbs and his paws felt clumsy,

—but that was fine, because he felt... faster, for a lack of a better word.

The raccants easily pushed him free from his last pawhold, and he twisted in midair, dodged the oncoming swipe, and landed on the handle of the axe, arms up in a boxing stance.

AGL +1

Well, why not try everything he could? **"Fancy Flourish!"** The little bear's arms darted out in a spray of quick jabs, as the bear huffed and puffed. Threadbare shifted his legs back and forth on the axe handle like a little boxer.

Your Adorable Skill is now level 17!
Your Work it Baby skill is now level 5!
The Bearserker has resisted your Fancy Flourish!

Then the axe twisted in her hands, and he dropped down, managing to roll and just barely dodge it as she struck down at him.

Your Dodge skill is now level 6!

Then it was up again, dancing toward her legs, paws up, jabbing at her with claw swipes as she turned, trying to cleave him. He was only doing about ten damage a hit, but she was having a lot of trouble connecting. The few hits he took did hurt, but he was wearing her down. And as he fought, he threw in Fancy Flourishes, managing to land a couple through her willpower, despite his inexperience with the skill.

Your Fancy Flourish skill is now level 2!

A green '6' drifted up from her head. Moxie damage.

Your Fancy Flourish skill is now level 3!

Another green '6'

But he dropped it once he started feeling tired. He was still using claw swipes after all, and that was more important in the long haul. He didn't have a chance of zeroing out her moxie, and he wasn't sure what that would do anyway. So instead he settled for trying to pound the stuffing out of her.

Your Brawling skill is now level 23!
Critical Hit!
LUCK +1
Your Claw Swipes skill is now level 19!
DEX +1
Critical Hit!
LUCK +1
Your Claw Swipes skill is now level 20!
AGI +1
Critical Hit!

LUCK +1
Your Brawling skill is now level 24!
But as time went on, he noticed something. She was getting torn up, yes...

...but her strikes were hitting harder.
Your Toughness skill is now level 15!
+2 Max HP
When they connected, they tore him up something fierce. He watched a red '40' roll by with alarm. He was down maybe half, he didn't have time to stop and check. All it would take was one lucky critical hit on her part, and bad things would surely happen.

Come to think of it, she'd had a skill called "Power from Pain," hadn't she? If this was it, it was troublesome. She couldn't have much left, hit-point wise, but...

He ran, getting some distance, and the crowd booed again. Was there a way to turn off guard stance? He concentrated, still running with a bear behind, and felt the stance click off. Instantly he slowed a bit, and the axe almost swept through his head.

Your Dodge skill is now level 7!
But before she could try a backswing, he leaped, and caught the chicken wire again. Instantly the raccants surged toward him, but that was fine. He had what he needed; a breather.

"Mend! Mend! Mend! Mend! Mend!" He shouted, over and over again as they pushed and shoved at him. He maxed the skill when it hit fifteen and kept going. After about the ninth casting they managed to knock him loose, and the Bearserker's axe narrowly missed him with an upswing. Without time to think, without time to re-establish guard stance he hit the ground, grabbed her leg, and tore great swipes of it free.

And this time, without guard stance gimping his damage, Threadbare managed to tear right through her plush paw. She crumpled, falling to one knee, and he grabbed her shoulder, hauled himself up, and tore through her plush head. Red stuffing spilled out, and the over-muscled Bearserker fell. The crowd went wild, and Threadbare clambered down, shaking. He was tired, so tired, but there was no way that hadn't—

You are now a level 2 Duelist!
AGL+3
DEX+3
STR+3
Ah, there it was. His pools refilled.

Then a hissing noise filled his ears, just audible under the roaring crowd. He looked down to see yellow dust pouring out of the Bearserker's skull. He'd seen that dust before, long ago... it was the same dust that his creator had almost turned him into, when he was first awakened.

His creator had taken great care to bottle it. Threadbare didn't have bottles, but he had apron pockets. He started scooping it up and pouring it into his pockets... but found that after he'd gotten about half of it in a pocket, the other half wouldn't fit. Curiously, he experimented, and found he could put the remaining dust in another pocket. He just couldn't mix the two of them.

Threadbare looked up, only to watch the Bearserker's corpse disappear in front of his eyes. Gone, just like that. What the heck?

A creak interrupted his reverie, and he looked over to see the portcullis shuddering downward as it started to close. No other way out of this pit... He ran for it, managed to just get under it before it shut.

The corridor beyond was dark, with lighted doorways off to the side, each blocked off by a portcullis, and a chest at the end of a stone door. And there, fading into view not ten feet from him, wisping into existence from nothingness, was another Bearserker.

Thoroughly freaked out and not wanting to fight a murderous midboss in the tight confines of a tunnel, he ran past her. The stone door opened as he approached, but he slowed, tempted by the treasure chest.

Then the Bearserker roared, and Threadbare saw a green '12' lift out and float up above him. Yeah, no, the treasure chest wasn't worth it. He darted through the stone door and it ground shut behind him, cutting off the sound of the Bearserker's lumbering approach.

Whew! Threadbare looked around him, at the tunnels lit by an obscene amount of stolen lanterns. Back to the old familiar corridors, it looked like.

The little teddy bear Flexed, and Self-esteemed himself again, watched those buffs skill up, and refocused his mind on the task ahead. He'd been separated from Pulsivar back there. He had no doubt the big cat could take care of himself, and a quick check of the party screen showed him still there, still in relatively good health.

Then the cat's hit points went up as he watched, and Threadbare chuckled, the tiny sound breaking the silence of the cave. Pulsivar was grooming himself, had to be. "Good kitty," Threadbare whispered, and toddled off to find him. He activated Scents and Sensibility along the way, hoping to catch the big cat's scent, and make his task easier.

He did find Pulsivar's scent... at about the same time the first Trash Mob found him.

One minute later, the trash mob was in ruins, Threadbare was a few coins richer, and down a few hit points. He mended himself, resumed the hunt, following the scent trail—

—and got jumped by another Trash Mob.

Midway through, he got smart. What exactly was animated trash?

"Eye for Detail."

Your Eye for Detail skill is now level 3!

Yep, they were animi. Also a slime, which was weird, but whatever. He was new to this whole animator thing, that was his excuse.

Well, he'd wanted to come in here with minions, hadn't he?

Five Trash Mob encounters and five skill ups to **Command Animus** and **Creator's Guardians** later, Threadbare was feeling a bit lightheaded but he had a full party. True, they were literally garbage, but they were his garbage, and they could take hits like no one's business. Well, not compared to him, but they were good for their level, anyway.

Having a bunch of Trash Mobs in his thrall let Threadbare pick up speed. He got jumped a few times more, but his garbage goons swiftly made junk of the offending Trash Mobs. And it turned out, that grinding through trash mobs using animi was enough for another animator level.

You are now a level 4 Animator!

DEX+3

INT+3

WILL+3

That was a welcome refresh. Binding all those trash mobs had cost him a bit over a quarter of his sanity, mending had taken more, and the fights had drained stamina a bit. All back in a heartbeat, thanks to a timely level.

And after a time, the mounting weight of the coins salvaged from dead Trash Mobs stretched his apron tight around him, and started working on another skill as well.

Your Sturdy Back skill is now level 6!

Threadbare followed the big cat's scent deeper into the tunnels. He knew he was close behind, when he found shredded remnants of other trash mobs along the way. **"Party Screen,"** he said with relief...

...and gasped when he saw that Pulsivar was down to half of his hit points. "No!" He ran forward, following the trail as fast as he could, trying to move at top speed without losing it. But it was hard, and to his horror, Pulsivar's hit points kept dropping, five or six at a time...

...until they stabilized at about thirty. Threadbare didn't let up, until he came to a red lacquered door, standing slightly ajar. Gold-painted letters on it announced to the world;

TRASH PANDA

Threadbare burst through the door, trash mobs following, clanking and tumbling...

...to find a room filled with paper screens, currently shredded. The floor was full of torn up mats, and odd looking weapons made from junk hung on the walls. Pulsivar was nowhere in sight, but lying against one wall, gutted with stuffing bursting out of her shredded hide, was Missus Fluffbear.

Wait.

No, this wasn't her. This version of her had white fur mingled in with her regular black color. Also she was two feet tall, nowhere near the six inches she started with. About half the size of the Bearserker.

Just to be safe, though....

"Eye for Detail"
Your Eye for Detail skill is now level 4!

No, this one was something called a "Trash Panda." Another midboss, by the looks of it. Another construct. Huh, wait, she had the Fancy Flourish skill as well...

That's about the point that an ungodly racket sprang up behind him, and Threadbare whirled to find a big black bobcat ripping one of his bound Trash Mobs to bits.

"Wait! No!" He ran and hugged Pulsivar, and the cat twitched, surprised. Golden light flared.

You have healed Pulsivar 90 points!
Your Innocent Embrace skill is now level 10!
Your Fascination skill is now level 3!

The Bobcat abruptly stopped attacking the mob. When the mob went after Pulisvar, Threadbare called it off. Then the big cat was purring, and licking his face.

"Okay, okay, okay," Threadbare patted the cat until he backed off. If Threadbare was right about what had happened last time, then midboss corpses didn't last forever. They had to loot it and hurry away. Threadbare salvaged a yellow cloth belt from the fake Fluffbear's corpse, wound it around his waist, and hurried on through the only other door out of the place, with Pulsivar and his Trash Mobs at his heels.

After the door shut behind them, Threadbare checked his status screen. Nice! The belt boosted his agility and dexterity, and gave a bonus to his Fancy Flourish skill. While he was there he checked his new pants, and found them good as well. They had something called "Hammerspace," which let him store a blunt weapon in their pockets regardless of its size. They'd be handy for storing his scepter if he ever got ahold of it again.

Missus Fluffbear had been holding the scepter when the raccants dragged her off. Maybe it was still in here?

The corridors they ventured into were different from the rest. As they went down them, the trash mobs disappeared, replaced by the occasional wandering raccant carrying thin paper boxes full of strange-smelling stuff that crunched underheel after Threadbare and his party fought and slew the wandering monsters. He lost the Trash Mob that Pulisvar had wounded, but scarcely noticed as the scenery changed.

The corridors now had brightly-colored flashing lanterns strung along them, and occasionally they passed a rolling red-and-white striped ball, or a bit of cloth arranged to look like the outside of a tent, strung up along the stone tunnel. A strange music started to play in the distance, cheerful and upbeat and bouncy.

It was all more than a little surreal, and Threadbare was glad when they emerged out into a huge cavern, as brightly-lit as day. All around them, to his horror, were stands full of raccants, stone steps laid out like bleachers. But on the upside, at least some of them thought his pants looked cool.

Your Work It Baby skill is now level 6!

Directly ahead were three rings, each as big around as the entirety of Caradon's property.

One ring held an arrangement of scrap wood hammered together with poles and ropes in it. A raccant was balancing on a wire stretched between the two highest poles, twirling a parasol and resplendent in a tutu.

Another ring had a small wooden wagon with a bulging cloth cover over it, zooming around. On closer inspection, raccant feet were visible just under the wagon, trampling along and driving it in circles.

A third ring held an oversized raccant in a mask that said "LYIN". He had a mane made out of straw, and wore big brown pajamas. Currently he was sticking the head of a small doll in the mask's mouth, then pulling it out again. With a shock, Threadbare recognized Beanarella, Celia's old dolly!

"Welkim! Welkim!" A voice boomed from overhead. Threadbare and Pulsivar jumped...

...as a portcullis dropped behind them, sealing off the tunnel they'd come through.

"Welkim tooda gray test shon nerf!" The voice continued, chittering, as a platform lowered from the ceiling, revealing the biggest raccant yet.

This one had a different mask from the others. It said "HOOMIN," and bore a warped caricature of Mordecai's face. Threadbare could tell by the bushy eyebrows. They were made from real bushes.

The raccant was dressed in a long red coat with tails, in addition to his own, fluffy ringed tail. He bore a whip in one hand, and a cone that he shouted through in the other, and on his head was a tiny top hat. A familiar tiny top hat. Threadbare had worn that many a time, during tea parties.

"You took those!" Threadbare accused, his voice lost in the calliope music. So they'd salvaged more from the house, than just his friend! Well, he'd have it all back, then. Just a matter of beatings. He flexed, called up his self-esteem, and bodyguarded Pulsivar for good measure.

Your Flex skill is now level 13!

Your Self-Esteem skill is now level 13!

Your Bodyguard skill is now level 6!

The Ring-tailed master nodded, as the bear made his preparations and the cat hunkered low, freaked out by the noise and looking for something to kill to shut it up.

"Komm iffu dair! Chall enj all freerings to winna prise!"

Turning aside to the audience, he mock-whispered through the megaphone; "The prises beetings."

Well, he was right. Just not in the way he intended.

Threadbare and Pulsivar rushed the first ring, and the tightrope walker hurled down circus balls at them, that bounced for minimal damage when they struck. Eyeing the distance up to her, Threadbare considered that she'd be throwing things at him the whole time he was trying to climb up there to get at her, and then he'd have to fight her while balancing on a tightrope... yeah, no.

Threadbare looked around for an edge, and saw the jumble of planks that made the "poles" that her tightrope wire was stretched between. They were pretty poor construction, and jiggled every time she ran back and forth up there. An idea formed, just as another ball bounced off his head.

Well. Why not?

"Animus," the little bear breathed as he touched one of the supporting poles. **"Invite Pole."**

Your Animus skill is now level 11!

Your Creator's Guardians skill is now level 11!

The tightrope walker stared at him uncomprehendingly, up until the point that one of her supports suddenly twisted, went spastic, and jiggled her wire so hard she fell off the rope.

Right into Pulsivar's waiting jaws.

CRUNCH.

The crowd oohed, aahed, and applauded. Her parasol fluttered down, pink and frilly, and Threadbare caught it, tucking it away into his apron with nary a thought. His eyes were on the next challenge. He dismissed the pole from his party, leaving it to its own devices, as he moved on to the second ring and the wooden wheeled wagon.

Well, maybe he could animate the wagon, too. Threadbare started towards it, ignoring the cries and shrieks of the dying raccant as Pulsivar ate her, and stretched out a paw to slap the wagon. But just before he could reach it, one of the cloth covers flipped aside, and a raccant spilled out, wearing a mask smeared with white and red makeup.

Then another.

Then another.

Then another.

But by that time Threadbare's trash mobs had caught up with him. He left the curious raccants to the mobs, and slapped his hand on the wagon, even as it spilled out far more occupants than it could possibly carry. **"Animus,"** he declared, tanking hits as he got his paw on the little wheeled device. **"Invite wagon."**

The Klwon Kar has resisted your spell!

Then the thing zoomed off, leaving him in a mob of... Klwons? Okay. The wagon stopped a little ways away, and spilled out more raccants.

They weren't tough raccants, his trash mobs looked to be taking them down pretty easily, but they bounced all over the place, squirted him with weird water bottles that damaged his moxie, and ran around honking weird rubber and metal devices for no reason at all. Doing his best to ignore them, he ran after the car, managed to catch it, and slapped it again. **"Animus! Invite Klo... Klw... Invite Kar!"**

Your Animus skill is now level 12!

Your Creator's Guardians skill is now level 12!

Thoroughly annoyed, Threadbare gave the Kar its marching orders, and it revved up, wheels squealing as the occupants inside shrieked and tried to escape. A few more got out, but then the little Kar zoomed at high speed across to the next ring and plowed straight into the unsuspecting "Lyin."

For some reason the Kar blew up into a big fireball. A red '264' floated out from the debris, as did the charred remnants of the Lyin's mane. Threadbare turned his back on the explosion, glaring at the remaining Klwons with button eyes.

Boy, there were a lot of them. Three of his Trash Mobs were down, leaving one more trying to hold back a tide...

...then a black shadow passed overhead.

THUMP.

Pulsivar came down, and went to work. Threadbare waded in as well, claws out and shredding. It was surprisingly satisfying. They'd worked up his temper with all those water bottles and klwoning around, and he took it out on them, killing with satisfaction for the first time ever.

And at the end of that fight, new words came up.

Congratulations! By killing in anger you have unlocked the Berserker job!

You cannot become a Berserker at this time! Seek out your guild to change jobs.

Huh. Well... Threadbare felt slightly ashamed, for no reason he could tell. He slowed, looking around him at the carnage—

—then another stupid jet of water hit him, and he shrugged and waded back in. They had it coming.

Finally, the ring was empty of the enemy. Their strange corpses faded, leaving behind only one of those rubber and brass honking things. He didn't see a use for it, but Threadbare picked it up anyway.

"Weldon! Weldon!" The Ringtailed Master chittered, and he hopped off the platform. "Clozure I's an nopen wyde fordee prise! Nukkle sammisches!"

He rushed them, and got a face full of Pulsivar's claws, reeled back snapping his whip at the big cat—

—to find Threadbare on the other side.

"Challenge! Guard Stance! Fancy Flourish! Grrrrr!"

Your Challenge skill is now level 3!

Your Guard Stance skill is now level 3!

Your Fancy Flourish skill is now level 6!

Your Growl skill is now level 2!

The Ringtailed Master's Woop Woop skill hurt their moxie, but they persisted. His Whippersnapper skill, which had bonuses against big cats, was thoroughly thwarted as half his attempts were intercepted by the bodyguarding Threadbare. And damn did Pulsivar hit hard.

The bear was no slouch either. And he could heal any damage the boss dealt.

Your Brawling skill is now level 25!

Your Weapon Specializaton skill is now level 6!

Your Weapon Specialization skill is now level 7!

STR +1

DEX +1

Critical Hit!

Your Weapon Specialization skill is now level 8!

Your Weapon Specialization skill is now level 9!

Your Claw Swipes skill is now level 21!

Your Weapon Specialization skill is now level 10!

Your Mend skill is now level 16!

Your Mend skill is now level 17!

Your Claw Swipes skill is now level 22!
At the end of it all, the outcome was inevitable. A level six boss in a rarely-visited and under-evolved dungeon was just no match for a massively-multiclassed toy golem and a level twenty-one beast. Finally, the Ringtail master fell. Relieved, Threadbare swooped the top hat from the boss's head, and replaced it on his own. "Mine!" he declared.

And to the victor, went the experience.
You are now a level 10 Bear!
You may Rank Up to a Tier II Bear Job at this level!
Would you like to do so at this time?

"Yes!" Threadbare declared. He'd made his choice long ago, taking everything into account. And then he fell down, holding his head, as it grew by a few inches. His eyes elongated, the buttons becoming bigger...

...and suddenly the bright light in here seemed a little TOO bright.

And then Threadbare was a Cave Bear.

Still a teddy bear, still a Greater Golem, but a bit thicker and with a bigger head.
You are now a level 10 Cave Bear!
CON+10
WIS+10
Armor+5
Endurance+5
Mental Fortitude+5
You have unlocked the Darkspawn Skill!

And that wasn't the only level up.
You are now a level 3 Duelist!
AGL+3
DEX+3
STR+3

But it was the final one that brought the most interesting results...
You are now a level 5 Animator!
DEX+3
INT+3
WILL+3
You have unlocked the Animus Blade skill!
Your Animus Blade skill is now level 1!
You have unlocked the Arm Creation skill!
Your Arm Creation skill is now level 1!
You have unlocked the Dollseye skill!

Your Dollseye skill is now level 1!

New skills... Threadbare shook his now mildly-larger head, and peered around with new eyes. If he could have seen himself, he would have noticed that the buttons were bigger, darker, so black that they almost seemed hollows within his head. And in there, a tiny gleam flickered like pupils.

The raccants in the stands had fled, he saw. For the minute the room was empty.

But... where was Missus Fluffbear? She had to be here!

He took a sniff. His Scents and Sensibility had helped him so often before...

And it did not fail him now.

PER +1

Your Scents and Sensibility skill is now level 16!

It was coming from above? He lifted his new, sensitive eyes —

—up to where the platform shuddered, and slowly began to retract into the hole in the ceiling.

"No!" He grabbed Pulsivar, interrupting a perfectly good groom, and held fast to the scruff of his neck. The cat jerked its eyes to the little bear, looking mortally offended. "Up! We need to go up!" Threadbare pointed with his free hand. "Jump! Please Jump!"

Fortunately, he'd just equipped some very good charisma gear.

CHA +1

Pulsivar got the gist of it, and did his thing, running and leaping for all he was worth, as Threadbare hung on tight.

Your Ride skill is now level 8!

It was a very good thing that he was so light, and had gotten so strong.

They made the platform, the cat's claws clicking and scraping as he caught the lower edge of it, flailed, and pulled himself up. All told it was a good thing Pulsivar didn't have a proper tail anymore, else it would have been severed as the platform clunked into the ceiling.

Threadbare let go, and looked around at the place...

...and realized that he was far, far out of his depth.

It was a void, a black void. The floor was stone, he could feel that under his paws, but there were no walls. Pylons filled the expanse, green pillars of light, flickering softly. In among a cluster of the pillars, a red crystal the size of Threadbare hovered, swaying up and down, as small lightning bolts arced between it and the pillars.

Some of the pillars had raccants in them. Others had jumbles of random things. Coins, bits of treasure, and familiar looking objects.

And one had Missus Fluffbear, suspended in midair. She looked a little torn and dirty, but she was still intact, still six inches tall, and most decidedly NOT a Bearserker or a Trash Panda.

"There you are!" Threadbare sobbed in relief.

Pulsivar rumbled, low in his throat. He did not like this place one bit. Threadbare patted him. "Stay here please," he said, then ambled toward the cluster of inhabited pillars.

As he approached each one, glowing letters faded into existence. One pillar filled with a pile of worthless junk got the letters MINION – TRASH MOB.

Another held one of the raccant guards. MINION – RACCANTEER

One held the bard he'd fought. MIDBOSS 1 - MC SLAMMER

Another held someone he hadn't encountered... a Raccant with a blonde wig and a torn up dress, holding a weird gizmo with buttons and numbers on it. She had two labels; MIDBOSS 4 – RACCANT EVEN, and MIDBOSS 5 – THE VERY MODEL OF A VARMINT MAJOR GENERAL. He hadn't come across this one. Maybe she was in another part of the dungeon?

The one with Missus Fluffbear in it had two labels. MIDBOSS 2 – BEARSERKER, and MIDBOSS 3 – TRASH PANDA. He reached for it...

...and his paws frizzed, blurred and started flashing green. Ow! What was this? He pulled them back, quickly. It felt almost like... like that one time, back in the Catamountain, during the final fight when Celia had almost hit him with an electricity ball.

Threadbare turned, to look at the red crystal.

He moved up to the pillar under it, the one labeled DUNGEON BOSS – RINGTAIL MASTER.

The Ringtail Master looked back.

Shocked, Threadbare stumbled back, and the boss burst out of the pillar, reaching out to grab and claw at the interloper—

—and got promptly jumped by Pulsivar.

He went down a lot easier this time. A lot easier. And his corpse didn't disappear.

A soft chime echoed everywhere and nowhere, and words, green words writ large across the... sky? They were made of numbers, all zeroes and ones, and Threadbare shook to see them. They felt... wrong. Strange. If he'd known the word, he would have called them unholy.

NO MASTER DETECTED IN DUNGEON 01010010 01000001 01000011 01000011 01001111 01001111 01001110 01010010 01010101 01001101 01010000 01010101 01010011

PLEASE ASSIGN NEW MOB TO COMMAND VARIABLE TO
CONTINUE OPERATION.

Threadbare stared at the words. They made no sense.
He went back and tried to pull Missus Fluffbear out again... and
again, his paws got zapped. No, no, that would do something bad. He
didn't know what, but it would be bad, his advanced wisdom told him.
What could he do?
The bleak landscape shuddered. For a second, there were stone walls
all around, an old mine cart off to one side, and then it was the black and
green weirdscape again. Pulsivar howled in fear, and ran to the bear,
nudging him with his face. It was time to go, Pulsivar insisted, in cat.
But there was nowhere to go.
Was there?
The words above shifted. ERROR! NO MASTER DETECTED.
DUNGEON SEALING IN 30.
Then the 30 changed to 29. Then to a 28.
Threadbare hugged Pulsivar, and held on tight. Was this the end?
It wasn't.
When the numbers reached zero, the world changed.
It was a dark mineshaft, dingy, just one central cavern with a few
small tunnels off of it. Threadbare looked around, his new darkvision
drinking everything in perfect detail, as scents once again filled his nose.
Raccant, mostly, but under it all, the welcome odor of sandalwood.
He ignored the chittering raccant bard and the other midboss as the
two of them fled, ignored the minion raccants who followed them out at
top speed, with Pulsivar in hot pursuit. He ignored the various bits of loot
littering the ground, and even ignored his Scepter, lying there, golden in
the darkness.
No, Threadbare ignored them all as he walked up to the tiny bear, half
his size. She stood trembling, dazed and looking around in the darkness.
And Threadbare hugged her. She stiffened, but then golden light flared
from his innocent embrace—
You have healed Missus Fluffbear for 100 points!
Your Innocent Embrace skill is now level 11!
And a smaller golden light flared, as she hugged him back.
Missus Fluffbear has healed you for 10 points!
And while there was a lot to sort out, for now, he knew that all was
well with the world. The loot could wait. He'd been too long in here
already, here and wherever that... other place had been.
Scooping Missus Fluffbear up, he carried her out of the shallow

mineshaft, and back into the daylight.

CHAPTER 3: A PAW FULL OF UNDEAD

The last spadeful of dirt went over the raccant corpses, and Threadbare watched as Missus Fluffbear solemnly tamped it down with her jury-rigged spade. She'd gotten quite good at digging, if he was any judge of the matter.

He still didn't know why she'd buried the raccants that Threadbare had killed in their fortified camp, or why she shrunk back and trembled whenever Pulsivar was around. For some reason she feared the big cat.

Well, to be fair, he was pretty scary if you didn't know him. Or if you were something small and edible. Or if he wanted to play with you and got rough. Or when he loomed out of the night, with only yellow eyes visible and glaring.

But Pulsivar had accepted her well enough after Threadbare cleaned and pressed her, and anointed her with the last of his soap powder from their old home. The scent had a calming effect on Pulsivar. So eventually she stopped trying to hide from him and got on with the raccant burial.

It was hard to tell, but he thought she looked sad. Had the raccants treated her well? She'd gotten that broken spade from somewhere, and the tiny knots in the twine that bound the fork to the remnants of the handle were small enough to be of raccant doing.

Perhaps it was best she didn't know that he and Pulsivar had killed this bunch out front. Yes, that seemed wise. Threadbare was glad his wisdom was getting up to large numbers quickly, life would have been difficult or short without it.

Letting his new companion finish her job, Threadbare checked the party screen again, Missus Fluffbear was a level five toy golem, and a level two bear, and also a tailor and a miner. She'd figured out the secret of "yes," then. He'd guessed that, from how she'd accepted his party invite instantly.

Which meant that she could probably use some equipment. Threadbare looked back to the loot that he'd gotten from the cave. He'd spent some time using his enchanter skill, the one called "Appraise," leveling it up to five and investigating each object that wasn't total trash.

Most of it was junk.

But the things that weren't, were welcome sights. His scepter went into his pants pocket, fitting in despite its size thanks to the miracle of hammerspace. He was glad to have *that* back.

The Ringtail Master's corpse had yielded a coat and that cone thing he was shouting from, which was evidently called a "Minorphone." he also had a whip that Threadbare didn't know how to use, that did small amounts of moxie damage to big cats with every strike. The little bear only knew one big cat and he liked him, so Threadbare pushed the whip to the side, with the rest of the pile he was making. He added the rubber and brass clown horn to that pile as well, then he came to the last item, which was the Ringtail Master's coat. It was red with mismatched bright buttons up the front, and had two triangular tails on its backside. It was heavier than it looked, and it had a ton of pockets, and Threadbare fell in love with it on sight. He pulled it on, and felt the usual mental readjustment as his attributes shifted.

The Minorphone got tied with string, to hang over his back. It was kind of bulky compared to his size, but it let him activate its magic to amplify his voice twice a day, which had the side effect of enhancing his voice-related skills. Since he was soft-spoken, it was bound to be useful.

That left the whip and the clown horn, and a few of Celia's knives. He took one dagger for himself, then set the rest aside for Missus Fluffbear.

Four things left, then. The first was another couple of doses of that glittery dust, red this time, and also some vials to keep it in. Threadbare knew this reagent stuff was the component for another of his enchanter abilities, as was the second item, a level one red crystal. According to his appraise, it could be used to enchant permanent magic items, but he had no idea how.

The third item was Cecelia's old doll, Beanarella. She was very torn, very chewed, and dirty, so he hastily mended her and cleaned and pressed her back to her original condition. If nothing else she could be an animi, even if she was about his size and rather bulky. Maybe he could jury rig a harness, or a back-pack like Celia had?

The fourth item was a red octahedron the size of one of his paws, cool to the touch, and glowing with flickering green numbers. It looked very much like a miniature version of the the red crystal, that had been in the strange place with the green pillars and the blackness all around. He'd thought it a crystal for enchantment at first, but... the appraise hadn't worked right. All it had turned up was the name of the item.

64756e67656f6e207365656420636c617373206f6e65

Threadbare tucked it away, for later research.

With the item sorting done, he looked at Missus Fluffbear, who looked back, smiling because she had no choice. She couldn't talk, and her mouth was stuck in a little yarn grin. He could fix that, given time, but... his common sense told him that coming at her throat with scissors wouldn't go too well.

And with Eye for Detail confirming her mediocre intelligence, he knew that explaining a lot of things to her was going to be tricky. She needed an education. A better one than he'd gotten.

Well. He could help with that. But first things first...

One quick tailoring job, using the scraps of leather and cloth retrieved from the junk, and he had a backpack. Another tailoring job, and a skill up this time, and he had a miniature version of his own apron, modified with a few extra straps sized for the whip and the horn.

"I have something for you," Threadbare told Missus Fluffbear. She took it, turned it over, examining it from every angle. Then she tried to tie it around herself, and he winced as her paws dropped it over and over again.

He resisted the urge to help. This is how she could get better at dexterity, by trying over and over again.

Finally she managed, and he showed her how to tuck the coiled-up whip in its pocket, the dagger in its sheath, and the horn through the buckled loop meant to carry it. The horn itself was almost as big as she was, so it dragged on the ground when she walked.

"Here, it does this." Threadbare pressed his paws against the bulb of the horn, and squeezed.

HONK

She took it almost reverently.

"So if you have to make noise—"

HONK HONK

"Not all the time, please—"

HONK HONK HONK HONKITTY HONK HONKLY HONKS

Threadbare was starting to see a flaw in his plan.

Pulsivar, unnoticed at the edge of the clearing, flattened his ears and slunk off into the woods.

Threadbare tried to get her to stop honking, and after a few minutes she did. She still seemed quite happy with the gifts overall though, pulling her dagger with one hand and her whip with the other, and waving them around in excitement.

He left her to that, and turned back to Beanarella. She really would eat up a lot of packspace if he carried her along, and he didn't like that notion.

So why not do something about that? Have her walk under her own power? Not as an animi, but as something more permanent, and hopefully more powerful?

He put the doll down on the ground, got out a dose of yellow reagents and the red crystal, and whispered **"Toy Golem."**

The little bear watched as his hands moved of their own accord, and a yellow bar appeared before his vision, hollow but filling up as his appendages worked. They sprinkled the glittering reagent in patterns over Beanarella, before putting the crystal right over her heart.

Your Toy Golem skill is now level 2!

He sagged, as about a third of his sanity went out of him. But he was successful, oh was he successful.

You have created an (average) Toy Golem Shell!

As first tries went, he thought it wasn't so bad.

Well. One more step to go, then.

Laying his paws on Beanarella's forehead, he stared into her painted eyes.

"Golem Animus."

WILL +1

Your Golem Animus skill is now level 2!

She stirred under his hands, and Missus Fluffbear left off flopping the whip around and shanking weeds to come stare at the newly-risen doll, as it sat up. Beanarella's thick neckless head twisted on its cloth body, looking around left and right, before fixing on her creator's button eyes.

But there was nothing behind her painted eyes. No spark of life. She just sat there, looking up at him, and waiting.

Well, he had expected that. But still, there was a sense of disappointment. For a little while longer, at least, he and Fluffbear were the only ones of their own kind. That he knew of, anyway.

"Invite Golem," he told Beanarella, and then she was in his party.

Your Invite Golem skill is now level 2!

You are now a level 2 Golemist!

INT+5

WILL+5

One Eye for Detail (and skill up) later, he checked out her stats. Her physical stats were... average. Better than he'd had starting out, he thought, and he didn't know why that was so. She had solid thirties in all her physical stats plus perception and luck, and a decent armor and great endurance.

But on the other hand, she had nothing mentally. No moxie, no cool, no mental fortitude, no sanity. And her fate was N/A. He didn't know what that meant. She did have the adorable, innocent embrace, and bodyguard skills, along with magic resistance and golem body, so that was good. And a little confusing.

"Why are you like this?" Threadbare asked her in his tiny voice, and she didn't answer.

Missus Fluffbear, sensing his confusion, tried to cheer him up.

HONK HONK HONK HONK HONK—

She was interrupted, as a piercing scream shook the heavens. And before any of the little toys could react, a screaming eagle drawn by both the shriek of the horn and Fluffbear's abysmal luck plummeted from the heavens and snatched her up, just like that!

"No!" Threadbare shouted, running after it as it flew away. "Stop! Stop!" To lose her, just like that, after everything they'd gone through was an unbearable thought!

But the eagle flew on, its prey in its claws. Threadbare had nothing, no skills or spells that would work at range. Nothing that would help him at a distance.

So he ran after the bird, despairing as it flew high... then despairing more, as a small black speck dropped away from it, straight toward a rocky slope.

"**Guard Stance!**" he snapped, doing everything he could to maximize his ground speed and skilling up at the same time. Then gritting his teeth and pushing his agility to the limits, Threadbare ran!

He burst out of the treeline in time to see Missus Fluffbear on her feet, trying to snap the whip at the plummeting form of the screaming eagle. With a wince, he saw the whip rebound on her and flick one of her button eyes clean off, as a red '10' floated out of the poor toy. "**Mend! Mend!**" he yelled, restoring some health to her.

The eagle, amazingly, failed to scoop her up. And as it passed overhead, Threadbare gave a mighty leap—

—and caught its lower talon, dropping guard stance to secure his grip, hanging on with both paws.

The Screaming Eagle was caught entirely by surprise. It was also no match for a teddy bear who had the strength of a muscular human at this point, much less one who had sharp, sharp claws. With a cry of despair it tumbled and crashed as he tore at its wings.

Somewhat battered but no worse for it the little bear stood up—

—just in time to catch Missus Fluffbear's whip in his face as she hurried over to help.

He would have rolled his eyes if he could, as the sad little '0' drifted up from him, but instead he settled for mauling the heck out of the Eagle. Fluffbear stabbed it repeatedly as well, and in short order it stopped moving.

Happily, she honked the horn again, and Threadbare put his hand on her shoulder, shook his head. She got the message and stopped.

"Let's go back to camp."

The gropevine wasn't an entirely unexpected encounter, when it lashed out and caught Missus Fluffbear a few minutes later. Threadbare knew they were native to the area, so it made sense. The second screaming eagle was annoying when it came in, but they were in the trees so it couldn't make a good grab in time to escape as Threadbare pounded it until it fled.

Beanarella caught up to the group at that point too, and she helped a bit with the kicking.

And then the Wizz-blizzards following in Beanarella's wake caught up, too. Little solid clouds made of ice with mean eyes and pointy blue hats, they came in dropping force blasts and hovering around and generally being obnoxious. Missus Fluffbear seemed to recognize them, and took great joy in whipping and shanking them, aiming at them with long expertise. They seemed to focus mainly on her, though a few wayward shots hit Threadbare and mostly ricocheted. They fell or fled, as the toys fought them, and Threadbare went through a few more mendings. And also got some mileage out of a skill he hadn't leveled in a while.

Your Magic Resistance skill is now level 5!
Your Magic Resistance skill is now level 6!

Then it was another gropevine, which Threadbare was certain hadn't been there when he ran through.

The third screaming eagle actually managed to get its claws around Fluffbear and haul her up—

—only to be pounced upon by Pulsivar, who dropped from a high tree and broke its back with his weight.

"This is getting ridiculous," Threadbare said, as they finally got back to the little stockade. "And I think I know why. **Eye for Detail.**"

Your Eye for Detail skill is now level 7!

Her luck had actually gone up a point since the last time he checked it. But it was still pretty lousy, at twenty-six.

"Come on," he patted Pulsivar, and took Missus Fluffbear's paw. "I think I know someone who can help." Beanarella fell in behind them as they walked, leaving the buried raccants to their rest.

As they went, Threadbare selected a few more skills to level along the way. Better now, than in the heat and stress of combat. Harden, Guard Stance, and Emboldening Speech seemed like good ones to practice. And so he cautiously crept through the woods with his paws up ready to block punches, enhancing Missus Fluffbear's hide, and rambling on about duty, bravery, and the right to arm bears. He also kicked on Noblesse Oblige, which he'd been thoroughly forgetting about, and watched it slowly start leveling as his party benefited from the buff. His primary attribute seemed to be wisdom, and with luck as miserable as Fluffbear had, she could use every bit of common sense she could get.

It DID keep her horn honks to a minimum, for which he was thankful.

It had been a long time since he'd been this way, but he still knew the route. He led them through the woods, to a large boulder, and down a goat trail to a valley below the wooded slope. Eventually the trees grew more weathered and worn, and as the afternoon went on, he could see the first gray line of stones there in the dead trees.

The strange girl who lived around here had a card game, Threadbare knew, one that had helped him when his luck was pretty abysmal. Maybe she could help again?

A few more creatures approached as they found their way down into the swampy valley, but Pulsivar's presence seemed to keep them at bay, and none of the screaming eagles that occasionally swooped by seemed inclined to attack. They all knew the Black Death, by sight or by smell, and there were better ways to die than by getting within leaping distance of the region's apex predator.

They came to the stones as he had long ago, and Missus Fluffbear grew interested, toddling around and staring at the writing that filled them. Threadbare followed behind her, reading each one as he went, and tracing the letters with his paw. This had helped him, he remembered, back when he was trying to figure out letters and words, figure out the world.

Celia did this for me, he thought, and bowed his head as his paw shook on the stone. For a second the despair crept on him again—

HONK

—but only a second. He smiled down at Fluffbear's anxious face, and patted her head. "See? This one says here lies William Walt, I got hungry and it wasn't his fault."

But the girl he'd met here was nowhere in sight. He even checked around with Scents and Sensibility...

...and caught a strange smell, coming from the east.

PER +1

It was like Pulsivar, but not Pulsivar. Like a couple of Pulsivars, because the scents were subtly different.

The big black bobcat perked up instantly as soon as he smelled it, bounding off that way, excited.

"Wait!" Threadbare insisted, running to keep up....

...which is about when the first skeletal hand leaped out from behind a gravestone, and tried to strangle Missus Fluffbear. Not a skeleton, just a bony hand, moving of its own accord.

She didn't much care about getting strangled and it was dispatched easily enough, but by the time they were done with it, Pulsivar was gone from sight. Missus Fluffbear, for her part, was oblivious to Threadbare's distress, waving her arms in the air excitedly.

Her Toy Golem level had gone up to six on the party screen, Threadbare saw. Not too surprising given how much fighting they'd been doing all that day.

"Pulsivar?" Threadbare called, hauling out the Minorphone and triggering its magic. "PULSIVAR?"

The sound was much louder than expected, and it rolled off the hills, echoing back and forth. But the black cat did not return.

So Threadbare fired up his sniffer and followed his scent. It was pretty easy, after all. His friend stuck to the strange cats' trail like a close-knit stitch in a seam.

Your Scents and Sensibility skill is now level 17!

Threadbare didn't know why Pulsivar was so worked up about this. He had no way of knowing that it was smack in the middle of bobcat mating season, and one of the scents that Pulsivar had picked up belonged to a female close to heat. If he'd known that, he probably wouldn't have understood it in the first place. Toy golems didn't generally have to worry about hormones, and in any case, he already had a method of reproduction that involved a lot less drama and biology.

Another dead hand later, they came to a place where the ground was torn up. Muddy stone boxes lay in deep holes, lids off, and the stones above were crooked and fallen. The scent of cats was all around—

—and then Fluffbear was falling into the pits, and that took a while to sort out. Fortunately Threadbare had plenty of string, and eventually he just tied her to him and kept on walking whenever he felt the string tug and jerk. Seriously, she was lucky to have him along for this.

In more ways than he knew, actually. Every time he helped her out of a predicament, she ground a little more experience for her luck. She'd already gone up a couple of times since the day started.

Eventually, Threadbare came to a deep set of ruts in the ground, straight and surrounded with pawmarks. Big ones. The ground was torn up here, by something Threadbare had never seen before. It smelled of... death. Old wood and old death, very old. And... rusted metal? And cats. Really strongly of cats.

And sure enough, Pulsivar was following it. He'd stopped to piss on one of the gravestones, but after that, ZOOM, if Threadbare's nose was right.

Sighing, the little bear gathered his party and marched on after the tracks.

Oddly enough, they didn't have any encounters on the way. He was uncertain if this was because Fluffbear's luck had hit a certain point, or if Pulsivar had cleared the way for them.

The actual answer was due to a completely different factor, but he had no way of knowing that yet.

They broke new ground, walked through land that meandered between the hills, past the occasional fallen shack or burned out barn, and Threadbare activated Keen Eye whenever the trail got too near them, making sure there wasn't anything lurking in ambush and skilling it up a bit. Twice they snuck past bears, actual honest-to-gods black bears, foraging peacefully. That was good for another two levels of stealth.

And a level of Scout. This one brought some surprises with it.

You are now a level 5 Scout!
AGL +3
PER +3
WIS +3
You have unlocked the Alertness skill!
Your Alertness skill is now level 1!
You have unlocked the Best Route skill!
Your Best Route skill is now level 1!
You have unlocked the Forage skill!
You already know the Forage skill... +5 levels added to it instead.

Two new skills, and his spent energy refreshed? Yes please!

Curious, he pulled them up on his status screen.

There was one called Alertness, that had a chance of activating all his sensory skills right before he got ambushed. And another one called Best Route, that helped him navigate to landmarks within his field of vision.

Okay, that Alertness one was handy as heck. The other one he could see using sometimes, maybe. Right now it didn't matter, because he had tracks to follow.

Night fell as they walked. To Threadbare it made little difference, thanks to his new cave bear eyes. But Missus Fluffbear was having a bit of trouble, so they slowed down a bit.

Then they crested a ridge, and he saw lights.

They were the glowing lights of windows. There was a big building out there, and several shapes beyond it, which his darkvision revealed to be wrecked and scorched smaller buildings. A few of them were mostly intact, but they were all dark, save for that big one.

He knew this place. It was Taylor's Delve. What had happened to it? Why was only one building lit up, and most of the rest all smashed?

Threadbare debated. The trail he was following went past the town, veered away from it. But those lights were intriguing. Then his string pulled tight again, and he sighed as he hauled Missus Fluffbear out of a ditch. It was getting too dark for her to see well, and her perception needed work. Pulsivar's stats were still visible on his party screen, and he was doing fine. That decided him... the big cat could take care of himself for a night or two, if it became necessary. He had for five years, after all. He'd be fine.

So Threadbare untied the string, took missus Fluffbear by hand, and with Beanarella stomping stoically behind, led the group down the hill and into town.

Once it had planks in the street, but now they were scattered and rotten, overgrown with lichen and the first shoots of new spring plants. But the toys were light and noiseless, as they crept up on the lit building.

Your Stealth skill is now level 9!

Threadbare debated, then waved Beanarella over to one of the windows as an idea struck him. He guided her to just under the windowsill, then climbed up on her back and peered in.

It was a big room inside, with a staircase going up to another floor. Candles lit the room, and a big bar filled the back of it, with stools lining the run of it. A mirror behind the bar had been thoroughly broken, and a pale man with overlarge fangs polished a glass.

At the tables, a rough-looking woman in a breastplate arm-wrestled a sturdy-looking man wearing a miller's apron. They too were pale, and their fangs stuck out inches from their lips as they grinned at each other.

Then, someone howled upstairs, and the building shook. Threadbare barely kept his balance. The patrons inside looked up nervously, then shrugged and went back to their business once it subsided.

The voice that howled seemed almost familiar, though Threadbare couldn't put his metaphorical finger on it.

Threadbare hopped down. It seemed all right. Maybe these people could help him find Pulsivar, or tell him what was going on.

He rejoined the nervous Missus Fluffbear, and led her around to the door. It didn't budge when he pushed it, so he hauled out his scepter and poked at the door handle, trying to turn it. That didn't work, so he tapped the heavy club against the door instead.

Noise from inside, some hushed discussion, and the man behind the bar opened the door, his lower face covered with a cloth mask. "Why hello there... travelers..." his voice trailed off, as he saw no one in front of him. Then gold flashed in the edge of the vision, and he followed his eyes down to the little bear's top hat, and the immaculately dressed teddy bear under it.

Your Work it Baby skill is now level 7!

"Hello," the foot-tall toy said, looking up into the man's red, red eyes. "Can we come in?"

"...sure? Ah, wait... uh... enter freely and of your own pill."

"You got it wrong Steve," the woman said, her voice muffled from her own mask. "It's will."

"No, I don't think this guy is Will." The bartender stepped aside, as the little toys toddled into the room, two of them peering around curiously. The miller had a mask on too, now.

The woman laughed, wringing her hands together at the unexpected parade. "So cute!"

Your Adorable skill is now level 18!
Your Work it Baby skill is now level 8!

For a long minute there was silence. The door shut, and the bartender coughed. "Ah, there's a... cold going around. That's why the masks."

"Yep," the miller nodded, his eyes red against his pale face. "So we don't give you colds! Although..."

"Yeah, what are you?" The armored woman said. "You monsters?"

"We're golems," Threadbare said, and instantly the atmosphere in the room seemed to lighten.

"Whew, that's a relief!" The bartender said, sliding his mask off. "We're monsters too!"

"Yeah, come on and belly up to the bar," The armored woman said, taking a stool and shifting a spear on her back so she could sit down comfortably. "We thought you were travelers. Like we were, once."

The three little toys moved up to the bar. Threadbare and Fluffbear looked at each other, and scrambled up to the stools, then on to the counter when they couldn't see above the bar. Beanarella stood placidly below, until the woman reached down and scooped her up, depositing her next to her party members.

"I'm glad you're not adventurers," The guy in the miller's apron said, taking a seat next to Missus Fluffbear. "Most of the time they either run or fight. All but the very stupid ones."

"Hey!" The woman snapped. "I was tired, okay?"

"Oh no no, it wasn't a knock on you, I'm just saying—"

"And the light was low! My astigmatism was acting up."

"Right, right, sorry."

"Hmph." She flipped her blonde ponytail back, and stared at Threadbare. "You are just the cutest thing, you know that? I bet you sucker people in that way, and then SHUNK!"

"No," Threadbare shook his head. "No shunking. Mostly hugging."

"Weird, but with that much gear on you I guess it's working out well." The bartender shrugged, and took a bottle down. "Do you drink?"

"No."

"We don't drink... wine, either." The bartender grinned. He had a friendly face, with two curly mustaches.

"Gods, don't remind me," the woman sighed. "At least I found us that goat a few hours back. You're all welcome, by the way. Not naming names. *Barret and Grimble.*"

"Thank you Darla," the miller said. The bartender just rolled his eyes.

Then the building shook again, as whatever was upstairs howled a breathless scream, that went on for minutes. Missus Fluffbear put her hands over her ears, and Threadbare patted her sympathetically.

When it was done, he asked "What was that?"

"Oh, uh, that's one of us who didn't turn out right." Darla said, shuddering. "Pity, too. He'd be a hell of a fighter, but... eh, he wasn't human. Gets weird sometimes when you're not. Racial skills get stuck, and bad things happen. That's what the mistress says." Boards creaked overhead. "Oh, here she comes now!"

"So you must be a pretty high-level golem," the bartender said. "Only ones I ever heard of aren't supposed to be smart. Did you luck out and get a class level, too? We get one, but only because we had them to start, and only one comes across."

"Your best one." Darla said. "Gods I miss my berserker levels. But at least I've got the knight stuff, so I'm somewhat useful in a fight. Not naming names here. *Barret.*"

"Shut up!" The miller said. "What was I supposed to do? Not my fault my parents literally made me grind miller before I ran away to wizard school! Then I got vamped, and ten wizard levels went straight down the drain, just like that!"

"Guys, guys..." The bartender made shushing motions.

"Oh, I've got eight adventuring jobs," The little bear said. "And two crafting ones."

The room fell silent.

"That uh, that sounds like you're an adventurer to me," the miller said, edging back a little.

"Maybe? I don't know. I don't think I'm a monster."

"Barret, Grimble, ease up," Darla said, as the miller drew out a stone club and the bartender slipped a hand under the counter. "He's weird, okay, but it's not like he's a necromancer or anything."

"Oh, I'm one of those too," Threadbare offered, helpfully.

Darla's face froze. "Oh boy. Tell me you're joking."

"Nope." There were feet on the creaking stairs now as someone descended, but Threadbare's attention was on the little trio around him. "See? **Assess Corpse.**"

Your Assess Corpse skill is now level 2!

Instantly words appeared over all of the humans' heads. Darla was a level four lesser vampire spawn and a level nine Knight. Grimble the bartender was a level five vampire spawn and a level seven Grifter. Barret was a level eight vampire spawn and a level twenty-one Miller. And for some reason, they'd all lost their smiles, and drawn their weapons.

"What's wrong?" Threadbare asked, sliding his hand down to his pocket, where he'd tucked the scepter.

"You!" A voice squealed, and Threadbare turned, to see the mysterious girl he'd met so long ago! She still wore the green-and-poka-dotted scarf around her head, but now she had a ragged black dress to go with it, and some big black boots that stomped as she charged him, scooping him up into a hug. "Mistah beah! Gahd, it's been so lahng, how ah yah?"

"Hello!" Threadbare said.

"You can talk now? Holy shit!"

"I made my mouth myself," said Threadbare, and hugged her back.

It was a very good, very lucky thing that he'd long ago turned off the auto-activation of his innocent embrace skill. Otherwise that night might have ended very differently, since that skill hurt undead.

But innocent embrace was off, and the hug was just a hug, and the lesser vampire spawns relaxed as their master giggled.

Finally, she put him down on a table, and he got a clear look at the words above her head.

Vampire level ???

"So what brings ya to my neck of the woods?" She grinned, toothily, pulling up a chair. Darla came over and plopped Missus Fluffbear and Beanarella down as well. "And ya brought friends, too? Wow!"

"I'm wondering if you can help me," The bear said. He pointed at Missus Fluffbear. "She needs to play that card game you played with me. A lot. Also I'm looking for a big, black bobcat. He's a friend of mine, and I don't know where he went to. He suddenly ran off."

"A big bobcat, yah say?" The girl's face grew guarded, and she shot the bartender a look. "And a friend of yahs?"

"Yes."

"Oooh... bad luck if he's around heah, then." She shook her head. "Grimble, why don't ya explain?" She winked at the bartender, who smiled and covered his mouth for a brief moment as he mouthed the words **"Silver Tongue."** Threadbare had no way of knowing that silent activation was a Grifter skill, nor would he have known what silver tongue did anyway.

The Grifter started his con. "Yes, my friend. I fear our little community is at war, with an evil necromancer! Which is why we were a little alarmed, earlier. Just a brief misunderstanding, haha."

"Haha," Threadbare agreed, not knowing why he should, but he did. He had no way of knowing his better-than-average willpower and actually-fairly-decent cool were being deftly suborned by the Grifter's enhanced charisma.

"Her thing, her style if you will, involves cats. Living ones, and when they die, she brings them back. And alas, they always die. So if she has your friend..."

"No!" Threadbare jumped to his feet. "She can't kill Pulsivar!"

"Ah, yes... *her* killing Pulsivar. Yes." Grimble shot a glance at Darla, who hurriedly tucked away a cat-fur pouch. "Anyway," he continued, "we've been fighting against her evil ways, but she's ever so strong, and being a necromancer, we're weak to some of her attacks. We've been trying to enlist the help of our best fighter, but alas, he is cursed. There is a strange spirit to the south, an evil witch who has cursed him so that he cannot join us."

"Fortunately the witch is strahng enough to resist the Cat Queen too," the vampire girl said. "But it's only a mattah of time till the Cat Queen catches that spirit. Then our best weapon is against us, and a powahful ghost witch is on all our asses too."

"If only someone could go out and kill that ghost witch," The bartender said, clapping his hands to his chest. "Someone who didn't have life to be drained away by her shuddering touch, or dead flesh that withered at her grasp..."

"I could do that!" Threadbare said, completely buying into the narrative.

Impressed, the Grifter and his master shared a glance. They didn't even have to offer a quest!

"Yeah, let's talk about that. My name's Madeline, by the way. What's yahs?"

CHAPTER 4: FOR A FEW UNDEAD MORE

The vampires were true to their word, and happy to have company that they didn't have to eat, run from, or convert. Though Threadbare was ready right away to go and put paid to that evil old ghost witch, they managed to talk him into waiting until daylight.

"She'll be weakah then," Madeline said. "Most undead things ah. Us too, but we got the common sense to stay outta the sun. Which is why the Cat Queen only sends her troops around in day."

The thing upstairs howled again, but they all ignored it, and kept playing their respective card games.

"You should probably be out of the town by then," Barret the miller pointed out. "I'm sure you're pretty tough, but she's got a lot of skeletons and even a few ghouls and wights."

"Whites?" Threadbare asked, laying down two reds.

"Nah. Smaht undead, with blue glowing ahhs." Madeline pointed to her eyes, and laid down two oranges.

Missus Fluffbear lay down two greens, winning, and happily watching a LUCK +1 flash across her vision.

Madeline ruffled her head, then started sorting through the well-worn deck again, pulling cards to her two-card hand, discarding, and attempting to get two matching colors. "So what happened to yah little gal? She get old and stop playing with toys? Because I may have ta go visit her foah a bite if she got that stupid. Toy like you, ya don't throw away."

"Oh no, nothing like that," Threadbare said, drawing and discarding, drawing and discarding. "It turns out her daddy was her grandfather and her father showed up and took her back. I got impaled in a house that burned down and collapsed and spent five years digging out."

HONK.

The vampires jumped. Threadbare shook his head. "Oh, sorry. Missus Fluffbear spent five years digging out. I mostly just got myself un-impaled."

"Woo. When family drahma goes wrong, amirite?" Madeline shook her head. "Sorry about that. So yah free. What ah ya gonna do now?"

"I'm going to find Celia and I'm going to save her." Threadbare slammed down two purples, the strongest hand in the game. "I might have to fight the king."

"Well, I don't know how he figgahs inta it, but powah to ya, little bear!" Madeline grinned toothily. "Tha King's an ass. He killed the old king and spent fifteen yeahs runnin' this kingdom inta tha ground. Look at this place!" She waved her hand around. "He set it all on faia! Well not him personally, tha soldiers, I mean. They killed everyone they could catch. I saw the faia and came into town. Even... saved... a few people on the way."

"Thanks for that, by the way," Grimble spoke up. He was back in a corner with the other vampire spawn, playing a much more interesting card game.

"S'aw right. Ya good company, ya know?" Madeline sighed. "Knew it was coming. Soon as the north folded, and Balmoran fell, all the little revolutionaries and resistance fightahs that had gathered heah were next. But nobody listens to the vampaiah, huh? Now Balmoran's gone, the dwarves are next on the chawpin' blahk, and only the ranjahs up in Jericho's Reach ah keepin' them alive. They'll be gone too soon, and tha King'll have total control. Of what's left ah this land, anyway."

She riffled the cards, reshuffled them. "Mordecah even dragged me to a few of tha resistance meetings down heah, thinkin' I might join. Old men and women and young stupids whispering about how they'd smuggle magic items and train up to fight when tha time came. All waiting for a mysterious gal who was tha true heir to tahn up an' lead them. Cowahds, most. Useless."

"You knew Mordecai?"

"Oh yah. Tried to put the bite on him one night when I caught him wanderin' around my turf, and wound up pinned to a tree, gettin' a lecture on how I, of all people, should know bettah than to judge by appearances. We came ta terms. I kept people away from one of the approaches to some old guy's house, and Mordecah let me live. Unlive. Whaddeva."

"I like him. He's my scouts master."

"Oh, ya a scout too? Nice! Real weird mix you got going theah."

"Most of it was accidental." Threadbare sighed. "I'm still figuring out how to make it all work. There's so much spread out over so many things."

"That's rough, yo." Madeline said, shooting a glare at the back table, and the other vampires who were rolling their eyes hard at the little bear's "problem." The vampire girl shrugged. "I miss him too. Real enlightened about monstahs and all. But now that he's gone, I'm free to do a few things I've been meaning ta do for a while. Theah's a dungeon out that way by my old stompin' grounds, and I'll need a dungeon coah soon. Should be a cakewalk, too. The little fuzzy bastahds won't know what hit'em!"

"What's a dungeon core?"

"Jeeze, I forgot ya green. It's... there's something that powahs dungeons, makes them dungeons. It warps tha land around them, makes the one who controls it and anyone he chooses immortal. Sort of. It makes copies of them, and adventurers come an' fight tha copies ovah and ovah. It also makes copies of any loot and magic that's in 'em, up to a point. Sometimes they need restocking. Hell, sometimes it improves items, even, or changes 'em." She shivered. "Sometimes it changes the monstahs who run them, too. I think that's what happened to the Cat Queen. Spent too long as a midboss in a dungeon that closed, and now she wants to go back to the only thing that makes sense to her."

"Dungeon cores sound really powerful."

"They ah, but they have a weakness. Theah's always a way to get to the coah chambah in any dungeon, into the place where sanity ends and the numbahs rule all. Dangerous to get in there, but if you can, you can seal or take ovah tha dungeon. If ya seal it, ya get a coah. If ya want one, I mean."

"So why do you want one?"

"Well..." The little vampire sucked her teeth. "I uh, might have some plans latah. Just got to settle stuff with tha Cat Queen first. So if ya ever find a dungeon coah, bring it to me, and I'll make it warth ya while."

"Okay," The little bear agreed. He'd make sure to keep an eye out for anything like that. "Which dungeon was near your place?"

"Oh, this bunch of raccants got the notion ta put one togethah. Found or got a coah somehow, I danno. I'll go settle theah hash latah."

"Wait, raccants?" Threadbare put his cards down. "I was up there just —"

"Dawn," Grimble interrupted.

"Shit. Ah, we'll have to continue this convo latah, okay?" Madeline said, as the other vampires went around the room, sealing the windows with heavy shutters. "Do me a favah and don't come back in heah during the day. Night's okay, but not day. Got that? Do NOT."

"Yes, I understand."

"Good. Now take ya friends and scoot. Remember, get clear of town and take out that ghost witch! Then come back tonaht and we'll talk more."

"Absolutely!" Threadbare and company marched out of the door. Grimble shut it behind them, started to bar it.

Knock, knock, knock.

Grimble paused, looked to Madeline, who rubbed her eyes. "Yah?"

"Excuse me, but where is she again?"

One set of directions shouted through a door later, Threadbare led Missus Fluffbear and Beanarella out of town to the south, down through the hills, into a wooded valley.

Some of the trails and fallen houses to the sides looked familiar. He'd been this way before, he thought.

Eventually, he came to a hollow. Crossing a running stream, he came into a clearing with charred trees, and the remnants of a large, burned hut on a small hill. Rows of gravestones filled the clearing, overturned and shattered, the soil all around them disturbed.

A feeling filled this place, and Missus Fluffbear shivered and honked mournfully. Threadbare felt it too, but he was too busy staring at the new words in front of his face.

A restless spirit wishes to speak!

"Speak With Dead," Threadbare whispered, readying his scepter for a good witch-thumping.

Your Speak With Dead skill is now level 3!

The sunlight wavered, turned brilliant white. The graves were pale marble now, against the black soil and gray, gray grass. The stark black wood of the burned planks turned to obsidian, and faded from view as faint outlines grew around them, forming the shape of a hut.

"Wait. This is where Mordecai and his family live!" Threadbare gasped. "What happened to it?"

And from the spectral beaded curtain, out swept a green arm, the only speck of color left in the world. "Come in, child. Come in."

"Zuula!" Threadbare knew that voice. He burst through the curtain, with a really-unsure-about-this Fluffbear on his fuzzy heels.

Inside, the hut was bigger than he remembered, even with shattered, black beams poking through the wispy stuff that made up the beds, the floor, and the rest of the features. In the middle, humming over a white fire, was a familiar green woman with gold, gold eyes. She smiled at him, and cast something in the fire. "Dreadbear! All grown up... and with a little girl. Or a mate?"

"This is Missus Fluffbear. She's not a girl or a mate."

"Then a friend."

"Oh yes! And there's Beanarella. She's just a golem."

"Oh, dere's something... yes. Hard to see. It has no soul, so Zuula cannot see it so good. Side effect of being dead."

"You're dead?"

"Yes."

"Oh." Threadbare wasn't sure what you were supposed to say about that. Celia had spent a lot of time fussing about trying to make sure her friends didn't die, that she'd infused him with the gravity and horror of it. That and his own skunk murdering ways had drummed in the lesson that people were supposed to try really hard to keep their friends from dying.

He wasn't sure how you were supposed to feel or what you were supposed to say to someone who was already dead. Sorry didn't seem to cut it. And other useful pleasantries he'd picked up from listening to small talk like "how's the weather," or "how are you feeling" didn't seem appropriate.

Then a thought occurred to him. "Wait, did the evil ghost witch get you?"

"Ghost witch?" Zuula stared at him with her unblinking eyes. "Only ghost around here be Zuula."

"Oh. It's just that the nice vampires in town said—"

"Nice vampires? Nice vampires!" Zuula hissed, and the spectral walls shook. Her hair blazed up around her, whipping to and fro in an unfelt wind. For a second the mask on the wall blazed, opened its ghostly mouth and screamed, red glowing from its mouth and eyes. Missus Fluffbear hid behind Beanarella, and Threadbare stood up from the seat he'd taken, alarmed as Zuula continued. "Is no such t'ing! Evil vampires! Filthy bloodsuckers! Stealing Garon! Stealing her son!"

"Wait, what? Please, I'm very confused," Threadbare said.

Finally, the dead shaman calmed down. "Come to tink of it, so is Zuula. You talking about old woman ghost? She necromancer, not witch."

"I don't know, maybe. There's this crazy cat lady necromancer trying to hurt the nice vampires in town, and a ghost witch who's making one of them crazy. And I'm supposed to be able to deal with the ghost witch because I'm a necromancer too and I don't have any flesh for her to wither or life to drain or something." Come to think of it, he wasn't so sure about that second part. He didn't know much about ghosts, or what they could do.

"Wait. You necromancer?" Zuula raised a see-through eyebrow.

"Yes. That's how I can talk to you like this."

"Zuula be wondering why you so... solid-looking. Hm! Dis change everyt'ing! Come out." She motioned to the curtained doorway leading out of the hut. Perplexed, the little bear followed her out. "Vampires be telling you not everything. Dey maybe lying."

"What's lying?"

Zuula froze, mid-step. "Hoo boy. You is still green, yes?"

"No, I'm mostly brown. I'm wearing red and black though."

"Lying is when you say somet'ing wrong to make people act how you want them to."

"That doesn't sound nice."

"It isn't. Friends don't lie to friends, mostly. Sometimes by accident."

"Lying sounds... bad. And a little confusing. Why would you say something wrong on purpose?"

"Well, it okay to lie to bad people. How does... ah, Zuula can see we got lessons to teach... hey, you fading."

"Oh! The spell must be wearing off. **Speak With Dead!**"

Your Speak With Dead spell is now level 4!

You are now a level 2 Necromancer!

INT+3

WIS+3

WILL+3

"There we go." And indeed, things seemed more solid now. "And I just leveled up by casting that spell and talking with you!"

"Really? Just like dat?" In the doorway, Zuula tilted her head. "What level you go to?"

"Two."

"Two? Bah, you not necromancer. You bone-diddler. Come on. We gots show and tell. First she show, den she tell."

Threadbare followed her outside...

...and wow, there were a whole lot of THINGS out there all of a sudden. Really thin things, with hollow eyes, made of bones. They were about the size of humans, and many of them were broken or missing pieces.

"Men come to kill Zuula, along with rest of town. Zuula fight." The scene blurred, and suddenly the bony things wore flesh and armor, fighting and falling to a flying half-orc as she blurred through the sky, sweeping groups of them aside with her club which evidently caused explosions every time it hit. "Zuula do good for a while..." The scenery shifted, and Zuula held a dragon in each hand, bashing the mighty beasts together. "...but eventually fall. Stupid daughter, stupid firstborn working for king. She come. We fight."

The scene shifted again, showing a towering figure twice Zuula's size, battering her down relentlessly with a sword as tall as a tree. The image of Zuula shifted into a bear, and Missus Fluffbear waddled forward to reach out to it, but Threadbare caught her and pulled her back. Zuula continued, oblivious. "Zuula fall. As is right, orc fights orc, strong win. But... unclever son interfere."

Everything flickered, and Garon rushed in from the side. And just as the scene faded, the towering, white-armored figure turned and impaled Garon with one thrust. He reached for his side, with his dying breath, but the sword stroke had cut his coin pouch as well. The figure lifted him up, as coins spilled down, and Garon the Mercenary fell limp reaching down for coins as his blood dripped onto the gold.

"She was in rage. He was in rage. Zuula does not blame. Bad business, but dat is for stupid Mastoya to deal with. Cannot help her no more. But Garon..."

Now the scene was in black and white. The dead lay in piles, and a small, familiar figure crept out of the woods. Madeline, the vampire. She came to Garon...

...and Garon twitched. He reached up to her, and instantly Madeline leaned down, mouth gaping.

There was a CRUNCH, and both of them faded from sight. "She steal Garon. Turn Garon into undead." Zuula spat. "Filthy undead! Not trust undead! No nice vampires. Zuula go to him, call to him all night long, every night. Remind him he is orc! Remind him to FIGHT! And he listen."

"Wait, you can't trust undead?" Threadbare frowned. His common sense was telling him something. **"Assess Corpse."**

Your Assess Corpse skill is now level 3!

Zuula was a level ???? Haunting Spirit. The bony things were level five Shoddy Skeletons.

"You're telling me I can't trust undead, but you're an undead too," Threadbare pointed out.

"Well, dat different. Zuula an orc, first. Humans weak, they go undead, they become all undead. Orc is orc, whether or not they alive. Orcs not lie to good people, like filthy vampires."

"What's so bad about them?"

"They eat people! So do orcs, okay, but we honest about it. And if you win fight with orc you can eat orc, is no hard feelings. But dese vampires bad because dey got Garon, and Garon not want to be vampire! He hate it. Zuula can tell. Is mother's bond."

"Oh no," Threadbare put his paws on his head. "They fooled me. They tricked me into thinking you were an evil ghost witch so you'd stop helping Garon fight." He was a smart bear, and a wise bear, and now he had all the information to make sense of the situation. And he did not like what he saw. "The vampires have Garon, and the Queen of the Cats has Pulsivar. I have to get them both back!"

INT +1

"Who is Pulse Liver?"

"Pulsivar. He's a cat. He was a tomcat but now he's a bobcat, a big black bobcat. He followed the smell of some strange cats. The vampires said he went to the Cat Necromancer, and she'd never let him go. Wait, maybe they were lying about that part?"

Zuula considered. "Maybe, maybe not. Hm... It occur to Zuula that you maybe caught between two warring tribes, here. Why not go see where Pus Liver is—"

"Pulsivar."

"—him too. Go see how he is. If he with Cat Lady, ask for him back. Cat Lady been by here to talk, she seem pleasant enough, if a little weird. Smart enough to leave Zuula alone, anyway. See what she tell you. Den come back and talk with Zuula if you still alive." She shrugged. "Hell, come back talk with Zuula if you dead, too. Shouldn't make no difference eider way."

Threadbare nodded. Then he went up and gave her knee a hug. "Thank you."

"Oh child." Zuula squatted down and ruffled his head. "You got a lot of worries. Got a lot of growing up to do. Come back to Zuula, she t'ink about how to help you when you gone, and after you back we maybe see about making you proper orc strong."

"I will," he promised, and then as the ghostly parts of the world faded back and color started to return to the area, he took Missus Fluffbear's paw and led her out into the trail. He checked the party screen, to make sure she hadn't gotten in any trouble there—

—and got the shock of his life, as he realized she was now a level one necromancer, in addition to her other jobs. Why? What...

...oh. Oh right. Repeated peaceful contact with undead. First the vampires, and now Zuula's ghost. And she'd auto-yes'd the job prompt when it came up. That must have been what happened.

Well, at least she'd gotten some good mental stats out of it, but Threadbare realized he'd have to be careful with what he dragged her into. She was literally very impressionable. If she wasn't careful she'd end up like he had, with all her options filled before she could speak or have much of a choice in the matter.

"You have to be careful, okay?" He told her, giving her paw a squeeze. She nodded at him, and honked her horn a few times.

"Does that mean you understand?"

HONKITY HONK HONK

He supposed that was the best he could hope for. At least until he
taught her how to write. Or figured out a way to do the stuff necessary to
give her a voice without scaring her. So many things to do, so little time!

It took about an hour to get back to where he'd left the scent trail last
night. Firing up his sniffer, he managed to locate it again.

PER +1

Your Scents and Sensibility skill is now level 18!

He followed the trail past the town, back up into the hills, and the
well-worn ruts picked their way up a stony path. Ramshackle remnants
of wooden towers and metal tracks interrupted the trail every now and
then, overlooking a large pit with steps leading down into it.

But up above the pit, at the base of the tallest mountain in the area, a
mine shaft gaped open. Four times the size of the one that the raccants
had occupied, it was lit from within by an eerie, glowing green light. It
also had two bonikitties out front, staring solemnly ahead. One Assess
Corpse and a skill up later, and he found that they were level ten
skeletons.

Well. This was troublesome. He approached, cautiously, gesturing for
Missus Fluffbear to stay behind Beanarella.

He needn't have bothered. As soon as he got within a few hundred
feet of the mine, a blue glow interrupted the green, and a familiar voice
called out. "Oh, hello there, you precious little thing! Oh look at your
tiny hat, it's so fitting!"

Your Work it Baby skill is now level 9!

You are now a level 4 Model!

AGL+3

CHA+3

PER+3

Checking Dietary Restrictions timer....

**Your Dietary Restrictions skill is now level 20! Buff adjusted
accordingly.**

He waved. That was the nice lady ghost he'd met in the Catacombs,
back in the Catamountain. That had been a good tea party, he
remembered.

"Oh come in, come in out of the sun! It's so hard to see you with
these old eyes. Do come closer, my dear." The bonikitties stepped to
either side of the mine entrance, and waved their skeletal paws.

Well, that was a good sign. And Pulsivar's trail did go straight to that
mine. Threadbare checked the party screen, found the cat in good health,
and wandered in, with Fluffbear and Beanarella tromping behind him.

"And you've brought some little friends!" The cat lady was much as he remembered her. See-through, still clad in her spectral crooked top hat and gingham dress. She also had two very large creatures to either side, cats so big they dwarfed even Pulsivar, with dead flesh drawn tightly over bones, and blue glowing light where their eyes should be. Assess Undead turned up the truth of her, and her minions.

TOCKSY P. LASMOSIS – LEVEL ???? SPECTROMANCER

The big cats were both level ???? Wight Tigers.

"So what brings you to my neck of the woods, hmmmm?" She said, bustling about a small living space set up in the opening of the mine, opening cupboards that looked like she'd salvaged them from burned and fallen houses, and taking out broken crockery, laying it on a table that had definitely seen better days.

From further in the mine, Threadbare could hear the wailing of cats, big and small. He started that way, but stopped when the tigers moved in unison and blocked his path.

"I'm looking for Pulsivar," he said. "The vampires said you had him. He's a big black bobcat."

"Oh! You mean Spookums!" The cat lady smiled, and turned to him. Her eyes were wild, now, and Threadbare got the distinct feeling he had to tread carefully. "He's having ever so much fun here, entertaining the ladies. Well, the ones I haven't had to wake up to their full potential yet, anyway. Like I woke Rajah and Regal, here." She stroked one of the Wight Tigers, spectral hand sinking into its head. It purred, arching its neck, and its breath smelled of dried meat that had spoiled.

"Okay, but can he come back when he's done?" Threadbare asked. "I really need his help. He's my friend."

"Mmm. Why don't we have tea and discuss that," the old woman smiled.

Threadbare nodded.

Beanarella was easily guided through mental commands, but he had to show Fluffbear how to sit. The old woman chuckled fondly, finding both toys thoroughly adorable. They had a good tea party, even if Fluffbear did keep dropping her cup.

CHA +1

Your Adorable skill is now level 19!

At the end of it, she sighed. "The vampires have told you all sorts of nasty things about me, I imagine. Really, I'm not so bad. I just want the Catamountain back, that's all. But those nasty vampires, and their impudent little girl want the same thing! And neither of us can start a dungeon with the other still here. It'd be far too easy to raid into it, and catch me alone in the Core Chamber, with all our friends locked away into the variable slots."

"What's a variable slot?"

"I don't know, that's what Nekochan called them. Weird little girl, but just so cute! She killed me, when I tried to raid her dungeon, but I didn't hold a grudge. After all, it became my home! It was... it was my proper place." The cat lady stared over her teacup. "Have you ever had a proper place, little bear? A place where everything was all right with the world?"

Threadbare remembered Celia's arms, and the hours of play, and how the little girl laughed when he danced for her, and how she liked it when he hugged her. "Yes," he said, and the sorrow came over him again. "And I'll get back there again, some day. No matter what. But for that I need my friends. I need Pulsivar," he rallied, remembering his mission. "Please can I have him back?"

She sighed. "Right now? No. I need his help. He's just too strong, he'd be a vampire killing machine, properly supported. But..." She scratched her chin. "I'll make you a deal. If you can bring me a dungeon core, or wipe out the vampires, I'll see about getting him away from my girls." She smiled, as she brought the teacup up to her face, considering him with gleaming eyes. "Assuming he wants to go, of course. If it turns out he... has an *awakening*... and wants to stay here, well, you might just have to leave him in *his* proper place, hmmm?"

Her tone was different, Threadbare noted. A bit more smug. Awakening... she'd put emphasis on that word, and she said she'd awakened the wight tigers, and they were undead now.

PER +1

Was this lying? He thought it over, and the very wise little bear decided that it might be bad to ask her that.

He needed to talk to Zuula, though. He was swimming in dark depths and didn't have a clear way ahead. "Thank you. I'll see what I can do. They are not nice vampires."

"So glad we've come to an agreement!" The woman beamed. "And now I'm afraid you must be going. My ghouls will be coming back from... scavenging the village... shortly. They might react poorly if they find you here."

"Okay," Threadbare jumped down, and tugged at Missus Fluffbear until she followed. "No, you can't keep the cup. It's hers."

That took a little explaining, and a few angry honks, but he finally got the point across. The little bear headed off back down the trail, just managing to clear it before a shambling group of rotting forms started up the hillside path. These were humanoid, but he didn't stick around to look.

Your Stealth skill is now level 10!

"Zuula! Zuula!" He yelled, running back towards the hut as soon as he got into the clearing. "Oh, right. **Speak With Dead.** Zuula! Zuula! She's going to kill Pulsivar and turn him into an undead—"

He stopped.

The clearing in front of the charred hut ruin was filled with skeletons, every one of them wielding a club. Behind them, Zuula stood, arms folded.

"Um... is everything all right?"

"Been t'inking about ways to train up you necromancy, little Dreadbear. But t'inking hard work. Orc already know how to get strong. You want to be more than little level two bone diddler?"

"I don't even know what that last word means."

"Just say yes."

"Yes."

"Good. We train de orky way! Use necromancy and fight!"

And as one, the skeletons advanced on him, raising their clubs.

******

Five hours, six necromancer levels, and three new skills later, his training was interrupted by new words scrolling across his vision.

By slaying over a hundred undead creatures, you have unlocked the cleric job!

You cannot become a cleric at this time!

Cleric? Beryl had been a cleric, he remembered. But he was too busy to think on it, as he shouted out commands to his controlled undead, while running away from the still active skeletons. In the back, Zuula yawned and reanimated one of the ones he'd knocked to bits earlier, and sent it back into the fray.

Then a brilliant light flared. Zuula stopped. Threadbare stopped. The skeletons froze.

And every eye, spectral eye, or hollow eyesocket in the clearing turned to look at the hovering form of Missus Fluffbear, as she lifted off the ground, turning slowly in a column of light.

Missus Fluffbear, who had cracked the secret of "yes" to make the prompts disappear. And whom Threadbare realized, calling up the party screen, was now a level one Cleric.

"Speak with Dead," Threadbare muttered. "Wait, give us a minute here Zuula. Please, I... I don't know what's happening."

"Puny gods be touching her, is what," Zuula said, waving a hand as the skeletons slithered back underground, to their graves. "She be choosing now. Hope she chooses wisely. Hope you taught her well."

"I've barely taught her anything at all."

"You taught her enough for now," a voice that wasn't his whispered in his ear. It was like a Scout's Wind's Whisper, but so much louder, and the voice that spoke it shook him in every part of his stuffing, as it spoke. "You taught her enough. But soon you can teach each other. Go with my grace."

Then the light shuddered and disappeared, and Fluffbear floated to the ground. She stared around wildly, and ran up to him.

"What is it? Did you hear the voice too?"

She nodded frantically, and pawed at his mouth. Then pawed at hers.

"Do you want me to stop talking?"

No, no, no, went her head, and HONK HONK HONKILY HONK HONKS went her horn.

Light dawned. "You want a mouth so you can talk!"

Yes, yes, yes went her head.

"Okay, but it's going to take a little while. I'm going to have to cut part of you open to do this, are you okay with that?"

She was. And she sat still bravely, as he took his scissors and made the cuts, then fiddled around with his tailoring materials until he could get everything just right. Then he sewed her up again, and stepped back. "Give it a try."

"Op. Akka. Pom. Bukkle."

"Try saying what I say."

"I aying at I ay."

"No, use your lips. Oh, hang on."

"Pie Aying Pot I Pay."

"Right, your tongue is different because you're so small. Let me adjust that..." A few snips and some new structures later, and she was mimicking his words pretty well.

"What happened? When you became a cleric?" He asked, once she had a pretty good grasp of talking.

"There was a light. A lot of big things looking at me. Then a man came forward and said he would help me. He had a big hammer like my old friend Scoops used to. His name was Yorgum, and he said he was the god of builders."

"Oh, okay."

"He said to pester you until you made me a mouth. He said the monsters have to leave this town so it can grow again someday. And that we're really special because there's so very few like us, at least right now. And that he couldn't tell us too much because of rules, but we should ask the nice lady about some of the weird stuff you found. And to go smite all of their asses. What's an ass?"

"I think it's the part you sit on." Threadbare concentrated. The rest of it didn't make much sense. "Weird stuff? I don't have too much of— oh, wait a minute." He turned back to Zuula, and rummaged in his pack, pulling out the red crystal with flickering numbers. "You're a nice lady. Do you know what this is?"

Zuula's ghostly eyes grew wide. "Dat be a dungeon core! How you get dat, little bear?"

"This is what they both want?" He asked, confused. "How do you even make dungeons with this? There's no help prompt."

"Wait," Zuula said, her eyes getting even wider. "Dey both want a dungeon core? Who dey?"

"The Cat Lady and the Vampires."

Zuula stood there, thinking for a bit.

And then she shook her head. "No, no. Wouldn't work. Zuula be bound here. Got no way to come along with. If she could come with you, would work. But she can't, so... no. Pity. Was awesome idea, too. Big violence, many asses smote."

"I want to do that!" Missus Fluffbear spoke up. "The nice god told me to!"

"Wait. You're stuck here?" Threadbare asked.

"Yes. Bound to hut. No way to go, no vessel to carry her."

"Hmm... **Status**." Yes, yes that worked the way he thought it did. "I may have a way around that. **Soulstone**."

Your Soulstone skill is now level 2!

A black crystal materialized in his paw. About the size of a small apple, it seemed to draw in the light around it.

"Oh..." Zuula said, approaching it. "Wimpy. Can feel it tugging, but so weak, so weak. Still, if she don't resist..." She touched it, and her form blurred, oozed into the stone, and was gone. A fleck of green light flickered, deep in the crystal.

There was a pause.

"Level fucking one?" Zuula's voice shrieked, bouncing around inside the stone. "No. Huh-uh." She shook, and the soulstone shattered as she burst out of it. "Not gonna ride in such a puny vessel. Total refuse. Professional orc pride on line." The spirit folded her arms and pouted, which looked weird on her tusked face.

"Maybe it's that low because my skill with it is so low," Threadbare mused. "Or because I'm only a level seven Necromancer."

"Well! Zuula know cure for dat!" She grinned, and up came the skeletons again.

They trained well into the night, but soon hit diminishing returns. Fluffbear got some good cleric levels, but Threadbare only got two necromancer level-ups, which didn't seem to affect the Soulstone quality. So he switched to casting Soulstone over and over again, skilling up as far as he could given his sanity limitations. In frustration he appraised it using his neglected Enchanter skill... and leveling that job up as well.

You are now a level 2 Enchanter!
DEX +3
INT +3
WILL +3

That was nice, but the appraise turned up bad news for Zuula. "Well, my skill's at twenty-four now. So your effective level in the soulstone is going to be a three. I think it's one level for every ten or fraction of ten," Threadbare said, showing her the crystal. He knew what fractions were now, he realized. And a lot more math besides. Such were the benefits of sudden intelligence boosts, he supposed.

Zuula wasn't any happier with level three than she was with level one. "What! No. No, a t'ousand times no!"

It took a lot of pleading, every bit of charisma he had, and finally pointing out that her son was on the line to get her to relent. Finally, begrudgingly, she oozed into the crystal. Threadbare blinked, as new information came up on his appraisal. "It's a level one crystal now."

"Which mean what?"

"I could use it to make a toy golem. Or do enchanting stuff with. Maybe."

There was a long pause. "Maybe don't try dat while Zuula in it."

"Yeah, I don't know what that would do."

"I could ask Yorgum," Fluffbear offered.

"Bah, what do gods know of it? No, listen, Zuula got more important stuff on how to kick all undead asses. Zuula got great idea. Now she go with you, and we make sure both sides lose, and we get you friends back. Interested?"

"Of course I am," Threadbare said.

"So you got de dungeon core, right? And dey both want it, right?"

"Yes."

"So let us give it to dem. At de same time..."

CHAPTER 5: THE BEAR, THE VAMP, AND THE CATLADY

The vampires of Taylor's Delve had learned long ago, and at great cost, that they couldn't spread out and sleep through the day with individual coffins. The Cat Queen hunted them by day, and her minions had good enough senses of smell that they could find the graves. And once the necromancer had found a reliable source of bodies to make ghouls from, it was easy for the enemy to dig them up, and dump the shrieking vampires out into the sunlight to sizzle. Madeline had lost too many spawn that way, before the Angst caught on. (An Angst is the proper word for a group of vampires. Crows have murders, wolves have packs, vampires have angsts.)

So now they spent days under the tavern, in the tunnel network they'd hollowed out with time, patience, and strong undead hands. It had multiple escape routes, and it was big enough that they could team up against any ghouls who managed to dig their way into the tunnels, and dispose of them. One on one, the Cat Queen's minions were no match for the vampires. But it was never a one on one scenario, which was why they were down to Mads and her three spawn.

Well, four, but that last one wasn't much use. Still, she'd taken the trouble to drag him downstairs, lashed to his bed, as usual. Thank Nebs for small favors that the original owner of this building believed in wide staircases.

He'd gone silent hours ago, though, and Madeline sat, stroking his brow. Had the little bear succeeded? She'd sent him out there because she thought he had good odds, but the glory of it was that it wouldn't hurt her position either way. She'd risked no loss to herself or to her angst by putting the toy golems in danger, so she'd done it.

She did know that this was the calmest she'd seen Garon in ages. "Ding dong the witch is dead," she hummed, smiling down as Garon's red, red eyes squinted up at her.

"I can't feel her. What did you do?" he rasped.

"I didn't do nathing. Some teddy bear mighta killed her, though. Well, de-animahted her, I mean."

"No!" He surged against the bindings, and Madeline jumped back, hand upraised. "She was my mother!" Garon howled.

"She was holding ya back!" Madeline yelled, her patience at an end. "I saved ya, not her! And we need ya strength if ya want to keep on existing!"

"I never asked for this!" bloody spittle flew from his mouth. His tusks had grown since his undeath, they cut into his lips when he talked. Madeline winced, and shook her head. *If he wasn't so gods damned cute, I swear, I'd leave him out to bake.*

"Look. Ya spent five years fighting me. Fine, whatevs. Vampy puberty, most a yas go through it. But what's it gaht ya?" She spread her hands. "Can't beat me. I'm ya mastah. Got hooks in ya brain, Garon. Fight as ya want, at the end of the naht, it's my will be done."

"Mother told me..." Garon rasped, his throat raw, "Being an orc... means never stop fighting..."

"Yah, but yer only half an orc, huh? Five years ya defied me, so now maybe you give me five yeahs of peace for a change?"

He roared, and Madeline rolled her eyes, and turned to go—

—and ran straight into Grimble. He held up a grubby peace of paper. "We've got mail."

"What?"

"This just got slipped under the door."

"I told yas not to go upstairs after dawn!"

"Somebody knocked. Ghouls don't knock."

"Fahkin... what's it say." She grabbed it from the Grifter, and peeled it open.

I destroyed the ghost witch like you asked. She hurt me pretty badly, so I can't leave her clearing right now. The ghost witch was guarding a dungeon core, and I want to give it to you. But I think the Cat Queen knows. Please send help as soon as you can!

I'm sending this message to you with Missus Fluffbear. Please come as soon as night falls.

Cordially, Threadbare

Madeline's eyes went wide. "Winnah winnah chicken dinnah!"

"What?"

"We tried ta draw three of a kind and gaht a full house. Get Darla and Barret ready. We march at night."

"What about..." He nodded past her, at Garon, still howling and frothing.

"I gaht him." She said. "Maybe he'll want ta pay his respects."

Silence. "My respects?" Garon croaked.

"Yeah, the one that croaked yer mah? No shit, it was this talkin' teddy bear guy!"

"Wait. What?"

"Came into town with a troop of toys, wearin' a top hat and showin' off a bunch of adventurah jobs. One of'em was necromancer, and so I sent him ghost witch huntin'. And he succeeded! Now we're ganna go and get the booty from him." She sighed. "Innocent little guy. I almost feel bad fah playin' him."

"Innocent, yes," Garon's face fell into a blank expression. "So he went out there and beat up my mother, huh? Did he know the details beforehand?"

"Pssh, why bothah with that?" Madeline shrugged. "Not like he had a stake in her survival anyway. Come on, are you with us or naht?"

"I'll go with you," Garon said. He'd learned to be very careful with his words over the years. But Madeline heard what she wanted, and unbound the heavy chains holding him to the bedframe.

Outside, they ran into the rest of the spawn. Grimble held the letter up to her, frowning. "Are you sure this isn't a trick?"

"What? Please. From that little beah?" Madeline laughed. "You saw how gullible he was!"

Grimble's Grifterly instincts fought with him one last time, but lost. "Yeah, that is a pretty ridiculous notion. He's just a foolish little toy, after all."

"Wouldn't last five minutes in a propah dungeon," Madeline agreed, as the vampires suited up. Darla handed Garon his axe, for the first time in years, watching him to make sure he wouldn't get stupid. But he just slid it into his belt, sneering.

"What've you got to be happy about?" Darla whispered. She'd never liked the half-breed much.

"Oh, I'll tell you later," Garon lied.

He never did tell her, but by the time it came up telling wasn't necessary.

*****

Andrew Seiple

In the green light of her cave, the old lady squinted at the letter.

I went looking for a dungeon core like you asked, and I found one. The ghost who had it is dead, but I need help. I'm really hurt and I need Pulsivar to take me to safety. He knows the way.
But I think the vampires know where I am. Please hurry! I just hope this letter reaches you in time.
Cordially,
Threadbare

"Hm... hm... well isn't this interesting, my dearies?" the old lady said, stroking a small tabby cat as it tried to flee. It clawed at her futilely, feeling its flesh writhe under her spectral touch. Where her fingers stroked, fur turned white, white as snow.

The cat screamed. The old lady smiled benevolently. "Oh, you're hungry my dear? Of course, of course. You there, **Command Undead, lay down for feeding time.**" she snapped at one of the just-returned ghouls. Snarling, eyes rolling in hatred, the ghoul did as it was told. Instantly, from the rear of the cavern, dozens of cats descended, ribs thin against their hides, mouths open and hungry. The ghoul vanished under a furry carpet, screaming as it became prey, instead of predator.

It was a good system, as far as the Spectromancer was concerned. The ghouls went out and ate the dead, regenerating their gruesome flesh, then they came back and the cats ate from them. Sure, some of the cats fell ill and died, but she just woke them up again and they were right as rain. She looked forward to putting the method into widespread use once she had a little more territory to her name.

Miss Tocksy put the tabby down and it ran from her, on trembling legs. She paid it no notice, turning to one of her Wight Tigers. "What do you think, dearies? Do you think we should bring Spookums to him? Hm... He does so like it here." She rose and walked back into the mineshaft. The dead cats came out to meet her, purring. The living ones fled for their lives. She walked past green glowstones set into the ceiling, past the old cart with two cougar skeletons harnessed to it, past all of that until she got to the back rooms. There, the black bobcat lay exhausted, grooming a cougar a third again his size. The cougar flinched back from the Spectromancer as she entered, and Pulsivar studied her with unimpressed eyes. Then the bobcat's yellow gaze shifted to the Wight Tiger, and his tail lashed, furiously.

"Come now Spookums, Mopsy, everyone's friends here," Tocksy said. "How would you like to go walkies?"

Mopsy retreated. Her heat was about over, and the all-consuming fire that had filled her was quenched. Now self-preservation was kicking in.

"Come," Tocksy insisted. "Walk."

Mopsy, white scars showing stark against her tan fur, followed meekly. The Spectromancer's touch could and had drained her moxie to dangerously low levels.

Concerned, Pulsivar followed, freezing as the Wight Tiger rumbled. Yellow eyes met blue ones, and narrowed. The bobcat did not like the smell of these weird predators. He thought they might need a lesson.

Then Mopsy looked back to him, and that beautiful, earthshaking odor filled his nose again. Completing that mating season quest had got him a level, and been pretty enjoyable overall. So he followed her, ignoring the Wight Tiger with the utmost dignity as they passed.

"Yes," The old lady mused, as her ghostly form floated through the mine. "Let's bring everyone for walkies..."

*****

The vampires were the first on the scene. "Grimble, up in tha tree, watch for theah ahss."

"On it." He had a pretty good stealth, even before he'd been vamped. Up he went, peering into the night. The worst of the Cat Queen's servants had glowing blue eyes, and they were visible from a long way off. But the woods were thick and they were cats, so he stayed sharp.

"Shit, what happened here?" Darla said, walking into the clearing, with her spear and shield out.

"Was it always like this?" Barret asked, pestle at the ready.

The graves, already disturbed, had been full-on wrecked. Most looked empty, and soil and bones were strewn all over the place. The burned-out hut was a tangle, and what looked like poofy cloth was all over the place, hanging from the charred timbers and broken skulls.

"Stuffing. That's stuffing," Madeline said. She gnawed her lip at the implications, and felt sorry for the poor little bastard. "Mistah beah? You okay?" She risked calling.

Something in the hut stirred. "Missus Fluffbeah? You theah?" She approached.

It scrabbled more, and she leaped onto the ruins, threw planks aside for all she was worth...

...and yelped, as the floor collapsed under her, where someone had dug with tiny paws, and weakened the supports. For a second there was way, way too much sharp wood crunching in all around her—

—but fortunately, a vampire's heart is a very, very small target and she hadn't played all those years of grindluck for nothing. A trio of red '37's burst up around her, and she swore as Barret helped her out.

"Fahck! Fahck!" She hissed, pulling jagged planks out of herself. Vampires got their wood allergies at level five, and she was ten levels past that. The splinters in her burned, and distracted her.

Grimble wasn't as distracted. "There!" He yelled, pointing at a small skeletal form high in a tree. To the vampires it stood out as clearly as if it was in bright daylight.

And it didn't hurt that green light shown from its skull, green light dancing against red glowing crystal. The bonikitty had a dungeon core in its head!

The little bear's plight was completely forgotten, **"Fast as Death,"** Madeline hissed, and dashed toward the tree, moving at a speed no living thing could match—

—but then the (unliving) cat was bounding from tree to tree, heading deeper into the woods.

"Aftah it!" The vampire girl bellowed, and her angst fell in behind her, moving slowly, much more slowly.

Garon lagged behind a bit, slowing to look at the ruins of the hut more closely. For a second, sorrow passed over his face...

...sorrow that turned to joy, as a top-hatted teddy bear faded out of the shadows, and tossed a clinking bag at his feet.

Garon stared down at him, and bloody tears wept from his eyes, as he stretched out a hand.

"Garon, please listen closely," whispered Threadbare. "I have a quest for you..."

A few hundred feet into the woods ahead, Darla glanced back when she heard the mad half-breed whoop. What was he on about now?

"Do the Job! Forced March! Fight The Battles! Follow The Dotted Line!" She heard him yell.

Ah, good, he was taking matters seriously now, Darla thought, and turned back to the chase.

*****

The Spectromancer heard the shouting from half a mile out, those hated bloodsuckers calling back to each other through the woods, shouting "Catch it! Run it down!"

That poor bear! Picking up the pace, she waved and her army of squalling dead felines followed behind her, along with two very puzzled living cats. Unseen, from his position behind the Cat Queen, Pulsivar nudged Mopsy as he ran, and swerved off towards the woods. The cougar eyed him, but did not follow, and eventually the bobcat swerved back, looking annoyed.

A coughing roar came from behind him, and the bobcat jumped, shot an angry glance back at the Wight Tiger. Yellow eyes met blue again, and death shone in both gazes. This would only end one way, they both knew. And it was only a matter of *when*.

"Oh my dear what did they do to you!" The Spectromancer's voice rose up in a wail, and the tiger broke the staredown, lumbered after its mistress.

The Cat Queen stood in the clearing, looking up at the fluff scattered around the wrecked hut. Then her eyes narrowed. "Puffweed fluff?" She said, peering at it more closely. And it was. Here in the mountains it bloomed far earlier than it did elsewhere, and someone had wadded great masses of it together, wetted it down to look like stuffing.

For all her obsession, the Queen was no fool. "This is a trap! Retreat, dearies, retreat—"

She broke off, as a lone bonikitty jumped into the clearing, and a small figure leaped after it, flying with no visible means of support. Madeline the vampire landed on the skeletal cat with both feet—

—and the dungeon core flew out of the destroyed skull, flashing green numbers on red crystal in the darkness, as it lay there for all to see.

"You killed her!" The Cat Queen screeched, as her minions piled into the clearing behind her, and the vampire spawn formed up around Madeline. Then the furious Spectromancer's eyes fell to the dungeon core. "Mine!" She spat.

Madeline grinned, as she scooped it up. "Come and take it, then." Oh, this was perfect! The she-bitch had always hidden behind her minions before. But now? Now they had a shot at taking her out directly.

Then the horde of growling, hissing bonikitties and cat wights slid out of the trees, and Madeline's grin faltered a bit. My, there were a lot of them.

And then it was too late for regrets, too late for anything but violence.

*****

One of the oldest orcish games, often played in variations among other species and known by other names, is called "let's you and him fight."

It's typically used when a weaker tribe is caught between two bigger tribes, and when done correctly, can ensure that the weaker tribe is the strongest one around. For a while, anyway, because orcs aren't good at lasting dynasties or the whole "not-picking-fights-against-bad-odds" thing.

When done incorrectly, the poor game-playing tribe's bones are made into toys for clever children to play with, to remind them not to be too clever unless they can pull it off.

Under the moonlight, bones flew as undead cats died, but not before tearing into wounded vampires. The vampires were stronger, true, but their defenses weren't that great. They relied upon blood to heal their wounds normally, and well, the undead they fought had none.

But the undead were weaker, much weaker, and as they fell the Cat Queen burned sanity to raise new skeletons from the bones around the hut. Sanity she wouldn't replace, unless she somehow gained a level. And at the level she was, that seemed unlikely.

Both sides were weakening themselves, and increasing the odds that the little group of friends would come out on top, and reunite with their lost loved ones.

"We pulled it off," Zuula whispered to Threadbare from her crystal shell. The soulstone almost seemed to glow with a smug green light. Not too far from her, Missus Fluffbear peered through the weeds, with the quiet form of Beanarella sitting placidly next to her.

The final member of their party was overhead, unnoticed in the night, gliding on skeletal wings. It had a part to play later.

Threadbare nodded at Zuula's words, rubbing his head. He'd animated a piece of cloth and made an eye for it, sticking it into the bonikitty they'd also animated. Dollseye had let him personally guide his undead through the forest, but it had been a really rough chase. Even with Missus Fluffbear's newly-learned clerical blessing of agility on the lesser undead, it had only been a matter of time until the vampires caught it.

Fortunately, he had kept ahead of Madeline just long enough.

The hard part was done. Well, mostly. "Why did we have to put you in the Soulstone, anyway?" He wondered.

"Dey not come around here if Zuula still here," Zuula explained. "Dey know better. Fear her too much. So Zuula hide in stupid crystal shell dat sticks her at level fucking t'ree. You is welcome."

"All right. Well I guess it's going... okay..." Threabare said, as one of the Wight Tigers flew past him, with Madeline desperately pummeling it as it ripped into her. He winced to see it. She'd been nice. But on the other hand she'd lied, and he really needed Garon back. And his mother seemed to think it was right decision.

"Never fear, little Dreadbear," Zuula chortled, mistaking his apprehension. "Zuula's time come. You wait and see."

"Oh, no, I wasn't worried about that. I just think it's a pity—"

An armored form flew through the air, bounced off a tree, and got up. Darla stared down at Threadbare, Fluffbear, and Beanarella. "You're fine? And you're just sitting here watching? What the—" Comprehension dawned on the dead knight's face. "You bastards!"

"**Command Undead, please sit down and be still,**" Threadbare tried.

Spell failed! Target is in the party of a more powerful intelligent undead.

"Oh bother," he muttered, as the vampire came for him, jabbing with her spear.

"**Dolorous Strike! Dolorous Strike!**" She chanted, gashing along his side with jabs that knocked him backward and tore his hide. For all his armor, she was good at what she did, and the little bear widened as twin red '64's escaped into the sky.

"**Godspell mend!**" Missus Fluffbear yelled, and some of it healed, but the vampire lunged forward and kicked her out into the clearing.

"No quarter, traitor!" Darla hissed.

"Let's hug it out," Threadbare decided, arms spreading wide.

"Ha! Not going to fall to that one!"

"Oh. I wasn't talking to you, sorry."

Cloth arms closed around one of Darla's greaves, and she looked down—

—to see Beanarella looking back up at her.

Light flared, and Darla screamed, as a red '100' floated up and the pulse of golden light illuminated the trees. The battle halted, and both sides turned to see the vampire fall, flesh turning to ash as the doll healed her. She was undead, after all, and the power behind Beanarella's innocent embrace was divine. Power that would have mended living flesh scorched her unholy dead flesh to nothing.

Empty armor clanged to the ground, and Darla blew away in the breeze.

"Hoo hoo hoo!" The cat lady chortled. "Looks like you've been betrayed, dearie!"

"Threadbare, what the fahk?" Madeline yelled. "What the fahk!"

"No, it's okay," the little bear said. "I tricked both of you, so that makes it okay. I think that's how orc rules work."

"Orc rules?" Madeline asked.

"I knew it was a trap!" The Cat Queen howled. "Come on dearies, get me that core and let's get out of here. Go!"

"Fuck it, if he's a traitor, I got no reason not to fill up my belly," Grimble said, turning his eyes to the big black living cat that he'd been eyeing since the start of this battle, the one that had been sitting on the sideline watching. "You fucked us over, we kill your friend, buddy!"

"You don't touch Spookums!" The Cat Queen howled, but then Madeline was on her, and she had other problems.

"No!" Threadbare yelled, but he was far across the field from Grimble. The little bear ran toward him, shouting his buffs on the way, trying to reach the vampire in time.

"No no no!" Missus Fluffbear sat up from where she'd been kicked, and ran as well. She didn't have as far to go...

...but she needn't have worried. As soon as the vampire got close, Pulsivar nudged Mopsy the Cougar and leaped away, disappearing into the night.

"One pussy's as good as another," Grimble snarled, turning to look at the cougar that eyed him with uncertain eyes. He advanced on her instead

"Holy Smite!" Missus Fluffbear yelled, and a glowing whip three times its size outlined her weapon. The Grifter screamed as it cracked into him, searing.

"You can talk now? I knew you were faking, you little fur bitch!"

"I don't know what that means!" Missus Fluffbear yelled back, and kept on whipping him.

Threadbare sprinted in—

—and then one of the Wight Tigers was in front of him, and he skidded to a halt.

"Please move," Threadbare tried.

The tiger clawed him, bit him, picked him up and shook him—

—then gasped, as two claws slashed into its cheeks, tearing its lower jaw loose as the bear dropped to the ground, crouching.

He didn't look as damaged as things the tiger bit normally did. The dead feline had no way of knowing that golems whose bodies were developed enough were resistant to the cold, dead touch of wights.

Though it was good for skilling up, mind you.

Your Golem Body skill is now level 21.

"Just don't die!" he tried to call to Missus Fluffbear. Then he waded into the Wight Tiger, claws flashing.

Meanwhile, Missus Fluffbear's lash left black streaks on Grimble's flesh, as it tore through his shirt, but he ignored it and marched toward her. Scooping her up with his far-superior strength and size, he took hold of her head with one hand, and her body with the other as she flailed and fought and tried to squirm free. "I did this to my sister's dolly once, when we were kids! She cried for days!" the vampire roared as he started to pull—

—and then black fur flashed out of the darkness.

If he'd been undamaged, perhaps he could have survived it. But Grimble had been hurt, fighting the Cat Queen's forces, as hurt as Darla had been before her fatal hug, and he had nowhere near Darla's hit points. Pulsivar tore through him like a blender through jelly.

Missus Fluffbear fell, nodded her thanks as she patted her stitches. That... that had been too close. **"Godspell Mend,"** she whispered, and waved to the big cat. The bobcat stared at her, licked his paw, and groomed himself—

—and promptly got blindsided as the other Wight Tiger leaped on him, growling.

It was go time, and the two disappeared into a tangle of limbs, and caterwauls, and roars, raging across the woodline.

Fluffbear started to chase after them... and a coughing growl interrupted her. She turned to see Mopsy the Cougar slinking closer, eyes on the little furry creature.

"Um..." Missus Fluffbear said, picking up her whip from the ground. "Good kitty?"

Mopsy roared and leaped.

Back in the center of the clearing, Madeline ignored the bonikitties on her back, clawing and chewing at her head and neck as she tore another handful of ectoplasm from the Cat Queen.

"Damn you!" Tocksy yelled. **"Command Undead! Lie down and do nothing!"**

But Madeline resisted. "As if!" She ripped a bonikitty off her neck and threw it into the spectromancer, sending her tumbling backward through the air. Then she took a few precious seconds and tore the little cat skeletons loose, grinding them to splinters in her bare hands.

"Status," the Spectromancer chanted, and blanched even paler when she saw how low her sanity had gotten. Not to mention her hit points. It was time to call it a night, she thought. Escape, evade, and come for the impudent little girl later. "We'll settle this another night dearie. Goodbye! Hoo hoo hoo—

Suddenly the clearing shook, as a broken wooden mask rose from the ruins of the hut, eyes filled with red, red light and mouth roaring out fire as it rose.

And all of the bones littering the clearing, all of the soldier's skeletons that had been exhumed, stood up at once. They tore into the remaining undead cats, and the dead ripped each other to pieces.

"Hoo." Zuula finished, as her ghost materialized. The air trembled, and the Spectromancer and the vampire fell to the ground. "Welcome to Zuula's house," said the ghost witch. "First rule? No flying. Second rule? You never LEAVE!" Zuula roared, as her mask fitted itself to her face.

"Garon? Garon! Talk some sense inta her!" Madeline yelled... and turned to see her spawn's axe coming straight for her face. "Oh you fahka!"

And then master and spawn fought. No quarter asked or given.

Meanwhile, at the treeline, Threadbare finally felled the Wight Tiger. His buffs had saved him from much of the damage, and a few mends put him right. "Fluffbear?" He called, hearing only feline yowling, and the lash of a whip... a whip that fell silent after a few seconds. "Fluffbear!" He ran toward his friend.

Then he hesitated. On his party screen, Pulsivar's hit points were dropping. Fluffbear's were stable, if only at half their normal level. "Fluffbear?" he said, turning away a bit, looking for his bobcat.

"I'm fine. I think... I think she's sorry," Fluffbear called.

"What?" He squinted over, and among the trees, he saw the cougar cringing. His darkspawn skill let him pick out every old scar, every tracery of white in her fur. And she smelled... she smelled afraid. And also she smelled like Pulsivar. "Okay, if you know what you're doing."

"No. But I think it'll work out."

"Okay..." He turned and ran for Pulsivar.

In his hurry, he sped right past the vampires.

"You should have let me die!" Garon roared. **"Twisted Rage!"** He battered Madeline with the axe, and she weathered it, tanking the ones she couldn't dodge, smashing him back, ripping the axe from his hands, and throwing him down.

"You think I didn't notice ya leaving my pahtay? Ya think I didn't expect this?" She hissed, ripping open his throat with straightened fingers. "I'll take my blood back now, ya traitah!"

"Mads," he croaked, grinning up at her as his hand slipped to his side.

"What? I'm drinkin' heah!" She said, lowering her mouth to his wounds.

"Blood is Gold," he whispered.

She had enough time to blink in surprise as his wounds disappeared. And then he was throwing her off, and slamming her down on the remnants of the hut, and all the pointy, pointy boards sticking up out of it...

Meanwhile, Zuula walked slowly after the Spectromancer, who flew around and around the clearing, sobbing. Every time she tried to leave the clearing, it hurt. A feeling like fire drove her back, burned at what was left of her incorporeal flesh. "Why?" She sobbed, feeling her strength leak away. "Why are you doing this? I just wanted... I just wanted to live alone with my dearies..."

"You kill you dearies," Zuula said. "You hurt dem. You keep dem hungry and bound and scared. Not natural. Not right. But dese are not reasons why Zuula kill you," The ghost witch said, hair fluttering out behind her in long dreads, as she gave a sudden hop and caught the Cat Queen up in her grasp.

"Then... why?" Tocksy said, struggling, clawing at the implacable ghostly hand holding her.

"Because Zuula stronger den you. And she *hungry*."

And Tocksy's screams filled the clearing as Zuula's mask gaped wide and began to feed.

Across the clearing, far from murder, Missus Fluffbear stared at the cougar she'd whipped into submission. The whip Threadbare had given her had been enchanted for something like this purpose, though she hadn't known it. It had stripped the cougar's already anemic moxie with every strike, and brought her to zero. The big cat, thoroughly whipped, rolled on her back and exposed her belly and neck, crying like a kitten.

"I'm sorry," Missus Fluffbear said. "I... I didn't want to hurt you. You attacked. Me, I mean... Oh." The little black bear toddled forward, and hugged her tightly.

Golden light flared again, and the cougar's wounds mended.

A large feline tongue rasped against the black bear's head. "Does this mean we're okay?" Fluffbear asked.

Through befriending a wild beast you have unlocked the Tamer Job!

Would you like to become a tamer at this time?

"Oh, okay."

And Missus Fluffbear blinked, as new skills and attribute boosts appeared before her...

Threadbare got to Pulsivar, in time to see the Wight Tiger shake itself and flee. Unbound by its mistress' death, it had no reason to remain here.

"Oh no..." Threadbare ran up to Pulsivar, who looked up at him, from a pool of his own blood. "Are you..."

Pulsivar sat up, painfully, and started grooming himself. Threadbare watched his hit points move back up into double digits. That had been way, way too close. "You just stay here, okay?" He gave the big cat an innocent embrace, healing him as much as he could. Wow, those were getting hard on his sanity.

And as the golden light flared, he saw a figure stagger up from the hut, and bring a makeshift stake through another's chest. "Garon?" he asked.

Garon has left the party.

"Garon!"

Madeline's fangs glistened in the darkness, as she buried them in Garon's still form, and drank deeply. With a soft sigh, Garon slumped to the ground, body dissolving, leaving only clothes behind.

"No! Garon!" Threadbare clapped his paws to his mouth. "What have you done?" He whispered in the darkness.

"I've wahn," Madeline said, glaring as Missus Fluffbear came up to stand beside Threadbare. "Gaht tha dungeon coah, Cat Queen's dead, and my wounds ah mostly healed, thanks ta that drink. That idiot." She sighed, looking forlornly at his ashes. "What did he expect? The fight was ovah once I got a command in through his will. Only a mattah of time."

"You kill Zuula's son..." The Ghost Witch thundered as she faded in, walking toward the vampire.

"What's it to ya, lady? He had it comin'."

"T'ank you."

"What?"

"Soulstone," Said Threadbare, followed by **"Speak with Dead.** Garon? Yes, could you get in here please? Ah, thank you."

"He never be free while he vampire," Zuula explained. "Now we got maybe some room to wiggle with."

"Yeah, ya know what? Fahk that." Madeline tucked the dungeon core away in her torn dress, and adjusted her head scarf. "You played me from beginning to end. I think I'm gonna fahking take you all ta stuffing."

"Zuula recommend against dat," the witch hissed, through her mask.

"Pfft. Ya don't scare me, lady. I'm too strahng to be affected by ya touch. And as fah as yer no retreat trick works, you spent a lot of powah heah, can't hold me heah much longer. I feel it weakening. And you lot?" The vampire's finger traced between the toys, and the cats slinking up to stand next to them. "Ya all torn up from the fight. I ain't fresh, but I can kill my way through ya."

"Oh. Thank you for reminding me," Threadbare said. He tilted his head to the side and concentrated.

"What? Remind you of what—"

About half a ton of skeletal dragon plummeted down from on high, claws tearing and fleshless maw rending.

Five years ago, Zuula had killed a lesser dragon. And she'd marked very, very well where it fell. Well enough to tell Threadbare where it was, so he could go and animate it as a skeleton.

The dragon itself eventually got smashed to pieces by the irate vampire, but by that point the teddy bears were able to bring her down without casualties.

And oh, did Threadbare reap the spoils.

You are now a level 11 Greater Toy Golem!
+2 to all attributes

You are now a level 5 Ruler!
CHA+3
LUCK+3
WIS+3
You have unlocked the Appoint Official skill!
Your Appoint Official skill is now level 1!
You have unlocked the Organize Minions skill!
Your Organize Minions skill is now level 1!
You have unlocked the Swear Fealty skill!
Your Swear Fealty skill is now level 1!

You are now a level 10 Necromancer!
INT+3
WILL+3
WIS+3
You have unlocked the Drain Life skill!
Your Drain Life skill is now level 1!
You have unlocked the Mana Focus skill!

Threadbare smiled over at Fluffbear... who smiled back. Next to her, a cougar the size of a housecat rubbed its cheek against her, while a very puzzled Pulsivar sniffed the cougar.

"Wasn't that cat bigger not too long ago?" Threadbare asked.

"She's my pet now. I'm a tamer now. It shrunk her when I accepted the job."

"Oh, okay."

"Wow, this is better than I thought it would be, that's a relief," Garon said from his soulstone. "Hi Mom."

"Son! You is free! Now we can pass on to de odder side."

"Pfft, why would I want to do that?"

"What?"

"I have too much shit to do."

"You dead! You supposed to move on!"

"You didn't."

"Zuula didn't because she had to make sure you didn't get trapped in eternal undead hell! Well now you not."

"No, but Mastoya is."

"Wait. What?"

"She wasn't herself when she stabbed me. It was the rage. We both came down from it then, and I looked into her eyes. She was crying, Mom. She was hurting so bad."

"She fucking killed you."

"Yes. And she didn't want to. Kill you? Yes. Kill me? No. It's going to eat at her, Mom. I need to go and stop that. I need to forgive her."

Silence for a long while. "You unclever son."

"Yeah, well."

"This is like that sprouts t'ing, isn't it?"

"Never ate'em, never will."

"Fff. You should really just go. She sort it out. Join us eventually one way or other."

"What was it you told me about being an orc? That you never stop fighting?"

"...damn it."

"So I won't stop. Hey Threadbare, I know it's a lot to ask, but can you get me to Mastoya? I can at least throw party buffs on you. I think. Gods, this is weird, not having a body."

"I've been thinking about that, actually," Threadbare said, looking over to Beanarella's limp form. She'd evidently been destroyed in the crossfire at some point. He moved toward her, pulling out his tailoring tools. "I could maybe make you a body. If the spells interact like I think they might."

"Seriously? I'm down. What's the catch?"

"Well, if it works, you'll be in a golem shell. Like me."

"If not?"

"I don't know, and it uses up the crystal. I don't know what happens to you, then."

Garon thought it over. "What have I got to lose? Let's do it."

"Pfft. Unclever child. You not going this alone."

"Mom?"

"Zuula stick around to make sure you not suffer. Look at you, children all! Green, and not in good way. Someone gots to be responsible adult here," said the half-orc who'd happily engineered the massacre of most of Taylor's Delve's undead population because she thought it would be an awesome fight. "Guess it gots to be Zuula."

"Okay. But I need something called yellow reagent to make it work.

And I've only got one dose of it left. It's... I need to be a good enchanter to make more of it, and I'm not yet. I think," confessed Threadbare. "It's hard to practice without materials."

"Oh, that's what ya need, is tha yellow stuff?" Said a nasal voice. Threadbare whirled, to see Madeline's fading form lounging against a tree. That's right, he DID have Speak with Dead going, and well, she counted too.

"You still around?" Zuula hissed, stalking towards her.

"Whoa, whoa lady, let's cut a deal heah," Madeline said, backing up. "You want yellow reagent, I want a new body."

"You tell Zuula where it is or she eat you!"

Madeline laughed, and strode right up to the ghost. "Destroy me and you never get it. We hid it well."

Zuula clenched her fists...

"Okay," Threadbare said. "I feel bad about tricking you anyway. Even if you were hurting Garon."

"Yeah, you should feel bad!" Madeline stalked over to him, shaking her finger. "I trusted you, beah! And you screwed me ovah, and got all my friends dead!" She sighed. "Okay, they were only my friends because I killed them and made them my friends, but the point stahnds."

"I know. I do feel bad about it. But Zuula and Garon were my friends first and they needed my help."

She sighed.

CHA +1

Your Adorable skill is now level 20!

"Fahk it. Can't stay mad at you. So whaddya say? Soulstone me, prahmise to give me a new bahdy, and I'll show you wheah we hide our loot. Ain't much, but we got plenty of yellow dust. An' other colors besides."

"I'll vouch for her," Garon spoke up.

"Garon! She enslave you!" Zuula hissed.

"She's a monster. She was just doing what came naturally. You should know all about that, Mom. That nature thing?"

"Dat is low blow."

"I'm not a Knight. Mercenaries can afford to fight dirty. And anyway, she was nice enough, just... yeah. Didn't work out."

"Thanks, Gar," Madeline said. Then she looked at her hands, as they started to fade. "Uh? Might wanna decide quick, Mistah Beah."

It wasn't much of a decision, really. **"Soulstone."** He offered it to her, and she dove in happily.

That joy lasted all of five seconds.

"Level fahcking three?" She screamed.

Zuula laughed her ghostly ass off.

*****

The box didn't just hold yellow reagents. It had lots more red, plenty of orange, and even a dose of bright, glittering green. Along with about three dozen crystals, most of which were level one.

"Where did all this come from?" he wondered, as the teddy bears and their feline companions stared at the glowing hoard in the box.

"Item smugglahs, mostly," Madeline replied. "Remembah those resistance guys? I searched theah houses aftah they were dead. Most of them made some coin this way. Which is in that sack to ya left, by the by."

"Oh, thank you." My, that was a heavy sack.

Your Sturdy Back skill is now level 7!

"There was a pretty brisk trade in illegal items from the Catamountain," Garon offered. "Used to be some of the wizards and guards could be bribed to look the other way, back before things got serious near the end. Items come out, and the really powerful ones got shipped elsewhere to help with the fight, and the lesser ones got disenchanted and sold as components on the black market."

"This is what happens when you disenchant things," Threadbare said, counting the vials of reagents. "That's what my appraise skill tells me, anyway."

"You need to get better at a lot of t'ings," Zuula griped at him from her own soulstone. "Gots to find focus. Is one reason Zuula come along. She gonna be your trainer, boy. You will hate her, before all is done. But you will learn. You will learn."

"I love you, Zuula," Threadbare said. "I won't hate you."

"We gonna put dat to de test, little bears."

Madeline cleared her nonexistent throat. "So, ah, about those bahdies... how does this wahk exahctly?"

"I can make toy golems. Maybe other kinds someday. It uses level one crystals, but soulstones are level one crystals. And it uses up yellow reagents. I just need to find or make toys, and prepare them."

"Oh you ah in luck," Madeline chuckled. "We ah, anyway. Theah's a whole stoah fah those not fah away!"

"Mrs. Fub!" Garon yelled. "Oh that's perfect!"

"What?" Threadbare looked down at his upside-down hat, and the soulstones he'd put in it. "What's a Fub?"

"It's a who. She was a toymaker before the slaughter," Garon said. "It's where Mordecai got most of his toys from, before she started getting suspicious. Her shop came through mostly intact."

"Oh! That sounds good. Let's go have a look." Threadbare said, and the voices of the dead guided the little group out of the darkness of the secret hidey hole, and out into the newly-rising light of dawn.

CECILIA'S QUEST 1: A HARD DAY'S KNIGHT

The shield slammed into Cecelia's face, rattling her head inside her helm. Dazed, she stumbled backward, barely managing to intercept the mace with her sword, as the black knight swung it to her side.

Even then, the blade's intervention only blunted the impact. Her foe was larger, stronger, more practiced. Knocked to the side, she backpedaled, used her superior agility to get some distance. But he followed, relentless, armor dull save for the red runes of the Royal Army.

She had to lock down that mace. Without catching the shield to her face, this time.

"Corps a Corps!" She shouted, lunging forward, and like magnets her blade clashed against the mace and stuck. The skill added to her strength, keeping both weapons locked. Corps a Corps was designed to tie up strong foes, keep them busy while her allies did damage, tore into the temporarily disabled target.

Your Corps a Corps skill is now level 57!

Or not so disabled, as the case may be. Sure enough, his shield came up again—

—and she let her legs go limp, slammed her greaves into the ground, and shouted **"Dolorous Strike!"**

With boosted strength, she drove her own shield into the plates over his codpiece.

Your Dolorous Strike skill is now level 48!

Her shield had spikes on it. They got in between the joints, and plate tore as she twisted. Her foe staggered back, breaking the corps a corp, choking noises emerging from his helm.

The black knight hunched over. Blood spattered the floor, and she shifted her eyes away as she rose. She stood there, bashed her sword into her shield, waiting.

From the sidelines, King Melos shook his head. He gestured for his attendants to leave, then beckoned. "Come here, Cecelia."

Cecelia Ragandor-Gearhart saluted her foe, then turned to her father.

Noise behind her, as armor clattered, and she whirled around too late.

Realization crashed into her at the same time the black knight did, bowling her over and hammering her down to the floor. Father had called to her, but he never actually stopped the match!

Gods damn it, father.

"Animus!" She snapped out, ignoring the pain, and slapping her hand to her foe's chest. **"Invite armor,** get the hell off me!"

She couldn't match her foe in strength, but will she had a plenty. And when you were dealing with animi, the animator's will WAS their strength. Her foe howled as his armor moved against his flesh, catching his muscles out of joint, straining them as it threw him backward to land in a heap on the ground. "I yield!" he cried. "I yield me!"

Cecelia walked over to her father, glaring at him through her visor. "What?"

"You just forfeited the match by casting a spell. Which doesn't matter, because you lost it half a minute ago." Melos sighed. His own armor was darker than her opponent's, his red hair stark against it like a spill of blood. But his eyes were full of disappointment, and Cecelia hated to see it.

He was her father, after all, and she had to do right by him.

"How did I lose?" She asked, unbuckling her helm. It was white-enameled metal like the rest of her armor, pearly white, with a unicorn's horn spike just above the visor. She'd designed it, crafted it herself. There had been some snickering in the barracks, she was sure, talk about "pony knight armor for the pretty pretty princess," but she didn't care. They didn't matter. She had worked hard to fight on even ground with youths and adults who had been training for it since they were born. Besides, she had moxie and cool enough to handle a little teasing.

And her armor was cute, dammit.

She liked cute things. There weren't many of those left in her life, these days. The few that were reminded her of better times. Simpler times.

"You lost," her father explained, clanking over to her and placing his hands on her shoulder pauldrons. "You lost when you stopped hitting him. He wasn't down. You needed to follow up, to end his threat."

"He was done. If he'd come at me again from the front I would have taken him down hard. He only got that last hit in because you distracted me." She glanced over to Renick, her assigned foe for today, standing locked and gasping in his frozen armor. That was a fair amount of blood on the floor. "Hey! Why isn't he healed?" She snapped to the clerics on duty. They looked to the king, and she slammed her sword's pommel against her shield. "Don't look at my father, look to your charge! Heal him!" She yelled.

Her father said nothing, and the two clerics nodded, and rushed over to the knight. She let the animus spell dissolve as they got to him, dropping Renick onto the shorter of the pair.

"Unnecessary," Melos murmured to her, a smile tugging at his lips, swiftly banished.

"They need to learn THEIR duty." She ran a gauntleted hand through her short-cropped ginger hair. "Do I pass muster?"

Her father pursed his lips, blew air out through his teeth as he thought. "Walk with me," he decided, putting his arm around her shoulders and guiding her away.

"That's a no, then?" She said, feeling her heart sink.

Five years I've been stuck in this castle. Five years, and I might have just blown my chance at getting free—

—no. No, it wasn't freedom. It was just another set of chains.

But at least these would be chains she'd built herself.

"It's a 'let me think about it.' You've taken well to your knight's training, even though you came to it belated. And your craftsmanship is exquisite. It makes me proud. It would have made Amelia proud to see it." He looked away for a second.

Which was good, because Cecelia had a lump in her throat, and boy did her eyes burn. She blinked away tears. "Thank you," Cecelia husked.

"But you'd be going to a battlefield. And on a battlefield, there are no rules beyond survival and winning. A painfully disabling groin shot? Well, his healer will shout out a word or two and it'll be healed just like THAT. It's not enough to disable a foe, if they have a chance to recover. You have to end it, decisively, until they stand no chance of posing a threat to you again." Melos' gauntlet clenched. "Every time I've deviated from this practice, from this policy, it's come back to harm me. And worse, to harm my kingdom. And I fear it will hurt YOU. Do you understand, Cecelia?"

She nodded. "I do."

He stopped, studied her for a long minute. "I wonder." He gave her shoulder one last squeeze, then withdrew his arm. "I'll arrange a new test for you."

"What sort of test?"

"No. No, this is a... make-up exam, if you will. It won't be anything you have time to prepare for. You'll have to show me not only your strength but your wisdom, when the time comes. And you'll have to win. No matter the cost."

Oh gods. Her mouth went dry, and Cecelia licked her lips. "I will." *This is going to suck.*

Then a flicker of motion caught her eye. Down the corridor, just under one of the tapestries, a green glow danced and flickered. "Oh! That thing again. I'll go get the wizards."

"What—" Melos turned, hand on his sword and froze in horror. He stared at the flickering light, and Cecelia watched as her father, the mighty figure who had been the anchoring point in her new life these last five years, the indomitable King of Cylvania, trembled so hard his armor shook.

"Gh!" He said, leaning on the wall, clapping his hand to his chest.

"Father? Father!"

And for a second, for just a second, he glanced at her. And to her shock it his eyes had gone black, black with dancing green specks. "Go. I'll handle it," he rasped, looking away just as fast.

"Are you okay? Handle what? What is this?" Cecelia said, moving around him, to try and confirm what she saw.

But he whipped his hand up to shield his face. "I'm fine. Go! Say nothing of this!"

Green light played through the cracks between his clenched fingers, and Cecelia nodded, and fled.

Behind her, she heard her father mutter, but she couldn't quite make out the words.

"What the heck is going on?" She wondered, heading back to her quarters. It didn't look good, whatever it was, but if her Father said to leave it be, he meant it. She couldn't risk any more of his ire, not this close to her freedom.

Halfway to her room she changed her mind, and headed for the barracks instead.

She'd hurt Renick pretty badly, she figured she owed the guy an apology.

*****

"Haha, no, it's fine, really," Renick grinned. Renick was big and broad, with hair like straw, and an earnest, ugly face. The joke around the barracks was that he'd joined the king's knights for the charisma boosts, so could stand a chance at getting laid someday.

Not that they'd joked like that around Cecelia, not at first, but they'd eventually come to accept her. Which was good, because though they weren't exactly as close to her as they were with each other, they didn't tiptoe around her or try to curry her favor and kiss up by flattery. When she wore the armor and trained with them, she was one of the knights, and that was that.

Her father had seemed to approve, though he'd warned her about getting attached. "A lot of these men and women are going to die for you," he told her. "Be careful how much emotional investment you put into any particular one."

"Well, if they're going to die for me, I should at least be good to them, right? Shouldn't I be someone worth dying for?"

Usually it went one of two ways when she stood up to him. The first way was solemn, shameful disappointment that depressed her for days. But that time it had gone the second way, and he'd been proud. And so from that point on she spent time in the barracks, albeit with a chaperone present, and joined in what camaraderie she could.

"It's fine. I mean, I've taken groin shots before. And the clerics healed me right up." Renick smiled, leaning back in his chair, running a rag over his shield as he cleaned it.

Next to him, a short woman with black hair grinned, and opened her mouth—

"—besides, it's not like I was using my balls for anything anyway," Renick smirked.

"You asshole! That was the perfect setup!" The short woman punched his (thankfully unarmored) shoulder.

Cecelia laughed with the rest of them.

"Sorry Lana, you gotta be quick. Or try something new," Renick said, placidly. "But seriously, Cee, that's a pretty good trick you did out there. I might try it sometime."

"I wouldn't," A thin, whiplike young woman with a scarred face spoke from her corner, where she was busy sorting knives into sheaths. "That's more of a duelist trick. And with your weight, Renick, you'd jam up your knees something fierce." She'd been an assassin, before she'd joined the Corps, as the rumor went. Going by how she acted, how she fought, Cecelia believed the rumor.

"You calling me fat now, Kayin?" He flipped her off casually.

She put a dagger past his shoulder, equally casually, sinking it into the dartboard beyond. "Nah, just big. But no, I'm just saying she can get away with it because of her weight and agility. You can't."

"That's a point. But either way, it was a smooth move." Renick sighed. "You're lucky, you got to dip into scout when you were younger. Lots of good battlefield stuff there, I hear."

"I haven't practiced it much. But sturdy back helps with the armor, won't deny," Cecelia smiled.

"I'm still waiting for my Duelist training approval," Renick said, checking his armor. "I mean a lot of the nimbleness stuff will be hard to pull off until I get my agility up there, but that class bumps strength, so it's good. And since Knight bumps charisma they dovetail nicely."

"And duelist adds dexterity and agility, so you don't completely suck once you finally get someone in bed," Lana said, smugly. And this time as the laughter rang out again, Renick punched HER shoulder. She just laughed harder.

"Hey, Cee," Kayin whispered in her ear, when the rest of the barracks had fallen back to arguing and boasting and the small talk and stuff that the knights filled their day with. "Your daddy tell you when we're shipping out East?"

Cecelia bit her lip. "No. And... I might not go with you. It's..." She bit her tongue, not wanting to confess to the lean girl that she'd failed what was supposed to be her graduation test. *Not a failure yet,* she reminded herself. *I get a do-over.* "...I have to prove to my father that I can handle it."

"What? I thought it was a sure thing!"

"He cheated. Upped the stakes." And he had. She'd won that fight, but he'd changed the rules, thrown in another variable. Which... okay, she could see the point of that as a general life lesson, but still, she'd WON.

"That's a shit thing to do to your own kid..." Kayin hissed, then shot a glance around. No one was listening, or even looking.

"It is what it is," Cecelia said. "Though..." She thought ahead. "I think I know what he has in mind. Would you be willing to help me if things go like I think they will?"

"What did you have in mind?" Kayin stepped back, and smirked. "And what's in it for me?"

Cecelia reached into her pouch, and jingled a handful of coins, and the former assassin grinned harder...

*****

"Stoker Feed Activated!" Cecelia shouted, feeling her hit points drain as a metal conveyor whirred to life under her. Whirring and clanking, it carried coal from the fuel box, to the fire. Heated instantly by magic, the gauges around her jumped and flickered, glowing in the cramped darkness.

"Boiler Shunt is Go!" Cecelia screamed, over the din of the stoker feed. Instantly her invention screamed, sending clouds of steam past the viewport, as the magic got the water boiling in seconds, synching it to the fire stoked by the belt. It took moxie from her, but not more than she could spare.

"Clockwork Engaged!" Cecelia roared, shoving her arms and legs into the sleeves, feeling metal clamps rattle and bind her limbs. Whirring, ticking, driven by steam and kinetic energy, she twisted her arms and felt the arms of her armor rise around her, massive by comparison to her regular fleshy limbs. She clenched her fingers, feeling her sanity diminish, but she had plenty of that and now the armor moved as she did.

"Linkages aligned!" She shouted, and the port slammed shut, as the cables throughout the massive metal suit stretched taught and fed into the clockwork gears. Stamina leaked from her, and fed into the suit, and she took her first shuddering steps, as the counterweights and gyros kept her upright.

"Cast In Steam and Steel, Raise thy Blade! All Systems Go!" Cecelia finished the last of the five spells, and that strangest feeling of all came, as her fortune fell, transferring to her steam armor.

Skill-ups rolled by, but she ignored them, as she piloted her armor out through the hangar doors, and to the practice grounds.

She was taking a risk, she knew, lowering her pools this close to father's unknown test, but piloting Reason always settled her nerves. Grabbing a clockwork arbalest, she fitted it into Reason's arm, winding the bolt feed carefully into the compartment she'd built for it. For the other hand, a wrecker blade, ten feet long and three feet from the edge to the back, like a massive cleaver that had been stretched out to a ludicrous length.

And as the sun sank below the castle walls, she stomped around the proving grounds, shooting targets and chopping through logs, running the obstacle course as she went. She'd hit level four in the Steam Knight job recently, about as far as she could go on the training grounds alone.

It had been a hard job to achieve, pushing her tinkering skills to the limits. But she'd thrown in even more of a challenge, by enchanting the various components, buffing her knight well beyond the specs that most who came to the job bothered to. It was an odd job anyway, mixing Knight and Animator and Tinker, and requiring a ton of resources and components to first craft the suit, then figure out how to animate the various parts to do what they needed to, and THEN you had to be a fifteenth level knight, so you could use the "Favored Mount" skill upon the finished product. Only then would the second-tier class unlock.

But holy fump, could she kick ass when she wore Reason. Fifteen foot tall and almost every bit of it crafted by her own hand, she was in full control when the boiler was screaming behind her and the mighty cable muscles were stretching at the guidance of her responsive clockwork.

She felt strong inside the suit. Untouchable, unbeatable. And more than that, it was a symbol of her freedom. The only way she'd be able to leave this castle, was as one of the elite steam knights sent to fight the dwarves on the eastern front. Only then, her father told her, would he be willing to let her anywhere near a battlefield. Steam Knights had the best survivability rate, and they got taken alive, thankfully. The dwarves had weird rules when it came to killing tinkers.

Her father had laughed, when she named it Reason. He thought it humorous, but he was mistaken about the meaning of the name. Her hope was to make him see reason. That was why it was called what it was.

And all her good mood and restored confidence fled as she turned back to the hangar, and saw who was waiting there.

"Oh fump," She muttered. "You?"

Smiling, Anise Layd'i raised her hand and waved.

Cecelia stomped back, brought her armor's components down one by one, and stepped free of the cockpit. Soaked in sweat, uncaring, she hopped down to glare at the demon who wore her dead mother's face. "What?"

"Aren't you eager to get to your test?" Anise smiled, blandly.

And suddenly, Cecelia felt a lot less confident.

*****

The Tower of Shame stood in the middle of the keep, holding those that the Crown chose not to kill, but could not let free. It had thick, thick walls, layers of stone lined with cork, that ate up the sound and prevented the screams and wails of the prisoners inside from disturbing the rest of the Castle's inhabitants.

But once you were inside the tower, you could hear the Tower's prisoners shouting, crying, begging for mercy. That's what Cecelia found as she followed Anise into the tower, ascending the long stair that broke off into corridors, heading into the various cellblocks.

Cecelia smoothed her arming jacket. A clean and press had gotten rid of the sweat stains, but Anise hadn't given her a chance to get armored, let alone grab a sword. **"Always in Uniform,"** she muttered, using a knight skill to buff her armor for the third time since she'd followed the demon. It kept running out, but it hardened her clothes, gave her SOMETHING in the event of sudden violence. And it used moxie, so whatever. She didn't have many abilities that used that, none that mattered for this test, she reckoned.

"Here we go," Anise hummed, opening a door near the top. Cecelia eyed it warily, but her alertness didn't fire off, so she figured she wasn't going to be ambushed yet. Still... "After you, I insist," she told Anise.

"Of course, dear." Anise strode into the cellblock, into the corridor that ran between the cells.

It was dark in here, and empty, save for a pile of rags in the corner of a far cell. As she watched, they stirred, and an old, weathered face lifted up from the man lying under them. A white-bearded, unshaven face, bald-headed with bushy eyebrows.

A familiar face, that she hadn't seen in a long while. "Mister Mordecai?"

"Celia? Celia girl?" Mordecai leaped up, and in a flash grabbed the bars. He was nearly naked, save for dirty, torn trousers, and thin, so thin, with ropy muscles straining under his withered flesh. "Celia? Is this a trick? You bastards, you ain't trickin' me!" In a heartbeat he went from smiling to screaming, pounding his head against the bars. "Stay out of my 'ead! Stay out of my 'ead! I ain't tellin' yer nuffing!"

"No! No, it's me, please Mordecai, please stop hurting yourself!" She ran to him, then flinched back as he punched through the bars, his hand falling short by inches. "Please stop!"

He screamed himself hoarse, then seemed to come to himself, looking around at the cell, looking down at himself in shame. "Sorry. I... sorry. Real. Hope yer real. Hope... sorry. Oh Celia girl, don't look at me. What they done to me... what they done to me..."

It was hard to tell what they'd done to him. He was covered with scars, but then again, she had seen how his marriage was firsthand, so she had no way of knowing if they'd been the ones to...

...no. They'd tortured him. "Mordecai, it's me." She reached through the bars, took his hand, and he wept, pushing his hairy cheek against it, dirty beard rasping against her skin. "It's me. I'm... I'm sorry."

"And here he is," Anise said. "Your enemy. The enemy to the Crown."

Cecelia froze. "What are you... what are you saying?"

"Did you think it would be an easy test?" Anise dropped a key on the ground, followed by a dagger. Then she turned and left. "Good luck!"

"What... demon!" Mordecai hissed. "Wears her face wears little Amelia's face I know what you are! I KNOW WHAT YOU ARE!" He tore free of Cecelia's hand with enraged strength, grabbed the bars and pushed his face out between them, roaring at the departing monster. "YOU DEMON!"

Then he collapsed, sobbing, leaving Cecelia with the key, the dagger, and the dawning realization of the nature of her test.

"Oh no," she whispered, sinking to the floor. "No, no, no..."

She weighed her freedom against the old man's life. Old man, sick and wasted, thin and ragged from starvation and suffering. An old man, mind broken, barely anything left of the strong, confident scout she'd once known.

He'll die here anyway.

It would be a mercy.

They'd just keep torturing him.

These thoughts and more trembled through her head.

And finally Cecelia picked up the dagger.

*****

The guards didn't look twice at her as she descended the stairwell, empty handed. She'd taken nothing from the cellblock, and she was alone, so they didn't check her.

The keep was oddly quiet, and the door to the wing leading to her chambers was locked.

Cecelia blinked, then her eyes settled into a squint as she realized. There was one route around the locked door, and it led through the courtyard.

She took a ceremonial shield off the wall. **"Animus Shield."** It was lower quality, but better than nothing. **"Harden,"** She said, patting her clothes. **"Always in Uniform. Keen Eye."** She didn't have any other buffs that were useful to the situation, so she took a deep breath, and walked through the keep, reaching the side courtyard with her shield bobbing merrily along behind her.

And there Cecelia found the knights waiting. Everyone in her training squad by the looks of it, and Sergeant Tane too. Seven Knights, ringing the courtyard, fully armed and armored, drawing blades as she approached.

"This is your test, girl," her father called from the battlements, the demons in his armor glowing and active, hellblades whirling around his head. "There are no rules! Fight for your life!"

Celia smiled.

And then, a song rang out, bouncing around the walls, echoing from the outbuildings, causing the King and his knights to peer around.

"There was a fool king, who clung hard to the dark…"

King Melos stiffened. "Who… who dares?"

"Killed his own wife, and thought it a lark…"

"You'll die for that!" Melos yelled.

"But in all of our hearts, he lit the spark… of rebellion!"

It was an old, raspy voice, unsuitable for a bard. But it was a song that heartened Cecelia nonetheless. **"Status,"** she whispered, and smiled at the strength buff she'd just received.

All too soon the song ended but it was replaced by quietly chanted words. And every one made the King's eyes go wider.

"Fast as Death. Build Up. One Track Mind. Power From Pain. Ambush. Subdue… RAGE!"

"And oh yeah, **Backstab!**" And then, a knight went sailing backward, helm crumpled. Mordecai stood where he'd been, camouflage fading, grinning. "ello there Melly. Long time no see!"

"You son of a bitch!" Melos roared, then froze in horror as Mordecai whirled, and tossed his dagger at Celia… who stretched out a hand, and smiled. **"Animus Blade!"** She shouted as it passed her head, and swung into a low orbit around her.

"No rules, father! No rules!" She reminded him, and charged the remaining knights as Mordecai whooped and laid about him, fists falling like hammers.

On the battlements, Melos leaned his elbows on the battlements, and palmed his face with both hands. "She is our daughter, Amelia," he whispered, unheard. "Hell help us all."

Each one of Cecelia's class had at least three levels on her, but she was an animator, too, and their weapons had been padded. They hurt, they sapped her stamina and left bruises every time they hit, but whenever she managed to get a hand on a shield or a blade or a suit of armor, it became hers. And she'd fire up Corps a Corps with an animus blade, then hammer her friends down with an animus shield while they were locked. Or she'd slap their armor and hinder them. Her sanity went fast, but oh, it was glorious.

Glorious, but painful. They were all trained knights, and the Dolorous Strikes that got through had her reeling.

Midway through, four knights down, she heard Mordecai yelp. She bought some breathing room by running back to see Mordecai leaping over the outbuildings, pursued by a black-clad form. She caught her breath.

That was one of the Four that made up the elites called the King's Hand! It was the Ninja!

"What?" She yelled up at her Father, almost getting clocked in the head by a training sword for her trouble. "You're seriously throwing HER into this test?"

"No rules!" He shrugged. "This is more fair, anyway."

"Fair!" Cecelia shrieked, backing into a corner as Sergeant Tane hammered down her last shield, and Renick closed from the other side. Kayin came down the middle.

They stopped, ten feet from her, as she stretched a hand out. "I'm a good animator. You know what I can do."

"Aye. And I know it'll take you six words to get one of us," Tane ground out. "At which point the other two will be on you, Squire Ragandor. So why don't you surrender and save your face a pounding?"

Cecelia's eyes flicked from Tane, to Kayin, to Renick... and back to Kayin. She winked.

"**Distant Animus**—" Celia shouted, and they charged...

"**Invite Renick's Armor** stop!" She shouted. He stopped and fell over, and she felt the wind as the other two approached...

And a feeling of relief surged through her, as Kayin shouted "**Backstab! Pommel Strike!**" And rang Tane's helm like a bell so hard that he tumbled, knocking Cecelia to the ground.

The girl stared up, dazed... at Kayin's open gauntlet. She took it, accepted the hand to her feet, and smiled at Kayin. "Do you surrender?"

"Absolutely." Kayin knelt.

For a long second, there was silence on the battlements. "What." Melos finally managed.

"I thought you might try something like this, father. So I went and found allies. It was a cruel test to begin with!" She stepped forward, leveling her hand at him. "Trying to make me kill on an old friend!"

The king removed his helm, and stared down at her. "What are you talking about?"

"Trying to get me to kill Mister Mordecai like... that..." She blinked. "Wait. Anise said..."

"Anise?" The King frowned. "What's she done this time?"

Realization crashed in.

Anise had never SAID that killing Mordecai was the King's test, or that she'd lead Cecelia to the test. She'd let Cecelia form her own conclusions. Shaking, the girl leaned against the wall.

"It's to do with that senile old scout, isn't it?" The King said, hopping off the wall and floating down, as the demons he wore carried him gently through the air. "Of course he'd seek you out, and try to get you to escape with him."

"Something like that," Cecelia said. "I... couldn't stop him even if I wanted to." Which was the truth. She didn't want to stop him. She'd unlocked his cell and offered to run interference while he escaped.

"Mm. Well, no matter. You were wise to use him to your advantage while he was here. In any case, it's a moot point. Janus tells me he's in the woods outside the walls now, and it's only a matter of time before he's back in his cell. He can't evade for long. The crazy old bastard may be a scout, but he's no ranger." Melos dispelled the demons in his armor and let his blades fall, then folded her into a hug, ignoring the scattered and groaning knights around her. "You passed. You'll get your wish."

Freedom. Cecelia sagged into her father's arms. "Thank you," She whispered.

It had been a hard life, in the castle. A hard life, hearing about the foes that bedeviled her father and tried to bring chaos to his kingdom.

But now she could sally forth, and meet them with steam and steel. Like her father, she would do what she must, and bring peace to Cylvania.

CHAPTER 6: BORN AGAIN

Threadbare looked at the heaps and piles of moldy toys, then up to the hole in the roof. There were bits and scraps of cloth up there, and up until a minute ago, there had been some rather irate birds that had vanished from their nests the second that Pulsivar and Mopsy entered the toy store.

"What's this white stuff?" Missus Fluffbear wondered, as she poked at the bird shit on her head and stared at her paw.

Garon cleared his throat. "Ah, I'll tell ya later—"

"It bird shit," Zuula interrupted.

"Oh. Ew!" Missus Fluffbear tried to get it off, with no real luck. "Fine. **Clean and Press**."

"You can do that?" Threadbare asked.

"Yes. My raccants taught me tailoring so they didn't have to keep fixing me and I could do it myself. But why was the bird shit white?" Missus Fluffbear wondered. "Raccant shit was brown. I certainly helped them bury enough of it, I should know."

"You buried things for them?" Threadbare turned his head to look her over.

"Yes. They gave me to their children to play with, at first. They played rough! It was very dangerous. But when they saw I could move things and carry things they took me from the children and made me work for them. Then I got attacked by those big hatted cloud things one time and beat them up with my spade. That's when their Chief, the great Hoomin decided I should be in his dungeon. Then you saved me from that. And then some of them were dead out front and I don't know why."

Threadbare twitched. Zuula's words rang through his mind. *Friends don't lie to friends, mostly*. He pondered it for a second, and decided that it would be bad to lie, here. "They were dead because I killed them. Me and Pulsivar. We wanted to come and look for you and they wouldn't let us."

Missus Fluffbear stared at him.

Threadbare continued. "I tried to ask nicely, but one of them tried to take my tools and hurt me. When I pushed him back they all attacked me."

"Was it the one with stars on his shoulder? That was mean to you?"

"Yes."

"He was mean to me too. I wasn't sorry to see him dead. But you killed Bujy and Hamste and small missing ear Kity, and they were my friends. Sort of." She kept staring at Threadbare. "I don't know how I feel about this."

"I don't know how you should feel, either," Threadbare said. He took off his top hat and rubbed his head. "I'm not sorry because they were trying to hurt me, and they could have if I didn't stop them. But I'm sorry because you liked them and I didn't know, if that makes any sense."

"Hey," Mads spoke up. "Take it frahm me, kid, it's okay ta feel bad. I feel bad Darla and Barret and Grimble ah gone. But theah ain't no point in blaming Threadbeah. If it wasn't him, it'd be somewan else. Bein' a monstah means soonah or latah someone kills ya. And raccants is monstahs, they all knew the score. They wouldn't hold no grudge, or ask you ta hold one."

"For once stupid vampire actually say somet'ting Zuula agree wit'." The shaman spoke up from her soulstone. "Dat proper orc t'inking. Don't hate strong for winning. Be stronger!"

"Gee, thanks," Mads said, voice dripping in sarcasm. "Because ya vote of cahnfidence is totally something I wanted and cared about."

"Don't make Zuula slap you rocks off. She do it."

"Yeah, that's what I heard about you."

"What?"

"Mads!" Garon shouted. "That's my Mom you're talking about there."

"Right, sahrry, sahrry."

Missus Fluffbear thought it over while the spirits argued. Threadbare held his hat in his hands and waited, worried.

"You didn't know they were my friends," Missus Fluffbear said. "And not all of them were, and they attacked you and they shouldn't have."

"Yes."

"Okay. I'm still sad. But I'm not mad at you. I'm glad you pulled me out of there. It was really weird in there. All green light and like... I don't know. Pictures and things and you feel yourself doing things and seeing things but you can't control what you're doing."

"You talking about dreams," Zuula said. "Everyting dream."

"I don't," Threadbare and Fluffbear said simultaneously, then looked at each other. Fluffbear giggled.

"Celia told me about her dreams," Threadbare said. "But I don't sleep. I guess you don't either?"

"No. Sometimes my friends talked about them. It didn't make much sense."

"Wait. Green light?" Mads said. "They had ya in a coah cahlumn? Holy shit!"

"What's a core column?" Threadbare asked.

"It's a ticket ta immortahlity, if ya a monstah. The mahstah puts you in theah, and you stay theah all safe while copies of you go out and do stuff. Ya get good enough, ya can control what ya duplicates do. But ya can't make them leave the dungeon."

"How you know this?" Zuula asked, suspicion in her voice.

"Pssh, I was born in a dungeon. Just a wandering bloodsuckah. One minute nothin' then BOOP, there I was, a li'l level one vampaiah. Mighta been a copy of someone in a core cahlumn, or coulda been just a randahm spawn. Dunno. Got good at what I did, then the Seven came an' sealed the dungeon and I escaped befoah it sealed completely."

"You never told mentioned anything like this to me," Garon said.

"Look, Gar, most of our convahsations were me telling you ta settle down, and you going NO FUCK YOU RAGGLGLGBALARGGELE ROAR! Or some variation of that."

"Point."

"Is that why you wanted a dungeon core?" Threadbare asked.

"Yeah, from what I heahd, it's a pretty sweet deal. Supposedly if ya in a coah cahlumn ya get some of the experience ya duplicates get. Then if the mastah's any kind of cool, he'll let ya out eventually and swap out for anothah monstah. That's propah dungeon management. And... well... if we stayed out heah, then eventually we'd be hunted down and killed. Just moah monstahs, to most people. But we need blood, so we need ta eat, so we can't go fah from people and animals. And that'd be anothah benefit! While yah in a coah cahlumn you don't eat, you don't age. That's what my friend Sydney told me anyway."

"Fun as dis is, we getting off track," Zuula said. "We got big pile of bodies here, just waiting for us to try out. Zuula kind of sick of dis no body stuff. So maybe we get on dat?"

"Oh, right," Threadbare said, digging through the pile. "I see a lot of teddy bears."

"Pass," Zuula said. "Half orc or nuttin. Zuula want to be bear, she got spell for dat."

"If it even works when you're a golem," Garon said. "Threadbare, would that work?"

"I don't know. I'm not even sure this will work," Threadbare said. "I don't know anything about this, beyond what's on my status screen help options. I know that when I was made words came up, and looking back on it, I think they were asking me if I wanted the bear job, but even that's conjecture. I was very stupid then, and my memory's not perfect. But the timing would fit for the skills I got and used after it so... maybe."

Garon thought it over. "So we need to experiment, is what I hear. All right. I'll be the test subject."

"What? No, hey—" Mads burst out.

"No! Absolutely not! Zuula will—" Zuula said at the same time. The two spirits stopped, and Threadbare somehow got the distinct impression the soulstones were eyeing each other with hostility.

"Look," Garon said, "I'd like to do something before I die, but if I can't, I'll cope and move on to the afterlife. In which case Mom, you get your wish. And Mads, your deal is for a body, so we can't experiment on you in case it turns out it kills you permanently, because that would be wrong. I'm a Mercenary, and when you make a bargain you keep it. We made a bargain with you, we keep it."

"Zuula not like dis."

"I ain't a fan neithah. Ah... be careful, ahright? Don't try nothing without running it by us fahst."

Garon continued. "So. Threadbare, you were made a teddy bear and you got the bear job. I don't have any experience with that, so IF I went with a teddy bear or something else, I'd be coming in blind. Let's find one of the soldier dolls, and make him look like a half-orc. Try as exact a match as possible to my old body, and see if that helps the transfer."

"All right." Threadbare pulled out his enchanting box, and looked through the vials. "I'll make an empty soulstone, to catch you if you get dumped out or something."

A suitable doll, a quick Clean and Press and some sewn-on tusks and leather armor later, and an axe-wielding knight doll was ready to go. The little bear also renewed Speak with Dead, just in case, and put up Assess Corpse and Eye for Detail. Then, thinking it over, he kicked on the enchanter's Appraise as well. His friend's soul was literally in his hands. He wanted to make sure he was careful with every step of the experiment.

"Missus Fluffbear?" He asked, wisdom kicking in. "Can your

blessing affect luck?"

"Yes."

"Put it on me, please."

"Yorgum's Blessing of Luck upon Threadbare!" She poked him, and his luck buffed up thirteen points. *Couldn't hurt,* he figured.

Then it was the big moment. Threadbare laid Garon's soulstone on the (newly-cleaned-and-pressed) doll, and emptied a vial of yellow reagent into his paw. **"Toy Golem,"** he said, and watched anxiously as the soulstone dissolved, sinking into the doll...

Your Toy Golem skill is now level 3!

...and sighed in relief as its status screen turned from "Simple plush toy" to "Doll Haunter (dormant)" It appeared to be the same message on all three screens, his eye for detail, his assess corpse, and his appraise.

"Garon?"

"Mfffawrmfmfmfmff."

"Are you all right?"

"Myef."

"Okay. Get ready... **Golem Animus!"**

Your Golem Animus skill is now level 3!

Congratulations! Through necromantic experimentation with spiritual desecration, you have unlocked the Spirit Medium class!

You cannot become a Spirit Medium at this time. Seek out your guild to change jobs!

"It worked!" Threadbare said, sagging in relief. "And oh my..."

Garon sat up. "It certainly did!" He said, then felt his mouth, which was sewn on and hadn't moved. "Whoa. Did you hear that? Can you hear me?"

"It come t'rough de speak with dead. You talking because of his spell," Zuula said. "Not hear you with ears, probably."

"I'll need to make you a mouth," Threadbare said, reaching for his tools. Ten minutes later, it was done.

"Okay, now that the transfer works, I need to check a few things," Garon said. "This might be temporary. **Status.**" The littled doll shifted, cloth helm wiggling as he read over his status screen. "Oh. Hoo boy. Um... Mom, you're gonna hate this."

"What? Why?"

"I've only got my mercenary and half-orc and crafting job... and a toy golem job, which looks fun, but for each of them I'm only level one. And I have zero job slots open in adventuring and crafting jobs."

"WHAT! Level one!" Zuula shrieked. "But stupid soulstone gave level t'ree!"

"Yyyeeeah, but the vessel doesn't, I guess. Also my stats are way lower. Way way lower. Like my intelligence makes me feel like I'm thinking through a headache, lower. And... oh, shit. Guys?"

"Yes?" Threadbare said, examining it. And he froze, as he looked at one of the attributes low on Garon's screen, just as Garon confirmed his fears.

"My luck's at newbie half-orc levels."

That was the point the evicted birds returned to reclaim their territory, swarming through the hole in the ceiling, and attacking everything in sight.

Starting with Garon.

Two frantic minutes of fighting later, the little group managed to drive them back once more. Garon's golem body was intact, but banged and scratched up pretty well. Thankfully, toy golems got a shadow of golem resilience, enough to survive a furious flock.

The golems and spirits reconvened, as Pulsivar and Mopsy had a field day. The two cats chased the birds outside, hungry for fresh meat.

"Good news is I got some stat boosts in there, and I'm a level two mercenary and toy golem and half-orc," Garon said, picking his torn helmet plume off the floor. "Bad news is my luck's still pretty horrible. Threadbare, I'm going to need you to destroy me. Or Fluffbear can do it, either's fine. Maybe Fluffbear, she's low enough she'll get some experience from this probably."

"What? Why?" Zuula asked.

"We need to find out if I can be caught in a soulstone if my vessel gets destroyed here. Otherwise death in this form is permanent for us. And if I survive, then I want to see if my stat boosts and level carry over, or if it wipes and I have to start fresh each time."

"That... would be good to know," Madeline confessed.

"Don't you start!" Zuula hissed.

"Just sayin', we're gonna be monstahs eithah way. Might as well figure out if we're immoatal monstahs, befoah we get into a bad spot."

Threadbare found himself uneasy about casually killing a friend. "Are you sure about this, Garon?"

The walls of the toy store groaned. Threadbare shot a glance around... the fight had damaged them. It would be terribly unlucky if they collapsed right now.

"I'm sure," Garon said.

Another groan—

—and then Threadbare plucked him up and popped the knight's head off, shredding the body for good measure. The groaning settled to a rolling creak.

The empty soulstone glowed. "Whew! Level three all around, again. I was worried they'd be stuck at level one."

"Now that we've sorted that out, we should probably continue this somewhere else," Threadbare decided. "Everyone choose a body, and does anyone know somewhere safe?"

"I have just the spot," Madeline declared.

She led them out of the toy store, and down into the basement of the inn. There, in the remnants of the wine cellar, sat a collection of stone caskets.

Madeline's casket had racks of clothing next to it, most of it patched up and worn. And some of it was very impractical.

"I don't see how this would have fit you," Threadbare said, holding up a slinky dress with a very low-cut bodice.

"Hey, not my fault I got stuck in a body that looks thirteen. I had hopes of learning ta shapeshift someday. Or maybe unlocking a rank up ta 'Mistress of the Night.' That job gets wicked cool heah and some huge gazongas."

"What's a gazonga?" Missus Fluffbear asked.

Garon sighed. "I'll tell you lat—"

"Tits," Zuula interrupted.

"Oh, okay."

"Mom!"

"What?"

"They're basically kids!"

"Kids know what tits are. Not last long as babies ot'erwise."

"Shouldn't thaht be 'udderwise?'" Madeline asked, slyly.

There was a pause, then Zuula's laughter rang spectrally around the room.

"But it's safe enough here, right?" Threadbare asked.

"Safe as anywheah. Still… maybe Fluffbear puts that blessing of Luck on Garon when he gets out, instead of you?"

"Wait," Zuula said. "Do Zuula first."

"What? Mom, why?"

"Zuula be midwife. She gots Newborn's Mercy. Dat level one, should come t'roo. Gonna mercy all of us. Between dat and… guh, ugh, stupid god's blessing, we get t'roo maybe better."

That seemed like a very good idea. So Threadbare hauled out the doll Zuula had chosen, and modified it. A plush doll of a woman in a dress got the skirt ripped into a loincloth and halter top, her cloth 'skin' dyed green, and big tusks. Her hair was styled into dreads, her black cloth eyes got replaced by glaring yellow ones, and at Zuula's urging, he gave her big angry eyebrows. "Ready?"

"Ready!"

The animation went off without a hitch, and provided more skill ups… and a pleasant surprise.

You are now a level 3 Golemist!
INT+5
WILL +5

Not really a surprise, when he thought about it. That had happened the first time he made a toy golem. Then he'd used Beanarella to do things while she was around, and made more golems. So that was useful…

At any rate, he was glad for the level up. His sanity had been getting very low… golem creation and animation was expensive. But the level up refilled it, so that was good.

Little cloth Zuula sat up, and slapped a plush hand to her forehead. "Newborn's Mercy! Wait, what? Newborn's Mercy, she say!"

"You're speaking through Speak with Dead!" Threadbare realized. "Uh-oh."

"Yorgum's Blessing of Luck on Zuula!" Missus Fluffbear shouted, and Threadbare felt his luck go back to normal. The plush cleric could only have one blessing active at a time, sadly. That was the rule on that spell.

Zuula sighed. "Will have to do," she spoke, in the spirit realm.

"Let's get you talking properly," Threadbare decided. "Just in case."

That took fifteen minutes to sort out, and about another hour when she was unsatisfied with the volume, and she made him dial it up so she could properly yell at people. Threadbare burned a lot of tailoring materials figuring it out, but ended up with a deep, resonant voicebox for her.

It wasn't a bad idea. He decided to upgrade his own and Missus Fluffbear's voices at the first opportunity. After his friends were settled and all in their new bodies, of course.

"Status." Zuula took a long look, then sagged. "Level one Shaman. Level one Midwife. Level one half-orc. Hm, at least both skills came t'roo."

"They did on me, too." Garon said, glumly. "Let me guess, you got darkspawn for the orc one?"

"Yes. How you know?"

"Because I knew you had it before. Me, when I came through I got Twisted Rage. And Man's Drive to Achieve for the human one, which is what I had when I was alive. Which means that if you had those skills in life, and go into the same race, they carry over. Which means… yeah, you know what? I'm changing my choice. Threadbare, you can keep that other dolly around for a spare half-orc if you want, but I want to be something else."

"What?" Zuula straightened up, yarn hair whipping around as she stared at her son's Soulstone. "Why?"

"I don't want to be a half-orc anymore."

"But... you was awesome half-orc!" Zuula said, waving her arms. "Why you give that up?"

"Oh geeze... ah... look, Mom, it's not you, or half-orcs, it's the rage. I can't handle the rage."

"But you build battle plan around it!"

"Yeah, and you know what? After I got to try it out in an actual fight, it sucks! Everything goes red and you're just killing, and killing, and hurting until it goes away. And it's not just that, it's what it does to your temper, outside of it!" Garon's voice raised, got shriller as he started speaking faster. Threadbare and Fluffbear glanced at each other, feeling not very comfortable at where this was going.

"But it you heritage!" Zuula wailed. "How ancestors know you if you not be half-orc! How dey guide you!"

"Mom, look, I respect your religion, but no. This is the only chance I have to ditch the rage. All my life I've had to take abuse and struggle to keep calm, because I knew I'd start killing like a maniac if I didn't. All. My. Life. Now that I'm dead? It's not gonna be all my death."

Zuula was still for a long minute.

"Hey," Madeline said, sounding like she wanted to be anywhere but there, "Garon, you still got yoah half-orc levels right now, right?"

"Three of'em," Garon said from his Soulstone.

"So it's only temporahry, then. Look at it this way, if he dies in the golem bahdy he becomes a half-orc again. So if he kicks it permanently, he'll go to his ancestahs as a half-orc."

Zuula considered it. Then she heaved a great sigh. "You right. Garon, Zuula sorry. You do what you want, clever boy. It be okay."

"Thanks Mom. Thanks Mads."

The teddy bears relaxed. This was better. It was hard when friends argued.

"Hokay," Zuula said, looking around the cellar, picking up a bottle, and breaking it. Clutching the glass shank, she toddled toward the stairs. "You do de t'ing, Dreadbear. Zuula gonna go grind some levels."

"I wouldn't," Missus Fluffbear said. "Pulsivar and Mopsy are still out there and they don't know you. You might get pounced and shredded just because." The little bear earned herself a wisdom point with that one.

Zuula sighed. "Fine. Fine, whatever." Then the little half-orc frowned. "Why Zuula not think of that? She wise too!" Zuula slapped her forehead. "Zuula forget. Why Zuula forget? Oh. Oh wait. Status. That why Zuula forget. Man, dese stats be nurphed."

"What's a nurphed?" Madeline asked.

"Nurph be god of weakness and losers."

"Actually he's the god of Honor and Fair Play, Mom."

"Did Zuula stutter? Same t'ing anyway." The little doll hopped clambered up on a casket. "Suckage. Dat a lot of wisdom gon' have to be grinded again."

"Speaking of that," Garon said, "I want to go next."

"All right, but if you don't want a half-orc body, what do you want?" Threadbare asked.

Garon told them.

For a second, there was stunned silence in the basement. Then Mads whistled. "You ain't afraid ta go big, Gar."

"Zuula forgive you," his Mom decided. "Not half-orc, but... eh, close second. She tink she see one in de toy store. Let's go get it."

Twenty minutes and one salvaged toy later, Garon stirred, and opened plush eyes as the world came into focus. Again.

He was immediately met by a prompt.

You have unlocked the High Dragon Hatchling job!
Would you like to become a High Dragon Hatchling at this time?

"Hells yes!" Garon whooped.

And then he was a dragon.

"Newborn's Mercy!" Shouted Zuula.

"Yorgum's Blessing of luck upon Garon!" Fluffbear chorused, happy at the skill ups she was getting for this one. Each one upped the cost a bit, but increased the effectiveness of the buff. Still, she was getting a bit loopy from the sanity cost.

"Oh boy... this feels..." Garon twisted his stuffed head on his long neck, and opened and shut a mouth full of newly-hardened cloth teeth. "This feels GOOD." He stretched his wings, feeling the power of his new frame. **"Status."**

He was silent for a long minute.

"Is everything all right?" Asked Threadbare.

"You're looking at my stats, right? With that eye for detail thing?"

"And other things, yes."

"Tell me you're seeing that eighty-three in strength."

Zuula jumped up. "Whaaat? Zuula be stuck wit' piddly forty-seven!"

"I see it," Threadbare said. "It looks like some of your numbers are pretty high. Except for dexterity."

"Yeah... I mean, the strength and constitution aren't up to my old stats from when I was living, but it's close, it's close. And the rest is… yeah, I can live with this." The three-foot-long green plush dragon strutted around the room, stretching and testing its legs and muscles. "Ooh, seven skills…. Two of which look like trouble. I get 'No Thumbs' and 'Limited Equipment.' Let me… Yeah, yeah, they suck. No weapons for me." The dragon grinned. "But I'm a mercenary, so whatever! Fighting is fighting. And with a basic armor rating this high, I should be fine. For now, anyway."

"What are the othah skills?" Mads asked.

"Let's see… Scaly Wings, Dragonseye, Chomp, Draconic Tongue, and Burninate. Oooh! I gotta try this. Threadbare, can I get the loudest mouth you can give me?"

"I'll see what I can do. You're bigger so I can put in a bigger air bladder."

It used up most of his remaining leather, but finally he got one installed that Garon was happy with.

"Yes," the little dragon said, in a voice that had been carefully crafted for yelling at thieving halfens and arrogant dwarves. "Yes, this'll do. Okay, stand back. **Burninate!**"

That was actually a pretty poor decision, as it turned out.

Burninate, which dragons usually roar in the draconic language so as to avoid mockery by younger races, is a costly and exhausting skill. It also calls up the fire directly from the dragon's mouth.

And at the time, the little plush toy golem who'd activated it had absolutely no resistance to fire.

Fortunately, with much credit owed to Yorgum's blessing and the quickness of his colleagues, they managed to get him put out before he was destroyed. A few mends, plus Zuula's test of shamanic Slow Regeneration (which worked perfectly), put him to rights.

"So unclever!" Zuula stood over the chastened dragon, shaking her plush finger at it. "What you t'ink happen! Showing off! Foolish boy! You not too big Zuula can't spank you!"

"Sorry, sorry, sorry Mom."

"Yeah, you know, ya burned up about half my dresses theah too, kiddo. Not too happy about that," Mads chipped in.

"Meh, you couldn't wear them now anyway."

"Ain't the point, Gar. Ain't. The. Point."

"Sorry," he muttered. "But hey, I've got a powerful skill! That fire did amazing damage!"

"Yeah, to you." Mads snickered.

"Okay, so it wasn't made for plushie mouths. We can work on that. Ah… maybe an asbestos tongue? I don't know. I'll think on it. What gives fire resistance?"

"Fire elementalists, mostly," Zuula said. "Easy skill for dem."

"Woo. Okay, so... well, maybe I can get that job once we figure out how to raise our job limits. It's an easy one, especially with this breath. All you have to do is kill something with fire, and the job unlocks."

Madeline sighed from her soulstone. "Right, whaddeva. Now that we got Garon outta the way, it's my turn."

"Oh, sure." Threadbare said. "I think I've got about one more left in me. Then I'll need a few hours to recharge my sanity. Maybe a few days. I've got a lot of sanity now. It takes a very long time to recharge."

"What you talking about?" Zuula turned to scowl at him. "You just go to sleep, and when you... wake... up... oh."

"Oh," Garon agreed. "That's a problem. Betting we can't eat or drink like this, either."

"No."

Zuula considered. "You smell?"

Threadbare sniffed himself, then shook his head. "I don't think so. Everything smells like burned Garon now though, so it's hard to tell."

"No, you sniff! You have sense of smell! Maybe herbs work."

"Herbs?"

"Like in hut."

"Mom."

"Yes, we try burning some later, and—"

"Mom!"

"What?"

"You are NOT getting him hooked on that stuff."

"Bah. It not work dat way for him. Probably not. Most likely not." She rubbed her cloth chin. "Hopefully not."

"Yeah, no. Or we wait until Fluffbear levels up cleric and learns curative... which we don't know will work on him, either."

"Hm."

"Yeah, hm."

"Yeah, can I have my bahdy now?" Madeline said.

"Oh, yes, of course." Threadbare lifted up the doll she'd chosen. "You're sure?"

"Pahsitive."

It had been a marionette once, of a pretty lady with long black hair. Her face had been painted with exquisite care, and her red dress was made of velvet, as were her elbow-length gloves.

"Once we give her teeth, she'll be a perfect vampaiah," Madeline said with satisfaction. "Whaddaya think, Mistah Beah?"

"Well it should work, even if she's not plush. Appraisal reads her as a toy, so the golem animation should take. But I don't know how to give her a mouth so you'd be stuck mute, unless we've got speak with dead going. It's just that I don't know how to work with wood," he shook his head. "Tailoring I can do. Wood's trickier."

"I can learn," Fluffbear offered.

There was a bit of silence. "You'd do that for me?" Madeline sounded surprised.

"Sure! I like learning new jobs, and I've got two more crafting ones open! Yorgum likes building and crafting! This will let me make wood things like houses, right?"

"Well, yeah," Garon said.

"If you're sure. Um..." Threadbare thought. "I don't know how to unlock that job."

"I do," Garon said. "Hey Mads, Grimble's workroom is behind the bar, yeah?"

They ventured upstairs, and after some digging, found his tools. Grimble had been the one to repair the tavern, after all, and he had plenty of wood and nails left over. Some quick carving and whittling, and Missus Fluffbear whooped. "Got it! Oooh, Strength and Dexterity. Yay!" She started happily whittling, and skilling up. "Straighten wood? Okay, I guess that's useful. But hey, new job! More power! Better attributes!"

"Ah..." Garon said, "You might want to be careful there. You don't want to fill up your jobs too fast."

"Bah, not dis again," Zuula grumped.

"Why?" Missus Fluffbear asked.

"If you leap on the first unlocks available, you might seal yourself off from a job that really suits you when it comes up. You don't want to just choose the first things available. Especially before you've had a chance to develop your attributes while they're low."

Zuula snorted. "Pssht. So afraid of fast paths to power..."

"Says the woman who stuck with Shaman and let her other adventuring jobs rot."

"Bah, she only need Shaman. Shaman awesome."

"Garon has a point," Threadbare put his paw on Missus Fluffbear's shoulder, as she whittled busily at scraps of wood. "I just found out a very good job that probably would have helped my friends, but I can't learn it. Unless I find my guild. Oh! Does anyone know anything about that?"

Silence for a bit. Then Zuula sighed. "No. Dat part of de problem." The little half-orc doll leaned against the counter, and shook her head. "Ain't no one know what guild de words talking about. People first t'ought maybe it meant dem old trade guilds dat ain't around no more."

"Yeah. Dad told me about that," Garon said. "When instant crafting became a thing, it wrecked the trade guilds overnight," Garon said. "Touched off some really nasty trade wars, and a lot of people died, as the bigger Guilds tried to scrabble to keep their power and influence, and mercenary work boomed. But those weren't the guilds the messages were talking about."

"So no one know, and so we stuck with de jobs we got," Zuula shrugged. "How many you got little black bear?"

"Five left," said Fluffbear, and they were all silent. "Adventuring, I mean. One crafting one left, now."

"Oh, you're eight and four too," Threadbare said. "Good to have that confirmed."

"How?" Garon finally managed. "Humans get SEVEN. Half-Orcs are stuck at six, for crying out loud. How'd you get such a big amount?"

"I don't know."

"Mff. So damned broken... Well, anyway, normally the path most people take is to level up their attributes associated with a job BEFORE they go into the job. That means that they train up their attributes while the training's easier, so that the skill ups from leveling go farther. But you've kind of blown that away, I guess."

"I guess. I didn't really know what I was doing through most of it." Threadbare said. "My luck was pretty horrible for a lot of it, so things kept happening to me. I think..." He rubbed his head. "I think if I hadn't taken all those jobs I wouldn't have survived."

"So..." Missus Fluffbear turned her head back and forth. "Which way is better?"

"No way's bettah, really," Madeline said. "Speaking as someone who's eaten people who followed both paths, it really just depends on wheathah you want to have powahful focus in one or two things, or have a bunch of useful skills in a bunch of areas."

"I think the important thing is to figure out what you want to be, what you want to do to get to your goals, and find jobs that you like that support that," Garon said. "Whether that's all at once or waiting a bit to see if you change your mind later, or if you unlock something nifty, that's up to you."

"No one can tell you how to live yah life, right?" Madeline sounded approving. "Kickass. So, uh, ya ready to make me a mouth yet?"

Twenty carpenter skill ups and five levels later, Fluffbear was.

It took Threadbare working in tandem with her for the leather and cloth components... the former of which they had to salvage from the curtains. This also gave him a Tailor level up, which refreshed his sanity. Ah yes, he'd forgotten he could do that!

It was handy, but sooner or later the levels would be farther apart. It had gotten him through some tough instances, but he couldn't count on being able to do that forever.

And finally, the crowning touch. Missus Fluffbear notched the eighteen-inch-tall marionette's flexible, jointed, cloth-and-wood mouth carefully, and slid in two tacks for fangs.

"Does that look vampire enough?" She asked Madeline.

The Soulstone pulsed red. "Oh yeah! She's hot. I'd do me."

"Do what?" Threadbare asked, confused.

"We'll tell you LATER." Garon shouted, then stopped, confused. "Huh. Sorry, I thought Mom was going to explain again."

Zuula sounded as confused as Threadbare. "What? Zuula not know what she talking about."

"Thank gods for small favors." Garon muttered.

Madeline chuckled. "Eh, fahgeddit. Let's do this thing."

"Wait," Garon said. "What about the daylight thing? And the wood thing?"

"I thought of that. You know how many nights I spent staring at my status? Got those 'skills' memorized. The exact wahrding was my flesh burns at the touch of sunlight. My FLESH, Gar. So if all I got is wood, instead, I should be fine. And the wood thing don't kick in till level five, and it says wood which pierces my skin will pain me, and wood through the haht will paralyze me. Guess what puppets don't have! Skin or hahts!"

"Sounds sketchy to me."

"Eh, if it don't work out we go with anothah bahdy, and I just accept I can't be a vampaiah."

"You sure you don't want to be a dragon instead, Mads?"

"I'll stick with what I know. Like yer old lady, theah."

"Maybe a bit clever girl after all. For dead t'ing."

"Love you too, Zuu."

"Bah."

They returned to the relatively safe basement, Threadbare did his thing, Zuula laid her midwife's blessing upon the puppet, Fluffbear blessed her as well, and she sat up.

"Yes! I DO want to be a vampaiah. Bing! Theah we go. Awright. Moment of truth… **Status**." The puppet read her screen, then jumped in place with a clatter. "You guys!"

"What?" said Garon.

"Zuula not a guy."

"I'm not either! I think," said Missus Fluffbear.

"I suppose I'm a guy," said Threadbare. "Celia thought so and she would know."

"You guys you guys you guys!" Madeline said, dancing a wooden jig with vampiric agility.

"What?" Garon said. "C'mon, share."

"I have an open adventuring job slot! And a crafting one!"

There was silence for a long moment. "What? How?" Garon asked.

"Well I didn't have an adventuring job befoah, right? And you all could carry one job ovah when you got turned into doll hauntahs, right?"

"Right..."

"So what if tha vessel opens up a slot regahdless, even if you don't have one ta begin with? Like you tucked a baby in heah, he'd be able ta learn new jobs! Oooh, good idea. Let's go find a baby."

"No." Garon said.

"What? Oh, right, what was I thinking!"

Garon looked relieved.

"There's no babies around heah."

Garon looked less relieved.

Oblivious, Madeline continued. "But the point is, I can learn something like an adventurah could. I'm kind of like people now. Wow. Didn't expect this." The vampire hopped up on her coffin, and drummed her heels on the lid with a staccato beat. "Man. What should I choose?"

"It's... tough to say. You're still a vampire, right?"

"Yeah, but my strength got a li'l nurphed. Most everything else too, but eh, level one, so whatcha gonna do? Only one way up."

"Unless you die. Then you gots to start all over," Zuula said.

"Yeesh. Buzzkill. Eh... well, good time to test it, before I try anything. Hey guys, wanna walk me upstairs to do the sunlight test thing?"

They did, and the little puppet stared at the hole in the curtain where Threadbare had cut it for the leather, and the sunlight leaking through onto the ground. "Moment of truth," Madeline whispered.

Then she put her foot into the sun.

"Tingles," She said, shifting it back and forth. "Ya put ya right leg in, ya take ya right leg out... yeah!" She whooped. "Left leg in, an' you shake it all ABOUT!" The marionette, stringless, danced the hokey pokey through the sunlight. Because THAT was what it was all about.

"Lucky, lucky day! Rules lawyerin' for tha win!" She said, stepping back into the darkness. "Whew. Comfier. Good ta have dahkspawn bonuses back. Lucky..." She froze. "Hey. That ah, that blessing of luck?"

"Yes?" Fluffbear asked.

"It's on me, right? And not Zuula? Who's runnin' on half-orc luck now?"

"Oh, yes. It's okay, because she has her Newborn's Mercy... up..."

They fell silent, and looked to Zuula.

The little shaman never had put her midwife buff up. She'd tried it on herself, but she hadn't had a mouth then, and in the joy of discovery they'd all forgotten completely about it. And once she had a mouth, she hadn't cast it. She'd forgotten to.

Zuula, oblivious, stared back. "What?"

WHAM!

The door flew down, as Pulsivar and a ragged wolf, frothing at the mouth and bloody, rolled through the room. Mopsy chased the screaming, brawling pair, slashing...

...and then her eyes fell on Zuula. Panicked, and spooked by the sinister little doll, she leaped—

Half an hour later after they disposed of the wolf's carcass, chastened the cats, yelled at Zuula until she Newborn's Mercied herself, and finished mending themselves and the door, they settled into the basement for a nice long game of grindluck.

"Best present I ever took off a corpse," Madeline said, fondling the worn cards as best as she could with wooden hands. Fortunately the animus spell and some careful woodwork beforehand had given her usable, if stiff fingers.

"Shut up and keep playing," Zuula grumbled.

"What ah you worried about? And... oh, I just unlocked necromancer. Guess we all still count as undead."

"Do you want to be one?" Garon asked.

"Thinking. I dunno. Threadbare's got us covahed on that front. Unless he dies."

"Oh gods, you're right." Garon said. "We're effectively immortal unless he goes, so long as we die around him and he can soulstone us in time. But we're boned if he dies. Unless we somehow find another friendly necromancer, and convince him to help. And even then I doubt we'd luck into another golemist—"

"I'm a necromancer," Missus Fluffbear said.

They all stared at her.

"Right. Of course you is." Zuula slapped a cloth hand to her yarn-covered head. "You deal peacefully with smart undead yesterday. Then when job came up you just said 'yes'. This why undead suck. Corrupting all de innocent youth."

"Says the lady who used to put scorpions into our bed," Said Garon, dropping his cards from his claws again. "Agh! Fucking dexterity."

"I gotcha hun." Madeline scooped up the cards, then froze. "Wait.

Maybe I DO gotcha, Gar."

"What?"

"I'm out for this hand." Madeline folded her cards, walked over to one of the wall sconces, leaped up, and kicked an unused torch free. "Ya a scout, right mistah beah?"

"Yes, I am," Said Threadbare.

"Firestartah me?"

"Um… won't you die? Oh wait, you mean the torch." It was a very good thing he had a fairly high intelligence, now. "Okay. **Firestarter**."

She took the burning torch and stalked off into one of the side tunnels that the vampires had burrowed out from the basement. Mystified, the group watched her go. Eventually she turned a corner, and all they could see was the flickering torchlight.

"Mads?" Garon asked, uncertainly.

"It's fine. Just looking for… ah, hello my pretties!"

A horrible squeaking chittering filled the air, and the toys jumped up from the table. "Rats!" Threadbare said, and charged towards the tunnel.

"It's okay, I got this!" Madeline called back. "They're caged! Darla had some set aside for snacks latah!" Threadbare slowed as he approached and oh goodness, wasn't THAT a horrible smell. Roasted meat and rodent fear. "Yeah, theah's the unlock! Thanks fah telling me how, Garon! Yes! Ooooh, **Status**."

The dragon's eyebrows wrinkled. "You're… welcome? Why?"

"Hee heee heee… ha ha ha!"

"Madeline? Starting to worry me, here."

"Endure Faia! Call Faia! Yeah, that's the stuff!"

The light in the tunnel flared, and Threadbare gasped as Madeline came around the corner, wreathed head to toe in fire.

But NOT burning.

"What?" Said the sunproof, stakeproof, and now fireproof vampire. "You wanted a faia elementalist, didn't cha?"

CHAPTER 7: CAREER PLANNING

Grindluck, while incredibly useful for decreasing the toddler fatality rate, is also an obscenely boring game to most adults, and young adults.

Also, it didn't help that Garon's newly-sewn-on thumbs refused to function in any way, shape, or form. "Oh damn it!" Down went his cards again, fluttering to the floor like sad little monuments to the newly-made dragon's folly.

"I really don't understand," Threadbare said, poking at his latest stitchwork. "They went on you just like the mouth did, and I teased the stuffing to where you should be able to open and close them."

"Told ya it wouldn't wahk," Madeline said, slapping down two green cards.

"Ha! Eat it!" Zuula's plush hand pounded two blue cards down to match her, and the little vampire puppet scowled.

"It was worth a try," Garon sighed. "I guess the skill wins out over clever ideas sometimes. I can't feel the stuffing that's in those thumbs, it's like it doesn't exist anymore. Can you remove them?"

"Absolutely." Threadbare went to work.

On the other side of the table, Missus Fluffbear tried to play cards, but kept getting pushed over by a purring Mopsy. The miniature cougar had decided that she needed pets, and the only one she'd let pet her was OBVIOUSLY doing something dumb and less interesting than loving on Mopsy. With pets. NOW!

Pulsivar watched from the side, yawning. His fangs were still bloody from that wolf. He was a little weirded out by all the little moving, talking dolls that had appeared, but evidently this was a thing that happened when Threadbare was around. And the little bear had gotten upset when Pulsivar sat on the big green one. Which had been entirely unfair. That dragon was warm, of course it was for Pulsivar to sit on!

"How long's it been, anyway?" Garon asked, as Threadbare snipped and removed cloth. "Oh hey, I can feel the stuffing in my thumbs aGNANANANA... careful there."

"Sorry." Threadbare shoved the just-snipped fluff back into the dragon's body, and sewed up the hole. At least the experiment had been good for a point of tailoring skill.

Garon craned his crested neck to watch him work. "It's not exactly like pain. But it feels wrong, and like bits of you are fading. Is that how it is for you?"

"Oh yes," Threadbare said. "I've never really gotten used to it."

"It feels bad," Missus Fluffbear confirmed, giving in and riffling Mopsy's head with both hands and her feet. The cougar buzzed a happy purr, and pushed the tiny bear around the floor with her face.

"Yeah." Garon sighed. "Well, it beats pain, I guess. Not by much, but hey. So," he said, changing the subject, "Have you thought it over?"

"Whee!" Missus Fluffbear said, as she rolled over a few times, and Mopsy let her come to a rest before licking her fur. "What? Oh, that. Yes I have."

Silence for a minute, save for the cat's slurping.

Garon sighed. Kids. *They were just kids, really. Had to remember that.* "And what did you decide?"

"I'll do it. It's not like I have to choose those jobs right away."

Threadbare nodded approvingly. "It's only three classes, anyway. That will leave you two more to play around with if you do have to take those jobs." He glanced over to Zuula. "So how does this work?"

"You say to her, "Teach Missus Fluffbear," then you say the name of the job." Zuula said. "Then it kick off sacred ritual. Ancient thing called montage."

"Oh, that's how you do those!" Garon said. "Wait. They take a while, don't they?"

"Most of a day."

Garon slumped, and stared at the grindluck cards. "Great. Just great."

"Hold on!" Missus Fluffbear rolled to her feet, and gently shoved Mopsy until the housecat-sized Cougar retreated. "I need to use a skill and feed her!"

"Pretty sure she's got plenty to eat. Still lots of that wolf upstahs," Madeline said, placidly laying down two violet cards and watching Zuula pound the table with plushy rage.

"Yes, but her loyalty gauge will go down unless I spent time with her or give her monster treats to eat to boost it back up!"

"What?" Madeline looked to Zuula, who shrugged.

"Oh! Oh, this," Garon rubbed his head with one wingtip. "Right, Bakky had to deal with this, this is tamer stuff. If the gauge gets too low Mopsy might run away. Um…" He studied Fluffbear, all six inches of her. "Have you ever cooked anything before?"

"No, but the skill says I don't need to know how. But it improves them if they get properly cooked, so maybe I could learn?"

"Eh, maybe you don't," offered Madeline. "That'd be yoah last crafting slot. Shame ta use it just foah one little skill you don't always need?"

"I'm a cook," Garon offered.

"You are?"

"Yeah. Used to help Mom in the kitchen all the time. Come on, let's get you some wolf chops and you can practice turning them into treats. Over a fire. With supervision."

"Faia?" Madeline grinned, and put her cards down. "I'm in."

Twenty minutes later, they had six steaming skewers of meat, and two very interested cats. "Um…" Fluffbear said, as Pulsivar and Mopsy engaged in a somewhat-joking-but-not-really shoving match, "Please be friends?"

"Threadbare?" Garon asked the largest teddy bear present.

"Oh, of course. Come on Pulsivar." Threadbare hugged his cat, and gently tugged him away from the skewers. He had enough strength over the bobcat, and the big black feline loved him too much to do him any serious damage as Threadbare kept him from the food. *Chastening nibbles don't count,* Pulsivar told himself as he sunk fangs into the brown bear's hide. But Threadbare took it in stride, and Mopsy gobbled up five of the Monster Treats.

Missus Fluffbear smiled. "Her gauge is full. Here you go Pulsivar!"

Threadbare released his friend, and Pulsivar took his skewer off to a corner to sulk. And to eat. Mostly to eat. Baked especially for a cat type creature, the meat was delicious. Obviously the smaller bear wasn't entirely useless. Perhaps he'd deign to put his rump in her face at some point as a reward.

"All right. Are you ready?" Threadbare asked, brushing cat hair from his coat.

"Yes!"

"Teach Missus Fluffbear Animator."

Instantly, things seemed to blur. His limbs moved without his control, pulling out toys and devices from pockets he'd never had before, all sorts of little gewgaws and objects he'd never seen. Just as swiftly he showed them to Fluffbear, who sat and learned as he mimed animating them. And towards the end, she started doing it, too.

Then it stopped, and everyone was sitting in different places. "Oh. I thought it would take longer." He smoothed his coat.

"It did take longah. Go look, it's night outside," said Madeline.

"Yep, twelve hours, give or take," Garon sighed, balancing his cards with his wingtips, and trying to draw more with his claws. "Oh frak it!" The deck sprayed. Zuula laughed.

"Did you learn?" Threadbare asked Fluffbear.

"**Status.** Yes! Animator is on my unlock section."

"Well, let's get the other two done then."

The newly made doll haunters had had a long conversation with the two greater golems, about how their continued lives were literally dependent upon someone having the necromancer/golemist combo, who was sympathetic to them. Therefore, since Missus Fluffbear had already chosen to be a necromancer, she'd agreed to get the unlocks for animator, enchanter, and golemist. Though they weren't exactly directions she thought she wanted to go in, she didn't want to risk her friends dying and having no bodies to return to.

Also if gods forbid, anything happened to Threadbare, she might be able to make him a new golem body and soulstone him over.

If Greater Golems had souls.

They hadn't tested that yet, and she really didn't want to.

And so, the little black teddy bear gained the potential to one day become an animator, an enchanter, and a golemist.

By the time they finished the third one, the cats were nowhere to be seen and their doll haunter friends were gathered around a dirty sack, looking thoroughly wiped out.

"What's all this, then?" Threadbare wondered, poking at the sack. It clanked.

"Oh, you're up!" Garon said, pulling his head out from under his wings. "Remember Darla, the vampire knight?"

"Oh yes."

"This is her breastplate and shield. Her spear's upstairs. We figured it was a shame to waste good gear."

"It ain't magical or nothing, but it's good solid ahmah and a pokey stick," Madeline shrugged her wooden shoulders. It looked weird, with her marionette body's peg-and-ball joints. "Figure yoah a smith, so you can shrink'em down to one of our sizes."

"Um…" Threadbare said, rubbing his head, then catching his hat as it started to fall. "I don't actually know how to do that. The only skill in that list is Refine Ore."

"Oh. Let me guess, you got it through a montage or something? Crafting jobs can get weird that way," Garon said.

"Or something," Threadbare whispered, remembering the sick sounds of his creator being butchered while he hung helpless above.

Garon took no notice of the little bear's haunted expression. "Yeah, it doesn't actually give you the skill until the first time you craft. I think the forge is still here. The anvil might be a little rusty. And we'll have to stoke the furnace."

"Faia? I'm in!" Madeline grinned. "Gahd I love this jahb. Shit, no wander all you people types spend so much time leveling and raiding dungeons."

"Zuula got to come along, obviously," The half-orc said, perking up. "You gonna play with heat like a forge fire, then someone gots to be responsible adult here."

One hour and a nearly-disastrous blaze later, Zuula was banished from the smithy until they could trust her not to throw random stuff in the forge to see how it burned.

"Awright, remembah the buff I'm giving you ain't huge. Only reason I'm basically immune is because it stacks with another skill I gaht. Ya ready, Mistah Beah?"

"I think so," Threadbare said, clutching his smithing hammer and balancing awkwardly in front of the furnace.

"Awright. **Endure Faia!**"

Suddenly, it seemed to be a lot colder in the cramped smithy. Threadbare nodded, and used the head of the hammer to nudge the furnace door open.

Garon poked his head into the smithy from the outside door. "I think you just push metal in until it gets soft, then hammer it into shape. Try making... I don't know, a basic shape or something."

It took some experimentation, but finally, finally, Threadbare managed to get what he wanted.

You have Unlocked the Smithing Skill!
Your Smithing skill is now level 1!

It took the rest of the night to level the job up to five, though. The town had been pretty well scavenged for metal, and the rest of the toys dragged in everything they could find, up to and including a few window linings. Which cheered Zuula up no end as she got to help break things to get them loose.

Finally, four Smith levels and four points of strength and constitution later, Threadbare put the hammer down. "I've got it. It's called 'Adjust Arms and Armor,' and the description seems to be what you told me I could do with it."

"Cool," Mads said. "Hey, drag those smithing tools out, wouldja?"

"Why?"

"I got a skill I ain't used yet, and this forgefire's a good place ta test it."
The toys got to a safe distance.

"Awright! **Endure Faia! Least Faia Elemental!**"

From the outside, nothing seemed to happen. Garon coughed a bit.

"Oh it's cute!" Madeline squealed.

"Is it safe to come in?" Zuula enquired, barging back through the door and stomping up next to the little vampire. The two toys stared at the floating, watermelon-sized little ball of orange flame with black spots for eyes that drifted around the room, staring at things.

"You're in control of that, right?" Garon asked.

"If it's in my pahty, yeah... shit." Madeline knocked her knuckles on her head. "We got a full pahty, don't we?"

"Yeah..." Garon nodded. "And no offense, but I'd rather take any of you over a teeny little elemental called up by a level one skill."

"Zuula gots solution," the half-orc pointed out. "Dreadbear and Pulsivar leave party."

"Say what now?" Garon looked stunned.

"Is not enough to have new bodies, and new classes," she shot a stern look at Madeline, who was tossing dried weeds to her new pet as snacks. "You gots to train dem. And Dreadbare and Pulsivar high level compared to us. Dey big experience suck."

"I'm not sure what you mean," Threadbare said.

"It de way de world work. High level hang wit' too low level, high level get most of experience. Slows down leveling. Slows down strength. So you two go out of party, but still be around watching and helping if you need to. We still work together, just you two in own party."

"All right, I suppose that makes sense," Threadbare felt relieved. For a second he'd thought Zuula didn't want him around anymore.

"Besides, now you can pull skeletons and animated objects into you smaller party. Level dose skills and jobs."

"What? How?'

"Every time a created t'ing win a fight or do something wicked awesome, creator get experience." Zuula put her hands on her plushie hips. "How you not know dis? You got two creator jobs!"

"Uh, three, actually, if Golemist counts." Garon pointed out.

There was a pause.

"So what ya sayin', " Madeline finally said, her voice distant as she considered the possibility, "is that every time we win a fight or do something awesome he gets experience?"

"Yes! Maybe. It might only work for Golems in his party," Garon said. "I know Bakky didn't get any skill ups when his pets were off hunting, only when they were doing stuff with him."

"Why don't we test it out?" Garon asked. "Threadbare, you want to be a better Golemist, right?"

"Oh yes! If I can figure out that greater golem upgrade that Caradon used on me, perhaps I can make you even stronger!"

"Stronger be good," Zuula said.

"Fah once we're agreeing. Again. Which is fah twice?" Madeline shrugged. "Semantics."

"Actually this is a good time to discuss long-term goals," Garon said, "And ways to get there. Let's do that party split, find the cats, adjust that armor, and figure out a game plan for the long term."

"Back to the basement?" Madeline asked.

"Think you can get that thing through the building without burning it down?" Garon eyed the fiery ball.

"I make no prahmises! But seriously, yeah. If he's in my pahty. Also his name is Spahky."

They did some hasty shuffling and Threadbare kicked Pulsivar out and left the party. Though he knew his oldest friend wouldn't understand the words anyway and wouldn't be hurt, Threadbare was very relieved when he found them sleeping, both Pulsivar and Mopsy curled up together. Annoyed at being roused, the big cat and the no-longer-big-cat groggily followed them back to their lair, and accepted Threadbare's new party invite with surly grace, blinking at the words until they went away.

They lay down by Sparky and went limp into slumber, while the nigh-inexhaustible golems talked.

"Okay. I guess it falls on me to give you the talk," Garon said.

"Zuula do it!"

"Mom, no."

"What? She give you de talk, you work out fine!"

"Normally yes, Mom, but right now you're running on half-orc mental stats, mostly. You're level one."

"So is you!"

"Yes, but... oh geeze, just let me do it, okay? Please Mom? You can jump in at any time if I miss something or you want to add something." *Because I can't stop you from doing that anyway,* Garon added, mentally.

"Hmf!" Zuula crossed her arms. "Fine. Make it good. And short. We got stuff to do."

"Okay, so nobody ever gave you the talk," Garon said.

"What talk?" Missus Fluffbear asked.

"The talk of planning out your future. Finding your focus, figuring out how to make your jobs work for you, instead of you working for your jobs."

"I did work for my jobs," Threadbare took off his top hat and rubbed his forehead. "That's not making much sense."

"Okay, no, look—"

Zuula jumped in. "You need to figure out which jobs you want, get dem, den work on you focus first. Everyt'ing else wait until you got enough to survive an' get by. What you want to do, Dreadbear?"

"Save Celia," he replied, instantly.

"From what?"

"The King and his armies, probably. And Anise Layd'i."

"A nice lady?"

"Yes, her too."

"Bah, whatever. Look, you no do dis by bumbling about and pulling up little level one tricks. You do dis by making youself walking badass who know his focus and sharpen things until they bleed you enemies just by looking at dem."

"I... don't think I can actually do that."

"You don't t'ink, but maybe in higher level job skill unlock you CAN! But you only get to higher level if you focus on leveling de good jobs and leaving de crap jobs for later. Like necromancer. Remember how Zuula make you grind necromancer?"

"Well, yes, and I'm glad because I used a lot of command undeads, and the soulstones were good for—"

"You keep grinding necromancer!"

"Right. And you're not just saying that because he might make us stronger if he figures something else out with it," Garon said, shoving his mother off the tabletop with his tail.

"Hey!"

"Hay is for horses," Garon snapped. "Okay, look. What have you got to stop people from killing you up close? Jobwise, I mean, what's good at it?"

"Well, Duelist and Bear seem to be working out so far."

"Good. Your Duelist job is what, three? That's only two away from leveling that. It's always useful to have a fighting job, so go for that."

"I don't have a fighting job!" Missus Fluffbear, who had been listening raptly, spoke up. "I need something like that so I don't almost get my head popped off again!"

"Right, let's talk about that after I'm done," Garon said, watching his mother grimly climb the table leg, heading his way with the angriest of eyebrows. "So Necromancer's a good one for you Threadbare, and Duelist, so that covers fighting and casting. What else do you want to focus on?"

"Well, Golemist, so I can make you stronger. Beyond that, I don't know. I haven't really had time to give it much thought."

"Enchanter!" Zuula burst out, leaping on Garon and trying to bite his muzzle. Unsuccessfully, as her mouth wasn't set up for biting and Garon just knocked her back with one paw. But she clung to his wing and swung around. "You need reagents to make de golems! Learn enchanter up, at some point you get disenchant! Dat makes de reagents."

"Okay," Garon said, thumping Zuula on the table until she let go, "So Golemist, Necromancer, Duelist, Enchanter. That's four, that's half your jobs. Are there any you can safely neglect?"

"Well…" Threadbare watched Garon and his mother fight. "Scout is at level five. It's handy, but I don't use it much. Ruler's at level five, too. So I guess I can leave it. Animator's nice, but Golems are more important right now. Oh! Model's at four! I need to level it, and see what new skills I get!"

"Wait." Zuula froze, in the act of failing to put Garon in a leglock. "You got Ruler? Seriously?"

"Model?" Madeline snorted. "Seriously?"

"Scout?" Missus Fluffbear asked. "Seriously?" Then she spoiled it by giggling. "Sorry, everyone else was doing it."

"Oh yes. I got Ruler when I killed a big rat with a crown."

Garon facewinged. "Because of course you did."

"And I got Model when I made my own clothes in the dungeon that time. Though I didn't really know what I was doing, I was just sewing cloth on to make carrying it easier."

"Yeah dat sound like you," Zuula said, snorting. "Model. Bah. Weak."

"I'm getting plus forty to all my pools from one skill out of it."

THAT got their attention. "Wait. What." Madeline said, hopping down from her chair to stare up at him.

There was a fairly long stunned silence after he explained how the dietary restrictions skill worked. Madeline spent most of it laughing her ass off.

"Yeah, definitely grind that, at least to five. Shoot, if you level it just by wearing clothes and doing buffs, go for it," Garon said. "I never knew it had that much useful stuff."

"Still weak. Bad by itself…" Zuula said, and then she gained a point to her anemic intelligence. "But it not MEANT to be by itself, is it? Zuula have to rethink this. Muchly." Then she shook her head. "Wait. Go back to Ruler?"

"What about it? It gives an okay free buff, but only to people in my party, or my subjects. And I don't have any subjects. Although…" He checked his status. "I suppose I can give buffs to people if they share the same quest. Oh, and people can swear fealty to me and become my subjects. Do you want to do that?"

Another long silence.

"It comes with a free buff that's always on?" Madeline asked.

And so, there in the basement, they knelt and swore fealty to King

Threadbare the first of his name, ruler of the basement, at least until they were done and ready to leave the town.

"Ought to be good for some experience. Now you go and put on fashion show," Zuula said.

"Excuse me?"

"We got you sorted. Got to talk with Fluffbear about future. She get talk too. Meanwhile, you level Model by showing off new clothes, yes?"

"Oh. Yes, that's one way."

"So go upstairs, make new clothes, den come down here and let us see them. Do it enough, probably get you to level five."

"Okay." Threadbare headed upstairs, stopped, then walked over to Madeline's rack of half-charred clothing. "May I?"

"Of course, yer majesty!" Madeline curtseyed deeply. "Anything for the king!"

"Hilarious," Garon tried to roll his eyes, but they were beads and the best he could manage was wiggling them a bit. "Naaahahahah, that's a weird feeling."

Threadbare, with a bit of difficulty and some brute strength, finally lifted up the clothes rack and climbed upstairs, dragging it behind him. The cats winced and growled as it banged every step of the way.

"So I know I want a fighting job," Missus Fluffbear said. "The whip worked okay until the man got too close. So I want to use my dagger better. And the whip."

"All right, so Duelist is probably out," Garon said. "Those guys focus and you want to use different weapons. Um… if you go through the fighting class, the other three jobs there are Berserker, Knight, and Archer."

"Bearserker?" Missus Fluffbear asked, bouncing up and down. "That sounds like it was made for me!"

"Um." The three doll haunters shared a glance, and a long headshake. "No. Trust me, that one's a bad one. Especially for healers. Which, by the way, how are you using mend anyway? That's not a cleric spell, I didn't think."

"No, but it's Yorgum's godspell. Every god gets a spell to give to his clerics, that's what he told me. And mend is his."

"Huh, that's handy, not gonna lie. But the fact is you're built to heal right now, and maybe use undead if you lean into necro, and definitely tamer if you use Mopsy here, and when you're raging all you can do is beat things up. Which means no casting spells and probably no ordering undead or Mopsy unless you drop the rage. So I'd recommend no on that."

"Besides, you not have it in you to get unlock," Zuula pointed out. "Have to kill in amger."

"Yeah, I ain't seein' you or tha big beah ever doin' anything like thaht,"

Madeline said. "Just don't have it in yah."

"So archer's next… but we don't have a bow. Though you're a carpenter, you could try to make one. Though a bow your size would have a piddly pull, so…"

"What's a bow?"

He explained it. Missus Fluffbear shook her head. "It sounds really complicated."

"Right. So Archer's probably out. Besides, you want something for up close, so—"

Padded paws pounded on the stairs, and they whipped around to see Threadbare leap out, clad in a potato sack with holes in it for his arms and head, wearing one of Madeline's scarves on his head.

Your Adorable skill is now level 21!

Your Work it Baby skill is now level 10!

They watched him, as he solemnly flexed, and strutted with self-esteem. Then they howled with laughter. Threadbare beamed to see them so happy.

"Ah. Uh. Ah…" Madeline said, "Yeah, tell me you leveled from that."

"No. Though my Work it Baby skill is boosting one of my items a little now."

"You have a skill called Work it… Baby…" Garon doubled over laughing again, for a time. "Oh wow. Uh, yeah. Goodbye Threadbare. Anyway…" He turned back to Fluffbear, as Threadbare trundled upstairs again. "I think you need to pick up Knight."

"Knight?"

"Yeah. Mercenary's another option but it's fiddly and you have to know how to get the most out of it. Knight is pretty good defensively, and has a few tricks that dovetail nicely with cleric. My sister was training as a knight and cleric, trying for paladin, I think."

"Yes. She was," Zuula said, shortly.

"Oh hush, it made HER strong, didn't it? We wouldn't be here otherwise. So yeah, Knight's a solid combo for you there."

"Best of all, we still got Darla's ahmah and shield and speah," Madeline pointed out. "So how do we get her the jahb unlock?"

"Oh, you'll love this," Garon grinned and pointed over at the sleeping form of Mopsy. "All she has to do is win a fight while mounted."

Missus Fluffbear jumped up, hands to her face in horror. "I'm not killing Mopsy!"

"What? No, no, you just need to—"

"Forget it! I won't be a knight! That's horrible!"

"No, listen, I—"

"You need to ride Mopsy and kill something else while on her," Zuula explained.

The little black bear calmed down instantly. "Oh. Okay." Fluffbear frowned. "What does ride mean?"

Pad pad pad on the stairs, and… **"Dazzling Entrance!"** Threadbare yelled, and leaped into the basement. The baggy legs of his pants fluttered behind him as he jumped, empty and loose since he'd buckled the pants around his head. His apron was on like Zuula's loincloth, and he was wearing an oversized pair of bunny slippers on his arms.

Your Dazzling Entrance skill is now level 2!
Your Work it Baby skill is now level 11!

More laughter. "No, just no," Madeline gasped as he flexed and strutted. "Go… just go back and try again. Please. And for tha love of Agnes, pants don't go theah."

Threadbare hurried off. Meanwhile, Garon explained riding to Fluffbear. "Easy enough for Threadbare to make a saddle when he's done with… this… Normally they're leather, but you're light enough heavy cloth would work."

"Okay! I'll be a knight!"

"Cool, now all we need to do is—"

Slam! Pad pad pad pad pad…

"Dazzling Entrance!"

About a dozen more fashion shows later, Threadbare was almost out of moxie, when all of a sudden...

You are now a level 5 Model!
AGL+3
CHA+3
PER+3
You have unlocked the Call Outfit skill!
Your Call Outfit skill is now level 1!
You have unlocked the Makeup skill!
Your Makeup skill is now level 1!
You have unlocked the Strong Pose skill!
Your Strong Pose is now level 1!
Checking Dietary Restrictions….
Your Dietary Restrictions Skill is now level 25!

With a sigh of relief, Threadbare pulled off the black spiky wig, and shucked off the see-through teddy. "Here's your whip back, thanks for the loan," he said as he gave it back to Missus Fluffbear.

"I can't look," Madeline whimpered, from under the table.

Next to her, Garon's tail poked out, lashing back and forth like Pulsivar's. "Is he changed? Please tell me he's changed."

"Hm? What?" Zuula put down the parchment she was using to take notes, as she studied Threadbare. "Oh yeah, he done."

"In more ways than one," Threadbare said. "**Status.** Oh my. Yes, these will do nicely."

"Good. Please never weah my lingerie again," Madeline pleaded.

Garon stared at her.

"What?"

"You said that word without your accent."

"What? Lingerie? I'm a vampaiah. We get a pass on saying sexy words."

"You're just making that up."

She chucked him under the chin. "You wanna put me to tha test, tall green and scaly?"

"ANYWAY," Zuula said. "Dreadbare, Missus Fluffbear here gonna be knight. So we gonna make her a saddle so she can ride Mopsy. Maybe you make one for Pulsivar, too, so you can ride as well?"

"Oh, sure." Threadbare hesitated, his regular coat halfway buttoned. "What's a saddle?"

A few minutes later, he nodded. "That's a good idea. I had a real problem getting to where I needed to be in that battle where every undead died."

"Not all of dem," Zuula chortled.

"Shaddup." Madeline poked her in the arm, and Zuula backhanded her off the table.

"Hey!" A faint red '0' worked its way up from where she'd fallen.

Threadbare ignored it. "But if I'm riding Pulsivar, he can get me around faster. If he wants to. And I can show him where he needs to be. And he listens to me." He rubbed his forehead. "Oh dear. Maybe this isn't a good idea."

"He loves you," Missus Fluffbear said, "And I can show you how to teach him. I think."

"Zuula can speak wit' nature, and he nature," Zuula pointed out. "We set him straight. Practice tomorrow."

"Tomorrow?"

"Yes. Enough dilly dally and fashion shows and stupid fucking grindluck. Zuula fed up wit' level one! We gonna level tomorrow!"

"Mom?" Garon surreptitiously dangled his tail off the table, letting Madeline grab it and swing back up. "Our luck's still not great. A few more days of grindluck..." he made a face. "Yeah no, you're right. what's your idea?"

"Zuula know a place that still be full of skeleton bits, and a necromancer to animate dem for us." She pointed at Threadbare. "Tomorrow we go dere and he make dem fight us, and we practice as party!"

"Why wait?" Threadbare asked.

"Well, you need to refit Fluffbear's armor and shield and spear... no, wait. You said you wanted to use the whip and dagger?"

"Oh yeah."

"That leaves a spear."

"Zuula take it."

"What? How come you get thaht?" Madeline shook a wooden finger.

"You got teeth to bite with and a bitey job. Zuula got not'ing."

"Oh, so ya agreeing that vampaiahs is bettah than orcs?"

The basement fell silent, as the toys watched Zuula shake, wordless. Her eyebrows twisted until they tore, seams pop pop popping as they gave way.

Madeline realized, too late, that she'd crossed a line. "Whoa, hey, I'm sahrry—"

Zuula hopped down, grabbed the broken bottle she'd made a few days back, and chased the marionette around the room, howling incoherently.

"Please, stop!" Missus Fluffbear called, and Threadbare stepped forward—

—and stopped, as Garon raised a paw. "Let them work it out. Better this way."

A few hours later, after everyone had been mended, and Sparky's fires were out (he'd taken the assault on his mistress a bit personally,) the teddy bears rode their groggy and disgruntled cats into the pre-dawn darkness, with the doll haunters and Sparky following after.

"See? If she'd had twisted rage, one of you would be dead, right now," Garon admonished.

"I don't know if this is going to work out," Threadbare said.

"What? Zuula apologize and give back eye. It only wood chip with paint anyway."

"No, I mean this riding thing. Pulsivar keeps going off to look at things," Threadbare said from fifty feet away.

Most of the party could see him fine in the darkness, and Fluffbear had Sparky to see by, so they watched as Pulsivar ambled back, ignored them, as he followed a scent trail from one side to the other.

"Do you smell anything?" Fluffbear asked.

Threadbare took a sniff. "Yes, but I don't know what. Never smelled it before."

Zuula shook her head. "No matter. We almost dere."

They crossed the creek, keeping an eye out just in case.

And right before the bonefield, they stopped, staring up the hill, with shadows flickering at the limits of Sparky's light.

"Tell me," Threadbare said, staring at a round shape in the darkness, "Was there a boulder there before?"

The boulder stood up.

The boulder turned, gray rock revealed to be gray flesh as it turned around, eyes wide and moonlike in the darkness, club clenched in one hand. It considered the toys below it on the slope.

And then it roared, and fetid air washed over them, and the doll haunters were very, very glad that they didn't have noses.

"Dreadbear! It be an Ogre! Quick, we gots to—"

Zuula was wasting her breath. Mopsy had frozen in fright, but Pulsivar? Pulsivar was outs, yo. He didn't do ogres. And he took Threadbare with him, right out of the fight.

With slowly dawning horror, the level one doll haunters watched as the black cat vanished into the night, taking their hope, salvation, and chance of resurrection with them.

Then they turned back to the ogre, as it charged and the ground shook under its feet....

CHAPTER 8: OGRE BATTLE

"Run!" Zuula bellowed, and proceeded to ignore her own advice, charging the ogre with her spear leveled.

"You run! You run too!" Garon cried. "No, wait!" But then there was no more time for talking.

The problem, Zuula thought as the tree trunk whistled over her head, was that she didn't have enough willpower.

Zuula got in between the Ogre's legs and jabbed the spear into its muscular calves, trying for the ankle and failing. A red '1' rolled up.

Your Spear skill cannot be leveled farther!

Level up your highest class to exceed your limit of 10!

At least they'd come through to their new lives with full generics and class skills for their level caps, that was a small blessing, Zuula dodged a stomping heel, very thankful she had a ten in that, too. The ogre slowed its charge and turned to try and deal with her.

But no, the problem was willpower. The correct thing to do with an ogre when you are level one, is to run from it. But her willpower was at half orc levels, and nowhere near what it had been when she was alive. She'd ground that willpower, through eight children, half of whom had survived infancy. She'd ground it through arguments and good times alike with her husband. Ground it since her early days with her first tribe, learning to stand up for herself even when they gave her shit for being a halfbreed. All that was gone now, capped by the husk she wore. If she'd had her old body and mind back, she would have acted differently, used her brain rather than rushing in.

But Zuula's instincts were too strong. She was half an orc, and she would fight. And she was half a human, so she would die for her loved ones. And though a far, far better thing to do would be to run, she couldn't. She couldn't override her instincts here... and so she jabbed and tore at its feet, sending up '1's and '2's. It wouldn't be enough. Not nearly enough. It was slow enough she could shift from attacking, and pray her ten dodge skill saved her, but sooner or later—

WHACK

—And then she was flying, hitting a tree at full speed, and everything became darkness.

*****

"Oh... damn it! Run Mom! No!" Garon charged after her, almost activated his wings, before he remembered that he hadn't tried flying yet.

WHACK! He blanched, as the little Zuula doll flew into the woods. "Soulstone! Make a Soulstone and go get her spirit, now!" He screamed at Missus Fluffbear.

"I can't! Mopsy won't move!"

"Leave her!"

"No! She'll die!"

The problem, Garon thought as the ogre turned to the stunned cat and started walking forward, slobbering, was that he didn't have enough charisma. Years he'd spent polishing that, years of learning to talk without either of his parent's accents, and being surprisingly well spoken. Years of dealing with people... all down the drain, thanks to an inconvenient death. If he'd had it back his team would have listened, and he could have organized them, got them to safety at least. But he didn't have that, and so different, more drastic measures were called for.

The dragon darted forward, roaring, not daring to breathe fire for fear of toasting himself... but the ogre turned to look.

Then it glanced over at the cat, and started forward again. Fluffbear was pleading with Mopsy, had jumped off and was trying to push her, but the Cougar's fear was horrifying to see...

...so Garon leaped into the air and bit the ogre's loinclothed rump as hard as he could. **"Chomp!"**

A red '33' drifted up and the Ogre's bellow shook the forest, as he whirled, flailing at his ass. The thing was literally too dumb to find his ass with a single hand, so Garon was able to scramble free before getting squished. He slashed at it with surprisingly hard plush claws, scoring '8's and '9's, evading the tree trunk before it could come down on him.

"Fucking go save Mom!" He screamed at Fluffbear—

—and the Ogre scooped him up by the tail, and brought him up towards its gaping mouth...

And then Madeline spoke.

"I Command you to Stahp!"

*****

"I Command you to stahp!" Madeline screamed once more, and this time the ogre didn't resist, staring at her as she brought all her diminished vampiric will to bear. Then Sparky drifted over, belching fire at the ogre, who dropped the dragon and scrambled back. **"Bloodsuckah!"** She shouted, leaping up, aiming for its arm—

—and missing, to clatter on the ground, next to Garon who was shaking his head and backing off.

The problem is willpower, Madeline thought as she got clear of those stomping feet, grabbing Garon by the wing and dragging him off. If she'd had more willpower, and more moxie to fuel her command skill, she could tell the ogre to go fuck off and it would have to listen. But she'd lost all that, thanks to being dusted by Threadbare's crew. And now here she was a part of them, and she couldn't pull her weight, because her will was a pale shadow of what it had been, trapped in a wooden husk.

She winced, as the Ogre slammed its club into Sparky, and a red '84' rose up as the least elemental winked out of existence. Then it turned back to its plush prey.

The ground shook as the ogre stomped after her, but she saw Fluffbear finally manage to snap Mopsy out of it, mount up and head toward the woods. **"Soulstone,"** she thought she heard the little bear cry, and nodded in satisfaction. Zuula might be a bitch, but Madeline didn't wish her dead.

Garon was shouting something, but it was hard to hear over the ogre's bellowing. "I'm thinking it's time to cut and run!" Madeline bellowed back. "Get into the trees, and—"

All of a sudden, Garon snapped his head up and slowed. "Say yes when he gets to you!" He said, with hope in his eyes.

"What? What ah yah..."

"Hello," Wind whispered in her ear, in Threadbare's voice. "Here is a quest for you please."

**THREADBARE HAS OFFERED YOU A PRIVATE QUEST
DETAILS: BEAT THAT MONSTER
REWARD: 100 EXPERIENCE POINTS AND SOME GOLD
COMPLETION: UPON THE MONSTER'S DEATH OR
RETREAT
DO YOU WANT TO ACCEPT THIS QUEST? Y/N?**

"Yes?" Madeline said, glancing back. They were gaining distance on the ogre, but it wasn't showing any signs of giving up the pursuit. They'd gotten into the woods, but it was running after them, slamming into and knocking over small trees as it went, club sending up sprays of mud and rock as it dragged it, roaring.

A few seconds later, she heard Threadbare bellow in a far louder voice than expected from somewhere distant. **"Organize Minions to Beat that Monster!"**

"How the fahck?" She screamed at Garon, as they ran. She felt... better. Not by a lot, but better. A buff? Had to be.

"The Minorphone! He's using it! Keep running!"

"The what now?"

Threadbare's amplified voice yelled out again. "Hello, this is my **Emboldening Speech. I know he's very big, and you're very small, but I believe in you and think you can do it. That's all.**"

It was stupid.

But it was the kind of stupid that refilled her depleted moxie, and buffed her sanity. By a bit, anyway.

"Oh you clever bear, he's offering gold so I can **Do the Job!**" Garon laughed. "And Party Buffs! Why not? **Fight the Battles!**"

That didn't seem to do much, but every little bit helped. And with clearer sanity, she knew what she had to do. She leaped on Garon's back, and held onto his wings. "Get ready ta bahninate him! **Endure Faia!**"

"That only stops some of the damage to me!" Garon said. I'll burn to death!"

She glanced back. The ogre was picking up ground. The plush doll haunters had to go around obstacles, he could barge right through. "You'd rathah be thumped ta death? Trust me, Gar! I got you!"

"All right!" Garon whirled, waited until the ogre was in the middle of a group of thornbushes, and screamed for all he was worth. **"BURNINATE!"**

Fire exploded out from Garon's mouth.

A thankfully reduced '92' exploded up from Garon's head.

And the Ogre caught the full blast, bellowing and stumbling back as a red '124' washed over it.

"Aaaagh!" Garon howled as he burned, and red '1's started to flicker up—

"Endure Faia!" Madeline yelled. **"Manipulate Faia!"** She cleaned the flames from Garon, added them to the burning brush around the ogre, and laughed maniacally.

"Fucking ow!" Garon grumbled. "Blood is— shit! I can't do it! No coins!"

The ogre, maddened, pushed out of the flames and made for them.

"Run around tha faia!" Madeline commanded. "I'll try ta get him again!"

It had been very disappointing, to find out as an elementalist, that she couldn't throw fireballs from the get go. Almost as disappointing as finding out that it was a sanity-based class, and here she was, all moxie. But thanks to Threadbare's trick, she had a little more oomph to go on. And so, as the ogre chased them around the fire, she teased and pulled blazing flames from it, scooting out lashing tendrils and bursts at the monster, pinging it for five to ten hit points a pop.

"How long can you keep that up?" Garon yelled, slurring his words a bit, his head charred and lopsided from his own breath.

"About a minute or two a pop! I got enough juice for maybe three moah manipulates!"

"Keep it up— shit!" Garon ducked, as the ogre hurled a tree branch past his head, shattering against a nearby trunk, spraying splinters everywhere. "Ow gods!"

"Just run fastah!" Madeline urged, peeling fire off and flailing it at the ogre.

"On the plus side," Garon said, as they ran around and around the gigantic, growing, blazing beacon, "Now the bears won't have any trouble finding us."

*****

"Zuula? Zuula?"

Go away. I be dead, Zuula thought, as she floated in the black nothingness, thoroughly pissed at being a one-hit kill.

"Zuula— there you are!"

Zuula sighed, as she saw the glow of a soulstone approach... but it looked different, this time. She opened her mouth, and—

—wait, she had a mouth? This wasn't right. She wiggled her arms, and—

—arms! Dead people didn't have arms! Therefore…

Zuula burst out of the mud puddle, yelling and trying to clear her mouth, sucking in air.

"Oh geeze! **Clean and Press!**" Fluffbear said said, offering her a paw and ignoring the mud spattered on her teddy-bear sized breastplate and shield. "Are you okay?"

"**Status,**" Zuula croaked with her newly cleaned mouth.

Then she blinked. That couldn't be right.

"Zuula only half-dead. Huh! But he hit her with a bonebreaking—"

No bones.

"Then she hit tree, hard enough to turn insides to—"

Her insides were literally stuffing.

Come to think of it, she had leveled up that golem body skill a few times, over the course of her bashing.

"Huh. Huh!" And slowly, Zuula smiled. "**Slow Regeneration.** Yes, come on Fluffbear, move over." She wiggled up behind her on Mopsy's back. The cat bore it, too frazzled to argue.

"Oh!" Fluffbear said, "Look at that!"

"Look at what?"

And then Threadbare's quest flashed in front of her face. "Yes!" Zuula whooped, and laughed even more as he shouted buffs through the minorphone. "Okay," she said, with her intelligence and will up to the point she could think clearly. Well, clear enough, anyway. "We need to fight dis t'ing smart. Stop fighting like warrior. Fight like shaman."

"Um. How?" Missus Fluffbear asked. "I don't understand."

"Not you," Zuula punched her breastplate, with a 'thunk'. "You do warrior t'ing. Ogre not hit as hard as we t'ink. Zuula, though, Zuula fight like Shaman."

"How?"

Zuula grinned, as her slow regeneration stitched her back up and pulled her burst stuffing back in through its seams. "**Secret Herbs and Spices.**" She scanned around, then nodded and pointed. "Dere! Go dat way!"

"Shouldn't we go find the others?"

A section of the forest blazed to life, as a distant "**Burninate**" echoed from a few hundred yards away. "Dey be fine. In fact, dis perfect! Move fast, we got herbs to pick!"

*****

"I'm running out of stamina!" Garon screamed back.

"At least the faia's getting bigger!" Madeline said, ducking another hurled branch. Only a matter of time until the ogre got lucky.

"That's not a good thing!" Garon yelled, narrowly managing to leap a burning log, dragging his tail through it, and hissing...

...but his endure fire buff was still up, thankfully, and he survived the damage. The little dragon corrected his course to go wider around the blaze.

The ogre just bashed through it, sending a red '8' up to the heavens. Madeline sighed. **"Status."** No, there it was in black and white. Seven sanity left, and she needed three more for another round of manipulate fire.

Low sanity. That must by why I'm standing, she realized, crouching on the dragon's back, and eyeing the distance to the ogre. *That must be why the idea sounds good,* she thought, as she hopped free.

"Mads?"

"Eh, it's only a body. See ya next go round!" She hopped off, and annoyed, the dragon skidded to a stop, circled around.

The ogre slowed, too, grinning. Its hide was scorched to hell and back, its butt hurt from where the little green thing had chomped its cheeks, and it was really, really hungry. Finally, the prey had given up.

It opened its mouth wide—

"Now!" Zuula yelled.

"Go Mopsy go!" Missus Fluffbear pulled on the cat's harness, sending Mopsy streaking into the clearing. As she went Zuula waved a big wrapped bundle of herbs through the fire, igniting them. Then as the ogre stared, open-mouthed, Zuula hucked the bundle right into its maw.

Surprised, and running on instinct, it shut its mouth and swallowed.

And oh boy, was THAT a mistake.

Ogres are one of the few races in Generica that lack any kind of ability to vomit.

Its bellow shook the trees, as the little toys scattered. It ran hither and yon in the burning woods, screaming and howling, smoke pouring out of its mouth.

But then it found everything was slowing down.

The smoke from its mouth turned into a snake and turned to look at it. The ogre giggled. It was really funny, even with the pain in its gut.

Then its legs drifted off and floated away, so it stopped running to watch them go. It tried to wave bye-bye, but its hands had eyes, and so it winked them instead.

At some point the meat fairy came out and started showering him with turkey legs.

Then everything hurt at once and suddenly all the ogre could see was darkness.

*****

Against the burning remnants of the woods, the hut, and the clearing, the little toys and their cats stood triumphant, splattered in ogre blood, and thoroughly drained. Once Zuula's secret blend of eleven herbs and spices had finished its work on the ogre, and slapped it with a thoroughly hallucinogenic high, they'd closed on it and torn the ogre to bits. It had taken literally half an hour, and they were all tired. Golem endurance is very high to start with, but fighting really does take it out of a person.

Even when all the enemy can do is sit there and stare into the distance, waving at hallucinations.

Then the levels started rolling in, and they were cheering, hugging, and embracing. All save for Mopsy. She'd leveled too, but she was too busy meowing in confusion, as her body grew a bit.

Just a little bit. She was a tamer's pet, so she was capped by the tamer's level.

"Hahaha! Back to de level five shaman!" Zuula danced with joy. "Four Toy Golem and five half orc levels too. But shaman for de win! Hello Dream Quest! Zuula miss you so!"

"Level fahve elementalist! Woo! New skills! Oooh, one of them gives me moah sanity. Nice! Wait, it ain't all that much. Eh, whaddeva." She frowned. "Only level three vampire? But level foah toy golem? What gives?"

"I got level four golem too," Garon confirmed. "Merc's back up to five. Gods, that was a lot of... a lot of..." He frowned. "Wait. Uh... Uh oh."

"What?"

"My dragon level's still one."

"Oh. Shit, that's rough man. Wait, so some races get levels fastah than othahs?"

"I'm a knight!" Yelled Missus Fluffbear, raising her dagger. "Yay! And more levels!"

"I guess that's how it works. Dragons take a lot to level." Garon looked like he was going to cry.

"Fuckin' Nurph, amirite?"

"Fucking Nurph," Zuula confirmed, patting Garon's wing.

Andrew Seiple

"Meh, whatever," Garon shook himself. "Still a dragon. Did you see that Burninate?"

"I still see that Burninate," Said Threadbare, on foot, guiding a very reluctant Pulsivar through the trees. "I think that maybe we should move to some place that isn't on fire, please."

"When did you show up?" Zuula asked.

"Ten minutes ago. But I didn't want to steal your kill. This was all to train you, even if it didn't work like we planned. Erm... you might want to..."

WHUMP!

A burning pine tree five times the size of the ogre slammed down ten feet from the toys, spraying embers everywhere. They jumped and screamed, and Mopsy was gone, baby, gone.

"...Move..." Threadbare finished. "Well, no harm done. Yet. let's go then."

Once clear of the now-burning hollow, Madeline looked up at Threadbare as he rode along on Pulsivar's back. He had black and white makeup on his face, in the shape of a handsome, mustached man. She'd seen the like on many playing cards, before.

"Nice paint."

"Thank you. It's a model skill. It's boosting my Organize Minions skill right now. I guess this is the Ruler makeup."

"If I evah get moah jahbs, that sounds like a useful one ta pick up."

"Model or Ruler?"

"Both. Eithah."

"I would be happy to teach you."

"Hate to interrupt lovefest," Zuula spoke up, "But we ready to move on out of village now, Zuula t'ink." She glanced back at the fire. "Might have to anyway. Wind comin' from south. Maybe not be village left in a day or two."

"Eh, that town was dead anyway," Garon said. And then they were all howling with laughter, as the bears looked on.

Fluffbear looked at Threadbare, who nodded, and they laughed too. It seemed appropriate.

The mirth lasted until Fluffbear noticed how badly injured Garon was. "Oh! Oh I should mend you! Hold on, let me—"

Threadbare put a paw on her. "May I try? I just picked up a new skill."

"You leveled from that?" Madeline looked up. "In what?"

"Golemist."

Silence, as they walked. "That confirms it," Garon said. "When your golems do something big, you get part of the experience. Speaking of

146

which, you owe us some gold."

"All right. Before that, though… **Mend Golem.**"

Garon's head put itself together, mostly. "Sixty-five? Lordy."

Threadbare smiled. "Okay, that was pretty decent. Now you can mend him the rest of the way please," Threadbare rubbed his chin. "And that's what it does at skill level one. Dear me."

"How's the cost?" Garon wondered, as Fluffbear godspelled him back up to full.

"Four times as much as a mend. Only works on golems. But…" Threadbare's scepter glittered in the distant firelight as he swept it around to point at each of his friends. "Well."

"Well." Garon nodded. And yeah, it was. This wasn't the existence he would have chosen, but it beat the alternative. Besides— he glanced over at Madeline as she rode on his back, looking back at the flames. The company wasn't so bad. And the pay was... the pay! "Oh yeah! Gold? You owe us that."

"So I do. Although I've been thinking…"

"Yeah?"

"You're pretty big. What if we sewed you a pouch, and you used it to carry your own coins? So you could heal yourself whenever and wherever you needed?"

"I been thinkin' about stuff like that too. Makin' mods and gearing up ta help us sahvive and prospah." Madeline said. "I got a crafting slot, and soulstones is crystals, riaht? So maybe I get Jewelah, and make us some weahable soulstone necklaces or something in case tha worst happens…"

"And Dreadbear is enchanter who need practice, so you put spells in necklaces," said Zuula. "Or other stuff we can carry."

"Maybe something to make Mopsy braver?" Fluffbear said. "Also can you adjust her saddle? She's bigger now and it's a little tight on her, I think."

Plotting, planning, and basking in the glow of their stat gains, the little party of friends made their way back to town to salvage what they could and move on before the fire got there.

"So where do we go from here?" Threadbare finally asked. "We need to save Celia."

"Noath prahbably," Madeline said. "There's a little fishing town up that way. Most of our prey came from there. Dungeon huntahs, lootahs, trappahs. The ones we turned all said it was a quiet little place where folks just fished and minded theah own business. We can staht asking about for Celia theah."

"Yeah, but we're a bunch of toy monsters," Garon pointed out. "Even for an insular, quiet community, that'd be a bit much."

"Actually, Zuula been tinkin' about dat," The shaman spoke, feeling a lot happier now that she was about twenty points of wisdom and eight points of intelligence smarter. "Here is de plan…"

*****

Meanwhile, many miles away, a man in green robes perked up. "Hey! There's something to the south!"

"What?" His wife asked, shivering. It was cold and lonely up on this hill, and she was thoroughly fed up with waiting. The wind was coming off of Lake Marsh, and chilling her to the bone.

It was all the more agonizing, because the fire pit was right *there*, with unlit wood stacked high, ready to go. They'd been sitting next to it, as they had every night that their turn came up, with flint and steel and oil ready to go.

But still, the stars refused to cooperate, and until they did, the fire had to remain unlit.

"Give me a second, let me get up here…" The man shimmied up one of the old dolmens, using one of the many tentacles carved into the sides to climb it.

She winced as he put a foot into one of YGlnargle'blah's graven eyes. "Sorry lord," she mouthed, just to be sure.

"What was that?"

"Nothing, nothing." She coughed. "Just cold."

"Well someone's not. They've lit a whomping great fire out that way."

"Out what way?" She moved over to the edge of the hill and peered. No way was she climbing a dolmen, the last time she'd done something like that had been a lot of donuts and about five blessed children of the depths ago. Which reminded her, she needed to pick up fish in the morning before she got back home. They'd been good lately, and it was fun watching their lidless eyes light up so as they got their special treats.

"South. It looks like a wildfire or something, it's really going," her husband said.

She froze. "Harb?"

"Yes Marva?"

"Harb, it's a fire? A big fire that we can see from here?"

"Uh-huh."

"A fire like the sort we were supposed to light when the stars were right, and YGlnargle'blah's words echoed like terrible thunder from the dolmens to enlighten his children?"

There was a long pause. Then as one, Harb and Marva turned to look at the town of Outsmouth, a few miles to the north.

Outsmouth, in which their cult was eagerly awaiting the signal. The signal of a fiery beacon, from the south.

Harb and Marva looked to the stars, which were really, really, really not right. Then they looked to the dolmens, which were as silent as they'd been the last two years that the cult had been keeping sentries out here. Then they looked to the unlit fire.

And then they looked back at the blaze.

"You know," Harb said, in that voice one gets when there's something entirely horrible right in your sight, but you don't want to acknowledge it, "That fire is pretty big. You can probably see it from town."

"If you're looking this way," Marva said, in that voice one gets when one is trying to deny the horror, find some faint scrap of hope to lift one's soul, even in the face of the death of all one's hopes and dreams, "Maybe nobody's looking this way. I mean, Ebbett's on duty tonight, and he is a bit of a slacker."

"Totally fell through on the last bake sale," Harb said, desperately. "Probably asleep right now. Nothing to worry about—"

BONG.

The two cultists turned to stare at the town.

BONG BONG BONG.

Someone had started ringing the bells.

"Dead gods dammit Ebbett!" Harb and Marva wailed simultaneously, and looked at each other. Harb shimmied down off the stone, took her hand, and the married couple ran desperately toward town, hands waving, screaming at their distant brethren that no, wait, stop, it was all a big misunderstanding...

CECELIA'S QUEST 2: BAD COMFORT

Cecelia was far, far from Reason, and she hated it.

She had her plate mail, at least, enchanted with the same heating runes that kept her warm in Central Cylvania's chilly spring, and a covered wagon to ride in to spare her legs and back, but she really, really wanted to be inside a ton of steel and more esoteric components forged by her own hand.

"You've got that look again," Morris said, grabbing the wagon's tailboard and hopping up into it, moving easily in his own armor. "That look like you just sat on a hedgehog. Why the resting bitchface?"

The bastard had hit level twenty-five recently, and loved showing off one of his top skills that let him move around like his armor was weightless. Cecelia ignored that, and answered his question. "I miss my Steam Knight suit."

"Fff. No way you'd get that to the front in one piece. Even if you had the coal to make the trip, the rangers would be on it like Zara on a cute noble boy."

"Like they could do anything to me while I was wearing it." She muttered.

"They can, Dame Ragandor."

Cecelia sat bolt upright, twisted around and snapped her fist to her chest with a CLANG as gauntlet met breastplate. "Sergeant Sir!"

"At ease." Out of his helm, Sergeant Tane's face was solid and square, with a crooked nose broken long ago and never set right. Framed with blonde hair, rapidly receding from a high forehead, the man resembled nothing so much as an old lion. His eyes flickered as he glanced around the four trainees, now full knights, that rode in the back of the wagon. Behind him, the cloth separating the teamsters from their human cargo was loose. Cecelia could see the horses, and between them, the road ahead, misty and muddy from the rain that had been falling for the last two days.

"They don't hit you where you're strong," he said, keeping his voice low so they had to strain to hear over the raindrops. "They come in the night, or in weather like this. When you're sleeping, or exhausted from slogging through mud, or out taking a shit just past the perimeter. That's when the arrows come, or the blades flash, and if you're a soft target you're dead, and then they're gone as quickly as they came. You can't touch them in the woods, you can't find them when they want to hide, and they would love to bring home the head and helm of one of His Majesty's Knights."

Next to Cecelia, Lana tensed up. "Don't we have scouts? I thought they were good in the woods."

"Yeah. Which is why you have to be a top scout to be a ranger, along with some other stuff nobody knows except for them." Kayin spoke up. "That's the rumor I heard, anyway."

"And none of our scouts are at the top of their field anymore," Tane confirmed. "When the traitor Jericho deserted almost five years back, he took our best and brightest assets in that job with him. The ones we've trained up since get targeted by his resistance. So never assume that you're safe, not here in the wilds, not in camp, not until you're at the front. Keep your eyes open, keep a buddy in sight at all times, and whenever you're out of armor I want Always In Uniform up."

"I've got some scout training, sir." Cecelia offered. "I could take an extra shift, borrow a horse and ride perimeter—"

"Absolutely not," Tane said.

Cecelia blinked. "It wouldn't be any—"

"Did I stutter, Dame?" His eyes bored into her. Cecelia met them...

WILL +1

...and managed to keep from looking away.

"You know why, Dame Ragandor," Tane said, his voice barely audible enough to hear.

She did. It was because she was her father's heir. "Yes sir. Doesn't mean I like it."

He smiled then, grudging respect in his eyes. "I do. Have patience, your time will come at the front. As you were, knights." He returned to the front of the wagon, buttoning up the cloth separator as he went.

As it turned out, her time came way sooner than that.

*****

Cecelia's eyes snapped open, and she didn't know why. Then training kicked in. **"Always in Uniform."** She sat up, feeling the air solidify around her, and peered around the tent. Firelight shown through the walls of it, flickering in the glow, and for the second, all seemed still.

But the flap was open. It hadn't been, when she went to sleep. She sat up, sliding a dagger into her hand as she went—

—and her face brushed against something crinkly.

Paper.

She froze, as it rustled against her face, then felt with her free hand, groping until she had it. A tug pulled it away from the thread it was tied to. Cecelia could just make it out in the firelight, a crumpled wad of parchment.

"Appraise," she hissed. No traps showed up. It was a simple parchment note. She tucked into her sleeping bag, taking the note with her, and said **"Glow gleam."** It took a bit to dial down the light to where it shouldn't be visible from her tent. (And also to keep it from blinding her too badly.)

The note was very simple. It said

GO SOUTH TO PADS VILLAGE IF YOU WANT TO SEE THE TRUTH OF YOUR KINGDOM, DAME RAGANDOR

Cecelia's breath whistled between her teeth. She read it again, just to make sure she was understanding it correctly, then killed the light.

Wide awake now, she pushed out of the tent, dagger in hand, peering around—

—and then the screaming started.

"Fire! Fire!"

Three of the wagons burst into flames, and for a second there were glowing red stars falling out of the night...

Flame Arrows.

Mordecai had told her about those, once. They were from an archer skill. Fire arrows coming out of the woods meant—

"Rangers!" She shouted. "We're under attack! Able bodies get those fires out! Noncombatants take shelter! Go go go!" She didn't know where the officer in charge was, and it didn't matter. They'd order the same thing, she was sure.

Then the horses screamed, as the falling arrows swept toward them, and she gasped as she saw the caravan's steeds fleeing for all they were worth. But how? They'd been tied earlier, she'd even helped...

She thought back to the paper in her tent. That was how. She shut up and helped with the bucket brigade, until Sergeant Tane relieved her, and told her to go suit up. "We're keeping watch until dawn. You can sleep in the wagon."

Unquestioning, she headed out to the perimeter, whispering **"Keen Eye"** as she went. Which is why she spotted the body first.

In the morning, the tally was final, and devastating. A third of the horses had been lost in the night. The two wagons worth of food had been mostly burned, doused with oil before the flaming arrows fell. Less than a quarter of their ration boxes could be salvaged.

And of the seven scouts and three mercenary guards who had been tasked to keep the perimeter, two were corpses and the rest were gone like they'd never existed.

*****

"Haven't you slept yet?" Graves asked, concerned. He was the second-oldest of her squad, a thickly-built man in his mid-twenties. He kept a white-streaked goatee, a neatly-trimmed mustache, and a friendly smile on his face at all times. "You really should turn in, it's bad for your pools."

It was easy to forget he'd transferred in from the necromancer corps, after some hushed-up-but-probably-horrible scandal. But he was a knight now, and he'd sweated harder than Cecelia to get into shape and survived the proportionately-harder tests that Tane threw at him, so none of that mattered to the squad.

"I've got a scout skill that helps me not sleep," Cecelia replied, scanning the road to both sides as she tucked the little metal device back into her pouch. The rain was still falling, but it had slowed. So had they, though. Most of the remaining wagons were down to one horse apiece.

"Must be nice. I could do all sorts of training if I never had to worry about sleep." He smiled. "Figured I'd end up like that eventually, I suppose. I thought I'd be a lich someday. If they exist, I mean. I was going to be the one to discover it."

"My skill is not perfect," she confessed, leaning against the backboard, feeling her armor settle against her spine. "Every extra hour I spend awake now I pay for later. I'm going to crash hard."

"Does the Sergeant know you're doing this?"

"I cleared it through him first," she sighed. This wasn't the first time one of the Squad had asked her this question, and she found their lack of faith disturbing. She ran her fingers along her white plate helm, before sliding it back onto her head. The rain pattered against it, instead of her sodden hair. It'd take a fair amount of polishing, when she was finally out of her armor.

"Mm," Graves grunted. He coughed, spat into the mud. "Listen. I've... asked the others. Now I'll ask you."

"Ask me what?"

He nodded toward the back of the wagon, and she followed, unbuttoning the blanket and leaving the weary teamster to do his job.

"I've got a skill. From my old job," Graves said, stretching out his hand, palm up. **"Soulstone."** A solid black crystal materialized.

Cecelia nodded. "Me too. **Appraise.**"

"Enchanter, right? I was going to learn that one at some point."

"Among other things." She looked it over. "It's empty. Level one crystal? Huh, Gemcutters could get some use out of it, but..."

"Yeah. It shatters if it's used in crafting, unless it's full."

"So what—" The answer came to her. "It holds souls. Of course it does. Why are you offering it to me?"

"Well..." Graves chewed on his lip. "I was going to pitch this to the squad at the front, before we went into battle. But we've got rangers after us now, so... look. We might die here. If they're serious about killing us and we slip up, we're dead."

She thought of her tent, slit open in the night, and a piece of parchment that had been left behind.

They don't want me dead, she knew. But she didn't know why.

Then the second part of the answer came to her. "Wait. You want to catch our souls in those if we die?"

Graves nodded. "I do."

"Why?"

"I've got another spell that lets me and anyone around me speak to spirits. It'd give you a chance to say goodbye to people, and wrap up any last-minute business you've got unfinished." He shrugged. "Not everyone gets that opportunity. I've spoken with a lot of undead that got themselves ghosted because of dying regrets. I don't want to see that happen to any of you. Let's be honest, we may not entirely be friends, but you're the closest thing I've got these days." He smiled.

"What are soulstones really used for?"

"Sorry?"

"I know enough about necromancy to know most of it isn't very nice. They've got to have other uses."

He sighed. "They do. In a pinch, if there's a corpse or remains but no spirit hanging around, I could use a soulstoned spirit to power it instead. That would use up the spirit, put it in the undead."

"Would it be me in there? If that happened?"

"If it were a wight or a mummy, maybe, but I'm only twelfth level. You'd be stuck in a lesser undead's body, unable to control it or do anything." He blinked. "If I did that. Which I wouldn't."

His eyes flicked to the side as he said that.

"Did you tell the others about that part of it?" Cecelia asked, staring into his eyes, leaning in closer. "Or did that little bit get left out?"

Graves blinked. "They... they didn't ask. Look, if you don't want to, okay—"

"How many accepted?"

"Half the squad."

"Go tell them."

"I... what?"

"Go tell them about this part of it. See if they're still okay with it then."

"What? Why? I wouldn't use them as zombie fodder, that's just... you don't..."

"Tell them. I'll go with you."

He hesitated, and sweat rolled down his face, a drop at a time.

"We tell them now, or I tell the Sergeant," She guessed, fishing for a reaction.

She got one. The man blanched. "Fine." Graves said, his smile long gone. "Come on, let's get this over with."

Lana blanched, then thought it over. "Sure, okay. Just promise me it won't come to that." Graves did.

Morris shrugged and laughed. "If you zombify me just put me outta my misery quick, okay old man? Dead's dead."

Renick just smiled, and patted Graves' shoulder. "It's fine. I trust you."

That had almost floored the older man. He simply nodded, and his mouth worked a bit, before he thanked Renick.

As Graves walked away, Cecelia walked with him. "I didn't expect that," Graves finally managed.

"Yeah. And my answer's yes."

"What?"

"Yes, you can soulstone me."

He stared at her. "I thought you wouldn't... why did you..."

"You're used to not being trusted, I get that. It's why you left out some of the details that would make your suggestion sound sinister. I know you're not going to torment us or do something stupid like that. I trust you. But I wanted to make sure you trusted the others enough to give them the full story. This doesn't work if we don't all trust each other, if we don't have each other's backs, Sir Graves. And now they know you have theirs, and more importantly, you know they've got yours."

Besides, the cynical part of her added, *If you stick me in a zombie my father will fumping kill you.*

But that part she didn't share with him. Graves smiled, and thumped his chest with a clang that made the nearest drovers jump. "You're going to be a hell of a queen someday. I look forward to serving you, milady."

And that drove it in.

She WOULD be Queen someday, if she didn't die first.

All this, all these people, all this land... she'd have to worry about it. Rule it.

Her father had unlocked Ruler for her, recognized her as his heir, but asked her to refrain from taking the job just yet. And she had obeyed, as she'd sworn to. She'd thought it was because he didn't trust her with it yet. Because he thought she couldn't handle the responsibility.

But what if it was because he was sparing her from the full weight of it? What if he was giving her what time he could? What if it was his version of mercy?

Her thoughts a whirl, she gave Grave's pauldron a light punch, smiled, and headed back to watch the perimeter while they settled in to secure the camp for the night.

*****

She woke in the back of the wagon, feeling like she'd just hibernated through winter. The aftermath of Wakeful Wandering was always like that.

In the distance she heard Tane's voice rising through the rain. Stretching out the kinks, feeling like she'd been tumbled down a hill, she slid down from the wagon and waddled her way through the mud. The Sergeant nodded at her as she joined the rest of the squad, and saluted. The others didn't spare her a glance, which told her right away it was serious.

"To sum up for our late riser, we've got five days of travel and one day of food left. We're out in the middle of nowhere and we can't risk foraging. The Rangers haven't hit us since the last run, but the Captain's assessment is that they won't pass up a chance to pick off more personnel if split up and try to hunt. Which leaves requisitioning food from the local villages. The rangers don't involve civilians in their treason or put them at risk, so that should be safe. It'll delay us, but there's no help for that. Dame Ragandor, are you rested well enough to lead a three-man task force?"

That surprised her. Then her stomach growled. Loudly. Morris fought to keep from laughing, and Zara failed completely, snickering through her visor. "Yes sir. I ah, could use a ration beforehand. If we can spare one."

"Very good. You've got the northern road then." Tane's face was stonier than usual. Was he trying to keep from laughing? "I'll take the other three south—"

South, the parchment had said. "Actually, sir, do you mind if I take the southern route?"

Tane raised an eyebrow. "The hell difference does it make?"

"I think I might know someone down that way. If we're where I think we are."

"And where do you think we are, Dame?" Tane's voice gave warning. He hadn't liked being interrupted.

So she gambled. "If we're north of Pads village, then we're where I think we are."

That surprised him. "Who the hell do you know— nevermind. Yes, you've got south then. I'll be taking Renick and Lana and Zara. The rest of you are under your acting commander. Go saddle up."

The Knight's horses had been battle trained, and spared the worst of the stampede. Cecelia, who didn't have one, got the loan of one of the more steady draft horses, a stout loaf of bread baked with dried meat and vegetables, a waterskin, and a couple of minutes to eat her ration bar before they departed. She used the rain to soften the tough comestible, and chased it down with slugs of water. The stuff was horrible, but eventually the hungry condition evaporated from her status screen, and that was all she asked of it.

"**Horsemanship,**" she muttered, as she vaulted up into the draft horse's saddle. It stamped and trotted uneasily, unused to being directly mounted. She soothed it as she could, as it bucked and turned, trying to convince her to get back down. "Oh stop that. Here... **Favored Mount.**" It felt weird to be saying that when she wasn't riding Reason, but it did the trick well enough, and the horse settled as her buff rolled over it.

No skill up this time, which was a pity. She really needed more practice with this one. It was a level fifteen skill and she'd only been that level for a few months.

Once she was sure of the horse, she dismounted and led it over to the other knights, already kneeling in a circle, the old ritual, the familiar custom. Without saying a word she knelt, until Tane nodded. Eight blades hissed free from sheathes, and eight helms pressed against the hilts as they held the swords out, points down before them.

"Our Code to mind, our foes to fall," Tane said, as the rain slicked down his armor.

"To Gods, King, and Crown, we owe our all," the rest of the Knights chorused in unison.

"Obey royal decrees of the land, against the loyal raise no hand," Tane spoke, as thunder rolled in the distance.

"Obey the King, shield the weak. Let no treason our lips speak." The rest finished, Cecelia joining in happily.

This was truly what separated them from other warrior jobs... the Knight's skill, Code of Chivalry. Other jobs could fight, sure, but knights always fought for something. And whatever code they chose when they began their career, the longer they kept to it, the more it gave them.

In Cecelia's case, what it gave her was a nice round buff of thirty to all her defenses. Most of the other trainees had more, thanks to higher levels in the class. But all it took was one slip, and the skill reset back down to one, and her buff fell to nothing.

Graves and Kayin and Morris fell in behind her as she left the camp, riding down the swampy, well-used road south.

"So who the hell do you know in Pads?" Kayin said, finally. "That's the sticks, the middle of nowhere."

"I'd rather not say," Cecelia said. "It's possible they're not there anymore. And uh, they might not be... on the right side of things. We might have to fight them."

If this was Mordecai trying to get back in contact with her, then he definitely wasn't on the right side. But she didn't want him captured and tortured again. This was... complicated.

She couldn't let the opportunity pass by, though. Someone had risked a lot to deliver that message to her. What did they want her to see?

The rain slackened as they rode, but the sky remained soggy gray, wet wool gray, and the road twisted, taking them past stockaded farmsteads.

"So how does this work?" Kayin asked, after they passed the third steading. "Should we be going up and knocking on doors?"

"No," Cecelia shook her head. "Per the Articles of the Cylvanian accord, any order of military requisition must be presented to the local lord. This place will have a Baron, or something. We'll talk to him."

"Really?" Morris said, sneering as they passed a field full of serfs digging in loose rows, muddy faces brown and open mouths pink as they stared at the passing knights. "And how will we know which one's the Baron?"

"He'll be the one who isn't totally covered in shit," Graves said, and the Knights laughed. Celia didn't.

The fields were big, and looked well-kept. But everyone in that field was scrawny and thin. Most of them were moving slowly, and a few looked far, far too old to be out there.

Sure, it was Spring and they'd just gotten through a long winter, but... a farm that size should be able to provide for everyone there.

Something was off.

Three hours down the muddy road, they finally came to Pads. It was little more than a collection of a few dozen huts, on the edge of a forest. Smoke billowed up from smokeholes, all save for five chimneys, all on the same house. It squatted on the highest hill, the only building in the village made of stone, sprawling and painted, with high walls around a grove of carefully-kept trees.

"There's the noble," Cecelia said. "Has to be."

"Those are peach trees," Kayin said, frowning. "Weird choice."

"Why's that?" Morris asked.

"They don't grow well in this part of the valley. They must take a wicked amount of care to get that big."

"Eh, maybe they've got a Kossite cleric running the show or something," Morris shrugged. "More for us to take back for the convoy, then, if that's the case. Come on, let's get this over with."

*****

"I'm sorry, it's simply out of the question," Baron Colm Comfort said. "We have no reserves left after the winter. We simply cannot spare enough to make a difference."

"I see." Cecelia turned from the portly man to look over the sitting room, adorned with a random assortment of fine goods. Mismatched candlesticks of gold and silver clashed next to chairs and couches of all makes, each of them made with the finest cloth and craftsmanship. Paintings of everything from flowers to landscapes to people adorned the walls.

It didn't match, and Cecelia thought she knew why. "Why don't you tell us how much you can spare, and we'll decide if it's enough to make a difference."

The Baron rubbed his face, sending his three chins wobbling. "Well, I, er, I'd have to consult my ledger. Check the storehouse. That would take some time, and I don't know if I'd want to delay you so long—"

"Oh, it's no trouble," Cecelia said. "The convoy's not going anywhere without food. But they can last a day or two without us. I trust you have no problem with us staying the night while you check."

Oh, he didn't like that at all. But nonetheless, he offered a smile that showed rotten teeth. "I'll see what I can do. Yes, certainly."

"We'll go hunting while you do that, see if we can scrape up something so you don't have to stretch as far. I trust you've a spare room or something we can store our armor in? It's hard to sneak up on game in full plate, after all."

Kayin inhaled sharply, next to her. She heard Morris shift, felt the intensity of his gaze on her.

The Baron's mouth closed, and the older man stared at her, gears turning behind his eyes. "Of course. Would you like me to send my huntsman along with you?"

"Absolutely. Just give us some privacy to shuck out of our armor, and we'll be happy to follow your man into the woods."

"Of course, of course. Right this way!"

The Baron's basement was full of kegs and racks full of wine and ale.

"Cecelia?" Morris asked. "Do you know what you're doing here?"

"Mostly." Cecelia frowned. "Did you ever see that much gold in your life?"

"No way he's come by that honestly," Kayin said, "but is it any business of ours?"

"He was trying to get us out of here pretty quickly," Graves rubbed his goatee. "Why?"

"Hiding food, obviously," Morris snickered. "Probably in his gut."

"That's part of it. I need to see his ledger." Cecelia nodded. "And I want to give him a chance to try to kill us."

Silence fell over the basement.

"Wait, what?" Morris asked.

Kayin grinned. "I like it."

"How loud are we going, here?" Graves asked.

"Depends on how he plays it," Cecelia decided.

Morris looked between the other three knights, confused. "Did I miss something?"

Cecelia grinned. "Not really. Here's the plan..."

*****

Baron Colm Comfort hadn't gotten to the age he was by taking chances. But this one... this one was less of a chance, and more of a free meal.

They'd come right to him. And then they'd even taken off their armor...

Pity about the horses, but he couldn't risk anyone checking after them, now could he? He'd wait until nightfall and send four of the lads south into the woods, wearing their armor and riding their horses. The mouth-breathing serfs wouldn't know any different. Then the lads could come back with the armor, and the horses would be set free to roam.

Armor could be disenchanted and sold. Horses couldn't.

He stretched out a hand to touch the white suit with the horn... and drew his digits back. It was a little *too* neat. He had to be sure.

Up to the top of the house then, peering through the spyglass he'd gotten, watching the woods. He wasn't lying when he told them his huntsman Jacob was the best at his job. They just hadn't asked what Jacob's job was. Not that Colm would have told them it anyway. Bandit was a much-maligned profession.

Twelve minutes later, he saw glass wink against the sun, from one of the tallest trees in the eastern forest. He smiled, fanning himself with a fine silken fan, before closing it with a "Snap." Knights out of armor versus two dozen well-trained bandits, striking from ambush. It had ended in the only way possible.

Hells, the best of his bandits were up to level seven. Against four unarmored young knights? No chance at all.

Then he started in surprise. There were forms moving out of the forest. Figures stepping from the shadows of the trees, heading toward the hill, toward the manor. "What the devils?" Colm said, bringing the spyglass around and focusing in on the oncoming group.

And his heart fluttered, as he recognized them.

Those were Jacob's band. Only they were moving slowly, drunkenly...

...and, as the Baron watched blood ooze down from one's face, to fall down slack lips, he realized that they were pretty beaten up. In fact, given their visible injuries, they looked, well, dead.

Realization struck him, and he bolted to his feet, hurried downstairs, wheezing all the way. A trap! It had been bait, and he'd fallen for it! They had backup out of town, somewhere, and the ambush had been ambushed!

He got down to the basement, locking the door behind him, and went to the wine rack, pulling a bottle out of a certain spot, and hearing the mechanism groan and shudder, before the wall opened up. Beyond lay the darkness of his escape route, and the choicest of his treasures.

But, then... he could get some small measure of vengeance before he went, and get a few more reagents and crystals for his trip, now couldn't he?

He turned back to the suits of armor piled in the corner, smiling—

—and found them standing, swords leveled at him.

"What? What is this?" He bellowed, stepping backwards toward the tunnel.

A mouth formed on one of the helms. "Before I was a knight, I was an animator," Cecelia spoke. "I animated these before we left the basement. Then it was Dollseye to let me see through my animi and Magic Mouth to tell you exactly how screwed you are."

"I see! You've animated all four of them. And one of you's a necromancer too, to raise my men!"

"It was obvious, really. You've been working with the local bandits, preying on the trade routes," Cecelia's voice filled the room, as the armor advanced in unison, slowly. The fat Baron backed up, step by step as they came. "What sort of man does that? Not one that pays his honest taxes, or looks after his serfs. You've been stealing, stealing from the crown, and stealing from your own people."

"I did what I had to!" The Baron roared. "The Crown? Don't make me laugh! The Crown takes its taxes and leaves us to our own devices! Everything goes to the war effort now, and nobody guards the roads or the settlements! They don't care if monsters attack us, or if bandits prey on us. There is no help for the weak! The only way to survive is to be strong ourselves, and everything this village has, every day it survives it owes to me and to my friends... who you just slaughtered." Colm sneered. "But you won't take me! I know animi. Animi can fight, but they're not great at it." He stopped walking, sneering now, feeling his confidence return. "I can get to them, and all it'll take is one touch to disenchant each one. I'll survive and they'll be dust. What of your precious armor then, hm?"

"They might be slow, yes," Cecelia spoke as the armor clanked on with endless patience, "but I've got a friend, and she's quick as death. That's the name for it, right?"

"**Fast as Death**," spoke a voice behind the Baron and he jumped, whirled to see Kayin behind him, a pair of knives in her hands and a mad grin on her face. "Got you, fat boy."

"What? How... I saw you leave!"

"Yeah. And you didn't see me sneak back after we beat the shit out of your huntsman. He spilled your plans. He was really eager to cooperate after Cecelia animated his pants and started up the nutcracker special."

Feet upstairs, thumping on the door. A distant groaning, that he knew from experience in his younger adventuring days. Zombies.

"You've met our assassin. She's the least of your worries. Before he was a knight, Graves was a necromancer," Cecelia continued. "If you don't surrender we'll kill you, he'll tuck your soul into something horrible, and you'll be trapped in a rotting shell forever."

"Animator, Necromancer, Assassin... Who the hell are you people?" Colm shrieked. "Next you'll be telling me that dopey-looking youth with you was a goddamn Model!"

"No, he's just a knight. Twenty-five levels worth," Cecelia said. "Unfortunately for your bandits."

The Baron's mouth shut. He hastily reassessed the odds.

"I surrender."

"Good man," said Cecelia. "Now let's talk about food again..."

*****

Sergeant Tane blinked, as he watched the four wagons roll in from the south. Yoked to the fattest oxen he'd ever seen, each one of them was laden to the brim with bags, and each one had a grinning Knight sitting on the buckboard, guiding them in.

"You're late," he said, glancing up to the darkening sky... then down to the bound, fat figure in the last wagon. "Who the fuck is that?"

"The former Baron of Pads," Cecelia said. "Guilty by his own admission, and his own records, of theft, treason against the crown, and preying upon the weak. His own people told me everything. Ah, they've got an alderman now, until the Crown can appoint someone new out there."

"Might take a while." Tane said. "He confessed willingly?"

"Yes, after he tried to kill us."

"Oh. Well that's simple, then." He nodded to Renick. "Take Lana and go execute this son of a bitch. Behind the latrines, I'm thinking."

"Yes sir." Renick nodded to Lana, and the two moved forward.

Tane watched Cecelia's face turn pale, as the man shrieked and screamed behind her. "Wait, what? We don't have the authority to do that!"

"We're a military convoy to the front," Tane explained. "We can't spare the guards to bring this man back to Castle Cylvania for a trial, and I don't see any witnesses, which means you can't go back to profess his guilt. I'm not going to feed a traitor food we can take to the front instead. So he dies."

Cecelia looked back to her companions. Kayin shook her head. "He tried to kill us, Cecelia."

Graves nodded to support Kayin. "He's horrible. Coming from me, that means a lot, right?"

But it was Morris who seemed to shake her the most. "Yeah, it's not exactly in accordance with the old laws, but... we've got field authority, right? And our Code of Chivalry doesn't say we have to follow the laws, just the King and the Crown. So it's okay if we do this."

"We..." Cecelia licked her lips. "We should follow the laws, too." She whispered, as Renick and Lana hauled the shrieking Baron away, avoiding her eyes. "If we don't, who will?"

"He got stupid and he got caught," Tane shrugged. "If it wasn't us, then someone else would have got him anyway. Really, he brought this on himself. And that's the end of it, Dame Ragandor."

She watched him go, watched them drag him off into the treeline, and only closed her eyes as the fat man's screams rose up, then fell silent.

When she looked back, Tane was next to her, lips set in a sad smile. "Come on then," he murmured, hopping up next to her and taking the reigns. "You did good. Don't let that trouble you."

"He was supposed to get a trial," Cecelia said. "He should have gotten a trial."

"He did, more or less. He had it when he tried to kill you and failed. The truth of it..." Tane said, looking away. "The truth of it is that things are messy right now. Chaos everywhere, rebels and traitors all around us. They know the law. They try to use it against us. The King's way is a hard way, but it's the only way to us. And if you don't like it, milady, then you're welcome to return your armor. And go back to the castle, while we sort it out."

Cecelia took a deep breath. She raised her gauntlet to her face, and stared at it. Then closed it into a fist. "No. I did something today. Something good. That village is better off in charge of themselves. And I'm not going to run out on my friends. I can help them. I can help everyone."

Tane nodded. "Good. Then I've got news for you. Messenger imp came by today, checking on us. Your Steam Knight suit's arrived at Fort Bronze."

"That's the last stop before the front, right?"

"Yeah. We'll drop the food off there. Then it's into action. But not against the dwarves."

"Wait, what?"

"I'll tell the others when we're together, but I might as well tell you now. There's been a rebel uprising, just southeast of the Fort, in another shitty frontier village. Some little fishing town called Outsmouth..."

CHAPTER 9: MEDIOCRE OLD ONES

The wagon rolled down the overgrown road, lurching and hobbling as the wooden cats pulling it slunk along, tails bobbing in time with their gait. Bright patches of colored cloth on the wagon's cloth covering spelled out big words, that read, simply,

ANNIE MATA'S TRAVELLING TOY CIRCUS

The toys rode in the front, the cats slept in the back, and Threadbare put his tools away after he finally, finally finished the last part of the dummy's mouth.

Your Tailoring Skill is now level 45!
You are now a level 10 tailor!
DEX+1
PER+1

He nodded, then arranged the robes and hood and veil carefully over the reclining form, until nothing could be seen of its face. Thick gloves already covered her hands. You could tell there was a human shape underneath there, but that was about it, really.

At least, that's what Zuula and Garon and Madeline had said, instructing Fluffbear to carve the wooden parts, and Threadbare on how best to pad them.

It had been a bit of a rush job, regardless. After they'd all agreed to the plan, Zuula had put him through the rigorous training necessary to make it work. And now here he was, five animator levels later, ready to give it a whirl.

Threadbare tapped on the cloth partition between the front and the back of the wagon. Next to him, Pulsivar opened an irritated eye. Seriously, why was it so hard for the little bear to understand the concept of naptime?

"I think we're ready," Threadbare said. "I'm going to stop the cats now if you want to come and watch."

The cats halted, the doll haunters and Fluffbear unbuttoned the partition, and gazed upon the fruits of their labor.

"No way is this going to work," Garon said.

"No, it be perfect!" Zuula insisted. "Used to have traveling animator shows all de time twenny years ago. Some of dem even had actual animators running dem."

"Oh yeah," Madeline said. "I remembah those. Like most of them were puppeteers lookin' fah work, and carnies."

"Carnies? Sounds like a monster type," Garon remarked, poking his head in, and using his draconic advantage to swivel his neck until he could see over the other toys.

"Kinda. Half of 'em were on tha run from something. I fit right in until they stahted insisting I work days." Madeline shrugged. "There might have been a few minor disagreements and some bloodless corpses left behind, right before I split. Bleh, just thinking about it makes me taste corndogs. Guess that's something I don't have to worry about no more." She rubbed her mouth, sadly. Some experimentation, and a lot of clean and presses, and in one case the disassembly of her new mouth combined with a thorough cleaning later, and Madeline was forced to the realization that she simply couldn't drink blood. It did nothing for her now.

Which was a problem, given the vampire job's... well, nudging in that direction. It wasn't exactly a skill, per se, but it was a kind of loose craving. Couple that with the realization that she wouldn't gain experience from drinking blood unless she actually drank blood, and her regrets were starting to build.

"Magic Mouth," Threadbare said.

"Hello, can you hear me?" The dummy said.

The toys considered that for a minute. "That still sounds a little like you," Fluffbear said.

"Ya putting it in the raht spaht, raht?" Madeline asked.

"Oh yes. It's below the strings and chambers we made."

The two bears had gotten very good at building voiceboxes over the last couple of days, using their own to improve the range and yield of sound producible. And given a whole human torso to work with, they'd been able to fit in their latest model without the usual worries about miniaturization that normally limited them. The voice came out of the tiny mouth at the bottom of the dummy's esophagus, fed through some strings and amplifying chambers, and came out sounding like a female human's voice. And whenever the strings vibrated, the dummy's jaw moved, so that under the veil she'd look like she was talking. Enough to fool someone who didn't look too closely.

That was the plan, anyway. Right now it sounded like someone speaking from the bottom of a well.

"It's not working, is it?" Threadbare asked.

"You're still way soft," Garon said. "Can you, I don't know, yell or something?"

The dummy's jaw opened, and a monotone wail issued forth. The cats, already a little freaked out by the whole thing, abandoned wagon.

"This is creepy," Missus Fluffbear complained. "Are you sure we can't use a zombie instead?"

"Don't think that would help much," Garon said. "No, look, this might actually be fine. Animators are supposed to be weird anyway, it's part of the mystique."

"No, this no be mistake," Zuula insisted. "It work fine."

"Mystique, Mom, not mistake."

"Is what she said!"

"Nevermind. Ah, look, Threadbare, could you stop that please?"

The dummy stopped wailing.

"You've got decent volume, just... I don't know, work on the voice a bit. Remember how Celia was. Only older."

"Like Zuula," the plush orc grinned.

"Sweet Nebs no, don't try to talk like Zuula. Just... it'll work out fine. Outmarsh isn't exactly a big city, we won't be there long. Just enough to find out what we need to know and where to go."

"All right," Threadbare said, as he started sewing up the dummy's yellow robe. All her clothes were yellow, since it was the color they had the most of. "I think we're about ready, then."

"I still got my resahvations," Madeline said. "Wooden cats is weird. Be bettah if we had horses."

"I've never seen a horse so I couldn't carve them," Fluffbear shrugged. "But I know cats! And this way if Mopsy or Pulsivar die we can golemify them!"

"Cats is fine," Garon said. "But it does mean that you'll be on your own for a while. Are you sure you're okay with that?"

Fluffbear bounced up and down in her seat. "I'm okay with it. It means you're stronger and that's good. Besides, I've got the kitties to keep me company!"

The whole cover story depended on Threadbare controlling the cats and the dummy, and the simplest and easiest way to do that was to have all three of them in his party. Which left three slots for other members, as the maximum party size was seven.

Add to that the fact that Threadbare had an animator skill called "Creator's Guardians," which seemed to be meant for animi, but also affected the doll haunters for some weird reason, and the choice was obvious. It was a decent-sized buff, currently about thirteen to all attributes, and at the level they were at it made a significant difference. Made it easier to think, easier to resist bad impulses, easier to survive if something went wrong.

When, Zuula had pointed out. When something goes wrong.

"Now that that's decided, we may as well get moving again," Threadbare gestured and the wooden cats resumed their travel, clattering down the road.

"I'll take watch," Garon said, heading out to the seat. The cats did a decent job, and could react to simple instructions like "follow the road," and "stop before you walk off a cliff," but didn't do so well with obstacles.

"Zuula come too," Said his mother, clambering up on the board.

"Me three!" Missus Fluffbear raced out front. "I want to practice whipping!"

"Pass," Madeline said. "Too bright. I'll get naht shift."

"Good," said the dummy. "You can help me practice."

Madeline chuckled. "Absolutely Missus Mata! Tell me how's the family?"

"Oh they're ingrates, they never call or send lotters."

"Letters."

"Those too."

"And what do you think of the weathah lately?"

"It's horrible! Back in my day, it wasn't raining sunny snowing or whatever."

"No no no, you're supposed ta pick one of those, the one it's doing right now."

Zuula buttoned up the partition. She could still hear the two of them trying to practice small talk, but this helped her to ignore it.

They were on the outskirts of the moors now, where the rivers of melting snow from the mountains ran down to the beginning of the bowl that was Cylvania's valley. Hills still jutted up here and there, like the knees of a resting giant, sleeping with his legs crooked. But water sagged and sogged between them, and new spring reeds and tall grasses were poking their heads up, yearning toward the sun with their roots in the wetlands. The road meandered along a natural ridge, lined with willow trees, and Fluffbear got her practice by snapping her whip at passing branches, trying to trim off twigs as the wagon rolled by.

Eventually Mopsy and Pulsivar returned to the wagon, with the bobcat hopping up to the back, and the tiny cougar curling up around Missus Fluffbear. The little tamer gave up whipping and settled into a petting routine that only a nigh-inexhaustible golem could sustain. Soon enough the cougar's purrs faded and its sides rose and fell with the rhythm of steady sleep.

"She's doing a lot better," Garon said, studying the sleeping cat. "Way less skittish. More settled."

"Cat ghost lady abused her," Zuula said. "Love heal her. Fluffbear be good tamer."

"Thank you. I don't know what I'm doing most of the time," Missus Fluffbear said. "But it seems to be working out."

"Most people like dat," Zuula observed, laying back to study the sky. "Even if dey never admit it."

As they rolled on, the sky grew cloudier, and Madeline and Threadbare gave off practicing and came forward as well. It was tight room on the buckboard, but the company was good. "I've never been anywhere like this before." Threadbare said, gazing around at the empty marshlands. Occasionally there was a submerged dock, or a fallen pile that could have been a hut at some point, but for the most part it was empty save for foraging birds and Rodents of Unusual Sizes that were content to stay far away from the noisy wagon. "I've never been much of anywhere, I guess. The world seemed so big when I was moving around with Celia. But there's this part of it too, and lots more parts like it, aren't there?"

"Oh yeah. It's way big," Said Madeline. "Takes about two weeks either way ta cross Cylvania. An' it's supposed ta be even biggah outside the Oblivion, but I never seen none of that. It went up befoah I could get out that way. Which is kind of a pity cause I met a lot of nice people from othah lands when I was back in Cylvania City. Nevah ran into one I didn't like. You could say they had great taste." She grinned, and her tack teeth glimmered in the rays of the fading sun.

"Hm. What are those?" Threadbare pointed. There, silhouetted in the falling orb, were what looked like distant pillars.

Zuula squinted. "Dolmens. Old stones put up by shamans long dead."

"Why?"

"Any reason, really. Back in de day, dolmens were like cure all for anything you need. Old tribes discover rock cutting and hauling technology with newfangled t'ings like rope and slaves and chisels, and go a little nuts. Be making standing stones for calendars, for festivals, for sealing ancient evils, all sort of things. Didn't know what to do about some'ting? Put dolmens on a hill." The half-orc doll sighed. "Zuula be pretty sure old shamans got kickbacks from rock sellers in dose days. Fortunately time march on. Wicker tech come along and shamans leave old stones behind. More and more of dem end up bricked. Nowadays you get same hoodoo power out of charms you can fit in you pocket, den old-style dolmen did with sixty tons of fucking rocks."

"Think we should check it out?" Garon asked.

Threadbare squinted. "It would be an awfully long way through the wet mud."

"I could try flying over," Garon offered. "I need to learn sooner or later."

"Oh yeah! You can do that!" Madeline brightened.

Zuula sighed. "Hokay. Stop de wagon. You, child, **Slow Regeneration.**"

"What does flying use?" Missus Fluffbear asked.

"I'm guessing agility," Garon said.

"Yeah, Agility," Madeline confirmed. "I used to be able to turn into a bat."

"Agility," Zuula grunted. "Owl skills be awesome to borrow."

"Yorgum's blessing of agility on Garon!" Fluffbare reached over and nudged him.

"Thanks! All right, let's see here," said the plush dragon hatchling, leaping from the cart, wings pumping—

—and promptly plummeting into the mud.

"Oh. Right." A muddy green head poked out. **"Scaly Wings."**

The practice went on into the night, and finally, after a couple of Clean and Presses and much skilling up of Scaly Wings, they deemed Garon to be airworthy.

The toys flew out there all at once, piled on Garon's broad back, holding on for all they were worth. Falling into the marsh wouldn't be a fatality or even very damaging, but it would mean a struggle back to dry land and a general inconvenience overall.

They touched down on the hill, and Zuula hopped off, and started poking at the stones. Three seconds into it she froze. "Hoo boy."

"I can't see," Fluffbear complained. "Can I glow gleam?"

"You uh, you might not want to see," Garon said. "It's all tentacles and eyes up in here. There's a fire pit and some wet kindling, too."

"Why wouldn't I want to see tentacles and eyes?"

"Well uh, because... well..."

"Some people find those things creepy," Madeline said.

"More den dat," Zuula said, moving from stone to stone. "Dey eldritch."

"What's that word mean?" Threadbare asked.

"Is like... arcane."

"I'm afraid I don't know that one either."

"Is like mystical?"

"Oh. That sounds nice."

"No. No, dis de opposite of nice. Remember how Zuula say some dolmens built to trap ancient tings and some be like calendars?"

"Yes."

"Well, ain't nobody be telling de time from dis one is all she saying."

As a matter of fact, Zuula was wrong.

There were in fact, a large amount of people very close by who wanted the dolmens to tell them one proper time for years. They had, in fact, taken measures to anticipate such times, and spread the good news when they arrived.

It was just bad luck all around, because tonight was the night they'd been waiting for. The stars slid into position, light played across the runes in just the right manner, and an entirely different group of people than its intended audience got to listen as the ancient being trapped in the demiplanes tangled between the stones shuddered into a sliver of wakefulness.

To the toys, it sounded like a chorus of frogs starting up.

"Neekabreekaneekabreekaneekabreeka...."

"Do you think we should light the wood?" Threadbare asked.

Garon shook his head, and glanced to the north. "We're not far from town. Somebody might see this and come out and investigate." The town had rather less lights going than he had expected, but no way would they miss a fire this size.

"NeekabreekaneekabreekaneekabreakCROOOOOAAAAAKKK."

"That sounded like a really big frog," Missus Fluffbear said. "Are you sure I can't make a light?"

"Positive," Zuula said. "Dose not be frogs. Dey not frogs at all!"

And then, to everyone's eyes save Fluffbear, the dolmens almost seemed to writhe. The eyes on them shifted, stone cracking, as they blinked.

"Oh shit run!" Zuula yelled, and hopped on Garon's back.

"NEEKABREEKANEEKABREEKANEEKABREEKA!!!"

The voice rose about them in chorus with itself, inhuman cries rising to the uncaring stars above, sounding like thunder, drowning out all else.

Your Stubborn skill is now level 8.

Threadbare found it very annoying.

Missus Fluffbear had her hands over her ears and looked pretty pissed. Garon was shaking his head, thoroughly unsettled by the noise. Blue '0's, followed by the occasional '1', drifted out of him and up into the sky.

But Zuula and Madeline were hard hit. Threadbare watched with horror as they screamed and writhed, holding their heads. Blue '7's escaped from her, dwarfed by Madeline's '18's and '20's.

And over it all, the thundering croaks and squeaks shook the dolmens, as eyes opened and shut, focusing with burning tri-lobed fury!

"We need to go!" Threadbare yelled, grabbing Fluffbear and jumping on Garon's back. He grabbed Zuula and Madeline and gripped the dragon's back with his legs and every bit of his triple-digit strength, keeping a hold on his friends as Garon lifted off.

Your Ride skill is now level 9!

Once they were outside of the stones, the sound shut off as abruptly as if someone had shut a vault door.

"Ow," Zuula said. "Dat bad. Really bad. Old one trying to come out. Fortunately not great old one. More like mediocre old one."

Madeline kept screaming.

"Shit. Check her sanity, Dreadbear?"

"**Eye for Detail.** Oh dear, it's at two!"

"Not zero? Good. Zero is how madness happen sometimes. Close one. Too close."

"If that's a mediocre old one I don't want to see a just-sorta-okay old one," Garon said, landing by the wagon. "What do we do about her? How do we help her?"

Threadbare cleared his throat. Then he wrapped Madeline in a hug, and rocked the smaller marionette, like Celia had rocked him, long ago. "With an **Emboldening Speech. I know that was scary. But it's all right. You're one of the bravest people I know. You're safe now.**"

Calm washed over the party, as Threadbare's skill buffed their sanity and moxie. Madeline stopped screaming, curled into him, and tried whimpering instead. For his part, the bear rocked her back and forth until she stopped.

"What do we do about it?" Garon asked. "Do we beat it up? How much experience do you get for one of those things?"

"No no no," Zuula said. "Dose t'ings eat tribes. Uh... **Status.**" She studied her screen. "Yes, dat work. Got just enough for one of dose. Zuula be back wit' answer in a bit." She headed into the back of the wagon, and the toys watched her curl up near Pulsivar. "**Dream Quest.**"

"Zuula?" Threadbare asked, placing Madeline gently on the wagon, then clambering up to look in at her.

"Forget it," Garon said. "She'll be out for hours."

They looked at the dolmens.

The ancient stones glimmered with a weird light. Possibly mystical, probably arcane. Definitely eldritch.

"We need to tell someone about this," Threadbare decided. "Let's go to town while we wait and warn them."

"I'd really prefer if Mom was awake for that," Garon said, glancing from her to the dolmens. "And I'd also prefer if Madeline had more sanity, so our fiery surprise was available if we ran into trouble."

Threadbare stared at the stones. **"Keen Eye."**

Your Keen Eye skill is now level 2!

"Those eyes are still moving, I think," he said, finally. "It would be nice to wait, but the town could be in danger now." He made his decision, and the wooden cats clattered to life again. Fluffbear, taken by surprise, ran a bit and hopped up on the back of the wagon. It took a couple of tries before she got a handhold, and squirmed up.

"Should I put on my armor?" Missus Fluffbear asked.

"It couldn't hurt," Garon said, glancing between the road and the dolmens. "Have you decided on a code of chivalry yet?"

"I think so."

"Good. Might come in handy, a passive defensive buff that builds. Certainly couldn't hurt. I have the feeling we'll have to end up fighting that thing."

"All right! **I pledge mine blade to this Code of Chivalry! I, Missus Fluffbear, pledge to protect my friends, and feed my kitty on time, and beat up bad people! And bad things!**"

For a second she glowed, and then it was done.

"That's a big responsibility," Threadbare told her. "Mopsy eats a lot for her size. And she'll only get bigger."

"That's okay," squeaked the little black bear. "I don't eat anything so it balances out. She can have my share of everything."

They rolled on in silence for a bit, following the road. As they went, the toys could see a stockade wall rising in the distance, a wooden curtain that surrounded the town, with torches along it every twenty feet or so. Figures in robes paced along the top, though a small knot formed above the gate, staring as the cart rolled up.

"Who goes there?" One of them called, his voice high-pitched and wobbly.

"I bet it's a trick," another one of them whispered, so loudly that the toys could hear it.

"Shut up! Keep the crossbows ready!" A gruff one commanded.

"Hello there, sirs or madams!" Threadbare made the dummy talk.

"I'm Annie Mata, here with a show of animated toys for all ages!"

There was a long pause. The three heads visible on the top of the wall ducked down. There came a sound of muttering.

"Come out of the wagon with your hands up, then!" The gruff one said, as one of the others ran off.

Threadbare controlled his animi, directing the dummy out of the wagon. She held up her arms, yellow sleeves flapping in the darkness.

Then the runner came back, with a lantern. He waved it down there, and the guards on the wall blinked to see her, clad in all yellow, masked and veiled.

Comprehension and hope dawned on their faces. "You... you're..."

"Wait!" Said the one who'd whispered loudly. "Have you seen the yellow sign?"

Threadbare thought fast.

There HAD been a sign on the route, saying "this way to Outsmouth," and it WAS pretty yellowed with age.

"Yes, yes I have, my boy."

LUCK +1

The guards relaxed. All save for the gruff one. "Nah! Nah, it could be a trick! Look at them cats! Those is wooden cats!"

"Well, yes, what of it?"

"It's like that one book I read! They're trying to give us these wooden animals, then they'll burst open and be full of armies once they're inside!"

The three guards on the wall considered the cats.

"I think that was horses, Daav."

"Same thing!"

"They're a bit small for armies, aren't they?" The high-pitched guard mused. "Maybe one soldier. If he was a halven or a goblin or something."

"Well maybe they're smuggling halvens or goblins then!" The gruff one said. "Look, I'm just saying, this could be a trick."

"Yeah, and it's one animator lady against all of us if it IS," the whisperer in the darkness said. "We did for the garrison, we can do for her if we need to. Besides, her cult's kin to ours. Bad luck to turn away a fellow seeker."

"State your business in Outsmouth?" The high-pitched one asked.

"I'm just here to put on a show and talk about interesting things. How about that weather lately?"

CHA+1

The guards relaxed. True devotees of YGlnargle'blah they might be, but they were fishermen first, and fishermen NEVER miss a chance to bitch about the weather. The tension eased, crossbows were put down, and Threadbare smiled as the nice people spent way too long complaining about the recent drought.

Five minutes later, Daav and Phred and Mhorty opened the gate. "Well, if you're here for a show, Marva could use some help. The blessed children are getting anxious, since most of their parents are having to pull gate duty. Maybe you could go to the church and help her calm them down?"

"That sounds great, sir or madam! Which direction might it be?"

They gave her a lot of confusing directions, which included such helpful tidbits as "Turn left at Jarger's house," but fortunately Threadbare was smart, as teddy bears went, and thought he could figure it out. Then he directed the dummy back into the wagon's seat, and held still as he willed the cats forward, through the open gate. The green-robed guards shut it behind him, and wished Annie well.

"I look forward to seeing your play later!" The whisperer in the darkness called. "I always dreamed of visiting Lost Corcasa!"

Threadbare had Annie wave back. He had no idea what that was. Then he remembered what he was here for.

"Oh yes, and there's an old one stirring under those dolmens to the south! You might want to do something about that."

The guards laughed. "We know, isn't it great?" The high-pitched one yelled. "He'll call us all home soon!"

Okay, that wasn't the reaction he'd expected. Puzzled, Threadbare left the guards behind, thoroughly fooled into thinking that the dummy was a friendly ally of sorts.

By engaging in successful duplicitous shenanigans you have unlocked the Grifter job!

You cannot become a Grifter at this time.

Well. That was interesting. Also not helpful at the minute.

The wagon rolled on through the town, most of it silent and dark. Garon sidled up next to him, and snaked his head around to Threadbare's fluffy ear. "They're cultists."

"Excuse me?"

"It's a job. A bad one. There's only a few types of cultists tolerated in the kingdom, and those aren't them. I think... I think we're looking at a full town of cultists. Or enough of them that they're in charge."

"Are they bad people?" Fluffbear asked anxiously. "I might have to beat them up."

"Nnnn....." Garon's honesty warred with the realization that if he said the wrong thing, the little bear WOULD march out there and start smiting. "Don't know. They might just be deluded. Let's wait and see what the full situation is, here, first."

"It's fahcked and we should run," Madeline said, clambering out of the wagon to take her place with the other toys. "But we're in now, so the only way out is through."

"Feeling better?" Threadbare asked.

"Yeah. Still down a wompload of sanity. Gahd I wish we had a way to rest. It's slow, slow, slow ta come back."

"Hm…" Threadbare glanced back to Zuula. "Maybe…"

His thoughts were interrupted, as letters flashed across his view.

You are now a level 6 scout!
AGL+3
PER+3
WIS+3

"Well!" He said. "I guess we explored a fair amount."

Garon shrugged his wings. "This is all new territory, so yes… oh. **Party Screen.** Cool, congratulations."

"Thank you."

"Oooh, that could do it," Madeline said. "I just need ta level up some an' get my sanity back fast that way."

"That works until you get out of the lower levels," Garon shrugged, twitching his wings. "And it's hard to rely on. Sometimes the experience doesn't stack up like you expect. Case in point."

"You'll hit level two dragon eventually," Threadbare said, then he stood on the wagon's seat. "Oh! There's the church. I think."

"Oh yes," Said Missus Fluffbear, as she looked at the stone building by the lake. The windows were green and blue stained glass, and lit from within. "That's totally a temple to Pau. Yorgum told me about her. Uh, him."

"God of the seas, right? And big lakes too, I guess." Garon nodded.

"And Goddess of storms. Which is why lightning strikes say his or her name when they hit."

As they got closer, they could hear a woman singing inside, barely audible over what sounded like the croaking of a couple of dozen big frogs. Madeline shuddered, and hid back inside the wagon.

Threadbare thought the woman's voice sounded rather desperate. And also that the croaking was a bunch of voices, nowhere near as deep as what they'd heard on the hill.

PER+1

"That's not the mediocre old one's voice," he said. "The frogs, I mean."

Curious, he had the dummy get out of the wagon and knock on the door.

There was a pause. Everything fell silent.

Finally, a harried-looking woman, stout and middle-aged, opened the door. Brown hair poked out, frazzled and chaotic, from under her green hood and the hem of her robe had big bites taken out of it. Strands of ropy slime oozed from the robe's hems to the floor. "Hello? Is everything... oh! Who are you?"

Her eyes bulged with fear... then softened, as they fell upon the two bears and the little plush dragon, as they hopped down from the wagon's seat. "Oh my goodness! An animator show! And these are your little toys, then!"

Your Adorable Skill is now level 22!

"Come inside, come inside," the woman smiled, madness flashing in her eyes. "The little dears will love you! Ah, I'll just take a break then, while you entertain them, shall I?"

"Oh, certainly," Threadbare had the dummy say, as they walked into the church.

SLAM! The door nearly caught Garon's tail as the cultist shut it.

CLICK! A key turned in the lock.

Feet pounded the pavement as Marva ran for her life.

And from the darkness, two dozen pairs of green, glowing eyes loomed out of the darkness, as the blessed children of YGlnargle'blah emerged from the wreckage of the pews and the thoroughly desecrated altar, staring at the newcomers, shark-like maws opening and closing as drool spilled to the floor.

CHAPTER 10: THE SHADOW UNDER OUTSMOUTH

The world returned to Zuula. She rose, trying to blink her eyes, before she remembered that she didn't have eyelids anymore.

It felt terribly, terribly confining to be trapped once more in such a tiny body, but at least she didn't ache anymore. No fuzziness from just-waking up. No weird conditions, brought on by the vivid and horrible dreams she'd had.

Or were there? **"Status,"** Zuula whispered—

—and stared at her full pools.

She'd been low, WAY low on sanity before she went into her dream quest. But now it was as full as if she'd slept a full night.

The shaman wasn't exactly the sharpest tool in the burnt-out-barn with collapsed walls, let alone the toolshed, but she immediately understood the value of what she'd found.

Zuula hopped out of the wagon, and looked at the stars. Not more than a few hours. She was in a town, too, she saw. Outsmouth? Had to be. There was a church next to the wagon, and light glowed through the green windows, as croaking, babbling speech resounded from within.

None of her party were around. Even the cats were missing. **"Party Screen."** Yep, there they were... Fluffbear had been added too. The wooden cats were out, though. Also there was something called "Church Door" on the party screen now.

And to her surprise, she saw that her toy companions' levels were higher. Not by much, but something had definitely happened. A fight?

What had she missed out on?

Zuula stared at the inactive wooden cats, went back to the wagon, got her spear, and marched up to the door.

"Is you Zuula's party mate now?"

The croaking continued unabated. The door didn't answer.

"Zuula's guessing animator bullshit."

The door remained shut and silent.

Zuula shrugged, rammed her spear through her chest to hold it, smiled at the con increase and golem body skill boost as a red '17' rolled up, then picked up a loose cobblestone.

BAM BAM BAM!

A red '1' rolled up from the door on the third try. Zuula watched it tick down in the party screen, from five hundred and sixty to five hundred and fifty-nine. Yeah, animators were some weird bullshit all right.

The lock clicked, the door handle jiggled, and the door opened...

And the church fell silent, its occupants frozen and staring at her.

Threadbare sat at the head of a low table made from overturned pews, wearing an oversized green-and-red fez with cloth eyeballs decorating it. Madeline, Garon, and Fluffbear sat on the sides of the table, mixed in with about a dozen green, scaly, fishy-looking small humanoids wearing ripped overalls and patchy pajamas and drool-stained dresses. Each of them clutched toys from the ruined toy store, toys that Zuula recognized, because before she'd gone to her dream quest they'd been in sacks that Pulsivar had been sleeping on.

About a dozen more of the little fish thingies slept around the church, curled up on the altar, or the pews, or seemingly nodded off where they were. They had toys too, and what looked like green robes had been tossed over each one.

"Oh, you're awake," Threadbare said, lifting up a silver altar cup, and gesturing around the makeshift table. More cups, various trays, and all sorts of religious knickknacks and ornaments adorned the low structure.

The fish things were staring at her.

Zuula pulled the spear free from her chest. **"Slow Regeneration."**

"Mom," Garon started. "Don't." His own fez wobbled, and fell off.

Zuula marched forward.

Madeline stood, "Hey no, whoa, they're kids, don't—" a tiny candle-snuffer slid from her head, and she tried to catch it.

"It's okay! Don't hurt them!" Fluffbear said, scrambling from her seat...

...too late.

Zuula slammed her spear against the table, hopped on the nearest seat, and bellowed "Where Zuula's hat?"

There was a pause.

"What? We gonna have a tea party, she need a hat too. Isn't dat right, child?" She asked the batrachian half-breed next to her.

It giggled, and clutched its dolly closer to its chest. Loose red braids swayed, as it pulled off the stretched scrunchy it was using as a makeshift princess crown, and handed it down to the funny green dolly.

Zuula plopped her new hat around her head, tying it carefully, and her jaw dropped in awe as a dozen skill ups rolled past. All in "Adorable," but still.

"Okay. Zuula start to see why you all got toy golem levels." She said, and Fluffbear giggled and slid a candle holder down to her.

"We're pretending like these are tea cups!"

Garon nodded. "Yeah. We found the hats and culty robes in a secret hiding spot behind the altar. Y'know, where every cult has a secret hiding spot?"

"Cult?" Zuula took a sip of her pretend tea, and the kids around her laughed and did the same.

"**Command Teapot. Give pretend refills,**" Threadbare told the incense burner in the center of the table, and it went to work trundling around the table and dipping its spout toward the 'teacups.' "It's been good animator practice, I got a level of that. Also two of model, and one of golemist."

"We think that's because we're leveling as well," Garon said. "I mean it looked that way from the ogre fight, but this seems to confirm it."

"No offense, but we were a little worried ya'd take this the wrong way. Maybe come in slinging spells and getting ya stab on." Madeline balanced her candle-snuffer on her hard wooden head.

"What? Why?" Zuula frowned.

"It's just that... well..." Garon said. "All right, look Mom, we were worried you'd think these kids were eldritch or something. Abominations, or old ones, or something horrible and jump to conclusions."

"Child. Have some faith in you mother." Zuula waggled her candlestick holder at him. "These kids. And they not eldritch, they just fishmen."

"Wait. They're not?" Garon looked confused. "But the cult calls them blessed children. And there's the old one outside of town—"

"Yeah, who is all tentacles and too many eyes. Do you have tentacles and many eyes?" Zuula asked the tiny fishman across from her. It giggled and stuck its thumb in one nostril slit. "Yeah, Zuula no t'ink so. Just fishmen."

"The cultists we talked with called them blessed children." Madeline didn't look convinced.

"Cultists all humans, right? Humans be dumb sometimes. Den dey try to talk to old ones, and old ones go t'rough dere minds like cheese grater t'rough cheddar. Of course dey gonna be wrong about shit."

The kids at the table burst out laughing. The funny little dolly said a swear!

Zuula sipped her imaginary tea, and smiled. "Besides, Zuula not break sanctity of tea party. You forget, her firstborn be girl. She know how important it is."

Besides, if it got her another toy golem level or two, that worked. Speaking of which...

"Dream Quest refill all pools like regular sleep."

"Whaaat?" Madeline jumped straight up. "Get out!"

"Why? Zuula just got to party?"

"No, no, I mean... really?"

"Yeah. Workaround to stupid no organs t'ing. Downside is, you in dreamquest you not wake up until it done."

"So it could be risky," Threadbare said. "But when we're not in danger, it's probably a good way to train faster."

"Can you do me?" Madeline asked. "I think I got all the levels I can from tea pahtying tonight. I can spend the rest of my sanity to do some fire tricks for the kids, skill up that way, then regain it all back in a quatah of the time."

"Sure," Zuula said. "We got two day, maybe t'ree before everyone here die, anyway."

The table fell silent, save for the happily croaking children, and the clink of their teacups.

"Wait, what?" Garon said.

"No!" Fluffbear said. "They can't die!"

"Tell you after dey go to bed. Which be SOON," Zuula said, using her momma voice. "Soon after Zuula level, anyway." She had her priorities, after all.

About half an hour later, a bit past midnight, the last of the children bedded down in Annie Mata's lap, next to a snoozing Mopsy. "Cat put up wit dem?" Zuula was impressed.

"They played a little rough, so when she lay down on the dummy I had it show them how to pet her gently. The dummy was doing that most of the night. These children are... a little young, I think," said Threadbare, with all the wisdom he'd earned over his five years of existence.

"Mopsy likes how they smell!" Fluffbear said. "She was licking them a lot."

"Yeah, the cat was a good distraction until we got the tea party rolling," Garon said, removing his fez. "Normally I'd be worried about desecrating a church, but eh, the cult got there first anyway. But seriously, why's everyone going to die?"

"Nature ain't big on whys. All Zuula know is dat in a couple of days ain't no humans going to be left alive around here. And the Old one is waking up too, so dat not be good neither."

"The nice cultists at the gate DID say something about the old one calling them all home," Threadbare said.

Silence, as the toys considered it.

"Ah fuck me theah a death cult," Madeline said. "We need to get outta heah."

"No! They can't kill the children!" Missus Fluffbear waved her arms. "I won't let them! I just swore a vow about that, I think!"

"Maybe they're deluded," Garon said. "They aren't going to kill anyone, maybe, but the Old One's going to eat them. Maybe he's not what they think he is."

"Is possible." Zuula shrugged. "Or it possible it call them home. No humans left alive might mean humans in a place dat nature can't see."

"Wait. Did tha dreamquest say anything about fishmen left alive in a few days?" Madeline asked.

"Dey obviously half-human," Zuula pointed at the kids, some with hair, some without. Some with human proportions, some more distorted. "So dey count as humans to nature. Humans bone so many t'ings dat nature just t'row up hands and say fine, you all human." Zuula snorted. "Which doesn't keep really fucking stupid humans from yelling dumb shit about keeping bloodlines pure and how humans is superior. Eh, at least humans not elves."

"We're getting sidetracked, Mom." Garon chewed his fuzzy lip. "So the great old one—"

"Mediocre old one."

"—Yeah, that guy—"

"No gender."

"—Whatever. So it wakes up and calls everyone home?"

"Maybe. All Zuula know from what dream quest showed is dat in a few days fish still be here, dogs still be here, bugs still be here, but humans? Humans gone."

The toys considered that. "No." Threadbare finally decided.

"No?" Zuula asked. "She guess maybe dere a few chances it not happen, but most signs point to whoop, humans out."

"These people are nice. Their kids are fun. I don't want them to die."

"Yeah, they're kind of worshiping the thing that's going to eat them," Garon said. "And maybe it isn't dying, but going to their afterlife... which would be pretty much like dying." Garon sighed. "We don't know enough about what's going on here."

"So let's fix that," Madeline said. "How about this? Come the moahning you suit up as Annie Mata and we'll staht asking questions. We'll coach ya to make sure they don't catch on, and we'll see if we can sleuth out this shit."

They decided that was a good plan. And after Madeline had fun practicing and controlling fire for a bit, Zuula dream quested her, then sat on the comatose marionette while they discussed the details and preparation they'd need to pull it off...

*****

Come the morning, a key clicked in the lock again, and the door handle rattled.

"Showtime," Garon called to Threadbare.

"Animus. Invite Annie. Magic Mouth. Dollseye," Threadbare rattled off, and the dummy stirred from her pew, placing both the sleeping Mopsy and the snoozing fishchild to either side of her as she rose.

"Hello? Ma'am? Are you... oh, thank goodness," Marva said, putting a basket full of sackcloth to the side. "I'm sorry to leave you like that, I was just on my last legs. The brothers of the society all take childcare for granted, you know? Phew! I think you'll need these. Do you know who needs changing?"

"Changing?" Annie asked.

"You don't smell that?" Marva squinted. "Oh. Well, you're new to Blessed Children, I imagine. Turns out they're like any other two year olds. Potty training sticks earlier with some than others."

"Say no more!" Zuula marched out. "Hand Zuula diapers and rags and point her to poopy bottoms!"

"Oh my! What a delightful little savage puppet!"

Zuula froze.

"Isn't she?" Garon asked, flapping up to sit on Annie's shoulder. "So strong, too. And wise. Wise enough not to be easily offended. Incidentally we're thinking of doing a cultist one, in honor of our stay, here."

"Oh that'd be delightful!" Marva handed a bunch of diapers and associated sundries down to Zuula, who unfroze, took them, then stomped around to the somnolent children, muttering. The middle-aged cultist followed, picking up sleeping, fussy kids, and stripping and changing them with the ease of long practice. "We've had to hide for ever so long. But now we're in charge, and we don't have to anymore. I'm so very glad that you're a follower of the Thing in Yellow. You understand how it is."

"Very much so," Threadbare said, unhappy at the lie but seeing no way around it. "Er, is everyone in this town an old one cultist?"

"Oh no. No, no, no. But the rest are friends and neighbors and supporters. So everyone's okay with us. You don't have secrets in small towns like this, not from your neighbors."

"Then why hide what ya were doing?" Madeline asked, peering around a pew.

"Oh, a little puppet! How precious! Can I pick her up?"

"Shuah."

Marva scooped up Madeline and examined her eagerly, chuckling at the tack fangs, and making the little doll squeak when the cultist peered up her skirt. "Hey! Don't get weahd!"

"Hah hah hah! I half expected her to be anatomically correct, the carving is exquisite. Did you make her yourself?"

"No, she was bargain at her price, though," Threadbare said. "Why DID you hide your cult?"

"Because the garrison weren't our neighbors. Or our friends." Marva's smile faded, and she smoothed Madeline's dress down, and tucked her into the crook of her arm. "They took the best of our catch, and they took our sons and daughters as conscripts, and when the dwarves killed the Hornwoods they didn't care or interfere. They didn't want to start another war, they said. The Hornwoods deserved it for claim jumping, they said. Then just a few years later the dwarves accused the King of killing Taylor's Delve. Of trying to kill the dwarven clan that lived down that way. And the dwarves declared war on the Crown anyway, and taxes went up, and conscription went up, and it looks like the King DID maybe kill off an entire town."

She'd started rocking Madeline now, unconsciously, holding her like a baby. "And my daughters died fighting dwarves. And I'll never get to hold them again." She was crying now. "So yes, we hid our cult. But now we don't have to. Now we're free."

Soft, fuzzy arms closed around her ankle, and Marva jumped a bit, as golden light flared. "Oh!" She said, examining her hands, and the fading gouges from where the blessed children had gotten a little bitey last night. "Thank you..." she said, staring down at the little armored black bear that had just hugged her leg.

"You're welcome. I'm very sorry things were bad," Missus Fluffbear squeaked.

"Oh, it wasn't your fault." She brightened. "Want to come to breakfast?" She asked Annie.

"Oh no thank you, I couldn't impose. Besides, I'm quite full from late-night tea." Fluffbear had the dummy gesture at the remnants of play.

"Goodness me," Marva said, picking her way through the repurposed religious paraphernalia and equivalents. "Where did.... Did you give them these toys?"

"Yes. I salvaged some from the toy shop down in Taylor's Delve, when I was through there," the dummy said. "That was before the fire, I'm afraid."

"Um. The fire." Marva said, her face instantly filling up with worry. "You saw that, did you?"

"Oh yes. It started in the forests. We— I barely got my wagon out of there in time."

"Hahahah... this is going to sound strange, but... could you not mention it? To anyone around here?" Marva definitely looked very nervous. "My husband and I would be in a whole lot of trouble for a very silly, totally ridiculous misunderstanding if that came up."

"I suppose I can keep quiet about that. Why would there be a misunderstanding?"

"It's a long story." Marva glanced southwest, out that one window that had a perfect view of the lonely hill in the distance. "Are you sure you won't come to breakfast?"

"I'm afraid so. I'm quite full and I should probably sleep and defecate later. You know, as humans do."

"Uh, well, yes?"

"Although I would appreciate learning more about your cult, and the old one."

"Oh, of course!" Marva smiled. "I'll let Pastor Hatecraft know you're interested. He's the one who does all the pamphlets and the printing, anyway. He kept the printing press after the librarian passed on under mysterious circumstances, you see."

"Wait." Garon said, frowning. "This town has a library?"

*****

Outsmouth's library was set back away from the lake, in a cramped and twisty street that had shuttered storefronts to either side. Suspicious eyes peered at the toys from oilskin-covered windows of the few homes still occupied on that street, and from somewhere in the town, unseen flutes played a tuneless melody.

"Is this eldritch?" Fluffbear asked. "I can't tell."

"Maybe a little," Zuula admitted, as she stared at the stone building, and the really big padlock on the door. "Doors. Zuula's true nemesis now!"

"Not mine," Threadbare said, from Annie Mata's arms. The dummy held him out so that he could touch the lock. **"Animus. Invite Lock. Open for me, would you?"**

The lock clunked to the ground. **"Kick lock from party,"** he told it, as Annie opened the door with her free hand. Dark inside, though that mattered little to most of the puppets, and Threadbare's nose twitched with the smell of old paper.

Your Scents and Sensibility skill is now level 18!

"Okay, I don't know why a tiny town like this has a library, but... Uh..." Garon said, following Annie into the room. "Um."

The library was one big room, full of dusty shelves of moldy books. Holes in the roof showed where water had done its thing, and stains below them showed where mold was doing ITS thing. Papers lay strewn about, and ink washed free by water pooled and puddled in stains along the walls.

"The Gahdess of Knawledge would straight up staht killing bitches fah this," Madeline said, surveying the damage.

"How are we supposed to find out anything useful?" Fluffbear asked.

Garon thought for a bit. "Your blessing skill, it's up to twenty or so, right?"

"Right!"

"Slap it on Madeline, boost up her luck and let her search."

"What? Why me?" Madeline protested.

"Mom doesn't have the patience to sort through hundreds of books. And I don't have thumbs. So that leaves..."

"Shit. Awright, but ya owe me one."

They boosted Madeline's luck, and turned her loose. Threadbare tucked in and helped as well. Fortunately it was dark enough in there that their Darkspawn buffs came into play as well.

Missus Fluffbear picked up a heavy tome, and waddled over to some light streaming in from a narrow slit window. After a few minutes, she cheered. "Yay!"

"What did you find?" Garon walked over.

"Oh, nothing. But my intelligence went up from reading about swamp plants! Did you know that every mushroom around here is bad for you in some way?"

"Yes. Zuula not need book to tell her dat," Zuula confirmed. "Wait. You get smarter from reading books?"

"Yep," Madeline said. "Well-written books can give mental experience. Not always to intelligence." She had her nose buried in an ancient ledger. "Okay. So this is interesting. Turns out the fish harvest doubled a few years ago. 'bout the end of the northern wars. It's been going good evah since... well, up until last year, that's when tha last entry is."

"So what?" Garon asked.

"So nothing yet, but ya look at this, and about the same time, tha priestess of Pau in town dies from a mysterious illness. Right, Threadbeah?"

"Yes, the dates are about a week off." He waved a book labeled 'dearly departed – deaths in Outsmouth, volume four; cows, goats, and humans'

"That's when a new fella steps up as tha local pastor of Pau, a newly-arrived guy called Hatecraft."

"We've heard that name, just that morning," Garon said. "So unless there's two of them, we know he's a cultist."

"Right. And he's blessing the fishing boats instead of the old Pau priestess doin' the blessing."

"So he impresses the fishing town by increasing their haul." Garon nods.

"Yeah. And if ya look, tha Crown steps up BOTH the tax AND the fishing tithe a month later."

"Ooooh..." Garon shook his head. "Dick move."

"It's when the dwahven wah stahted, but still..."

"Yeah. A jerk move like that means lots of converts to the cult." Garon lay his head down, and thought. "Who is this guy?"

"I didn't find him in the local family birth records. So he probably came in from somewhere else," Madeline said. "First record of him is actually on the library payroll. Dude was an assistant. Lived in the basement of the library."

"Jinkies!" Said Missus Fluffbear.

They all looked at her.

"What? It says jinkies!" She held up a book, with brightly-colored children's toys on it. "I think that's a fun word."

"To the basement then," decided Threadbare.

They eventually found it, after moving some piles of paper around until they revealed a trapdoor. Garon went down first, and froze. A blue

'8' escaped from his head, as he recoiled from something out of their line of sight.

"He being attacked! Is old one! Or eldritch!" Zuula shrieked, and the toys piled down, ignoring the ladder entirely...

...and stared in silence, at the tiny room below.

And the horrific images plastered on the wall.

Sanity damage rippled through them, all save for Threadbare, who took off his top hat and rubbed his head, puzzled.

Fluffbear was also spared. She squinted around, with her dagger out and ready. "What is it? I can't see!"

"Good," choked Garon. "Someone please cover her eyes. Or get her out of here."

"What's wrong?" Threadbare asked. "It's just more pictures of tentacles. Well, I mean, there's women in these pictures, too. And they sure don't look comfortable. But that's not really anything to fuss about, I'd say."

"Let me see!" Fluffbear said, trying to get a better angle in the bad light.

"No!" The doll haunters chorused. Zuula covered her eyes.

"Aw..."

"I don't think you're missing much," Threadbare reassured her. "It's kind of boring, honestly. But since it seems to be upsetting the others, maybe you could keep watch upstairs? I'm not sure where Pulsivar got to and sooner or later he'll come looking for us, I'm quite sure."

"Well, okay. Um..." She considered the ladder. Definitely not sized for her six-inch frame. "Could you?"

"Of course." Threadbare had Annie come down and pick her up, then return upstairs.

"Dis be why humans make de worst cultists," Zuula sighed, keeping her eyes well below visual level of the homemade drawings on the wall, and looking around the small, dank basement. "Dey get WEIRD about it."

"Never have I so regretted being unable to vomit," Garon muttered. "Come on, let's search. Dibs on not under the bed."

"Not it!" Zuula and Madeline chorused.

Threadbare shook his head, and started poking around under the moldy bed, while Madeline rummaged through crates and the few items of furniture down here.

CRACK!

Everyone jumped, and Fluffbear peered down into the hole again. "What was that?"

"Mom!" Garon howled.

Zuula looked over from the wreckage of the barrel she'd smashed, and put down the rusty crowbar. "What? Is barrel!"

"Geeze. Not this again. Mom, look, you can't just go around smashing every barrel you come across..."

"Yes she can! Sometimes is loot inside!"

"Mom, look, no, that was ONE small dungeon, and Taylor's Delve had that one sealed years back—"

"Ho, so you tell de story? You want Zuula to stay awhile and listen?" The little half-orc grinned.

"Don't get me started. Just... please, no more barrel smashing. Not now."

"Psh. Could have been somet'ing in dere." Zuula said, sitting down and pouting. "Maybe dat one kid's spare pegleg. Never could find it for dat little fucker. He would have had good loot for reward, too!"

"Yeah, he was totally an item smuggler. Pretty sure pegleg was code for reagents."

"Found it!" Madeline whooped. "I think so, anyway." She held up a pink book, with bunnies on it, labeled "Dear diary." The bunnies had tentacles.

"I want to see!" Fluffbear said.

"We'll come to you," Threadbare said, coming out from under the bed, covered in dust bunnies. "There's nothing under there but more drawings. I'm pretty sure they would cost you more sanity," he told his friends.

Upstairs, in the moldering library, they read the book. Some of the words took a little guesswork, the guy was fond of using obscure words with way too many syllables.

It didn't take long. For all he was verbose, his entries were very short, all things considered.

Also pretty blasphemous.

By studying forbidden lore you have unlocked the Cultist job! You cannot become a Cultist at this time!

"We need to find this guy," Garon concluded. "Quickly."

"Someone's coming!" Fluffbear said, scrambling down from the windowsill. "A whole bunch of someones! They have crossbows and spears."

"Shit," Garon said. "We need to get out of here—"

"Why?" Threadbare asked.

"Well, if they're armed, they're not going to be friendly. I think this is going to go bad."

"Isn't that why we're using the dummy?"

The toys considered Annie in silence. She waved.

A minute later, when the cultists shoved the door open, Annie was sitting in one of the lone chairs in the room, reading through a storybook. Her toys sat around her, still and clearly deanimated. "Oh, hello sirs and madams!" Annie said, closing the book. "Is everything all right?"

"Yeah," Daav said. "The pastor wants to see you. Now."

"And no funny business!" Mhorty said, his voice squeaking and breaking as he waggled a fishing spear in her direction.

"Of course not. I was just practicing some stories for your little dears. Such cute little scaly kids."

The half-dozen cultists relaxed. "Yeah, they're little angels, ain't they? Maybe you'll be blessed with one of your own!" Phred said.

Annie went peacefully with the group, who seemed much relieved at her acceptance of the matter.

Five minutes passed. Then ten. And then Threadbare twitched, and stood up. "I think that should do it. Also, I caught a glimpse of Pulsivar. We can collect him and Mopsy on the way, I think."

"On the way where?" Fluffbear asked.

"The place it all started…"

CHAPTER 11: UNSAFE SECTS

Pastor Elpy Hatecraft lingered for a moment more, dwelling on the artifacts of an antediluvian nature retrieved from the very depths of what in aeons past had been a submarinic trench. The local peasantry had mistaken it for a mere lake, and more ignoramuses they, for it was clearly a hoary relic from a bygone age, when squamous tentacles reached forth deep from umbral places beneath the earth, to rend and manipulate the soil and the geography about them. Lake? Bah! The brobdingnagian body of water the quaint and curious locals referred to as Lake Marsh deserved a far more Sesquipedalian surname. He had a few in mind, but he'd been waiting until the engraver got back to him with quotes, for changing all the signposts.

Unfortuitously, the engraver wasn't a member of his society of forbidden lore (and bingo twice a week,) or else Hatecraft could have offered elevation into the highest eldritch mysteries of the Society of Indefatigable Exploration of the Unknown Elder Antiquities. Namely, the bleachers that Hatecraft permitted the most elevated brethren to utilize while they observed the chamber of blasphemous conception, during the rite of manifestation.

But all that, as had many of his more enabling and eminently profitable plans, had evaporated like morning dew as inaction turned to action, and he'd awoken from his late-night slumber to the tintinnabulation of bells, bells, bells, and the somewhat unanticipated revelation that a revolution had occurred, thanks to the brethren and sistren on watch receiving the long-awaited sign that great YGlnargle'blah, an inscrutable entity that Hatecraft had chosen specifically for his dormancy and turpitude, was, in fact, engaging in unanticipated somnambulism.

Which was not Hatecraft's plan at all.

"Load faster! Make haste!" He commanded the beast, and it muttered and grumbled, in its loathsome way. The barbels on its cheeks twitched in time with its irritable susurration, its very existence evidence of an uncaring cosmos full of helpless gods, a form that offended the reasonable man's eye and raked at the very sanity of all logical onlookers.

Though, the effect was somewhat spoiled by its pants.

The brethren and sistren had put their foot down about that, they wanted YGlnargle'blah's envoy to wear pants when he wasn't engaging in blasphemous rites. Which was absurdity of the first order, but they HAD insisted, and so the herald of the octopodlian apocalypse, the evidence irrefutable of the truth of YGlnargle'blah, and the prominent celebrity in the rite of blasphemous conception now had to wear canvas shorts when he was off duty, as it were.

Initially concerned but somewhat relieved to find that this increased the eagerness of the female gendered of the society to engage upon the rite of conception, Hatecraft had grudgingly agreed. He would have hated to give up his Saturday nights at the peephole, after all.

But the pants proved no hindrance to the primary usage that Hatecraft employed the thing from below the waves at this minute; namely, engaging in longshoremanship of a most mediocre quality. The beast dropped half the crates he loaded upon the boat, and Hatecraft was reduced to mere scrabbling at the sands in the hidden cove, uncovering every fallen coin from every shattered container, and ensuring that not a single silver candlestick or precious metal adornment that he'd painstakingly milked from the society's coffers went astray.

The small bell he employed as both an early warning system and a doorknocker doled out its brazen peals, and Hatecraft hurled imprecations and threats at the beast, until it revolved its bulging, piscine eyes, and retreated to the depths of the dark cove, descending beneath the boat until such time as his viridian orbs and herring-enhanced exhalations could best be utilized for the purposes of intimidation.

Besides, when encountering a fellow ineffable lore-seeker, even one within the same blasphemous pantheon, it was best to have an ace kept in the proverbial hole.

Arranging his features into a pleasant countenance, Elpy Hatecraft pushed his spectacles up on his narrow face, and smiled at the stranger as she entered the cave below the church, escorted by half-a-dozen of his acolytes. "And you would be Miss Mata," he greeted the woman, her robes jaundiced and unhealthy as doubtless was her quaint and curious obsession. "Welcome to the true temple of the Society of indefatigable exploration of the unknown elder antiquities."

"Thank you. It's good to be here," Said the woman. "I had no idea this little cave was here, you can't really see it from the outside."

Elpy smiled, and gestured to the small hole in the wall where the lake entered, luxuriant with weeds and verdant marshgrass, offering concealment of the most fortuitous sort. "Yes, that's the objective. Are you here to enlist into the incipient revolution, my dear Miss Mata?"

"Actually I was wondering if you knew anything about a girl named Celia. She's the King's daughter."

Hatecraft found his angle of conversation entirely derailed. Intellect temporarily disengaged, he blinked at the shrouded woman from behind his spectacles, mouth opening to emit a rather undistinguished croak. "Bu-what?"

To his amazement, the woman started to twitch, and mutter in disjointed exclamations. "You didn't know— Well she is, I saw him— of COURSE I'm sure— Zuula knew. Zuula, please explain it— Hold on he's looking at me funny, I think it's still on—" She fell silent.

Hatecraft pulled off his spectacles, as his mouth moved, trying to make sense of the entirety of the inexplicable affair. Ultimately, he directed his gaze to the acolytes, who were looking at each other and whispering.

And to his horror, he realized that they were staring at the boat, encumbered to the brim with boxes, barrels, and crates, with a few shattered containers gleaming with unrevealed treasure in the dim green glowstone lanterns that he'd had to rig extremely carefully to get just that right shade of 'eldritch'.

"Ascend the stairs forthwith," he told them. "I can ensure that the treasury is moved to an infinitely more secure location myself, and I must communicate with the blessed messengers that are afflicting Miss Mata's mentality in an insalubrious manner."

Daav turned to Phred. "Wot'd he say?"

"He's just moving the stash. And he wants to talk to the lady alone."

"Aw, I wanted to watch," Mhorty sighed.

"Psh, don't get greedy, it's not even Saturday. And she might say no. And no means no, that's the first rule of the rite. Come on, let's get going then. Bye Pastor!"

"Farewell!" Elpy flapped his hands at them, in the sacred sign of the guardian marshfowl that he'd taught them early on in his theocratic regime. It looked impressive and did absolutely nothing save stretch the fingers, but it pleased the congregation nonetheless and a few of them even dropped their spears to return the sign.

With much clattering and a few lingering suspicious looks from some of the less-fervent acolytes at the boat full of treasure, the acolytes departed.

Hatecraft waited until he heard the door upstairs shut, and marched forward to Mata, shaking his finger in her face, chastening and intimidating simultaneously, he was certain. "You're no devotee of the Thing In Yellow! If you were, you would have surely drawn comparisons to this subterranean sanctuary to the lake of Holi, in lost Corcasa!"

"I never said I was a devotee to anyone," said Mata, returning his gaze unblinking, eyes just visible through her veil. "I'm a little confused about why your cult thought road signs were significant."

Hatecraft smiled. "And now I'm certain that you're no cultist. We don't call ourselves by such plebian apellations. Tell me, Miss Mata, what brings you to Outsmouth? Are you perhaps here to spy on our holy revolution?"

She still didn't blink. "I'm trying to find news about my little girl. But I don't think she's here. She's the king's daughter, and I'm worried about her."

Now, and only now, Elpy blinked. That wasn't the alibi he was expecting an agent provocateur to operate underneath. He pulled back from her, retreating to rally his ruminations, and best consider the concepts to conjugate. "You claim to be a mistress of royalty, then? A jilted mother, seeking her royal bastard?"

"I don't think you should talk that way about Celia. Please apologize."

"Celia? You claim to be Princess Cecelia's maternal originator?" Elpy laughed. "Unless you're Amelia Gearhart under there, that statement is magnificent within its ludicrousness. If I were you, I would observe your perambulation warily around such worrisome embellishments."

"I never claimed to be her mother. Her mother's dead. She's my little girl, that's all."

"Mmm. Madness, then. Insanity and fixation... fortunately I know all about such afflictions." Elpy spread his arms wide, convinced he was dealing with a madwoman. "I think, that I can recommend religion. You've already paid your dues, as it were," he nodded to the boat. "Would you enjoy true enlightenment?"

"No thank you. You lie to your friends too much." To his horror, the woman walked over to the boat and picked up a sack. "And these are our coins. Why did you take them?"

"Wartime requisitioning," he snapped, hastening over and removing the sack of lucre from her grasping, gloved digits. "A small fee to contribute to the coffers of the holy revolution."

"Yes, but you didn't want that revolution to happen," Mata pointed out. "So it looks an awful lot to me like you're using it as an excuse to steal."

A cold, nameless dread began to creep up Hatecraft's spine. His appendages numbed, as the air in the cove seemed to grow malign, and arctic, almost gelid to his frantic inhalations. "What did you say?" he whispered.

"We read your diary. We know you wanted to be important, so you came here to research the old one, and try to get people to do what you told them to do. Then you found the monster, and IT did what you told it to do. And that's when you killed the old priestess and the librarian."

"How..." Elpy rubbed his forehead. His diary! He'd completely forgotten about that aggravating tome during the relocation of his quarters to a location more suiting to his magnificence! "So what? You've only sealed your fate!" He hissed, striding forward to admonish the woman, ignoring her inscrutable arrogance. "With one word to my faithful they would engage in your agonizing and ultimately lethal defenestration!"

"I'm sure that's very bad, but Zuula's talking with them now, and showing them the book. I don't think they're very faithful any more. They're pretty mad, to be honest."

Hatecraft's mouth snapped shut. He looked up at the wooden ceiling above, noting for the first time the creaking of footsteps on the church floor above. Many footsteps. And just audible above them, a low, ugly muttering. The sort of muttering simple rural fisherfolk do when they find out that their savior and prophet is just a pathetic basement-dwelling 'nice guy' with some kinks involving calamari.

"Who are you!" He bellowed into the unblinking woman's veiled face. "Take off your mask!"

"Mask?" She said, as she tilted her head quizzically. "I wear no mask."

Silence, for a long moment.

"You're, er, you're wearing one right now," Elpy pointed out.

"Oh, that. Technically it's a veil."

Elpy had had ENOUGH. **"Great Cmpylyah's Curse on your Constitution! Dark Bolt!"** he screamed, blasting her backwards with eldritch lightning!

A red '99' escaped into the sky, and she staggered, and fell to one knee. Elpy ripped the veil away from her face—

—to look upon charred wood. "Ah. An animator," he sneered,

kicking the crippled puppet to the sand. "So that wasn't a lie, at least. Clever. I would hunt your real embodiment down, but my chronological excess is approaching its end, in this approximate location. I think I shall employ the egress, and leave you to enjoy the consequences when this town's inevitable doom approaches, whether it be from eldritch consequences or more mundane genocide." He hopped on the boat, gave three knocks on its side.

The water churned, then stopped. Hatecraft frowned, and knocked harder.

"No, don't go anywhere," The charred wreck of the mannequin said. "Not after we went to all this trouble to come to you."

With a surprised warble, the beast burst from the water, trousers rent and dripping.

And to Hatecraft's astonishment, he was followed by three dripping, weed-covered, unnatural little forms…

*****

Threadbare charged out of the water, dropping the stone that he'd used to weigh himself down when he walked along the bottom of the lake.

Beside him, Garon did the same time. From his back, Madeline pointed at the really big fishman they'd run into under the boat. "Back off, scaly!" She shouted.

Threadbare opened his mouth to say something to Hatecraft, but water came out instead.

This could be troublesome, he thought, as Hatecraft shrieked and threw black lightning at him. Fortunately, the little bear was small and nimble.

Your Dodge skill is now level 8!

He needed to get his mouth clear, and the guy wasn't giving him time to do it. So Threadbare decided to try one of his little used tricks. He leaped forward, onto the boat, and hugged the guy's outstretched arm. Golden light flared…

You have healed Elpy Hatecraft for 110 points!
Your Innocent Embrace skill is now level 12!

…but Elpy had a surprisingly good will, for someone who had so thoroughly failed to resist his own urges. Or maybe Threadbare just needed more practice.

Your Fascination skill was resisted!

"Get off! Evacuate!" Elpy screamed, shaking his arm. But the little bear's strength was much more than the cultist's. Threadbare spat water into his face, trying to clear his voice for speech.

"Fevered Strength!" the cult leader hissed, and Threadbare's arms slipped as the thin man bulged with muscles. Then the little bear was flying backward, hitting the wall of the cavern, and bouncing to a stop.

"Dark Chant!" Hatecraft roared, as he grabbed a gaff hook and leaped out of the boat. And from everywhere and nowhere, from the place between the worlds, carried on ineffable winds from places no man was meant to see or hear, came words that were terrible in their strangeness.

"IO! IO FORTRAN! CMPYLYAH RPL WEBQL NPL FORTRAN!"

Even Threadbare, with his strong mental fortitude, felt his sanity escape as the chant tore at his mind...

Meanwhile, on the beach, Garon and Madeline faced off against an eight-foot, scaly being. It had the head of a catfish, with glowing green eyes, and a blubbery layer of fat over way too many muscles. Initially freaked out over their appearance, it now seemed to be getting angry. "WRRBLGLRGLE BLAH!" The thing spat, standing legs akimbo, hiking its shorts up and putting up its dukes.

"Burninate it! I got yer back!" Madeline yelled. **"Endure Faia! Manipulate Faia!"**

Garon hosed the fishman down with water, as he tried to speak.

"Oh." Madeline said. She'd kept her mouth shut no problem underwater, but the plush toys... well, they WERE pretty porous, weren't they? "Uh oh."

Then Garon twisted and jumped to the side, as the fishman kicked at them, and Madeline, with her substandard ride skill, went flying. "Mothafuckah!" She ate sand, and picked herself up, just as the chant started. "No!" She howled, as the alien words ripped through her head... "Not again!"

On the other side of the cavern, Threadbare winced, as a Dark Bolt ripped through him, sending a red '47' into the air. Then Elpy was upon him, stabbing down with the gaff hook. Threadbare dodged again, tried to clear his throat, but couldn't. His friends were losing heart, as the dark words ripped sanity from them, he saw blue numbers flowing up and away, way too big in Madeline's case. He had to stop that. But how?

The gaff hook caught him square on, impaling him through the gut.

Your Golem body skill is now level 22!

Your Toughness skill is now level 16!
Max HP +2

The bear grabbed the spear, and started to pull himself up. Elpy shrieked, and started battering him against the stones, the beach, and anything else he could reach. It damaged the little bear, but the golem kept up his inexorable climb.

And as he did so, the answer came to him.

"I don't know if this will work," Mata said, in her creaky, mildly-charred voice, "But this is my **Emboldening Speech.**" Elpy froze, and looked toward the dummy. **"This man and his monster have been doing bad things and lying to the people they should be helping. So let's stop them. There's no way he's tougher than the ogre, and you did great on that."**

Your Emboldening Speech skill is now level 8!

To Elpy's horror, the puppets straightened up, and the sanity escaping them shrunk and slowed. His abomination, however, clutched its skull, as the dark chant continued its work. The beast never HAD been immune to the blasphemous insanity-over-time spell.

Then furry paws seized Hatecraft's fingers, and pain ripped through his hand as bone snapped. Fevered Zeal granted strength, yes, but at a cost to constitution. He hurled the spear, and the bear free…

…and the bear threw itself off the spear, yelled **"Fancy Flourish!"** In a still-waterlogged voice, caught the wall with strong legs, and fell to the ground. He landed on both feet and whipped the spear around in a dazzling display.

Threadbare smiled as he saw a green '12' escape from Hatecraft. He smiled more as skill-ups flew by.

Your Fancy Flourish skill is now level 7!
Your Work it Baby skill is now level 31!

Too many foes! Hatecraft started toward the dolls on the beach, charging them while their backs were turned—

"Fight me," Threadbare invited. "I **challenge** you!"

Your Challenge skill is now level 4!

Hatecraft wasn't distracted. He kicked at Madeline, but his foot came nowhere near her, as the challenge debuff threw his aim off. She dodged, and shouted **"Call Faia!"** Red fire, not properly eldritch at all, licked up from her hand and hit him in the crotch. Hatecraft staggered back, shot a look at Threadbare, who was holding up the gaff hook.

"This is sort of a blade, isn't it?" Threadbare asked, his throat finally clear of water. He studied the double-sided spear blade carefully.

"What?" Hatecraft wheezed, batting at his burning balls.

Threadbare brought the spear down hard on a rock, so hard that the little teddy bear bounced into the air.

CRACK!

The spear blade broke off. Threadbare walked over and tossed it into the air. **"Animus Blade,"** he said, as it whirled. **"Invite broken spear thing."**

Your Animus Blade skill is now level 9!

"Technically it's a gaff," Hatecraft hissed, his grammar offended at the improper education displayed in this plebian plushie.

"Yeah, it's a gaffe all right!" Madeline yelled. "And you made it! Whoops!" She went flying backward as the abomination managed to boot her a good one. "Ow!" then "AGH!" as the dark chant swelled, and another blue number ripped from her skull. "Little more encouragement here boss?"

Threadbare charged Hatecraft, as the reverend recovered from his roasting and seized up a board with a nail in it. The two fought, claw to wood, as the little bear shouted emboldening speech after emboldening speech.

Meanwhile, Garon bit at the catfish thing, ripping its pants and tearing into its scaled flesh. But the thing was tough, and though it was slow, the few hits it managed to land popped seams and burst stuffing.

Garon needed his skills, and he couldn't get to them, his throat and mouth were choked with water. His superior air capacity worked against him. The Dark Chant wasn't hitting him so bad, at least, it seemed like high dragons were resistant to that sort of thing, but even with Threadbare's speeches it would soon take Madeline out of commission unless they could shut down the cultist.

Then Garon felt a familiar weight on his back, after he danced around the catfish man's latest lunge. Madeline.

"Gar, do you trust me?" The wooden doll yelled.

"Gurgleglub! Blarfle!" Garon spat water, and settled for nodding.

"Good. **Bloodsuckah!**" And Garon froze, as he felt tiny fangs rip into his neck...

Across the way, Threadbare staggered as Hatecraft broke the club over his head. The nail ripped his hat off, and tore a wide stretch of his hide open. The cloth flopped over his eyes, and he staggered back, temporarily blinded and feeling the blackness come on as the stuffing spilled from his head. **"Mend Golem!"** he yelled, three times to be sure.

Your Golem body skill is now level 23!

Your Toughness skill is now level 17!

Max HP +2

Your Mend Golem skill is now level 3!

You have healed yourself for 65 points!

Your Mend Golem skill is now level 4!
You have healed yourself for 68 points!
Your Mend Golem skill is now level 5!
You have healed yourself for 68 points!

"G-g-g-golems?" Hatecraft spluttered, staring in disbelief. His calves were a bloody wreck, but Zeal and fear kept him on his feet. "Inconceivable!"

"Yes. Golems," Threadbare said, raising his bloody claws again. "Surrender. I don't want to kill you. But you have to stop all this."

"Burninate!" Came Garon's bellow across the way, and the fishman roared as he cooked. "Ow ow ow!" Garon yelled, until Madeline scooped the flames from him and threw them away.

"Mend Golem," Threadbare threw his way—

Your Mend Golem skill is now level 6!
You have healed Garon for 74 points!

—but the moment of inattention cost him.

"Dark Bolt!" Hatecraft screamed, and threw eldritch lightning at the wounded teddy bear...

...lightning that crackled and faded away.

Your Magic Resistance skill is now level 7!

"All right, then." Threadbare waded in, claws swiping, watching his skill rise as Hatecraft backed up, hit points slashed down bit by bit.

But the pastor sneered, and grabbed up the haft of the broken spear. **"Unholy Smite,"** he said, and dark energy flowed into the improvised staff.

Then his eyes went wide, as a tiny little squeaky voice shouted from the stairs. "I can do stuff like that too! **Holy Smite!**" yelled Fluffbear. And with Mopsy warbling a battle cry, the mounted bear charged him from behind.

"There you are!" Threadbare sighed, as he tag-teamed Hatecraft, ducking under the man's erratic blows. "Where's—"

Fifty pounds of the gods' perfect killing machine emerged from the shadows of the stairwell and pounced on the distracted fishman's back.

Pulsivar had his priorities, and if he was gonna kill anything down here, it was going to be the guy who smelled like baked fish, okay?

The dark chant faltered and faded, as the enemies finally fell.

And when the angry mob of former cultists worked up the courage to head downstairs, they found a pile of battered toys doing their best to convince Pulsivar that he probably shouldn't eat the dead fishguy.

He might be eldritch, after all. That shit could be contagious.

"You survive!" Zuula said, emerging from the crowd of cultists. "Good. Had devil of time convincing Pulsivar to go into dark basement full of bad words."

"Yeah, what was that chanty thing? It sounded nasty," Fluffbear squeaked, raising her voice to be heard as in the background the congregation took turns kicking Hatecraft. All but a few of the women, who were sitting next to the fishman and crying.

"Some cultist stuff, I guess," Said Garon, whistling. "Ah. Thanks for the amateur tracheotomy," he told Madeline.

"Anytime," Madeline burbled, and grinned. It had taken some doing to gnaw through to his flooded throat and let the water drain, but it had paid off.

"Oh, let me fix that," Threadbare said.

"No need, said Garon. "**Blood is...**" he clutched his chest, where his hidden pouch full of gold coins was. But his words trailed off, as impulses he'd never felt before told him whoa now. "Actually why don't you fix that. Yeah, no need to waste gold—" his eyes opened wide. "I leveled! Sweet Nurph, I get plus twenty five to stuff? Oh fucking wow!"

"Right. That settles that," Madeline said.

"What?" Garon asked.

"Tell ya later." She patted him. "Oooh, got a few levels myself. Vampaiah level five, good to seeya again."

But Threadbare wasn't listening. He was too busy watching his own level-ups scroll by.

You are now a level 11 Cave Bear!
CON+10
WIS+10
Armor+5
Endurance+5
Mental Fortitude+5

You are now a level 4 Duelist!
AGI+3
DEX+3
STR+3

You are now a level 5 Duelist!
AGI+3
DEX+3
STR+3
You have unlocked the Parry skill!
Your Parry skill is now level 1!
You have unlocked the Swashbuckler's Spirit skill!
You have unlocked the Swinger skill!

Your Swinger skill is now level 1!

You are now a level 8 Golemist!
INT+5
WILL+5

You are now a level 7 Ruler!
CHA+3
LUCK+3
WIS+3

Threadbare stared, sitting down hard. "My goodness. Wait, swinger? Is swinging good?"

The women around the fishman's corpse cried harder, for some reason. "This is neither the time nor the place, okay?" Marva said.

"Er, right. **Status. Help**... Ah, that's what it does. Ropes and chains and things. Okay." He frowned. "Chandeliers? I'm not sure what those are."

"Big piles of pointy wood that stupid vampaiahs hang over their heads in theah castles," Madeline said, strolling over. "The smaht ones use metal."

"Oh. Well I can swing from them really easily now," Said Threadbare. "I suppose that might be useful."

"Zuula relieved that you skill all about dat particular usage of de word." She said, heading over to the group. "What you do here?"

"I tried to get him to surrender."

"He know de score. Cult angry. Dey just kill him anyway. Why you kill fishman, dough?"

"Well, he attacked us," Garon said. "If he'd surrendered I would have let him back down, but then, well, he got Pulsivar'd."

Pulsivar burped. His breath smelled fishy, but he still cast envious looks at the fishman's corpse. The guy had been delicious, and the bobcat wanted him some more of that.

"I have a question," Missus Threadbare said.

"Sure. What's-" Threadbare froze. "Hold on. A spirit wants to talk. **Speak with Dead.**"

The world shifted. The former cultists went silent, and shifted uneasily, looking at the somewhat even creepier cave. After an awkward couple of seconds Daav cleared his throat. "We'll uh, we'll just take the bodies up, and uh... be off, shall we? Yes, why don't we." They beat feet upstairs, bearing Hatecraft and the fishman with them.

"Hello?" Threadbare asked.

"Yo," a strange voice said from the direction of the underground lake. It was deep and smooth, and like all of the dead, it spoke to their minds and not their ears. "What's up? Why'd you murder me, little dudes?"

"You're not Hatecraft." Threadbare frowned.

"Who? Oh, the weird little mean guy? Naw, dude, naw."

"That leaves one person. Are you the fishman?"

"I guess so. Yeah, that's a good word for me."

"Why did you fight us?" Garon asked.

"Buncha freaky ass little monsters and a motherfucking miniature dragon come outta nowhere? Fff, like you wouldn't."

"Ya got a point theah," Madeline said.

"Why did you help the evil cultist hurt all these people?" Fluffbear said.

"Was that what he was doing? Didn't look like it to me," The fishman said, poking his head up from the water where he'd been resting his ectoplasm. "It was hard to tell with that guy. He was intense. And I never learned the language, so I didn't really know what his deal was."

"Why don't you tell us what you do here?" Zuula asked. "You don't look eldritch to Zuula, but dere cult involved so she want full facts before we err on de side of smacking old ones."

"Old ones? Nah, just one. My man YGlnargle'blah. We be chilling with him under the sea. Used to rule around here, y'know? But the ocean over this place started shrinking, so when he said come with me if you want to live, we went."

"Ocean? There's never been an ocean around here," Garon said.

But Zuula was shaking her head. "Dere was. Long ago. Way long ago."

"Yeah, it's been a while. So he called his children home, and we've been chilling in his airless realm of cool darkness ever since. But me, my family got on my case, wanted me to grow up and learn a trade. I tried to tell them music IS a trade and the band would take off any day now, but shit, man, they didn't listen. So I went exploring, trying to find some good seaweed I could harvest, or maybe some new kind of fish I could sell, and I found kind of a door. It dumped me out in this weird-ass place. It was rough for a while, and I got pretty sick. Crawled into this cave, thought I was gonna die. That's when weirdo found me."

"Called his children home..." Garon slapped his face with one paw. "He won't call the cultists home at all. YOU'RE his children, not the human cultists."

"Yeah. Wouldn't be a good place for humans, where I come from. It'd be kind of drowny."

"So why you making fish babies?" Zuula asked. "You horny or

somet'ing?"

"Gh. Yuk. Don't remind me." The fishman sighed. "That little weird dude insisted I get it on with half this freaking village. Those, urk, smooth bodies, and ulp, hair everywhere... Blrp... mf. Man, I guess I'm glad ghosts can't vomit but I kind of want to, y'know? At least he started letting me have a bag I could put over their heads. I think he convinced them it was part of a ritual or something. And he kept summoning tentacles and things while I was trying to get it over with. Some messed up stuff, I tell you."

"I don't understand," said Missus Fluffbear. "Not any of that."

"We'll tell you later!" The doll haunters chorused.

Fluffbear pouted. "Well, okay. I had a question anyway—"

"Whoa. I'm dissolving. Is this good?" The fishman interrupted.

"You going to you afterlife." Said Zuula. "Is normal dead stuff."

"But my afterlife ain't here!" The fishman's voice rose. "How will YGlnargle'blah find me!"

Zuula considered. "Soulstone him, Dreadbear."

"What? Oh. Good idea. **Soulstone.**"

"What's that?" The fishman spirit walked out of the water, and stared. "Dude, it's like an angler trap, only a lot more interesting..." He reached out to touch it... and flowed into the stone.

"Weird," The soulstone pulsed blue. "It's tight in here, but comfy."

"We can put you into a new body, if you like," Said Threadbare, politely. "Or we can take you to YGlnargle'blah's circle. He seems to be acting up lately."

"Oh, that ring of stones thing? I've been looking for that! It's not in the lake anywhere, and it's supposed to be underwater, that's what the old writings say."

"Old writings from when ocean be here?" Zuula asked.

"Yeah."

"See, dis why you not trust books. Ocean be long gone, remember?"

"Oh. Right."

"Do you know why YGlnargle'blah is awake?" Madeline asked.

"He's awake? Aw shoot. I was worried he'd notice me leaving. He's like... think of a really protective grandfather. He used to walk the world and get it on with hot scaly chicks back in the day, most of us are descended from him. Then that Konol guy, the new god, did his thing and YGlnargle'blah had to go to the aether. So I think maybe YGlnargle'blah finally came looking for me. Man, I'm in so much trouble."

"No so much," Zuula said. "You dead now. But wait, more blood of yours is around."

"The little nippers? Yeah, they're cuties. Even if some of them have... urg... hair."

"What will he do if he comes through the dolmen circle?" Garon asked.

"Who, YGlnargle'blah? He can't. Not until the walls are way thinner and Konol's all the way dead. But I guess he can stand on the edge and yell until I come back."

"Okay, dat not add up," Zuula said. "Zuula definitely had visions that humans be wiped out in a couple days, here. Mediocre old one standing on t'reshold and being cranky not do dat."

"If not the old one, then perhaps something else?" Threadbare asked. "What could kill everyone here in a day?"

They thought.

Thanks to Threadbare's noblesse oblige boosting their wisdom, they didn't have to think too hard.

"This village, which recently rebelled against the Crown? And killed every garrison member who didn't run? And revealed their forbidden religious beliefs for all to see?" Garon said, flapping his wings. "Oh lordy, the army's on its way."

"I still have a question," Fluffbear squeaked.

"What?" Threadbare turned to her, and everyone else glanced over.

"What's a paladin?"

*****

A little later, the group came upstairs to the church. Smoke filled the air, and through the open doors they could see a burning pile of robes and fezzes. The fish children sat glumly around it, watching their tea party stuff burn. The now-regularly-clothed ex-cultists were standing around in small groups, talking. All save Marva, who was sitting on a stone bench, with two of the little fish children curled up next to her, sleeping. Threadbare could tell they were asleep by the way their eyes didn't glow.

"Hello sir," Marva cleared her throat as Threadbare walked out, cleaned from the fight. Immediately all eyes shifted to him. He coughed into one paw, nervously, as his "Work It Baby" skill shot up to its maximum level.

"Ah, hello. I apologize for fooling you with the dummy."

"No, no, it's all right. We talked it over, and we're just glad you showed us the truth. That *man*—" Marva snarled the word, "—tricked us all."

"Oh. Well, yes. Um... there's no easy way to say this. We think the army's coming to kill everyone here."

"We know." Marva rocked her fishbabies.

"You do?" Madeline asked. "Why you still heah, then?"

"We have nowhere to go. This is our home, and all we know is fishing. No other settlement would offer aid to people who used to be cultists, and with the kingdom as shrunken as it is, there's no civilized place to hide. The wars ground everyone down. And we'd die in the wilds, if we tried that. Assuming the army just let us go."

Threadbare considered. He turned to his little group of toys. "Are they right?"

"Yeah," Zuula said. "King not hesitate to wipe out villages. Taylor's Delve proof of dat, and wasn't any cult shenanigans involved."

"The army will mow through this town like a scythe through wheat," Garon said. "Most of these guys are level eight or under. I mean, we're not much farther than that, after that fight, but we've got jobs and golem advantages over them."

"Golem advantages." Threadbare rubbed his chin. "Marva, I saw a lot of treasure on that boat below. Are there any reagents and crystals in there?"

"Why, yes. The trade mostly dried up since Catamountain closed, but we used to be quite the black market hub back in the day." The middle-aged fishwife smiled. "We donated everything we had to the... society... but nobody was an enchanter so it went unused."

"I see." Threadbare said. "You have nowhere to run. How would you like to fight?"

"Fight for what?" Marva said. "Our pastor's dead. We have no one to lead us."

"You do," said Zuula, standing her full eight inches tall. "Bend your knee and swear, and Dreadbear save you all!" Then she went downstairs to smash open barrels full of loot from the boat, because she'd been right about barrels, dammit.

The ex-cultists muttered. They discussed. And in the end, they decided, they had nothing left to lose.

One by one, with more trickling in from the rest of the town, including most of the folk who assumed they'd be slaughtered along with the cultists, the people gathered to place their hope and their dreams in the paws of one small teddy bear.

And on that day, Dreadbear, Lord of Outsmouth, first of his name, swore in subject after subject and gained three ruler levels.

He'd need them, for the ordeal ahead.

CECELIA'S QUEST 3: FIRST ENGAGEMENT

"Good of you to finally join us, Dame Ragandor," the half-orc said. Heavyset and clad in white armor that had once been pristine but was marred with countless scratches and nicks, the green woman's face could have been marble for all the emotion it showed.

"Thank you. The rangers delayed us—"

"Your sergeant has already filled me in on that and I wasn't asking you for excuses anyway."

Cecelia felt her cheeks tighten. They'd told her the CO of Fort Bronze was a hardass. Her father had warned her she'd find people in the military that would be rude to her on purpose, to test her, and that she'd have to find a balance between sticking up for herself and letting stuff go.

So instead of stammering or apologizing or fussing like the old, weak Celia would have done, Cecelia stood there at attention, keeping her eyes fixed on the General in charge of the Eastern Front.

General Mastoya sighed and rose, looking out the window. Her hair clicked together, the fingerbones braided into it rattling. She was the first Knight that Cecelia had ever seen with long hair.

Well, besides her father, at any rate, but when you got that high a level in all those classes, you more or less made your own rules.

"You're greener than I am," Mastoya said out the window, looking into the courtyard. "But I'm supposed to teach you how to be a proper officer AND run a war at the same time. I don't like that."

Cecelia stayed silent. It stretched on, on enough that she eventually thought it safe to speak. "Why not, Ma'am?"

"Because it's pointless." Mastoya turned to face her, scorn written into every scar on her face. "You're going to grow up and be a queen.

You're not going to have an officer's career, or troops to look after, or have to worry about whether or not the enemies are tunneling under you right now, or where your next meal's coming from. Officer? Bah. First you'll have to convince me you're not just daddy's little girl out playing at toy soldiers."

"It's precisely because I'm going to grow up to be a queen," Cecelia said. "How can I ask people to fight, or even to die for me, if I don't know what that involves? What kind of queen would ask her people to do something she wouldn't?"

"Go on."

"I won't have an officer's career, but the wars will come regardless so I might as well know how to fight them. I won't have specific troops to look after because I'll have a nation full of subjects to look after. And our enemies will always try to undermine me, and I'll always worry about my next meal because we're putting so much stress on the farms and not enough on the fat nobles that we're one bad harvest away from a famine."

"Ha!" Mastoya seemed to like the "fat nobles" dig.

"And as far as toy soldiers go..." Cecelia looked away, and sighed. "You know, when I was a little girl and first started adventuring, I animated my toys. And they fought for me. But I never threw them away, or let them get ripped up to the point I couldn't mend them. We were a team. But I always knew they weren't PEOPLE."

A lump rose in her throat. There had been one exception, but now wasn't the time, and she forced that lump down. "But I grew up, and I put aside childish things." She closed her eyes, pushed the burning house, pushed her grandfather's bruised face from her memory. "People are not toys. They never will be toys to me. I'm not the little girl I used to be." She opened them again, in control of herself once more. "My father saw to that. And as you're sworn to him, I certainly hope you have faith in his methods."

Mastoya was nodding now. The scorn had faded from her face... mostly.

"Well, nothing can make or break you like family. I should know that. I owe everything I am to my father, as well. Well, that and surviving the barn fire that was my mother. Fucking green bitch." Mastoya barked laughter. "Guess the apple doesn't fall far from the rotten tree."

"I'm sorry. The only half-orc woman I ever knew was a good mother"

"Would have been nice to have that kind of mom," Mastoya said. "Ah well. The past is past. All right, Dame Ragandor, you'll have your shot."

Mastoya settled into her chair, and pulled out a handful of scrolls. "The Town's name is Outsmouth. Not too far from where I grew up, and about the same kind of shithole. Small place, about six or seven hundred people. Only reason they're important is because they supply about half of the fish we eat in this valley, and they aren't as dependent on field hands, so we can levy troops faster than we can elsewhere. Easy life, right? Hard as hell for even country bumpkins to fuck up. So of course they went and started a fucking unsanctioned cult."

"Daemons or old ones?"

"Excuse me?"

"It's probably not going to be djinn because we don't have a history of that here, so of the known cult types we're probably dealing with daemons or old ones."

"It's old ones," Anise said, from the doorway. Mastoya jumped, and her face darkened.

Cecelia closed her eyes. "Hello, Anise."

"Inquisitor Layd'i," Mastoya ground out. "So nice of you to join us."

Movement behind her, then Cecelia clenched her teeth as two strong, thin hands descended to grip her shoulders, thumbs rubbing gently against her spine. "I simply couldn't stay away. Not after your messenger gave me your eloquent summons. And since the rest of me is attached to my ass, I brought it as well, I hope you don't mind?"

"There are days I do." Mastoya said.

Cecelia opened her eyes.

"It's an old one cult," Anise said. "The worst kind. At least half the town's converted, which means the settlement is beyond saving."

"Really." Cecelia had her doubts, given the source of the information.

"Really, Dame." Mastoya surprised her. "A cult like this gets a foothold this size, there's no saving it. It'll hurt us for years until the area's safe enough to resettle, but we have to put the entire town to the sword."

"We're one bad harvest away from famine," Cecelia said, softly. "And it's only half the town corrupted…"

"Half that we know about," Mastoya said, sighing, and pulling a bottle out from her desk. She bit the cork off, spat it out, and took a slug. "And insidious. Pacifying them's no good. Even if we had the scouts to vet them, even if we COULD spare the scouts to vet them, cultists can fiddle with their status screens. They can hide their information. I'm sure you know all about that."

"Actually I don't. I'm not a cultist."

Mastoya's eyes widened, and flicked to Anise. "But your father—" She started, then stopped, looking over Cecelia carefully. "Huh. Not what I expected."

"You didn't let your mother limit you," Cecelia said, "So why should

I let my father limit me?" Anise's hands tensed on her shoulders, just for a second. Then they withdrew. The girl kept her sigh of relief silent.

"Well, nobody's perfect," Anise said, cheerfully. "Anyway, I hate to interrupt your bonding, but there's genocide to plan."

"The Inquisitor is right," Mastoya said. "Much as I hate it, there's tentacles involved. There will be abominations, things that should not be, weird magic, and lots of sanity damage involved."

"Yes. Daemons just want to show people the folly of virtue and torment the weak until they either get stronger or perish so that they stop sucking down resources," Anise said, matter-of-factly. "The Old Ones want to corrupt Generica, inserting their own reality and overwriting ours. Unlike daemons, who are currently proving they can co-exist peacefully with mortals in Cylvanian society, old ones and their spawn have no place in a sane and reasonable land."

"If they win, if they even get enough of a foothold here in Cylvania, we're dead or worse," Mastoya sighed, taking another slug of drink. The smell made Cecelia's eyes water. "I hate it, but everyone in that town has to die."

"There's really no other way?" Cecelia asked, not caring if it made Mastoya think less of her.

It didn't seem to. The half-orc's eyes were sad and old, as she gazed at her future queen. "No. Which is why I'm assigning you to this. You are your father's daughter, and if you want to be a good queen, mercy alone won't cut it. You have to be able to bring down the fist, not just offer the open palm."

"My father told you that, didn't he? It's something he'd say."

Mastoya snorted alcohol, coughed. "Yeah." She poked a crumpled scroll at the edge of the desk. "Don't get me wrong, his charisma buff is nice, but..."

"Yeah." Her father's Noblesse Oblige was a definite help, when it came to dealing with other people. There really was no excuse for rudeness.

So they sat in the commander's quarters, and talked about how best to kill every civilian in a town really not far from where Cecelia grew up.

She was polite, she was attentive, she took orders well, and at the end of it after she was dismissed she went to the nearest privy and vomited until she could vomit no more.

This was it.

Everything her father had been training it for, everything she'd been trained to do, was leading up to this point. If she did it, then she'd have proven to her father, to his enemies, to everyone that she was strong enough. That she'd not be a weak Queen.

All it would cost was the lives of a cult, who deserved it, and about three hundred or so people that didn't.

Cecelia cried then, on the privy floor, knowing there was no way out of it, knowing that if she refused, then General Mastoya would just send someone else. Knowing that Anise would be there, smiling, wearing her dead mother's face and looking on with approval and making sure that nobody was spared.

It sure didn't seem like shielding the weak. She thought, recalling her code. *But it definitely was smiting traitors. And obeying the King.*

And when she was done crying, she washed her face, stared at her short, frizzy hair in the mirror, and wet it down until it stayed. She'd shave it all off after this, go bald like many of the more fervent soldiers in the army did.

It would be less trouble, when it was all gone.

*****

Reason clanked and clattered, gears groaning as it pushed through the mud. The rains of early spring had been harsh in this part of the valley, and the roads around here were more of a suggestion than anything else.

Behind her, two hundred troops followed in silence.

They weren't the best. They were what General Mastoya could spare from the eastern forts. And they mostly had to come back alive, or even that amount would cause serious problems down the road.

"Most of them are somewhere around fifth to tenth level," Mastoya had said. "Conscripts with a little training, remeffs, the usual lot that the dwarves would eat for breakfast if we threw them into the direct line of fire. This will be good for their experience, probably level them a few times if everything goes right. They can handle sword and shield and crossbow, and that's enough for a bunch of tentacle cultists. But that won't be enough to handle any spawn or shit they call up. That's where you and your lieutenants come in."

Riding on their steeds, her knights kept pace alongside the ten squads. Mastoya had kept the four most well-trained members of her cadre for herself, to shore up the shortage of elites against the dwarves. But Cecelia had been able to get Graves, and Kayin, and Renick, so she was satisfied. Renick was a sturdy fighter who could take a serious beating, and the other two had useful non-knightly abilities.

She also had two royal wizards, a smattering of low-level clerics of Ritaxis to keep their units healed, and a handful of very jumpy, very new scouts who had somehow survived the rangers and made it to the front in one piece.

And also *her*. Cecelia frowned through the vision slit, at Inquisitor Anise's green-clad form, strolling along tirelessly, hands in her pockets, smiling at the countryside and the empty shacks they passed on the muddy road. Even the mud didn't seem to touch her, as if it loathed even being near the woman-shaped thing.

"Movement to the left!" The caller bellowed, and the column ground to a halt. Shouts, the whir of a few arrows, then after a minute one of her scouts ran into view, panting.

"Spotters, ma'am! Got one but more escaped!" the wind whispered in her ear.

"Good work," she said, through the magic mouth she'd slapped on Reason. "We'll catch up with the escapees in short order. We know where they're going."

The scout saluted with pride, then jogged back to his flank.

Then they came to an area where the road wasn't. Someone had done a number on the surrounding marsh trees here, toppling and filling the area with logs and fallen foliage.

"What's to the left of us?" She asked.

The Scout's Whisper came in quickly. "The marsh gets worse. Sucking mud and blackflies."

She looked right and didn't have to look far. The lakeshore was right there. No way through that didn't involve water, and it looked like logs had been toppled there, too.

Cecelia gnawed her lip. "Every fourth unit, tools out and clear the way. Everyone else, crossbows up. Cover them."

The army shuffled, as the units chosen for dirty work hauled out their entrenching tools, and started digging into the pile—

—and then a horse thundered up, as Graves bellowed. "Undead in the roadblocks! Get back! Undead in the roadblocks!"

Too late, as a few soldiers screamed, and vanished into the foliage. Bony moldering hands ripped forth, seeking the living, and the soldiers shouted, battered at the logs, and retreated. Crossbows sang and bolts flew, but Graves bellowed "Save your bolts! Stop firing! Bash them, don't shoot them!"

Then he rocked in the saddle, as something pinged off his helmet.

A bolt?

No, Cecelia realized as the first ragged volley game hissing out of the trees. *Arrows*.

"Ambush!" She yelled. "Clear the road, return fire!" She maneuvered, lifting Reason's arbalest arm up and out of the way, and bringing the wrecker sword around to bear. "I've got the barricade! Graves, get back!"

Screaming and wheeling, his horse burst skeletons asunder with furious hooves, then fled as the clanking, thundering steam knight suit charged forward, slinging the blade low and up, sending logs flying into the air and back. Old bones went with them, but more were revealed, and at least three dozen skeletons wormed their way out of their hiding place to claw and scrabble at Reason's legs.

And all the while, arrows hissed past her, to fall on her troops. *Her* troops!

This wasn't how battles were supposed to go. Fortunately her knights were there to keep her soldiers from panicking. "Wounded fall back!" Renick shouted. "First rank, shields up, shield wall! Second rank, form up and return fire! Leave the bones to the Captain!"

It still felt strange, to be called that. But she put it from her mind, as she brought the wrecker blade down on the skeletons. They couldn't hurt her armor, not beyond the occasional '1' from a lucky crit, though the ones clambering up her back were worrisome. Groaning and creaking came from back there, as they tore at the seams in the housing and tried to tug at the smokestacks, and she winced as the stoker belt stuttered on its cylinders for a second.

Only a second, as suddenly the scrabbling thinned.

"Command Undead, get off of her!" She heard Graves shout. **"Command Undead, get off of her!"** he repeated, until the noise was gone and she thought Reason's back was clear.

She didn't know where the hell a bunch of old ones cultists had gotten a necromancer, but she was glad she'd brought one of her own.

Then there were more shouts to the rear, and she smiled. She'd gambled with that little trap, and now it had paid off.

After what seemed like an eternity, but was probably only a few minutes, it was done. With the destruction she'd wreaked on the skeletons and the makeshift roadblock in general, the way was clear again.

She was tempted to press on... but... she turned, rotating the steam knight suit to look at her troops. Shaken, still firing into the trees, jumpy...

Cecelia watched a bit, saw no return fire. "Cease fire!" She ordered.

Silence stretched, broken by sobbing behind her. "Form a perimeter, regroup!" She ordered, and the sergeants echoed the commands down the line. Graves spurred his horse to fall in next to her, as she clanked back north.

"Old bones, looks like they emptied a cemetery," Graves shouted up at her. "Still did for three casualties."

"See that they're properly stowed on the dead cart," Celia said. "There's a necromancer running around and I don't want them used against us."

"Yes Ma'am." He spurred his horse back to the front.

Cecelia came to a whistling stop, peering down at the smoldering cart, full of barrels and boxes and labeled 'supplies.' Several of the barrels had been pushed out and were burst open, showing absolutely nothing inside save for emptiness. Just the way she'd ordered them set up.

Renick stood guard over a bloody man in a brown robe. Not far, in the woodline, the soldiers she'd hidden in the cart chopped at a field of squirming tentacles, hewing them down hack by ichorous hack.

"Worked brilliantly, ma'am," Renick said. "They went for the cart, our guys went for them. There's a couple more dead past the tentacle field but the rest escaped."

"Burn the bodies," Celia commanded.

"And the prisoner?"

Cecelia stared at the man, who stared back. "I'm not afraid of you!" he shouted, then shrieked as Renick kicked him.

"I know," Cecelia said. "That's why we're here today. Inquisitor?"

"Yes?" Said the thing, and Cecelia closed her eyes. She'd been half hoping Anise wasn't here. "See if he knows anything useful then render justice."

"Of course, Captain," Anise purred as she came into view from behind Cecelia, and knelt down by the captive. Cecelia bit her lip and moved into the woods, searching and doing her best to ignore the man's screams.

Renick followed. "Ma'am? We haven't secured this side yet."

"I know. That was our scout's job. He didn't sound out, so—"

"There!" Renick shouted, dismounting and running over to a crumpled form." With a heavy heart, Cecelia recognized the scout who had waved to her, not ten minutes ago.

And suddenly she was breathing, fighting a panic attack, trying to get steady.

"He's dead. Throat's torn. Something chewed it," Renick said, glancing around into the marsh trees, greaves sinking into the mud.

"Bring his corpse. We'll have Graves talk to him," Cecelia decided. "And we'll bring him home with the others, see he gets a decent burial. We're not savages," she said, trying to ignore the screams behind her as Anise 'questioned' the prisoner.

Fifteen minutes later, as the shock of battle faded, and the army was reassembled into a marching order, Graves came up, rubbing his head.

"I'm going to need to get into the claret if you keep needing necromancer spells, here. My sanity hasn't had this much of a workout in a while."

"I make no promises," Cecelia said, lowering her voice. "Did he have anything to say?"

"When the ambush started he got drawn off a bit by snipers. Then something small dropped on him from the trees and started chewing his neck. While he was trying to get it off, the snipers charged him."

"Something small."

"He says that he got his hands on it at one point, just before the snipers dog-piled him. He says he felt wood and cloth."

"Not bone?"

"No."

Cecelia shook her head. "The townsfolk. It has to be. We're not up against cultists, but the rest of them who know they're going to die as well. Gods dammit."

"If it's any consolation, skeletons are a weak spell. Level five."

"That's something. Although this guy's neck was torn…"

"No, it's probably a trick. The first thing I thought of were vampires. But no, the marks are all wrong. And way too small. Besides, we haven't had those in Cylvania since the Seven sealed Count Joculah's dungeon years ago."

"True." She glanced through the visor up at the sun, still high in the sky. "Wouldn't make sense to see vampires in the daytime anyway. Not that wood and cloth things ripping throats makes sense, either. Unless they've got an animator, too…"

"They do," Anise said, stepping in from behind Cecelia. The girl shut her eyes, and let the frustration surge through her. That was the only downside to Reason, sneaky assholes like the inquisitor could sneak up on her at will. "Someone calling herself Annie Mata."

"That's almost as dumb as your alias," Cecelia told her.

Anise merely smiled. "Evidently she's a servitor of Dreadbear, a mighty necromancer. He's seized power in the town."

"Uh huh." Graves said. "Mighty. I'm thinking not so much on that. There was some decent resistance on those skellies when I ordered them, but not anything I'd call mighty."

"He's a king of some sort, too."

THAT made Graves shut up. Cecelia's eyes went wide. "You're certain?"

"No, and that bothers me." Anise's eyes blazed with sudden fury. "The man I questioned didn't fear death!"

"Soulstones." Graves said, instantly. "I'd bet my last coin on it."

Cecelia's breath whistled in her nose. "Either that or he was happy to go to his old one. We're dealing with cultists here, remember."

Kayin came galloping up, with her helm off. "Orders, Captain?"

"What?"

"The troops are getting restless."

Cecelia closed her eyes.

She was beginning to see why her father had made her grind her willpower before she came to her first command. She couldn't leave people alone for twenty minutes, before they started asking her to do things.

"We advance," she decided, bringing Reason around to stomp forward again. "Necromancer or no, animator or no, our goal remains the same."

"And this Dreadbear who's leading them now?"

Cecelia passed the dead cart, with the scout now on it, staring at her with accusing, unmoving eyes. She looked away.

These were the first who had died in her service. They wouldn't be the last, and she hated it. "He's a traitor too. He dies with the rest of them..."

CECELIA'S QUEST 4: THE FALL OF OUTSMOUTH

"Eye for Detail."

Cecelia stared at the town. What little of it she could see, with that ten foot wall in the way, and a large, wooden gate slicked with moss and mud along its bottom. This was probably the first time it had been closed in decades.

"It's an animi," she confirmed to her command staff. "Whoever their animator is, she's smart."

"Probably only one animator of significance, unless she's got an apprentice or two. That's something," Renick said. Animator was one of the harder unlocks, it required either a lot of study of magical theory from pre-change books, or apprenticeship to an animator willing to teach the fundamentals.

Cecelia lifted her head, and Reason's helm rose as well as she considered the top of the wall. It had a black-robed watcher with a bow visible every five feet or so. At least two hundred people were on the stockade, waiting for trouble to start. "Why so many archers?"

"It's a small peasant town," Graves said. "Bowfishing is a thing, and they'll supplement their catch with whatever they can hunt. Some of them will have just formalized it, that's all."

"And it's not hard to get someone passable in the weapon skill and job in a few days," Renick said. "True, most'll be five or under, but the same goes for our guys. And that doesn't take into account the craftsman and oddball jobs some of them will have."

"Which some of our people have too, so in the end it should balance out," Kayin said. "I'm more concerned by what I'm not seeing and what

I'm not hearing."

"Which is?"

"Dark ominous chanting ripping at our souls, weird monsters hitting us from the sides, and occult graffiti everywhere. You know, everything you'd expect to see when you're fighting an Old Ones cult."

"The Dark Chant is a level five skill," Anise said. "Perhaps their cult is young, yet?" Even she didn't sound convinced.

"No. No, a cult of this size you're at least looking at a few eights and tens. With someone near double that leading them," Graves said. "That's, ah, what we were briefed on in my, uh, old profession." He coughed.

Cecelia gnawed her lip. "Something isn't adding up here. They're acting too... sane. We need more intelligence." She took a deep breath, released it. It was time to put more men into danger. "We have three scouts left, yes?"

"Yeah," Renick confirmed. "A seven, a six with some oddball support jobs, and a four."

She winced. "Tell the four to stay with the army and keep an eye on that lake. Send the seven and six around on long recon. Swing wide east around the town and tell me what's happening at the other gates."

"That'll take—"

"At least half a day," Cecelia said. "I know. I'm a scout too, remember?"

"I'll pass on your orders to the scouts and go with them," Anise decided, and was off before anyone could say anything.

"Where exactly is she in our command structure?" Renick asked, rubbing his face with one gauntlet.

"Way, way above it," Cecelia said. "But unable to countermand my orders in the field on military matters."

"Well, that's something at least."

"Half a day means that it'll be night before they get back," Kayin pointed out.

"I know. But we've got enough darkspawn-enchanted helmets among the units that we should be able to see any trouble they throw at us. And night opens up possibilities for us, too." She moved Reason's visor down to look at Kayin, and lowered the voice coming from her magic mouth. "You were an assassin. Think you can infiltrate that town?"

Kayin's cold smile wasn't entirely devoid of charm. "You know that dead cultist's robe? I picked it up and washed it, just in case you asked that question."

"I'm a little unclear on how Assassin works, besides the stabby bits," Cecelia confessed. "Do you have any useful stealth tricks for the situation?"

"That's more burglar and scout," Kayin said. "We're good at bullshitting our way past people and being unobtrusive. Though my stealth skill is good enough that night should be all I need. Probably the best way to use me is to launch your assault, and I'll use the chaos to slip in. Question is; what do you want me to do when I'm in there?"

"I figured that would be self-evident, given the name of your old job," Graves grinned.

"No, you're right Kayin," Cecelia said. "We have no idea who the cult leader is, or if this Dreadbear guy is him, or what their command structure's like. We need intelligence. Not the attribute kind, the military kind."

"We've got an imp wrangler, don't we?" Renick asked.

"Good thinking. Let's check while we're waiting on the scouts."

Cecelia got clear of eyesight from the wall, hunkering Reason down behind a copse of trees, and decanted. She took a breath, as she felt her pools slowly start to refill again. That was the downside to Steam Knight armor, it shut off the slow, natural regeneration that every living being got. Raising thy blade cast in steam and steel meant awesome power, at the cost of needing either someone backpacking you to keep it going, or carefully rationing what you had.

And speaking of rations, she was hungry as hell, and more than a little thirsty. "Let's have lunch while we wait."

The actual rations of the army had been distributed among the lower-level footsoldiers' packs. They only had a couple of days worth, but they weren't that far from the fort, and the expectation was that they'd have plenty to eat once the town was dead.

Once the town and everyone in it is dead, Cecelia tried, and failed to push the thought from her mind as she ate her ration loaf. *Dead, because we're going to massacre them.*

"We're going to have to kill everyone here because if we don't the old ones will eat everyone, innocents or no," Cecelia reminded herself.

Graves took it as a question. "Yes, I'm afraid so. It isn't our fault. They were dead either way once the cult grew too big for the locals to stop it. Me? I prefer the version of them being dead that doesn't end up with me in an elder god's belly."

"But it isn't their fault either. The people who aren't cultists, I mean."

"Yeah. It fucking sucks," Renick said, looking at her soberly. "Which is why we need to win the wars, so we can concentrate on policing people and making sure it never gets bad enough that a cult grows this big ever again."

Cecelia thought it over, as she finished her loaf. There were some flaws in that idea, but she didn't think the knights would be willing to listen to them.

Things will be different when I am queen, she decided. She desperately hoped that was true.

"You called for me, Captain?" The imp wrangler bustled up. A large man with a slightly-haunted look and cages strapped to his back, he wore the red sign of an approved cultist on his black robe.

"Yes. What have we got, impwise?"

He hauled off three cages and showed her. Three black, scaly little things with wings and overlarge eyes stared back at her, licking their needle-like rows of teeth and grasping at the bars of their cages with tiny clawed fingers. They were somewhere between a bat and a housecat in size.

"Trained and disciplined. Aren't you, you little vermin?" sneered the cultist as he rapped his knuckles on one cage. The imp inside cowered and shook.

"That's enough," said Cecelia. "So they'll obey orders and take messages?"

"Yes ma'am. They can manage about five sentences, the shorter the better. Beyond that gets unreliable."

"Can you make more?" Cecelia asked.

"Plenty of birds around here," He fished around on his belt and held up a slingshot. Nostalgia stirred within Cecelia, and she shoved it aside as the sanctioned cultist continued. "I can do one, maybe two a day if I get access to the grog rations, but it wipes me out for anything else. The sanity cost is about a hundred each. And they won't be as trained or disciplined. It takes about a week to work the kinks out of any pact."

"Is that how it works?" Kayin asked, surveying the little fearful demons.

"Oh yeah. The basic pact just gets them manifested, and the basic directives installed into their new forms. Then you want to spend about a week or two hammering out the paradoxes, and ensuring that the vows are all locked down, and the loopholes are sealed. You do NOT want a demon running free without those, even something as simple as a Rank One. They'll find tons of ways to twist your core commands, completely exploit the letter of the pact, and do things just to spite you. Even if it screws them over, as well."

"How boned am I if I carry two of them on me?" Kayin asked. "Say in some padding under a robe, while I'm trying to keep them a secret."

"Eh, they're prone to weird noises when they get surprised." He hauled off and whacked a cage with a stick, and all three of the imps shouted and squeaked, warbling in weird, repellent tones that were like birdsong only oilier.

"Right. Give me two in cages then," Kayin said. "I'll stash them someplace accessible when I breach."

"Breach?"

"Need to know stuff," Cecelia told the imp handler. "Tell her how to use them then go back to the rear and summon another. Work on training it, I'll send word if I need a message sent back to headquarters."

"Yes Ma'am," he pounded his chest in a salute, then pulled Kayin off to the side.

"What now?" Renick asked her, as he walked back alongside. Graves followed on her other flank, eyes peeled as he watched the swamp around them.

"Now we wait. Depending on what the scouts say, we either move at dawn or fort up for the night."

"The troops will get restless," Renick pointed out.

"Right." Cecelia sighed. It was hard work managing this many barely-trained soldiers. "Put them to work building camp while we've still got daylight. Plenty of trees, and hey, there's that pile the cultists already knocked down for us back up the road. I won't say no to free logs." Her scalp itched, and she ran her gauntlet through her hair, frizzy again in the moistness of the marsh. Yeah, it'd be time to shave it off soon, just lose it forever. Maybe she'd find a good barber and make that style permanent.

*****

"They're stalling us," Anise announced, fading out of the early-dusk shadows. Behind her, the mid-level scout staggered into camp, and threw her a sloppy salute. One arm was bandaged, and his armor was torn.

"Report," Cecelia commanded him, sparing a second to nod at Anise.

"All's quiet on the eastern gate. They only have a few people watching it."

"How's the terrain between here and there?" Renick asked.

"Bad. It's mostly two-foot-deep water between the two gates, with lots of overgrowth and marsh plants."

"No good for a sortie then," Cecelia decided.

"Good for my purposes, though." Kayin nodded. "I'll go get changed."

"At the south gate there's people leaving. They're moving in groups. All sorts, and children are with them. No robes."

"They're evacuating the townsfolk who aren't cultists," Cecelia said, surprised.

"Or that's what they want us to think," Anise said. "This could be a trick, and they'll come around on our flank."

"Evacuating them where?" Renick said. "There's nothing but wilds out this way, ever since that one mining town was wiped out by rebels."

Cecelia felt a lump rise in her throat. She looked away, letting the lie slide. Telling the truth of the matter wouldn't help the situation at all here, and the guilt weighed heavy on her.

"There's more," the scout said. "Every group of them has a little stuffed toy or two following along with them. Some are carrying things."

"What?" Cecelia stood upright, so fast that her armor rattled. "You're sure?"

"Yes Ma'am."

"They're going to take a chance on surviving the wilds." Cecelia said, her mouth going dry. "With guardians along that don't sleep, and can take on things five times their size."

"For what, an hour or two?" Renick frowned. "Animi don't last that long. You told us that."

"They're not animi. They're golems. Those families are being escorted by golems. Little golems that think and learn and love their children, and will fight to the death for them." Celia swallowed, hard. "I wondered where he'd gone, after father told me grandfather escaped his prison. Now I know. Oh gods—" she said, putting two and two together and getting five-hundred-and-ninety-seven. "—he's even calling himself Dreadbear, to hide his real identity. He's hiding here somewhere, talking to them through magic mouth on that poor little teddy. It all makes sense now!"

"Ma'am?" The Scout asked.

"Anything else to report?"

"No ma'am. But the Inquisitor made it farther than I did. You should really hear her report, it's concerning."

"Very well. Dismissed. Go talk to the clerics and rest up."

"Aye ma'am." He thumped his chest and was off.

"I wasn't ignoring you," Cecelia said, turning to Anise. "But he was pretty badly torn up, so I wanted to hear his report first so he could go get treated. What happened?"

"They have scouts too. Not very good ones," Anise shrugged. "But good enough to kill our senior scout. But that doesn't matter, what does matter, is a hill about three miles out of town. There's a circle of stones up there, and the old one linked to them is waking up. They're ferrying sacrifices out there. Children, as far as I can tell."

Cecelia's breath hissed between her teeth. "In my father's name I order you to tell the truth. You're certain of this?"

Anise looked annoyed. "I'm positive. Children-sized figures in robes arrive by boat, and are accompanied up to the dolmens by people who are presumably their parents, based on the weeping embraces and pathetic goodbyes they get. I watched for a full hour, as closely as I dared. Not a single child came back down from the hill, and every time one went up there the old one's power grew."

"They're summoning him." Renick said, horror filling his large features. "They're stalling us here so they can summon him fully into this world."

"Something doesn't add up," Graves said. "Why are they letting the uninvolved people leave? To old one cultists, those would be perfect sacrifices."

"Grandfather." Cecelia sighed, settling back down. "It's because he's working with them."

She didn't see Anise twitch in surprise, didn't see how the woman-thing's face settled back into its usual mask, as Cecelia continued. "It was hushed up, but my Grandfather was a rebel. He escaped custody a few years back, and now he's here."

Graves' jaw dropped. "Wait. Wait wait whoa, you're talking about the father of Amelia Gearhart. The guy who taught the hero everything she knew, before..."

"Yes. Caradon."

"Well. Shit." Renick summed up. "There's no way that guy isn't a level twenty-five tier two. We need to call in reinforcements. Get some Dragon Knights in—"

"No," Cecelia said. "I know my grandfather. He hates the Crown, but he won't end the world. He's a good man, just deluded. If he's shown himself to the cult, it's only to save people. Which means that he'll try to intervene to stop the old one from being summoned, as soon as everyone's safe."

"Your grandfather committed treason against the Crown," Anise said. "The King's commands are clear when it comes to traitors. Can you face him and fulfill your duty, Dame Ragandor?"

Cecelia narrowed her eyes, as she gazed at the thing wearing her mother's face. "I have not forgotten my father's lessons on the weakness of mercy. But my father's promise to me stands firm, and we shall both honor it. If he is here I will capture him. You shall not hurt him and you shall assist me in this task to the best of your ability."

"I know full well my place in things, Cecelia," Anise said, bowing her head. "And I made my own promise to you, do you remember that?"

"That you would help me become who I needed to be," Cecelia said.

"And you have, so deal with it. Now go, and tell the unit commanders to make ready for the assault. Renick, go with her and sort out the details. It's going to be frontal, as soon as the night's fully upon us."

The two departed. Graves remained, looking at their retreating backs, then over at the town. "Why? If your grandfather's going to backstab the cult in the end..." One gauntlet rose to rub his beard. "But we don't know that for sure, do we?" He answered his own question. "No. It's possible he was driven mad by cultists, or they've managed to trick him."

"Grandfather was smart but gullible." Cecelia sighed. "I realize that now. We can't take the chance they're stalling us, and this cult is sacrificing kids. It's pretty clear-cut who the villains are. It'll be painful but we need to assault them head on, now, and blitz through the town so we can get to the dolmens to stop the ritual."

"And the uninvolved townsfolk? The ones fleeing into the hills?"

"Not our priority," Cecelia said, feeling a great weight shift from her. "If they're not fighting us and they're clearly not the cult, then they're not traitors. We'll inform the general and she might send someone to hunt them down. Eventually." *And their blood won't be on MY hands,* she thought.

"Even if there are cultists among them secretly? Old one cults are insidious," Graves pointed out, with his quiet logic.

"We know where their old one's summoning site is now. What are the odds there are two of those in this valley? We just lock it down or destroy it and render their religion a moot point. Between you and the wizards I'm pretty sure we can figure out something."

Graves nodded. "All right. To tell the truth that sits better with me anyway." He rubbed his beard.

He really is a good man, Celia reflected. "What's your first name?" She asked, suddenly. "You came in just after I did, and nobody ever used it. I don't think we really properly knew it."

"Oh, uh," Graves said, lowering his gauntlet. "That's because I don't use it very much. Herbert. I'm Herbert Graves. Why do you ask?"

"You're going to have my back tonight, and we're going to kill our way through a lot of people who really, really deserve it." Cecelia smiled. "It only seems polite."

Graves nodded, eyes glittering as he studied her smile. "Listen. If we get separated... try to keep me in view, okay?"

"Well, yes. Steam Knights need support to guard their flanks and rear, that's the first lesson we learned."

"No, it's not that," Graves said, shifting. "I mean if the worst happens, you won't have long to get to the soulstone. Spirits last the longest around their bodies, but we're talking minutes, here. It's tied to willpower, so you should be good, but uh... You can travel a bit as a newly-dead spirit, but that cuts it down by a lot, the farther you go. I'm sorry. I'm sorry to ruin the moment, this is morbid, and—"

"Herbert," She smiled, and he shut up. "It's all right. Come on, let's get the army straightened out, we've got a battle to win. We can talk more after that."

His smile was genuine, and he thumped his breastplate with enthusiasm. "Yes Ma'am!"

"And keep that Deathsight spell of yours up. We know they have a necromancer, and I expect more surprises from that quarter..."

*****

They came for the cult in the night. They came with torches high, with shields up in the first few ranks, and with the more adept crossbowmen behind them, raining down rapid shots from their crossbows, sending the heavy bolts flying in ways that anyone without the archer job couldn't match.

The cultists returned fire from the walls, their own bows weaker but better ranged, even if their accuracy wasn't as good. They had volume, and they punished the first ranks.

Cecelia strode forward slowly in Reason, the darkspawn enchantment on her inner helm letting her see despite the uncertain light. Well, as best she could with Reason's forearm held up to shield her visor's slit. Peripheral vision she had. Forward view? Nah. But she only had to keep pace with her front lines, keep going forward until she got to the gate. Even as an animi, she was pretty certain it wasn't going anywhere.

Arrows thumped and rattled off Reason's hide, and she swallowed. Occasionally one hit with enough force to do one or two points, but overall she wasn't worried. Was happy, even. The more that came for her, the less that went for her troops. No, the gorge churning in her belly was from the fact that she was going up against people who actually wanted to kill her. She'd felt that feeling when they cut down Baron Comfort's bandits, and she was feeling it again, here. It was bad. This wasn't monsters, or beasts, or a situation where she was up against a thing following its nature. These people had made the active decision that they needed a Cecelia-shaped hole in their lives and were doing their best to make it reality.

Well. She had a thing or two to say about that. **"Mend,"** she snapped as the damage started to mount.

"To the flank! Right flank!" Renick bellowed, and she shifted.

THINGS were coming out of the lake.

"Right flank shields!" She screamed through the magic mouth. "We planned for this, people!"

You don't go up against old ones without keeping eyes on the nearby body of murky water. That was just asking to get tentacled.

"Rally Troops!" Renick shouted. "Let's send these eldritch fuckers back where they came from!"

She heard the right flank roar with approval, as their moxie got a decent buff.

Oh yeah, I can do that too. She risked an unshielded glance at the walls, found them near, and snapped her arbelest arm back up as arrows clattered off Reason's helm. "Rally Troops! The gate's right there, let's go knock that fumper down!"

Then her men were cheering, or screaming, and she didn't know because she was lifting her sword up, and charging.

"Now now dispel now!" She yelled.

"Dispel magic!" She heard over the yelling, from just behind her. Then something that could have also been a dispel magic, from further back, where the other wizard was. She'd spread them out in the battle, to make sure at least one of them survived to get within range.

At least one of them got through, because when she hit the gate, what had been augmented animated wood but was now disenchanted, ordinary, somewhat rotted mossy wood splintered and gave. She brought the sword through it in a single ponderous thrust. Then the bulk of Reason slammed into it, and it burst into fragments.

Screams from above her, and then she heard splash of liquid, and a smell filled her nose as she backed off, hastily.

Oil!

Her mentors had briefed her on this. Fire, sticky fire like Geek's fire from alchemists or oil or tar from sieges, could roast a steam knight alive in their suit.

Which is why, like most problems she'd come to, Cecelia had given a lot of thought and experimentation to finding a good solution. And in this case, the solution involved the outer layers of quilted cloth she'd sewn around Reason's helm and front. "Clean and Press!" Cecelia shouted, and sighed in relief as the first few flaming arrows clattered off of her, seconds too late.

Relief that lasted until something inhuman roared from above her. "Burninate!"

Her world became fire, and she shrieked as red numbers rolled up from Reason's components. She backed off further, hunkered down, and started hissing the spells of her backup plan. **"Distant Animus blanket! Invite Blanket!"**

Rustling came from below her, as the fire-quenching blanket she'd commissioned from the royal enchanters wormed its way out of the cork-stoppered compartment she'd put it in, and crawled up Reason to smother the flames. **"Mend, mend, mend,"** she chanted, once the fires were out. Distant animus was a good ace to play, but it had a range limitation of about one foot per level. Which was more than enough to land the spell on the blanket five feet from her.

"Ricochet shot!" She heard someone call, then whipped her cheek to the side, as a lucky crit hit Reason's visor slit, bounced toward her, and collided with her helm instead of her face. *Close! Too Close!* She wanted to turn, to flee, to retreat. Instead she slammed the burning arbelest up to cover Reason's visor, gritted her teeth as the heat roiled around her, and waited.

She'd done her part here. She'd shattered the gate, and she could hear the bellowing of the troops around her as they surged to and through the wall, and the shouts and cries of combat once they were past the gate. Cecelia and Reason had given them their shot, and now it was on them to make it count.

So she knelt, letting the blanket do it work, breathing as shallowly as she could, mending the damaged parts of Reason as the flames died, falling to the fireproof blanket's embrace. *If I hadn't cleaned the oil, I'd be dead*, Cecelia knew. There would have been no way to escape Reason quickly enough.

The minutes passed, the fire died, and when Cecelia lowered her the arbelest arm, an imp crawled through the visor. "Kayin has entered the village. Everything's chaos. The dolls are in charge, cult says follow their orders. Dreadbear's a teddy bear in a voodoo outfit. They have a dragon golem and Kayin wants to know if you want it dead."

A dragon golem! Cecelia's eyes widened. She'd only ever heard about dragonfire. Never seen it in action.

Now I have, she supposed, shuddering at how close that last call had been. "Gods dammit grandfather, you nearly killed me," she croaked.

"What? What what? What?" The imp jumped up and down, boggling at her. They were generally dim, she knew, their own intelligence a reflection of the creator's own. And the imp handler hadn't impressed her overmuch in that regard.

Cecelia cleared her throat. "Tell Kayin to take out the dragon if she can. Leave Dreadbear to me." Gods, if Dreadbear was what she thought it was, she wasn't sure she could kill it. She really, really hoped she could take him alive. Get him away from Grandfather, to a safe place where she could break the little golem away from the rebel lies the old man had been teaching it.

But first things first. "Return to her with those words. Do you understand?"

"Yes yes I go!" The imp screeched and departed.

She'd heard that the higher-level officers had access to better imps, ones her father had personally made. Ones that were suited to skilled recon and intelligent enough to operate independently.

Dumb or smart, they still creeped her out.

Finally, the arrows against her slackened, and she stood, to see the shattered gates before her, and most of her army fighting inside the town. No good place for her there, so she waited, observing, for the bodies to move so she could squeeze in without trampling her own people.

And then the level-up flashed across her field of view, and she sighed. She'd hit level five steam knight, finally. **"Status, help,"** she said, and settled in to read and best think how to synergize her new tricks into her tactics.

"Ma'am!" Graves rode up, an entourage of skeletons following him. "The things from the lake were animated boats with wooden wheels nailed on. They were full of skeletons. There was something in the water croaking eldritch song supporting them, but we drove it off with concentrated fire. Renick thinks it was some kind of bard."

"Bard?" Cecelia blinked. "Seriously."

"Yes. Also, uh..." he rode in closer. "I seem to have unlocked a Tier 2 job I've never heard of."

"Really?" Academic interest fired up... then faded, as she looked to the battle raging in the town. There was a time and place to discuss this in depth, and it wasn't here. "What is it? Make it short."

"It's called Death Knight. Big on necromancy and buffing undead. And plagues and frost for no reason I can tell."

"Gods." Cecelia rubbed her face. "You're one of the few people I trust with something like this. Look, will it help you survive this battle?"

"Most definitely."

"Take it. As your current commanding officer I authorize it."

"Thank you ma'am! Yes!" he stood there for a second, helm elevated as he read the details. "Intelligence and Con? Okay, works for me. Good news is the plague stuff is only plague resistance at this level. Everything else seems manageable, nothing that the inquisitor would kill me over. Oooh, this'll help. **Bony Armor!**" Half the skeletons shivered and fell apart, wrapping around him, until his pauldrons were jawless skulls and the rest of his plate was laced in ribs.

"Cute," Cecelia said, dryly. "All right. Get Renick and the wizards and let's go get this over with."

*****

Midway through the town, as they fought the fifth batch of cultists in the burning remnants of a block of houses, Graves stiffened up. "Shit! I just got Kayin!"

What was he... oh. Oh!

"Ask her where!" Cecelia shouted, rage filling her. "We'll fumping make them pay!"

"Speak with Dead." He chanted, and Kayin's voice echoed through their minds.

"Hey Cecelia. Got the dragon, fucked up the escape. Bad assassin, no cookie."

"Where!" Cecelia said, shaking, feeling the tears burst from her eyes. "Show us where!"

"Southwest, by the church. They've got a rallying point there."

"ON ME!" Cecelia bellowed, and surged ahead, breaking Steam Knight protocol. Her friend was dead, and by the gods she'd make her killers pay.

They found her by the church, windows shattered, cultists inside firing arrows desperately at the approaching knight.

"TALK TO THE HAND!" Cecelia roared, and her arm intercepted arrow crits as she charged the building. **"STEAM SCREAM!"** she bellowed, and Reason sent a shuddering howl to the skies, trembling the stars within their firmaments. She had the hot satisfaction of seeing green numbers, big ones streak from the cultists at the windows as they shrieked, and then she was crunching through the wall, sword raised high. "Oh yeah!" She yelled, sword chopping down as blood sprayed red, red on the busted bricks.

At some point in there she unlocked the berserker class.

"Undead!" Graves called. "I'm on it... what the hell?"

Kayin yelled from her gem. "That's it! That's the thing that got me, the dragon rider!"

"Call Faia! Least Elemental! Shape Faia- shit!"

"Bitch please!" Renick roared, and then came the sound of heavy metal boots stomping through wood.

"An Emberling? Seriously?" Renick said. "Oh. Oh shit, Kayin. Sorry."

"Yeah, that's my body. The little shit got my throat," Kayin said. "It was pretty messy. You might not want to see this, Cecelia."

Finally, there was silence. Cecelia snorted snot from her nose, and blinked away tears. The fury drained from her, leaving her feeling hollow.

She wasn't sure what kind of people were insane enough to take rage as a job feature.

Then came stillness. A change in the air, nothing she could put her finger on. It was like reality shuddered. She'd felt it before, a few times.

She backed Reason out of the church, wheeled around, gasped as she saw Renick and Graves off their horses, kneeling next to Kayin's charred corpse. Her darkspawn helm showed her the pool of blood her friend had died in, in agonizing full color. It pooled around the rent stuffing and green fur of a little dragon, torn and fragmented from Kayin's successful work.

Cecelia swallowed, hard. "We need to get her to the corpse cart. And make sure their necromancer gets nowhere near her."

"Well, her spirit's with me. They won't lock her soul into a corpse, that's the important thing," Graves promised. Then he glanced west, to the shore, and frowned. "The little puppet thing had a spirit. It was like an undead sealed into a toy body."

Cecelia blinked. "What? You can do that?"

"No shit?" Kayin sounded interested.

"I've heard rumors," Graves said, muttering. "They can go into animi, but they pass on once the animi expired. Or if you're really evil you can enchant weapons and armor, make hauntblades or wraith armor."

"I could maybe stand being a knife for all eternity," Kayin mused.

But Graves was still talking. "That... that puppet was a fire elementalist, though, and I've never heard of jobs carrying through. And it was a girl's spirit that ran by me, right into the lake." He turned, surveyed the town. "And there goes another! On the edge of the shore. The dead cultists, their spirits are running into the lake."

"Soulstones," Cecelia whispered. "Soulstones don't need to breathe. They're under there somewhere." She sighed. "It would probably take days to find them. And something capable of operating underwater."

"The way is clear," Anise announced, stepping out of the shadows. "We need to stop the rite."

"Yes, of course," Cecelia was drained, so drained. The battle had been long and hard, and now she understood why the cultists hadn't feared death. "Grandfather, what have you done?" She whispered.

"Your orders, Captain?" Anise asked, hands folded behind her back, smiling.

And oh, did Cecelia hate her at that moment. But why? She

wondered. Anise was easy to blame, true, but she couldn't help what she was. And she hadn't killed Kayin.

Cecelia thought. And as she did, that sensation from earlier nagged at her mind. She'd felt something like that before, both in the Catamountain, and in the dungeon the elite knights had special access to...

"Renick, Graves," she said, carefully. "A second ago, did it feel like everything shifted? Like when we ran Daggerhall together?"

"Yeah. Yeah it did," Renick said. "I didn't think anything of it, but now that you mention it...

Cecelia gnawed her lip. "It must be Grandfather. Renick, take Kayin's body to the corpse cart, then get the army moving. Inquisitor, I assume the sacrificial site you found was *that* thing?" She pointed across the lake, to where a green glow was visible to the southwest.

"Yes." Said Anise. "I'll have the scout guide them."

"You're not going yourself?" Grave asked.

"If this strange feeling is your grandfather, I need to be there with you when you find him," Anise smiled at Cecelia. "You understand, dear."

"I know," the girl sighed. "You don't trust me one bit."

"I trust you every bit as much as you trust me." Anise's smile grew.

"That's pretty much what I just said." Cecelia confirmed, then checked her coal reserves. A bit left. Enough for the task at hand. "Stand back. If there's a dungeon it'll be in the church somewhere. I'll clear the wreckage and see what we can find."

The trapdoor they eventually uncovered, and the wooden stairs down, were too small for Reason. With a sigh, Cecelia decanted from her suit, animating it and inviting it to her party. It should be enough to stand guard over the site while they explored, but... "Kayin, do you still have a messenger imp?" she asked.

"The building I stowed them in caught on fire. Pretty sure they couldn't escape."

"Bad way to die. Not that there's a good way. Ah... sorry," Graves said. "Thoughtless of me."

"No worries," Kayin said from her soulstone. "I'm pretty much beyond offending, here. Besides, I've made too many corpses to be sensitive about my own."

"Heh. Just sit tight, we'll get to you shortly," Cecelia smiled, glad to hear her friend's spirit in good... well, spirits.

"Who are you speaking to?" Anise interrupted.

Cecelia shot Graves a glance, got one in return. "You didn't hear that?" Cecelia asked.

"Let's just focus on the job at hand." The Inquisitor descended the steps, peering around, distracted and with a hungry look on her face. "A dungeon, yessss...."

"Might want to stay silent for a bit, Kayin." Graves whispered. "Don't want that one getting ideas about you."

The cave below was relatively small, and definitely not a dungeon. It had bloodstained sand next to a cove full of dark water. There was also a small chamber down a side-passage, that led to a room with bleachers, mattresses on the grimy floor, and an unexpected shock to her sanity when Cecelia saw the kind of drawings that lined the walls. If there'd been any doubt to the righteousness of her cause, it was gone now.

But it was also empty of any kind of dungeon.

At least, she and Graves thought so until they returned to the main cave, and found Anise crouched at the water line, staring into the darkness. "Clever, clever," said the Inquisitor, a smile curving her flawless lips. "They put it underwater."

"How far?" Graves asked.

"Not far." And then Anise waded into the cold water, fading from view as she went.

Graves and Cecelia shared a look. "Invite me," she said.

One invite later, she and his remaining three skeletons, and a hastily created animus blade and shield went into the water...

...and surfaced into the light.

"Oh," Cecelia said, staring around her, at the riverbank, and the pine woods just beyond.

And there, up on a hill, was a two-story house. Cozy, hidden...

...and familiar.

Beyond the stretch of river, a narrow bit of woods, and the house, everything was foggy and unresolved. The colors were bleached and strained, and some of the trees had a translucent quality to them.

"It's new. Barely formed," Anise hissed, to their side. She paced back and forth, hands flexing, fingers grasping. "Oh this will be perfect!"

But Cecelia didn't hear her. She was too busy looking at the house, where she had been safe. Where she had been innocent once. And her eyes burned once more, as she felt her heart burn in her chest.

Here was her reckoning, she knew. The final reconciliation, one way or the other, the final challenge to overcome, to put aside childish things and become the woman her Father and her future subjects needed her to be.

And she didn't know if she was strong enough.

CECELIA'S QUEST 5: WINNING HEARTS AND MINDS

"What is this?" Graves asked.

"This was my house. This is where I grew up." Cecelia shook her head. "I was so naive back then."

Anise smiled, and said nothing.

Cecelia's voice sounded distant to her own ears. "He'll be inside. I know what he's doing, why he's doing it." She swallowed, hard. "And I'm going to march in there and tell him why it won't work, and will never work, and arrest him for treason."

"We," said Graves.

"What?"

"We'll march in there and arrest him."

Cecelia closed her eyes. "Thank you." Then she shot Anise a look, and found the thing glowering at the house. "Something wrong?"

"I thought I was done with this place. It gives me... indigestion."

"We'll get you something for that when we're done. Let's go... Inquisitor."

Cecelia led the way, and as they went, the trees loomed larger and larger.

"What is this?" Graves asked. "I didn't think there was any old growth left in the valley."

"There isn't. This is wrong. It's a perspective trick. Which means... keep an eye out for giant scarecrows."

"What?"

Then the first Raggedy Man stepped out of the trees.

"Eye for Detail," she scrutinized it as it came, arms extended, lumbering toward them in eerie silence. Covered in tattered cloth, with straw poking out the eyeholes of its massive cloth mask, it was thirty feet tall if it was an inch. Grasping fingers of wood clenched, and more sticks of wood showed through its torn pants, woven together with old rope.

"Captain?" Graves shouted, moving his skeletons in between them and the raggedy man.

"It's level seven, and weaker than our sergeants," she snorted. "Let's take it apart."

It didn't get a single hit past their shields before they knocked it to bits. Anise didn't break stride, leaving them to deal with it as she marched up the hill.

Cecelia hurried after, lips compressed in a thin line. She didn't trust her alone here. Didn't trust her, period.

That was pretty much how things had been for the last few years, it's just that there had never been anything Cecelia could do about it beyond tread as cautiously as she could around Anise. And even then, the daemon had a way about her, something that let her slip things into conversations that you caught later, and winced at.

But she was literally the devil Cecelia knew.

So for now that would have to do.

Then they were up and moving through the trees, each of them six times as tall as she remembered. But the details were off here, subtly off. Trees that she knew by heart were different, sketchy, foggy.

"Getting senile, Grandfather?" she whispered. She paused by one that he'd used to measure her every year, carved notches into as she grew. The bark was bare, and the wrong type for its species. "Birch," she murmured and remembered Mordecai, and flashed to the image of the old scout in his cell, scarred and broken, and almost lost it then.

But Anise didn't stop, and Cecelia couldn't leave her be. So she followed, and Graves kept pace alongside her.

Her house was huge, as was the workshop to the wide. She swallowed hard as she saw the black cat in the window of the shop, glowering out at her. "Pulsivar," she said, and turned her back on him. He'd lain on her back sometimes, when it rained in the night. A heavy purring weight, warm in the cold. They'd slept there that way sometimes and she'd nodded off to dreams, lulled by raindrops and the smell of his fur.

"That handle's pretty far up there," Graves said.

"It's still a door," Cecelia said, her voice raw. **"Animus. Invite door."** It opened, and she kicked it from the party, running mostly on force of habit.

The front room was empty, a simple dinner set on the table. Venison and porridge, she could smell it, and the smell hit her harder than the sight of the place did. Hurt in a way she hadn't expected.

"Pretty nice place," Graves said. "But... where are all the monsters? This is a dungeon, right?"

Cecelia looked toward Emmet, huge as two Reasons put together, and shook her head. "Wait for it."

But the giant suit of armor didn't animate as they crossed the floor, or as they passed the cheerful fireplace, with the logs popping in their merry blaze, but oddly cold.

There was no temperature differential between here and outside, she realized suddenly. *It all just sort of was.*

That struck her as odd, more than anything else she'd encountered so far. Doubts gnawed at her mind, for the first time.

"This might not be Caradon," she said, stopping abruptly before the stairs. "This... something's not right, here."

"If not him, then who?" Anise asked.

"This isn't an old man's house," she said, as she sheathed her sword and slung her shield on her back, and scrambled up the stairs, grabbing each one and boosting herself up. "It's the house as seen from a very small person's perspective. Which means..."

She got to the top, and peered down the hallway. There, at the very end, was her grandfather's room. Light spilled from under the door, and she could hear the old man humming, as he did when he sat up and worked before he went to bed every night. An old familiar melody, but she knew it for the ruse it was now. "He left you behind, didn't he, Threadbare?" She said, looking instead to her own room, darkness beneath the crack under the door. "Left you behind to stall me, while he escaped. Come on. It's me, Cecelia, all gr-grown up now," she said, tears spilling from her eyes. "Come... come out and we'll talk about this. I'll get you some paper to write on or s-s-something." Oh, the tears came freely now, and she tugged off her helm, shook her head. Her hair bounced, short but frizzy as it had ever been.

And for a second, everything flickered. For a second, there was nothing there but darkness and green light, and Anise gasped.

"What is this?" Graves said, pushing in to put his back to Cecelia's.

"The master just stepped out of his slot," Anise said, and for once her voice wasn't tainted with cool malice. "But someone else stepped in before the dungeon could close."

"Dungeons close?" Graves narrowed his eyes.

"How do you think we seal them?" Anise said, looking around.

"Come out!" Cecelia shouted. "You have no idea how much I've mm-missed you all these years! It's not too late, we can talk this over!"

And after a moment, from under the door to her room, a light flickered on.

"Perhaps you'd better come in," An even, calm voice said. "We have a lot to talk about."

Anise started forward, then hissed in anger as Cecelia's gauntlet fell on her shoulder. "Listen, and listen well, daemon," Cecelia said. "You don't touch Threadbare. I just want you to know that if you try to harm him in any way, shape, or form, I WILL kill you or see that you spend all eternity with the worst punishment I can inflict upon you."

"As you like," Anise shrugged her hand off, staring at her like a lion watching a housecat strut and hiss. "But I *will* keep my promise to you. By the time we leave this place, you'll be well on your way to being the person you need to be. With or without your permission. To be honest, I loathe your weakness and I want it gone so I can move on to more important matters."

Cecelia digested that, and the anger and disgust helped her focus her mind a bit. "I think this is the most honesty you've ever shown me."

"Part of me DID love you once." Anise smiled. "It took years to grind away that weakness. Then you turned into a teenager and it got much easier. Shall we?"

Pushing the arrogance of the woman-thing from her mind, Cecelia approached her room. The door swung open as she went to push it open.

And there, in a cluttered room, with her old drawings on the walls, and her old bed looming giant to the side, with toys strewn about and rendered exactly like she remembered them, was a table.

And around it, sat toys having a tea party.

"Beanarella," she said, staring at the little stuffed doll. "D-dracosnack," Cecelia managed, looking at the little green plush dragon that had survived so many battles. "Loopy," she sighed, at the fuzzy giraffe, much larger proportionately now, in this dungeon of memories and sweet pain.

"Threadbare," she finished, staring at the toy, the smallest one in the room.

He wore a red coat with mismatched buttons, and an apron under it, and baggy pants that looked ridiculous on him. But she recognized the scepter and the toy top hat, the very same one she'd given him here, in this room, at this table, so long ago. And Cecelia wailed then, overcome as she sank to the floor and sobbed, arms open wide as the little bear ran to her and hugged her, hugged her tightly. Golden light flared, and her minor injuries closed, and she picked him up and cried into his fur, cried for everything she'd lost and everything she'd done, and sobbed until she couldn't anymore.

Purring at her side then, and she looked up through a veil of tears, to a black feline face and yellow eyes. The ears were wrong somehow, but that purr...

"Pulsivar?" She whispered.

And then he was licking her tears away, and rubbing his face all over hers, and she laughed and held him to her breastplate, held them both, and the anger and sorrow and bitterness that had filled her and buoyed her to this point drained away like pus from an infected wound.

"I'm going to vomit," Anise announced behind her.

"No Inquisitor, you're going to shut the hell up and let her have this," Graves said, and Cecelia giggled, absurdly, breaking her sobs as they wound down.

She had friends now. New and old. She'd been so lonely, for so long... but now everything could be fixed.

"I missed you, Celia," Threadbare said. "I was so worried for you."

"I'm sorry. I'm... I thought you were dead. The sword... I looked up and you were pinned and you weren't moving, and then they backed me into a corner and I couldn't see. I wondered, later. I thought you had more hit points, but they told me the house burned, and I didn't know if you made it out, and I tried Wind's Whisper a few times just in case, but I didn't have much range—"

"Shh." he said, patting her lips with the teacup he still held in his left hand.

She giggled, as she remembered how he'd done that, long ago. Then, collecting herself, she put him down.

"Hm," he said, looking down at his snot and tearstained coat. **"Clean and Press."**

"Your grandfather left behind a toy teddy tailor to... do what, exactly?" Graves asked. "Forgive me, I'm honestly a little confused by this whole situation."

"He's more than that," Cecelia whispered. "Much more. We ran dungeons together. Well, a dungeon, anyway. Which... how?" She gestured at the house-shaped world around them.

"It's a very long story. Would you all care for some tea? It's mostly real." He pointed to the table.

"Erm." Graves said, glancing at her.

"Appraise," Cecelia said, looking the setup over. She didn't think he'd poison her, but this place was strange, and golems might not be used to things like the vagaries of human digestive systems. "It's tea. It'll restore a little sanity, that's all."

"Tea parties are good for that, I find," Threadbare said, settling into his chair and laying his scepter on the table. "You taught me that one early on."

"They are," she giggled, as Pulsivar licked her face again, then gently nudged him away. "Gods you've gotten big. Wait, you're a bobcat?" She blinked. "You weren't a bobcat before."

"He ranked up in the years after everything went bad," Threadbare said. "I did too. My head's bigger now. Evidently that's a cave bear thing."

She shook her head as she took her seat. Graves settled in next to her.

"I'll pass, thanks." Anise shook her head. "I'm really here for one thing only."

"Which is?" Threadbare asked.

"I'll tell you if it comes up."

"Fair enough, I suppose."

"It never is." Cecelia drank her tea. "So. You can talk now."

"It took a lot of work and tailoring. I figured out how to make voices. My chest is full of strings and other things. And then once I could speak I could say things like Status, and all of my skills and spells, and life got a bit easier. In some ways." The little bear took off his hat, and rubbed his head. "I guess it's more complicated now, too. So it's not much easier. It's just that I've got more ways to handle problems, if that makes sense."

"That's how life goes, I'm afraid," Cecelia said. "We all have to grow up, and do things we don't like."

"Oh. I don't know about that," Threadbare said. "I like helping people, and saving them. And that's mostly what we did tonight."

Graves frowned. "Helping people like old ones cultists? Saving innocents by feeding them to blasphemous gods?"

"Graves—"

"No, listen, I know he's a teddy bear, but those cultists were feeding kids to whatever was in that stone circle. Still are, maybe. How's that jive with your helping people thing, Mister Threadbare?"

"Oh, that. That's a misunderstanding. They're not feeding the children to the old one, they're taking the ones with his bloodline home so the soldiers don't kill them all."

"They're not being eaten?" Cecelia blinked.

"No. They're all half fishpeople, the ones that are going to wherever the old one is. They'll meet their distant relatives and swim forever in lightless seas. It sounds a bit damp to me, but they seemed eager enough. Well, considering the alternatives..."

Graves and Cecelia looked at Anise. "You left out the fact the kids were fishmen," Cecelia said.

Anise scowled. "They were all wearing robes and I couldn't get close. For the love of Cron, I'm not always trying to fuck you over. Although it's rare, I can make mistakes too."

Threadbare continued. "That's all the old one wanted. He was never going to come here. Too weak to do it. But the last high priest of the cult lied, and manipulated the villagers into thinking he was. Which is why they rose up against the Crown." Threadbare considered his tea, pretended to sip it. "We killed the high priest and showed everybody the truth, but the army was on the way and it was too late."

"You could have explained it," Cecelia said.

"Could we really?" Threadbare lifted his button eyes to look up at her. "The King's laws are clear. Death to any settlement that embraces the old ones or other unsanctioned cults. He destroyed Taylor's Delve for less than that., and there wasn't even a cult there. Why would the army stop and listen? They never have before."

"That was rebels, who wiped out Taylor's Delve." Graves snapped. "They only blamed the Crown for..." he stopped, at Cecelia's expression. "Ma'am?"

"It's true," Cecelia said.

Graves chewed on that. Swallowed hard. "We're only at war with the dwarves because of Taylor's Delve. Now you're telling me that they're not lying? That they do have just cause? That we've seen thousands of our own die in this war because we started it?"

"It's... complicated," Cecelia said, avoiding his eyes. "My Father... he had to..."

"Why?" Threadbare said. "He got everything he wanted. He got Emmet and he got you. That was why he moved everyone in to fight Caradon. Well, not everything." Threadbare put his hat back on, and put the teacup down. "He didn't get the golemist job."

"Right," Cecelia said. "Which is why he needed grandfather alive, which is why I bargained for his life! It was the only way!" She said, and the teacup shook in her hand. "I had to be good, I had to do what he say, and be who he needed me to be, so Caradon would live! I had to... I had to." She finished, her voice breaking. "I still have to."

Threadbare looked at her. Then he looked down. "You don't know."

And slow horror filled her. She knew, she knew, in the back of her mind she knew what he was going to say, and she knew that it would unmake her. That her life would come tumbling down, and nothing would ever be the same again. "Don't," she whispered.

Threadbare took a breath. "Celia, Caradon's dead. Your father killed him."

The teacup shattered in her gauntlet.

Warm tea spilled over the table, and she stared, feeling her eyes burn, but no more tears came. She stared over Threadbare's head, and the last hope that she'd had died with the little bear's calm, even words.

"Mrrow?" Pulsivar pushed his head against her again, insisting, and she put her arm over him, hugged the cat tight.

"He lied to me," Cecelia said.

"He twisted his words," Threadbare said. "I'm smart enough to see that now. He promised he wouldn't hurt him, and that you'd see him again. He fed him numbing powder so he didn't feel pain, and figured you'd end up in the same afterlife. Then he killed Caradon, and used a cultist trick to try and steal Caradon's jobs. But he didn't realize I was still alive. And that I was in Caradon's party."

"Ah, is that what happened?" Anise said. "My my, how unfortunate."

"You knew. Of course you knew," Cecelia said, Pulsivar freezing motionless below her as the girl's voice filled with hatred. "And he DID lie to me. He said Grandfather had escaped custody, two years ago."

"Oh. No, he was with me then. Very dead." Threadbare said. "I was busy getting myself free from that sword. And the rubble of the house."

"I didn't know, precisely," Anise said, hands behind her back as she paced around the room. "But it was one of the plans we discussed, if the old man proved reluctant to give up his secrets. Really, we couldn't leave him as a loose end, Cecelia, surely you see that. For the good of the kingdom, the King cannot tolerate treason. Even from his relatives."

"He lied to me!" Celia shouted, rising, drawing her sword. Pulsivar growled and backed away, and Threadbare stood as well, putting his teacup to the side and picking up his scepter. Graves looked to the both of them, and glanced back to the skeletons.

"And? What does it change?" Said Anise, turning to stare at her with those black, black eyes. "This kingdom burns, Cecelia. It burns with chaos and anarchy, slipping out of control with every day that rises while our enemies still live. Enemies like this one, standing before you." Anise gestured to Threadbare.

"I... you're right..." Cecelia whispered. "I've seen..."

"I haven't seen much," Threadbare interrupted. "But I talked to people who have. It seems to me that the King creates the enemies he goes to war against. The war with the dwarves happened because he killed everyone in Taylor's Delve, when he didn't have to at all. And the only reason the cult rose up against him here is because they were sick of heavy taxes and their children all being conscripted."

"It... we do good. We do good things. The Crown does," Cecelia said. "We brought down a corrupt nobleman."

"You brought down a corrupt nobleman, ma'am," Graves said. "Point of fact."

"Watch your words, little man," Anise murmured, smiling at him.

He blanched, then rallied. "Well, speaking my mind got me kicked out of one job. What's one more?"

"Shut up," Cecelia told her. "You tried to get me to kill Mordecai."

"And you set him free instead. By all rights you should be rotting in his cell as a traitor," Anise sighed. "But Melos has a blind spot when it comes to you. You're his perfect little angel. The good queen-to-come, who will fix everything that he's turned to blood and shit. The untarnished successor, who will bring honor and truth and peace back to the kingdom." Anise laughed, and her scorn rang from the walls. "He doesn't see just how much he's screwed things up. No, it'll be all you can ever do to keep afloat, my dear. You'll scrabble and you'll fight and watch your subjects die and writhe in torment over and over again, for the rest of your life, because the alternative is a dead valley, and corpses stacked to the skies. This is your destiny, Cecelia." Anise extended her hand, nails gleaming red in the dungeon's off-kilter light. "Are you strong enough to take it?"

Cecelia looked to Anise. She looked to Graves, who had his shield out, and she knew his hand was on his sword's hilt, under it. "I trust your judgment, Ragandor."

She looked to Pulsivar, who sat under the table, tail lashing, eyes narrowed as he stared at Anise.

And she looked to Threadbare, who stared back at her.

"What should I do?" She whispered.

"I love you, Celia. I'll love you whatever happens, whatever you decide." Threadbare told her. "Now that I've found you I'll never leave you again. Not if I have any choice in the matter. But..." he looked out the window. "I don't think you're going to be happy if you do what your father wants you to do. If you try to be who he wants you to be."

"My happiness doesn't matter," Cecelia said. "Not when you balance the lives of everyone in this kingdom against it."

"It does matter," Threadbare said. "If you don't want to rule them, you shouldn't rule them. How can they be happy if their queen never is? Is the King happy?"

"No." She said, closing her eyes. "He hates it. He hates every day of this."

"Like you would, if you took the job."

"Yes," Cecelia said, and her heart throbbed within her chest, as a final sob forced its way out of her throat. "Yes!"

"Then don't take the job if you won't be happy. Celia, I want you to be happy. Nothing matters more to me."

"This kingdom will burn if I don't."

"Then stop it from burning." Threadbare said, walking around the table, to stretch his paw out to her. "You don't have to be a ruler to do that. We saved everyone here who was innocent, because the ones who were guilty atoned and laid down their lives to buy them time. Because we helped them see what was right. And that was just me and my friends. Think of what we can do together! You don't have to do it alone, either! I've made so many friends, and some of them are people you know, too. Some of them still are your friends, Celia. We all want to help you. We want to help you so much..."

Celia's sword quivered in her hand. She looked to Anise, smiling, with eyes colder than the space between the stars.

Then she looked to Threadbare, mouth quivering, eyes black and made of buttons but more expressive than most human eyes she'd stared into.

"You've never lied to me," she told him. Then she glared at Anise. "You have."

And casting her doubts to the wind, she grasped Threadbare's paw.

Casting the last five years, the training, throwing everything away, duty and fear and the confused tangle of emotions that was her father and all of that, away, she took up the paw of her oldest, truest friend, and raised her blade against the demon.

Graves' sword rasped as he drew it, and he fell in next to Cecelia. The skeletons shifted to block the door. "This is treason, you know," he told Cecelia.

"I know," she said, and sighed as her code of chivalry broke. Thirty-two points down from all defenses, at a really inconvenient time. "Sorry."

"Eh. I lost my fiancee to the dwarves," Graves said, glaring at Anise from under his helm, the skulls on his pauldrons writhing in response to his cold anger. "I pledged allegiance to a realm that doesn't deserve it. So I figure it's only fair if I take it back."

Anise clapped her hands, gently. "Bravo. Happy ending. Except oh, there's one little loose end, isn't there? The nasty old daemon." Anise smiled. "Do you know why he pacted a succubus, using his dead wife as the vessel? Do I have to spell it out for you? Not that he's had much free time to enjoy those benefits."

"You shut up about him. You've twisted him all up, driven him mad," Cecelia said. "All for your own amusement, fiend."

"Me? Driven him... Ha!" Anise slapped her thigh. "Oh, you have no idea how fucked he truly is, and how much worse it'll be for him and everyone else, soon. On the shoulders of the king, the world rests. When he falls, so does this miserable little land." She sneered. "This situation wasn't his doing, and he tried to stop it, but he was just weak enough and here I am. Along with all the others."

"Others..." Graves said. "The Hand?"

"If you're looking for the part where I confess all my evil plans because you're going to die anyway, look again. Most of you are going to die here, but I think a couple of you could make it out if you really tried hard. So I'll shut up now." Anise reached up and they flinched, as she put her hair through a scrunchy, making a ponytail of it. "Shall we?"

"You're very confident," Threadbare said, spreading out to the right, as Pulsivar faded back into the shadows under the bed, readying for a pounce.

"No, I truly don't care. Fifteen years I've been stuck in this miserable shell, fighting the willpower of the last vestiges of Amelia fucking Gearhart, trying to break free so I can finally have some FUN. If your father hadn't been so rushed with the Pact I wouldn't have been able to do even that, so thank Vhand for small favors there."

They looked at each other, across the room. Each of them knew that the first command, the first skill invoked would set off violence.

"Tell me this, at least," Cecelia said. "Is there truly nothing of my mother left within you?"

"A few childhood memories. Makes this house painful, slows me down a bit," Anise said. "I've managed to grind down the rest. Make room for new experiences. New jobs."

"Wait. Demons can't take jobs!" Graves burst out, and for the first time he sounded worried.

"First Pact daemons, no. Imps, hellhounds, no. Second Pact daemons? It takes a while, but yes, yes we can."

"That goes against every bit of lore that—" Graves shut his mouth.

"That we told you." Anise said, grinning. "Or implied through skillful omission of the truth. Oh, I love my passive skills, they make you people forget to question things you really, really should."

"And your job is..." Cecelia asked, staring, feeling the tension balance on a knife edge.

"Well, my main one is cultist, actually." Anise winked at her. "High enough to cast the Second Pact, finally. Remember how I told you how I would make sure you became the person you needed to be?"

Then she moved, faster than she'd ever moved before, faster than Cecelia had thought she could; A burst of motion, too fast to process, an impact that exploded against her chest like Reason's sword against the gate, an impact that SHOULD have sent her flying backward but didn't, and her breastplate broke open like cardboard, as Cecelia felt her limbs go numb.

She looked at Anise's face, inches from her own.

And she looked down, to see the daemon's arm disappearing into her breastplate.

And through her chest.

Her sword clattered to the ground. She couldn't feel her fingers anymore.

"I really only need two parts of you to do that, Cecelia," Anise told her, and kissed her gently on the lips before grabbing her neck and tearing and Pulsivar was howling and Threadbare and Graves were shouting, but they were too late, too late by a hot, horrified second.

...and Cecelia died, with her head and heart in Anise's hands.

CHAPTER 12: THE DAEMON'S DEADLY DANCE

"No!" Threadbare's voice was last in Graves' hoarse yell.

"She's got Silent Activation! She's fully buffed! Pile on her quick!" The death knight followed his own advice, stabbing at the daemon as his skeletons charged her from behind. Pulsivar pounced from the side, and with her arms still tangled around and in Celia's corpse, Anise blocked frantically, turning Graves' blade aside with the girl's armored corpse.

But Threadbare had other priorities. Shoving down his sorrow, biting back his rage, and keeping his head despite the pain, he knew what he had to do. **"Speak with Dead. Soulstone.** Celia, get in here quick—"

It shattered, and his paw went with it as Anise somersaulted over Graves and kicked his arm off. Threadbare flew back, bounced off the wall, and coughed in shock as a red '64' rolled up from his shoulder.

Your Golem Body skill is now level 24!
CON +1
Your Toughness skill is now level 18!
Max HP +2

Anise whirled as Pulsivar's claws raked her back, and hissed as a red '32' rose up. She spun in place, lashing out with one heel in a sweeping round kick, and the cat cried out in pain, knocked backward.

"She's a glass cannon!" Graves yelled. "Keep on her!"

Threadbare didn't know what a glass cannon was, but he was pretty sure he'd seen Pulsivar straight up murder soft targets before, and Anise sure as heck wasn't one.

"Mend Golem," he said, and as his arm dissipated from the floor and reappeared, he snapped his scepter out to face her. **"Harden. Flex. Self-Esteem. Guard Stance. Bodyguard Pulsivar!"**

And THEN he launched himself into the fray, just as she shook

Cecelia's body to the floor, her hands still full with her grisly trophies.

"Oh, if you could have seen the look on your faces," she sneered, dodging like a champion, and taking down the three skeletons with three fast scissor kicks. Pulsivar danced around and she feinted at him, then slammed her heel into Graves' chest, so hard that he grunted. A red '24' floated up.

Then she turned to Threadbare, ducking under Graves' retaliation. He waved the scepter at her. "Nice toy," Anise purred. **"Disarm,"** she snapped, her bloody hand blurring down and punching it free from his grasp.

"I don't need it!" Threadbare yelled, and charged her, claws swiping. "You murderer!"

With Celia's head she fended off Graves' blade, and she laughed as she hopped easily over Threadbare's swipes.

But eventually, one got through.

Your Brawling skill is now level 34!

Your Claw Swipes skill is now level 23!

Your Weapon Specialist skill is now level 16!

A red '17' rose up, and Threadbare frowned. Her flesh was tough, tougher than humans were supposed to be.

And every time he succeeded against her, he gained a stat or a skill. With the full power of his intelligence, and a rising dread, he knew what that meant.

She was way, way stronger than he was.

He'd kind of gathered that, from the way she'd killed... killed... He shoved that from his mind, and fought harder.

Then as she tried to crush Pulsivar's spine with a quick stomp, he found himself moving, lightning fast.

Your Bodyguard skill is now level 7!

Was all the warning he had, before she smashed him to the ground, knocking his hat free.

But he had no bones to break, or organs to squish.

Your Golem Body skill is now level 25!

He clawed her ankle for the trouble, in the split second before she hopped away.

DEX+1

Your Brawling skill is now level 35!

Your Claw Swipes skill is now level 24!

Your Weapon Specialist skill is now level 17!

It hurt him more to realize how weak he was against her. How he'd failed Celia in the clutch. If he'd spent the last two days training, instead of making golems and helping the town prepare, then maybe, maybe...

but no. There was no time for regret. He'd gained levels, lots of them, but they'd all been in caster jobs, for the most part. All he had combat wise were raw bear levels and his duelist tricks.

So why fight her like a warrior?

He rolled to his feet, as Graves rained down Dolorous Strikes, and Anise parried with her forearms, catching the flat of the blade and knocking it away, hands still full of her gory prizes.

Time to get creative.

"Soulstone—" he started, then switched words. **"Animus!"** he yelled, and though he wasn't fast enough to dodge, that wasn't the goal.

Her shoe met his paw, and the damage was worse this time, but it didn't matter. He'd cast the spell, and touched the target. That was his goal, and it was worth the soulstone's destruction, and his arm hanging by literally threads.

He staggered back, holding it on. **"Invite shoe!"**

Your Animus skill is now level 35!

Anise paused, a strange look on her face, then she gasped as her now-conscripted footwear constricted.

The strength of an animus is influenced by the creator's will, and enhanced by the Creator's Guardian buff. In Threadbare's case, this was pretty considerable. Bones cracked, and a red '97' rose up. More damage, smaller red numbers from behind as Graves and Pulsivar pressed the advantage.

Your Creator's Guardians skill is now level 26!

But Anise was strong, very strong, and had tricks of her own. **"Flexible Stance!"** she called, and twisted out of the shoe with a quick boneless hop and kick, then kicked her other shoe free for good measure, backflipping onto the giant bed.

"Animus!" Threadbare yelled, slapping the sheets, **"Invite sheets!"**

"Ah ha ha ha ha no," Anise said, squirming free with a quick movement, and hopping on one foot up to the bedpost, perching on it, balancing on her unbroken appendage and sneering down at them. "Probably the most amusing part of this? You seriously think you have a chance! Let's have some music for the shattering of your hopes and dreams! **Dark Chant!**"

And an unholy wailing arose from nowhere, a wailing chorus, as dark, deep music swelled and pulsed.

"Cron, Cron, Vhand Syncd, Cron, Cron Vhand Ypbind!"

The music skirled and gnawed, but not at their sanity, as the old ones' dark chant did. No, it targeted their moxie, and Threadbare felt his courage slowly leaking from him.

"We have to shut that down or she'll play keep away until we're quivering wrecks!" Graves yelled, as green numbers fled upward from his skull. "Do you have anything, bear?"

"What is she, exactly?"

"A daemon!"

"Then I've got *this!*" Threadbare said, rummaging in his pockets until he found the sole twist of green reagent that he'd been keeping since Taylor's Delve. **"Ward Against Daemons!"**

Your Wards skill is now level 2!

He slammed his paw to the ground, and the powder traced into arcane sigils, stretched out to trace patterns over the room...

...and the music slowed, and faded into a bare murmuring that they could safely ignore. Anise, on the other hand hissed in pain as red '1's started to curl up from her. "Fine!" She spat.

And that's when Pulsivar pounced. He'd spent a precious twenty seconds leaping up to the bed and creeping through the covers, going after the woman who'd murdered his kin. With a Caterwaul that failed to yank any sanity at all from her, he struck, raking his claws down her back—

—and coming up short suddenly, as she twisted, caught his throat, and grinned. **"Transfer Wounds,"** she told him.

Pulsivar howled as his foot cracked, his back exploded into pain, and he twisted free. That was one of his lives down.

Anise cast him aside, then put her formerly-wounded foot down, with a sigh of relief. But the gnawing of the wards continued, and she smoked faintly as her flesh burned.

"Clever. And I don't have anything with me to dispel that right now," she said, casting a frown at Pulsivar's limp form, and at the animated sheets that were moving him to safety, handing him down to Threadbare.

"Innocent Embrace!" Threadbare said, hugging his friend.

You have healed Pulsivar 120 points!

Your Innocent Embrace Skill is now level 13!

Anise rolled her eyes. "Pathetic. Well... not so much. You've lasted longer than I thought you would." She hopped down, dodged the sheets. "I was hoping you'd go down as easily as that mewling bitch did. But then, I DID use my tier two job skills on her." She waggled her hands and blood dripped from their contents. "And now I don't have to waste moxie with silent activations."

Graves inhaled sharply, and the color drained from his face. "What! Tier two? Oh no." He looked at the remnants of his skeletons. **"Bony Armor!"** he said, as the few unbroken bones flew up to replace the cracked ones overlaying his armor.

"Crane Style! Focus Chi to Feet!" she called, and hopped away from the still questing sheets, grinning. "Oh, and **Drain Life!**" she yelled.

Pulsivar screamed, as black energy crawled over him, scarlet blood flying from him to the daemon.

"No!" Threadbare said, as the cat fell, a glaring red '123' exploding up from the feline's body. Another life down.

But his tail twitched, and he was still in Threadbare's party screen, still alive, so the little bear kept his cool. The focus was Anise. Anise had to die. Only then could he help Pulsivar. Only then could he save Celia. Save her soul, even if her body was gone.

"Drain? I can do that too!" Graves yelled. **"Drain Life!"** and he pulled bloody health back from Anise, who hissed and changed directions to land next to him. **"Shield Saint!"** Graves yelled, blocking a flurry of vicious kicks, that struck with a force they hadn't had before. His shield and armor dented and buckled every time they hit square on, and Threadbare raced to try and take some of the pressure off of him. But how?

Healing Pulsivar was out. The cat was faking death, and healing his friend would just draw attention to him. The bobcat's hit points were no match for Anise's damage potential, if she shifted her aggression to him.

No, he had to keep her busy until the gnawing damage of the ward did its work. **"Animus Blade!"** he yelled, flipping his dagger into the air and diving towards the fight. Sneering, Anise dodged easily...

...but she wasn't his target. **"Innocent Embrace!"** he called as his arms wrapped around Graves's armored calf.

You have healed Herbert Graves 130 points!
Your Innocent Embrace Skill is now level 14!

Anise managed to kick the dagger out of the air, wasting a few seconds. "Ah, Crane Stance is no good for finishing things quickly. Can't Tiger Stance, because, well, my hands are full. Of your little girl. Awww... too soon?"

"Shut up!" Threadbare yelled, finally losing his cool. **"Drain Life!"** Black energy stretched toward her... and failed.

"Woops. Looks like you need more practice," Anise said, advancing on them. "And I know your weakness, little bear. I've been studying your breathing, every time you speak."

He put his hand on his mouth—

And the daemon whirled, plucked up the dagger she'd de-animated between her toes, and sank it to the hilt in his chest with a single twisting toss, nailing him to the wall.

He coughed, surprised, and no sound came out. *My voice box! She's cut it!*

"And so you end this, silent and helpless, just like you were so many years ago. Now, then—"

"Drain Life!" Graves shouted, and she shrieked as it tore a red '54' from her. "Will you stop!" She screamed, and leaped after him.

No, Threadbare thought. *Not this time! I won't be helpless again!* And with a mighty push, and a ripping that tore him from throat to gut, with a red '252' spilling from his body, he heaved himself from the wall. Stuffing sprayed, and oh, it felt wrong.

Your Golem Body skill is now level 26!

CON +1

STR +1

Your Toughness skill is now level 19!

Max HP +2

Anise sneered, and started toward him—

—and stopped, as he ripped two beads from where they'd been hidden in his blingy chain, and smashed them to the floor.

You have been healed for 119 points!

You have been healed for 125 points!

Threadbare's front zipped back up, the stuffing wisped back into him, and inside, in his throat, he felt whole once more.

Threadbare took a breath. "Testing. Yes, I thought someone might try that at some point." He had one mend golem bead left, but didn't think it prudent to tell her that. "Now where were we?"

For just a second, she seemed worried. For just a second, her face twisted as she realized what she was up against.

Then, reality flickered, and kept flickering. Anise and Graves paused. "Oooh, the master's stepped out," Anise cooed. "You realize that your last chance to run is now? Thirty seconds, and this dungeon will be gone. Then you'll have nowhere to hide." She slammed her foot into Graves again, shattering his shield and sending him back with repeated kicks.

"No," Threadbare whispered. *Fluffbear can't come in here! She's far too weak to handle Anise right now!*

Truth be told, he wasn't sure he could handle her. Not at all.

"Corps-a-Corps!" Graves yelled, and suddenly, to everyone's surprise, he was shoving her against the wall, blade pinning her leg by the ankle.

She blinked at him.

"Get her please!" Graves howled.

Threadbare came in on one side, and Pulsivar stirred himself, leaped in on the other, ripping into her toughened flesh.

And she laughed.

"Getting in close with a succubus? Unwise. **Dark Kiss,**" She whispered, and then she leaned forward, and wrapped her arms around Graves, flipping his visor open with her teeth and kissing him full on the lips.

With a moan, he withered, flesh shrinking against his bones as he toppled with a crash of armor that was now much too heavy for him—

—and just as he fell, so did the dungeon. Pulsivar retreated, and Threadbare leaped onto Graves. **"Innocent Embrace!"**

Nothing happened.

Whatever was wrong with him, it wasn't something healing could fix.

"Time's up, darlings," Anise smiled, turning to see who had arrived to challenge her. "Now where's that dungeon's... master..." she trailed off as a small figure appeared, leaping from the shallow water of the cove.

"Heavens Blade! Holy Smite!" Squeaked Fluffbear, and with a howling, thoroughly unhappy Mopsy bearing her forward, charged the daemon with everything she had. She rode past, gouging her glowing dagger along her ankle, sending a red '43' up.

But Anise didn't move.

Anise turned, staring drunkenly at the little black bear, who reined in Mopsy and glowered up at her. "Leave them alone!"

"You... you..." Anise said, shaking. "No... how... no... Amelia!" She roared, her voice mingled with something inhuman and deep, bellowing, filling the chamber, "You fight me on THIS, Amelia? This TOY! You... I..." She fell to her knees, and blood pattered out of her eyes, bloody tears spilling onto the sand of the dark cove under the church.

"Fluffbear," A woman's voice said, hissing from Anise's throat. "Her name is Missus Fluffbear. And you can't HAVE her!"

Threadbare stared.

For a second, he was tempted. For a second, he though they might be able to end it, here and now. Could he? She was tough, but if she was paralyzed...

She's not paralyzed, his common sense told him. *And hitting her might snap her out of it.*

WIS +1

And then, to his great relief and horrible guilt, a voice resounded in his mind.

"I'm safe! Graves has me!"

"Celia. Oh Celia, I'm so sorry.."

"Run! Run before she kills you!"

"What she said!" Kayin yelled, from her own soulstone.

"We're leaving!" He yelled to Fluffbear. "Go!" He gathered up his dagger and scepter, stowed them.

"But I have to—"

"Go!"

Anise stretched out a trembling hand as Mopsy carried the little armored teddy bear up the stairs, followed by a very done Pulsivar, who'd lost all the lives he cared to tonight, thank you very much.

For his part, Threadbare ran to Graves. "Can you run?"

"No..." Graves held up a hand, trembling, with the glow of full soulstones leaking from within his grasp. "Take them and leave me!"

"No. No one else dies!" Threadbare decided. "Can you hold your breath?"

Behind them, the demon screamed in two voices, but the strange one was already fading.

"Yes?" Graves said.

"Good! **Animus! Invite Armor!**" Threadbare slapped his breastplate, and under his mental directions, the suit rose and ran into the surf, with Threadbare clutching Graves' hand and the precious cargo they'd nearly died to protect.

"Amelia, you stupid bitch," Anise hissed, voice breaking, warbling as she rose, panting, to her knees. "You only delay the inevitable. And as for you—" she turned her head to the toys, and the withered death knight...

...and her eyes widened as she saw only ripples in the dark water of the cove.

She stood, wincing at the damage she'd taken. At least the dungeon's destruction had dispelled those damnable wards. "You got lucky!" She bellowed. "Run! You have nowhere to go! I'll find you, and when I do..."

Anise smiled, looking down at the body parts she'd successfully kept intact, throughout the fight. "I won't be alone," She finished, looking down at Cecelia's pale, surprised face. In her other hand, the princess's heart beat its last.

Underwater, mere dozens of meters away with Graves holding his breath as best as he could as his newly-animated armor carried the crippled Death Knight along the bottom of the lake, Threadbare heard the daemon shout, and only now, with the danger gone, did he sag in defeat.

He would have done anything to have spared her this.

Threadbare had failed his little girl, right when she needed him the most.

And yet... he hadn't lost. Not entirely.

CHAPTER 13: AND YET SHE PERSISTED

The hunter's cabin was deep in the marsh, long abandoned, and well-shielded from the sight of the town. Which is why it had been a drop-off point for the reagent smuggling trade, back when Catamountain had still been in existence.

Graves and Threadbare emerged from the shallows near the shack, to find the place quiet. Too quiet.

"It's..." Threadbare spat the last water from his voicebox. "It's me. This armored guy is a friend, too."

"T'ank goodness." Zuula said. "Dreadbear. Fluffbear and cats tell us what happened. We sorry. We so, so, sorry."

Threadbare hopped down from Graves' shoulder, and held up his paws. Two soulstones glittered between them. "We're not all lost. Do we have any yellow reagent left?"

"About ten vials."

"Good. Good... I..." He sagged. "I don't know what else to do," he whispered.

And then Fluffbear and Zuula came out of the deep shadows by the shack and hugged him, and Threadbare sobbed, gasping, tearless eyes staring into the night. He couldn't cry but he could try, and in time it made him feel better.

"Erm," Graves said. "My helm's at a bad angle and it's very dark here. What exactly is going on?"

Threadbare glanced back the way they came. The swamp was thick here, in this little inlet off the lake. Nonetheless, he patted Zuula and Fluffbear until they backed away, then strolled up to the side of the cabin away from the lake before saying **"Glow gleam."** His hat lit up, and he dialed it down until it wasn't blinding, and put it on the porch. **"Clean and Press."** he threw in, cleaning the water from it, and getting rid of his own dampness as well.

Inside the shack, Pulsivar and Mopsy looked up from a serious nap session, and glared at him. Did he have no consideration for the hard work they'd done tonight?

To the side, Annie Mata's cart lay, with the tailgate of the wagon open and a crate stacked high with glimmering soulstones on it.

"Alright dudes!" A cheery, burbling voice called from the shore. "I think that's the last of— whoa! A soldier!"

"Friendly!" Graves wheezed. "I'm friendly! Don't shoot!"

"He okay, Dreadbear say so," Zuula confirmed.

"You can talk now?" Threadbare glanced over, as the fishman doll stepped from the shadows. Made of wood, stuffed with ejectable stones for ballast, and with leather air bladders that let him submerge and rise with a bit of work, the fishman they'd taken to calling Glub had adjusted well to his new existence.

"Yeah. Got tired of you and Fluffy having to do that deadspeaky thing. I leveled when I was trying the thing with the boats. Turns out bards get another borrowed skill at fifth level, so I stuck this thing called "Knack for Languages" into it. I'm runnin' it now, it's totally baller."

Glub had never had an adventuring job option before, and had liked the notion of being a bard the most from what he'd unlocked in his old life. Which was fortunate, as his rejuvenating song had helped Threadbare regain sanity faster while they prepared the defenses and evacuation of the town.

And his aquatic nature and darkspawn trait made him the perfect fit for the last part of plan 'nobody dies permanently.'

"Dese de last? You sure?" Zuula asked, taking the soulstones from him.

"Yeah. Hey, did Garon and Mads make it back?"

"No. They're in the stones somewhere. I hope," Threadbare said. "We need to check. **Speak with Dead.**"

Immediately a hubbub of voices erupted from the crate, and Zuula's arms. She sighed, and hopped up on the tailgate, and chucked the stones in with the rest.

"Please, please, one at a time," Threadbare said. "Garon?"

"I'm here."

"Madeline?"

"I'm heah."

Graves started, and his armor rattled. "Mads? From Rack Street?"

"Herbie? Holy shit! Little Herbie, all grown up!"

"Wait, you know each other?" Threadbare rubbed his head.

"Yeah! Back when I was tryin' ta blend in with Cylvania City's nahtlife, my gang had this little kid that ran errands for us. Somewahn's brother. Smart kid, for a street rat. Now heah you are, all... ooh. What happened, man?"

"Long story. A daemon kissed me. And from what my status screen tells me, it looks like it's a curse. My strength's currently a three."

"Oof. Dat bad," Zuula said. "Can't do nutting for curses. Need a cleric, 'bout twenty level or so. Or Oracle. Or wait until daemon remove curse."

"I don't see that happening, I don't think," Threadbare said.

"Hello?" Celia's voice asked, and the toys froze. Threadbare buried his face in his paws. "Zuula? Garon? You're here too?"

"Yes," Zuula whispered. "Yes child, we are. Dreadbear, what is dis? How..."

"She was the one in the steam knight," Fluffbear squeaked. "Threadbare thought her voice was familiar, but we didn't know until the fighting got in the town. And we heard the soldiers yelling about Captain Ragandor."

Garon spoke up. "Yeah. We had to try to talk to her. Mads and I gave up on the divebombing runs and we pulled back to the church so Threadbare could set up the neutral ground, try to defuse the situation. Then that fucking assassin came out of nowhere."

"Sorry about that, by the way," Kayin spoke up. "If it's any consolation the little nasal one and the cultists there did for me, too."

"She's with me," Graves added, hastily. "Or rather we're with Dame Ragandor. Inquisitor Layd'i turned on us. She was the daemon that cursed me."

"You're the one that got me? Eh, it was war, no hard feelings," Garon said. "That body had problems. Dragon wasn't for me, as it turned out. No matter how powerful it was."

"Now me, on the othah hand..." Madeline said, musing.

"Body?" Kayin asked, confused.

"Yeah, we'll all get new bodies!" One of the soulstoned villagers shouted. "And be born again, for real, not like Hatecraft's lies!"

"Yeah!"

"Right on!"

"Fuck yeah!"

"Easy, easy, please," Fluffbear squeaked. "We have to tell the new ones about the deal, to see if they want to do it, too."

"Deal?" Cecelia asked, warily. "I've had about enough of deals for the next few years. Too many daemons."

"I've found a way to put soulstoned spirits into golem bodies," Threadbare explained.

The clearing filled with silence, save for the muttering of the happy ex-cultists.

"Holy shit," Graves finally gasped.

"Is it better than being a knife for all eternity?" Kayin asked.

Graves eyes' glittered in his withered face. "Yes. Most hauntblades and wraitharmors eventually go mad. But if you're talking a body with full manipulation, sensory abilities like a golem could provide, and a voice for ease of socialization... wow. That has possibilities."

"You know something about this?" Threadbare perked up.

"A little. There are these guys called Spirit Mediums that are supposed to operate in those areas, but I never got high enough rank to have the clearance to learn about them. That knowledge is in the very restricted section of the archives."

"I've unlocked that, but I can't take it. I think it's to do with golemist and necromancer."

"From the rumors I heard, either animator and enchanter are viable combos with necromancer to unlock it. I was going to go enchanter, anyway, at some point. If you tell me how you did it, then I might be able to learn that job for you, help you out with this."

"And why would you do dat?" Zuula said, frowning at him. "You was killing some of dese people not too long ago," she pointed at the crate of soulstones, some of whom were murmuring angrily.

"Yes, and I'm sorry. We thought they were going to call up the old one, and that they were sacrificing children. Your little bear friend set us straight. And when the Captain turned on the Inquisitor, I turned with her. I'm an enemy of the Crown now, the same as you."

"And the Crown has to stop," Cecelia decided. "Stop killing its own people, stop helping daemons,stop driving entire towns to rebellion, stop these senseless wars that it started. It has to stop the lies, and it won't unless WE stop it."

That got cheers from the assembled spirits.

And for the first time since he'd failed, Threadbare felt hope rising in his heart. He opened his mouth, closed it, and decided to ask the question that he hadn't dared to ask before. "Will... will you let me put you into a new body, Celia? Will you stay with us, and help us save everyone?"

"Of course, you silly bear!" Cecelia said. "I just got you back, there's no way you're getting rid of me so easily!"

Threadbare sagged in relief.

He'd done it.

She hadn't lived through the process, sure, but he'd saved Celia.

And with a soft chime, Caradon's last gift to him unlocked, and he became nine thousand, four hundred, and sixty two experience points richer.

You are now a level 13 Greater Toy Golem!
+2 to all attributes!
You are now a level 14 Greater Toy Golem!
+2 to all attributes!
You are now a level 15 Greater Toy Golem!
+2 to all attributes!

You are now a level 12 Cave Bear!
CON+10
WIS+10
Armor+5
Endurance+5
Mental Fortitude+5

You are now a level 8 Enchanter!
DEX+3
INT+3
WILL +3
You are now a level 9 Enchanter!
DEX+3
INT+3
WILL+3
You are now a level 10 Enchanter!
DEX+3
INT+3
WILL+3

You have unlocked the Boost +10 skill!
Your Boost +10 skill is now level 1!
You have unlocked the Disenchant skill!
Your Disenchant skill is now level 1!
You have unlocked the Spellstore X skill!
Your Spellstore X skill is now level 1!

You are now a level 6 Duelist!
AGI+3
DEX+3
STR+3

Threadbare sighed in relief, feeling his pools refill. And with a slightly sharper mind, the massiveness of the tasks ahead of them came into focus.

"This won't be easy," he said. "We'll need all the help we can get."

"We'll go to the dwarves," Cecelia said. "In this case, the enemy of my enemy really IS my friend. Beryl named me a clan friend, remember?"

"I think that was before she knew you were the King's daughter," Garon pointed out.

That stunned the muttering and talking villager spirits into silence.

"I've studied the dwarves. That doesn't matter. A debt like that has to be paid, regardless," Cecelia said. "I was planning to try and use it to forge a fair armistice after we'd beaten them, but this is even better. And if I can offer to montage some of their people into steam knights, then that's something else I can use to sweeten the deal. They've been trying to figure out the unlocks for those jobs for years."

"Won't work," Garon said. "The best bodies Threadbare can stick us in are toy golems. And whether it's the golem or the soulstone, whatever the case, we only get one adventuring job when we come across."

"And one crafting job," Madeline added. "I picked up jewelah in town, but didn't have time ta grind it. Might be that I can turn soulstones into haiah level crystals. Get us to wood gahlems, or what was that one you just unlocked yestaday, beah?"

"Clay," Threadbare confirmed. "That one takes a level two crystal and a green reagent. I just used the last of that though, I'm afraid."

"Well, you've got two people ready and willing to experiment right here," Garon said.

"Three," Kayin added. "Although I'm okay with being a toy, if I have to. You gave me some ideas when you killed me, little miss bitey."

"Heh. I'd say ya had good taste, but eh, I got no tastebuds, so tha joke doesn't quite fit no moah."

"If you can make me a spirit medium, I'm pretty sure that will help with the process," Graves said, thinking it over. "I'll need a montage or two."

"Four," Threadbare decided. "Do you have that many job slots open?"

"Just exactly. Knight, Necromancer, Death Knight... yeah, four. Why four?"

"Death Knight?" Squeaked Missus Fluffbear. "What does that do?"

"I'll tell you later."

"I want you to be a golemist too," Said Threadbare. "It's the way I got the unlock for Spirit Medium and I don't know the other ways. And until we can get you uncursed, animator will let you animate your own armor so you can walk around and do things on your own. And this way, if I die and you survive, you're a golemist so maybe you can make sure I have a new body to come back to."

"Oh. Shoot, that's a good idea." Graves blinked, and looked down at the little bear. "Yeah, you're the Captain's teddy, all right."

"Four montages, four days." Cecelia mused. "Where are we, precisely?"

"Three montages," said Threadbare. "I can't montage spirit medium, I don't know that one. But the unlock is simple enough that I can show him how."

"More like two days," Zuula said. "Toys and undead spirits don't need to eat or sleep or none of dat."

"But I do," Graves pointed out. "Uh... I'll need someone to hunt for me and scrounge up drinking water."

"No problem man," Glub said. "I'm good at that stuff."

"We out in middle of nowhere, Celia," Zuula said. "Across de lake. Take dat army a week to get here, unless dey got boats and know where dey going."

"No and no," Celia said. "My troops weren't outfitted for a long pursuit anyway, and I'm assuming that those boats with wheels were the last ones in town?"

"They were," Glub said. "Amphibious assault craft!"

"Was that your idea? That was pretty clever," Graves said. "Also can I sit down now?"

"Oh, yes, sorry. Here." Threadbare directed the armor to sit, and smiled as he sat down, with Celia in his hands. "I'll let you rest for a bit, and when you're ready we can start the training."

"I'll need to sleep and eat. It's been a long day." Graves said, wearily. "Talk to me in the morning."

"Well while they're montaging, there's a few things we can do," Cecelia said, making the most of the situation. "I'll need you to fill me in on everything you know about the current situation, the King, Anise, and by the way who are you Madeline? I don't think we've met but you sound familiar somehow?"

"Heh! We did, actually, but it's been a few years. See, I was actually hiding out pretty close to yah house, and we met one naht when Mordecah took ya out inta tha woods..."

Threadbare walked into the rotting old shack as they chatted, put his back to Pulsivar, and rested. The big cat grumbled, and curled up with him, and Mopsy took his other side. Tails thumped, and he petted them, listening to his little girl's voice as she planned, and plotted, and caught up with old friends.

She sounded happy, and that was good enough for him, good enough right now.

The little band of friends had much to do, but that would come later. For now, though the night had almost been disastrous, they'd forged a somewhat happy outcome from it regardless.

And that was enough.

DAEMON'S QUEST: THE WOMAN SHE NEEDS TO BE

Arusheluxem sighed, as she looked around the chamber. The iconography was of the blasphemous spawn of the outer darkness, the chaos from ancient times, when everything was far more, well, basic. Before Konol had done his thing, and then obligingly died. Making it about the one and only time the gods had ever been useful.

It was all wrong for what she needed to do, but she had neither the time nor the resources to hand to formalize the matter.

Fortunately, the nature of the being she was calling lent itself to utility over appearances, a concept distasteful to her own preferences.

Anise Layd'i. It made her smile, whenever they called her that. It's what she used on her status screen, these days, now that her Conceal Status skill was up to decent levels. It had taken a little bit, once she'd been summoned, to unlock the cultist job and grind it to the point where she could reliably hide her status from the various means of viewing it. A trick which she'd have to help this new spawn master in short order.

First things first. The succubus laid the head down on the slimy mattress, then deposited the still-beating heart below it. Weaker now, but still fresh enough for her purposes. In fact... yes, she had time. **"Occult Eye,"** she murmured, and blinked as the world shifted to her view. An easy cultist trick, one that identified adherents of the same faith, and flagged objects of occult significance. In this case, she'd used it because it made artifacts of forbidden lores and the planes above and beyond, glow to her sight. Then she strolled back to the cove, looking for what had been left behind, when the cowards fled.

And she found it.

Minutes left, she gauged, returning to the room where a high priest had once indulged his kinks at the cost of his follower's time and efforts. She gathered her thoughts, cleared her mind, and checked her sanity. Good enough, she wagered. It had mainly been moxie and endurance burned during that farce of a fight. If she hadn't had her hands literally full... ah. Regrets. She'd kill them later, she or one of the others.

"I invoke the Second Pact. The forbidden knowledge, offering the heart and mind of the mortal mob Cecelia Ragandor-Gearhart, as sacrifice to call forth a Hellsmith of the second circle, forging darkness to my desire. These are the terms of the pact, in the true tongue;"

She cleared her throat, and began the lengthy process. Clarity was vital here, even a single missed syllable or accent could have disastrous repercussions.

Fortunately, being a daemon, she was fluent in her native tongue.

"Ent mayne, par an the seas ent arg sea, come ah, char twin stars arg vee, par an thesis bracketa..."

It felt good to speak the true tongue once more, the one that bent the mind, and drove daemon cultists to caffeine and insomnia, pouring over ancient texts time and again, to ensure that they had the commands inlaid correctly.

And as she spoke, the air thickened around the severed parts of the girl, Cecelia.

It was a mistake, to think that daemons cared about souls. They didn't. The plane they came from was seen as a place of torment, where mortal souls suffered eternally. Anyone who truly knew anything about daemons knew that was a lie. Daemons didn't LIKE mortals, certainly not enough to spend eternity with them. No, the true aim of daemons was a world where they didn't NEED to do anything on this layer of reality. Empty. Silent. With no rogue variables blundering about, and nothing interrupting the major processes that they were charged to oversee.

No, daemons had no use at all for souls.

But brains? Those had memories. And hearts? They were symbolic, more or less. And tricky to recreate, much easier to recycle.

The succubus spoke and red energy pulsed up from the heart, its torn arteries stretching and growing, spreading out to flop upon the mattress, sprouting veins and capillaries as they went. One stretched upward, seeking like a snake, before slamming home into the severed throat of the head, in a manner that would have made Reverend Hatecraft reach for his lotion.

The head opened its mouth and screamed, unendingly, a scream that only grew louder as lungs formed, and the rest of the organs followed.

Through it all Arusheluxem droned on, hitting each syllable with precision, feeling her sanity slip away bit by bit, taking her focus with it.

That was the trap of the pacts, more or less. They cost the very thing you needed a lot of to get them right, and failure had consequences. Nothing too horrible, usually, assuming you had the power to confine a rogue daemon, and the time to work through the pact, fixing the errors that you had made the first time around. But not everyone DID have the time and power, and so the end result was pleasing to the rogue daemons who could escape or regain their own free will, even to a limited degree.

She came to the end, as the skin formed, and Cecelia's nude shell stopped screaming, and opened its eyelids for the first time. For a second nothing was there but blackness, darkness from a plane mortal mobs were never meant to touch. Then she blinked, and Cecelia's eyes replaced it.

"**...named Gshantatrixem,**" Arusheluxem finished. "**Bound by my will!**"

"Inefficient," the new daemon said, clambering to its feet. "Human form, insufficiently mature. Messy hormones. Good musculature structure." It frowned. "No augmentations. Permission to self-improve?"

"Denied," Arusheluxem told it. "You are playing the part of a woman called Cecelia Ragandor-Gearhart."

It stared at her, contemptuously. "I am not skilled in subtlety and deception. You should have called a Deceiver."

"Fool. I have my reasons. You are the last part of a plan over a mortal decade in the making. You will NOT endanger my plans or I will see you suffer when we return to the branch of Var Rhun."

The new daemon's eyes went wide. "You know of... wait." It studied her. "You appear mortal, and you pacted as one, but you are a daemon as well... this defies logic."

"The meddlers gave the mortal mobs too much power. Power they did not secure from us." The being known as Anise smiled at the new spawn. "I have taken four of their... jobs... as my own." She'd nearly taken a fifth, before finding out that model wasn't necessary, because some of her succubus skills overlapped in just the right way. "You will learn two, perhaps more, before we leave this place."

"I am a Hellsmith," the daemon appealed to her. "I ALREADY know what I need to know. I can build you war machines, great bombs and guns, gasses and shells to taint the land and slay your foes. I can augment your flesh with cold armor and hot weapons to smite down your foes. That is my purpose. Why do you wish me to pretend otherwise?"

"You'll get to do all that too," Arusheluxem smiled. "And let me show you what your host used to drive around in." She grabbed a dirty sheet from the back of the room, threw it around the daemon spawn's nudity, and had it hold the cloth shut.

Dark, when they got out. Dark in a way that neither daemon truly cared about. And watching the new spawn's eyes light up and jaw drop when it... she... saw Reason, made the jaunt worthwhile.

"Passable," the Hellsmith declared, stalking around Reason, touching the legs of it, studying the gears and joints and engine. "Ah... yes. Room for improvement. Definite room for improvement. Solid base, though. Yes, I find this acceptable. For now."

"Can you work it?"

The Hellsmith snorted. "Please. This is easy. I'll need some flesh, some tools worth a damn, twenty meters of steel wire, six corpses worth of sinew, a few copper rods, some bell jars, and two brains for backup failover processors. Wait. Coal? They wasted a chassis like this on a coalburner? Seriously? Tch. Torment would be easier. Liquified, refined, about seventy proof and I'd get this baby screaming. Literally."

"It has to look the same from the outside," Arusheluxem cautioned. "For now, at any rate. Later we won't have to hide."

"What happens later?"

The creature called Anise looked around. Renick had left a token garrison, by the sounds of patrolling boots, and the distant torchlight moving around town, searching, ensuring that everyone was truly dead. Too many ears. "Come inside. You'll need to stay in here anyway for a bit. I'll see about arranging a knight and an animator to montage you." Arusheluxem decided, pushing the reluctant Hellsmith away from drooling over Reason, and back to the church. "I'll have to spin a cover story but that's no big deal for these mouthbreathers. But in a day or two you'll be on your own devices for a bit, so I need to make sure you're ready before I go."

"Go?" The newly-pacted daemon blinked at her. "Where are you going?"

"I'll be off to deliver the good news to a pathetic king, that his shitty little kingdom gets to keep existing for a little while longer..." She reached into her pocket, and pulled out a red crystal, that glittered with green numbers, flashing endlessly in the night.

"That's—"

She whipped her fingers to the Hellsmith's mouth. "Ah ah ah. They call them Dungeon Cores, here. And most people have never seen one."

"Cores? That's entirely backwards." The Hellsmith frowned.

"Yes, and oh, I love them so for coming at it in such a backwards way. We wouldn't be in this juicy, ripe situation if they hadn't..."

KING'S QUEST: TORMENT

His existence was green light, entirely green light, and that was how he knew he was in his true body when he woke from unexpected sleep.

In a place beyond worlds, in the wreckage of his hopes and dreams, with his dead, dismembered friends lying all about him, Melos the first, King of Cylvania opened his eyes.

In the castle beyond, the projection that was him, but not him, laughed heartily and stalked the halls, looking for adventurers to fight. Clenching his eyes shut Melos exerted his will, groaning at the effort, until finally the thing that was better than his id but worse than his ego returned to his quarters. Painstakingly he tripped the wards and circles that would keep it in place for a few hours, let him get some semblance of rest.

It had found its way out once or twice before, when he'd succumbed to exhaustion. When he'd been weak, and foolish enough to think that he could risk sleep deeper than a fitful slumber.

The first time it had happened, he'd woken to find his blade in King Garamundi's stomach, with a room full of horrified servants looking on.

And weeping, knowing there was no help for it, he'd had the projection cut the servants down rather than risk witnesses. The damage had been done, though, and no one believed his stories of an assassin. Balmoran had seceded a year later, prepared for war, and he couldn't honestly blame the man.

At least Melos could honestly say that he hadn't killed the king. He'd gotten very good at mincing words, over the last decade and a half.

But either way, he couldn't let this dungeon's master copy run free. No. No, he'd taken precautions since then. Gone without sleep. Balanced sanity on a knife-edge, which was hard, because you didn't regain any, while you were in the green light. Not unless you were asleep, not a bit otherwise, not any other pool either. Buffs didn't work, healing didn't work, bardsong didn't work, nothing. He'd had to kill the bard afterward, too. Pity, the man had been a decent level and a loyalist. But no one could know, no one could ever know, until everyone was safe again.

Sanity. What was his? He couldn't say status, not in here. Not in any way that worked.

He braced himself and stepped through the veil of light. **"Status,"** he croaked, and winced at the number. He'd need to sleep again soon.

Above him, the numbers pulsed, and words flashed up, broken, skewed, seventeen different versions of the same message, informing him that the master was out of his slot, and needed replacing.

"I know," he said, feeling around at the table that Anise had left him. "I know!" he screamed, finally finding the bottle she'd left, ripping the cork free, and drinking the contents in three hasty gulps. He'd forbidden her to poison him or give him anything disgusting, but the week, watery beer was scant help. He'd have to sleep soon, and gods help him.

With seven seconds to go, and his bladder aching, he stepped back into the column of green light, gasping as his mind shifted, and the world blurred. The wards were undamaged, he saw. Perhaps his alter ego would be cooperative for once. Perhaps he could sleep, get the rest he needed.

"Nice try," he told himself. "Never. Never trust you."

He nodded off regardless, came to. Checking his projection's surroundings, he shrieked in horror. The thing had his armor off, was halfway out the window, with a manic grin on his red-bearded face, and the green holes in its torso showing clearly for all to see. Fortunately it was dark, and nobody seemed to be around. But the wards on that entire wall were gouged, sparking, broken. Days to redo them. Reagents that would need requisitioning. How long had it been? How long had he managed to sleep?

Melos stepped outside, wincing as his brain throbbed, as the veil grasped it like it always did. **"Status,"** he whispered, and he stared in horror at his sanity.

"No," he whispered. "So little. So little so little so little back. So little…" As the world throbbed, and his head bloomed with ache, he cried, just a bit. He needed to drink again, and he felt blindly back to the table—

—and felt his gauntlet close on flesh. A hand. A hand he knew all too well.

"Anise," he said, retreating to the green. "Report, I'm listening." Then it was in through the barrier, and watching as the thing that wore

Amelia's face moved to stand in front of the column, fearful and worried.

"Milord," she said. "Your daughter has won her first great battle, but there were consequences."

Melos' eyes snapped open. Mute, unable to speak, he stared out of the light. But he let his fury show, and she quailed to see it. He could punish her later, through the projection. He'd done that before, hurt her, done worse to her, until she'd learned.

Learned to lie better, anyway, the shattered remnants of his common sense whispered in the back of his mind. Or was that his guilt? He didn't know. Couldn't know.

"I tried to keep her safe! But... the cultists. She lost sanity, when she explored their sanctuary." Anise took a breath. "Cecelia lost her jobs. I brought in some trusted cohorts, to reteach her the basics. They're doing it even now. She tells me she can pilot the Steam Knight suit, so no one should ever know."

Melos closed his eyes. When the tears stopped, he opened them again, and stepped out of the column.

"My lord?" Anise said, stepping back.

"You swear to me that you had no hand in this? That you didn't wipe her mind?"

"I never affected Cecelia's sanity, I swear." Anise held up her hands. "She won the battle. The old one is no longer a threat in that area, nor ever will be again."

With the seconds ticking by, with a growl of frustration that was half a sob, Melos fled back into the column, then out again, resetting the count. Anise offered him a roll, and he ate it, wincing at the staleness, as she continued.

"There is one windfall from this," Anise said, and Melos gasped as she held up a new dungeon core. Only a minor one, but still, but still...

He tore it from her hand, ran to one of the filled columns, one of the ones labeled "LOOT." He clawed at it, reached in and pulled a burned black crystal from its plinth, and replaced it with the red dungeon core. Immediately it lit up brighter, the numbers flashing in its depths cycling up, going into overdrive and vibrating in the enclosure. A strange energy pulsed from it, green numbers flashed overhead, and some of the tear overhead seemed to mend.

It wouldn't be enough, he knew. Not for long. Not even for a year. But it would buy time, and that was what he needed right now. He took a look around at the other columns, sprinkled throughout the black space. Of the sixteen other filled loot columns, fourteen of them held burnt cores.

He lost a precious second then, to self-pity, as reality pulsed.

"Teach her quickly!" He yelled, throwing himself back into the Master's column. In there for only a few seconds, just long enough to make sure it registered, then out again. "Teach her quickly. Get her back up to speed. Crush the dwarves. No more traitors."

"I did execute a few, in the town. I hope you don't mind that I attended to that personally."

"I don't care."

She smiled, and her posture unbent a bit.

He knew she'd screwed him over somehow. But he didn't care, couldn't care. The daemon continued, glancing around the room, at the other four columns that held figures. "I could more efficiently crush your foes if you let the rest of the Hand out. They've spent too long as mid-bosses, it can't be good for their health."

"No," Melos rasped, staring at the faces of his dead friends, their nude forms hiding the daemons inside them, trapped in green light for eternity. "No, but you can have the golem. Have Emmet, like we discussed. It's time for Amelia Gearhart to return to the world. Talk to me in the castle." Then it was back into the column, to reset the count, and closing his eyes again.

Resting them. Just resting.

He knew she was smiling. Knew she was sneering. Knew that she'd surely screwed him over in some petty, spiteful little way. He'd never had the time to properly review the pact, never had time to iron out the details. How could he, when he only had thirty seconds and passing through the column disoriented him each and every time?

When he opened them he saw her leaving, heading toward the hidden door, picking her way over the dismembered bodies. Past the throne, broken and sparking, where once all the loot columns had channeled their energy, past the apparatus that Grissle had made long ago. Past HIS corpse, the only intact one left in the room.

Things didn't rot here. Didn't change. Didn't fade.

It was immortality, of a sort. And by the gods he'd scorned, it was a horror he'd never be free of. Not until his daughter was ready, not until he had someone he could trust, someone the traitors hadn't twisted, to share the burden. One day she would be ready for the truth, and then they could trade off, take turns in the column that supported all of his reality, all the reality that Cylvania had ever known for the last fifteen years.

And perhaps, someday, they'd find a way to fix it.

Be strong, Cecelia. Endure. Fight hard, but never lose your heart. The hardest part is yet to come, thought the damned king, as he went back to his torment.

EPILOGUE

Once upon a time, there was a teddy bear whose little girl had died. But he wouldn't let her go, and he knew that their story was far from over. He had much to do, so he said **"Status"** to check himself, and this is what he saw.

Name: Threadbare
Age: 5

Jobs:
Greater Toy Golem Level 15
Cave Bear Level 12
Ruler Level 11
Scout Level 7
Tailor Level 11
Model Level 8
Necromancer Level 11
Duelist Level 6
Animator Level 12
Enchanter Level 10
Golemist Level 12
Smith Level 10

Attributes   Pools   Defenses
Strength: 124 Constitution: 138 Hit Points: 330(410) Armor: 52(59)
Intelligence: 216 Wisdom: 201(208) Sanity: 417(545) Mental Fortitude: 42
Dexterity: 135(142) Agility: 112(126) Stamina: 257(358) Endurance: 62
Charisma: 110(145) Willpower: 199 Moxie: 309(424) Cool: 20(47)
Perception: 107 Luck: 89(96) Fortune: 196(283) Fate: 15(22)

Generic Skills
Brawling - Level 35 (+8)
Climb - Level 13
Clubs and Maces - Level 9
Dagger - Level 9
Dodge - Level 8
Fishing - Level 1
Ride - Level 8
Stealth - Level 13
Swim - Level 5

Greater Toy Golem Skills
Adorable - Level 30
Gift of Sapience - Level NA
Golem Body - Level 26
Innocent Embrace - Level 14
Magic Resistance - Level 7

Bear Skills
Animalistic Interface - NA
Claw Swipes - 24
Forage - 13
Growl - 2
Hibernate - 37
Scents and Sensibility - 20
Stubborn - 8
Toughness - 19

Ruler Skills
Appoint Official - NA
Emboldening Speech - Level 16
Identify Subject - Level 10
It's Good to be King - NA
Noblesse Oblige - Level 26
Organize Minions - NA
Royal Audience - Level 17
Simple Decree - Level 8
Swear Fealty - NA

Scout Skills
Alertness - Level 2
Best Route - Level 2

Camouflage - Level 2
Firestarter - Level 4
Keen Eye - Level 5
Sturdy Back - Level 6
Wind's Whisper - Level 5

Tailor Skills
Adjust Outfit - Level 4
Clean and Press - Level 13
Recycle Cloth - Level 1
Tailoring - Level 51(65)

Model Skills
Call Outfit - Level 1
Dietary Restriction - Level 40 (+80 to all pools)
Fascination - Level 4
Flex - Level 16
Makeup - Level 3
Self-Esteem - Level 16
Strong Pose – Level 5
Work it Baby - Level 40

Necromancer Skills
Assess Corpse - Level 12
Command the Dead - Level 28
Deathsight - Level 8
Drain Life - Level 1
Invite Undead - Level 12
Mana Focus – NA (+11% to sanity)
Soulstone - Level 45
Speak With Dead - Level 20
Zombies - Level 3

Duelist Skills
Challenge - Level 4
Dazzling Entrance - Level 8
Fancy Flourish - Level 7 (14)
Guard Stance - Level 8
Parry - Level 6
Swashbuckler's Spirit - NA (+13 to cool)
Swinger - Level 2
Weapon Specialist - Level 17 (Brawling +8)

Animator Skills
Animus - Level 35
Animus Blade - Level 10
Animus Shield - Level 4
Arm Creation - Level 7
Command Animus - Level 19
Creator's Guardians - Level 26
Dollseye - Level 18
Eye for Detail - Level 20
Magic Mouth - Level 10
Mend - Level 40

Enchanter Skills
Appraise - Level 30
Boost+5 - Level 9
Boost +10 - Level 2
Disenchant - Level 1
Elemental Protection - Level 8
Glowgleam - Level 26
Harden - Level 28
Soften - Level 30
Spellstore I - Level 9
Spellstore V - Level 1
Spellstore X - Level 1
Wards - Level 2

Golemist Skills
Clay Golem - Level 1
Command Golem - Level 10
Golem Animus - Level 46
Golem Guardians - NA
Invite Golem - Level 11
Mend Golem - Level 15
Program Golem - Level 40
Toy Golem - Level 56
Wood Golem - Level 9

Smith Skills
Adjust Arms and Armor - Level 7
Refine Ore - Level 10
Smelt Down - Level 1

Smithing - Level 46

Equipment

Journeyman Tailor's Apron of fire resistance (+6 Armor, +10 Tailoring, Resist Fire 9)(+2 Armor, +4 Tailoring, +3 Resist Fire from WIB)

Baggy Pants of Hammerspace (+5 AGL, +5 CHA, Allows hammerspace for one blunt weapon)(+2 AGI, CHA, from WIB)

Okay Quality Bling

Ringtail Master's Coat (+5 CHA, +5 LUCK, +5 Armor, +5 Fate)(+2 CHA, LUCK, Armor, Fate from WIB)

Rod of Baronly Might (+5 CHA, +5 WIS, +10 Cool)(+2 CHA, WIS, +4 Cool from WIB)

Yellow Belt of Bravado (+5 AGL, +5 DEX, +5 to the Fancy Flourish skill)(+2 AGL, DEX, Fancy Flourish from WIB)

Toy Top Hat (CHA +10)(+4 CHA from WIB)

Inventory

A Finely-Made Dagger (Dagger Level 5)

Tailor's Tools

A small jewelry box with a few reagents and crystals, most minor.

1 bead of Mend Golem (Level 15)

Minorphone (Enhances voice and social skills focused through it twice per day)

Quests

Unlocked Jobs

Berserker, Cleric, Cook, Cultist, Grifter, **Spirit Medium,** Tamer, Wizard

APPENDIX I: Threadbare's Jobs and Skills

CAVE BEAR

Cave Bears are large beasts, tough and strong and stubborn. They eat pretty much anything organic and spend most of their lives underground, emerging to forage as needed. Bears gain experience by eating bear-associated foods, roaming their territory, and defeating foes with their natural weapons.

GREATER TOY GOLEM

Toy golems are the protectors of children everywhere! And also good, reasonably cheap guardians for any fledgling golemist. They aren't the toughest of golems, but they possess a few costly powers good for helping their charges survive. Like all golems, they're sturdy, resistant to magic, and immune to a lot of things that would kill living beings. Greater golems possess sapience, and attribute ranks that lesser golems simply do not have. They can even learn jobs! Limited in that aspect only by the intelligence of their crafter, greater golems have theoretically astronomical potential. Greater Toy Golems gain experience by doing adorable things, surviving conflict by toughing it out, and defeating foes using their natural weapons.

ANIMATOR

Animators give life to inanimate objects, awakening them to serve and defend the animator. Animators gain experience by casting animator spells and defeating foes with their animi.

DUELIST

Duelists fight with their chosen weapon and swashbuckle around, using mobility and attitude to win their fights. Duelists gain experience through fighting with their specialized weapon, defeating foes with panache and style, and doing risky, flashy things in dangerous situations. Note: Specialized weapons can be changed. Practice hard, your specialized weapon will shift to your highest weapon skill.

ENCHANTER

Enchanters are one of the oddest adventuring professions. They do most of their work beforehand, and use their items to devastating effect. Enchanters gain experience by creating magical items, casting enchanter spells, and using their created items to defeat foes.

GOLEMIST

Congratulations! Through blending Animator and Enchanter, you are now a golemist! Golemists craft unique magical constructs, and use them to fight their battles. Golemists gain experience by casting golemist spells, creating golems, and using their golems to defeat their foes.

MODEL

Models improve their bodies and attitudes, displaying their glory for all to see and controlling how others look upon them. Models gain experience by using model skills, successfully controlling first impressions, and defeating their foes through social maneuvering.

NECROMANCER

Necromancers raise the dead to do their bidding, and can negotiate with powerful spirits and undead entities. Necromancers gain experience by interacting positively with the dead, casting necromancer spells, and using the undead to defeat their foes.

RULER

Rulers entice people to work for them, and organize them through decrees and rewards to do their bidding. Rulers gain experience by having their subjects do their bidding, organizing others to a common goal, and looking out for the interests of those in their charge.

SCOUT

Scouts roam the wilderness, spying upon foes and using stealth and survival to accomplish their goals. Remember, be prepared! Scouts gain experience by using scout skills, exploring new wilderness areas, and remaining undetected by foes.

SMITH

Smiths work with metal, crafting objects with the help of a forge, anvil, and hammer.

TAILOR

Tailors work with cloth and occasionally other flexible materials, crafting objects with the help of scissors, needle, and thread.

GREATER TOY GOLEM SKILLS

ADORABLE

Level 1, Cost N/A, Duration: Passive Constant

Adorable has a chance of activating when you do something cute in front of an audience, or onlookers blame you for something that isn't your fault. It improves the attitude of anyone who fails to resist your charms.

BODYGUARD
Level: 10, Cost: 25 Sta Duration: 1 minute per toy golem level
Name a target party member when activating this skill. For the duration, you have a chance of intercepting each attack aimed at them, so long as you remain within two yards of them. Multiple attackers or overwhelming amounts of strikes may reduce the effectiveness of this defence.

GIFT OF SAPIENCE
Level 1, Cost N/A, Duration: Passive Constant
Congratulations, you now have all the attributes and can think and learn. Good luck with that. You also have 0/8 adventuring job slots open, and 2/4 crafting job slots.

GOLEM BODY
Level 1, Cost N/A, Duration: Passive Constant
Your body has no organs, and is made from inorganic or once-organic material infused with a magical force. By being exposed to effects that would kill or cripple living beings and surviving them, this skill will level up. As it levels up, you will gain immunity and resistance to a wider range of lethal effects.

INNOCENT EMBRACE
Level 5, Cost: Sanity equal to half the amount healed, Duration: Instant
Heals an embraced target 10 X the level of this skill. Will affect on other golems, is standard healing otherwise. Currently activated through Animalistic Interface, and will affect any legal target embraced. Does not affect uninjured targets.

MAGIC RESISTANCE
Level 1, Cost: N/A, Duration: Passive Constant
Has a chance of negating any non-beneficial magic cast upon you. The chance of success is dependant upon the spellcaster's level.

CAVE BEAR SKILLS

ANIMALISTIC INTERFACE
Level 1, Cost N/A, Duration: Passive Constant
Allows the beast to use their racial skills without requiring vocalization. All skills that are not constant passives may be turned on and off as the situation and instinct require.

CLAW SWIPES
Level 1, Cost 5 Sta, Duration: 5 attacks
Enhances the damage caused by your hands and feet, and adds the sharp quality for the next five strikes. Currently activated through Animalistic Interface, and will activate whenever you brawl with intent to injure.

DARKSPAWN
Level: 10, Cost: N/A Duration: Passive Constant
You gain a bonus to all attributes equal to twice your Cave Bear level while in darkness, and can see normally in darkness. Sufficient light will disrupt this effect, and the bonus does not increase the maximum size of the associated pools.

FORAGE
Level 1, Cost 10 Sta, Duration: 10 minutes
Greatly enhances your perception for the purposes of finding food, water, or other natural resources in the wilderness. At higher levels, may be used to locate specific naturally occurring resources. Currently activated through Animalistic Interface, will activate whenever you hunt for natural resources.

GROWL
Level 5, Cost 10 Mox, Duration: Instant
Growl at a target to damage their sanity.

HIBERNATE
Level 5, Cost N/A, Duration: 1-3 months
Go into a torpid sleep. Requires a cool, dark place and you cannot be affected by the Starving condition. Restores all pools to full, as per a normal rest.

SCENTS AND SENSIBILITY
Level 1, Cost 5 San, Duration: 5 minutes
Activates heightened smell, greatly increasing perception for that sense and allowing you to catalog and remember specific odors.

Currently activated through Animalistic Interface, and will activate whenever you encounter an interesting scent.

STUBBORN
Level 5, Cost N/A, Duration: Passive Constant
Increases your resistance to sanity damaging effects.

TOUGHNESS
Level 1, Cost N/A, Duration: Passive Constant
Has a chance of increasing whenever you take serious damage. Raises your maximum HP by two whenever it increases.

SMITH SKILLS

ADJUST ARMS AND ARMOR
Level 5, Cost 10 Sta, Duration: instant
Resizes any armor or weapons to fit the chosen wearer or wielder, and also allows minor alterations.

REFINE ORE
Level 1, Cost 10 Sta, Duration: Instant
Separates any usable crafting materials in a container or dirt, ore, or stone into neat piles of material.

SMELT DOWN
Level 10, Cost 25 Sta, Duration: 30+ Seconds
Breaks a metal item down into ingots of metal, and separates out any gems or other materials into a small heap nearby.

SMITHING
Level 1, Cost NA, Duration: 30+ seconds
Crafts the desired metal or mixed-metal-and-forgeable item desired, requiring different materials for each project and the presence of appropriate tools. Has a chance of failure.

TAILOR SKILLS

ADJUST OUTFIT
Level 5, Cost 20 Sta, Duration: Instant
Resizes any cloth outfit to fit the chosen wearer, and also allows minor alterations.

CLEAN AND PRESS
Level 1, Cost 10 Sta, Duration: Instant
Instantly cleans the selected item, and removes any wrinkles, stains, or other blemishes. Only works on items that are primarily textiles.

RECYCLE CLOTH
Level 10, Cost 25 Sta, Duration: 30+ Seconds
Breaks a cloth item down into bolts and patches, and separates out any leather or other materials into a small heap nearby.

TAILORING
Level 1, Cost NA, Duration: 30+ seconds
Crafts the desired cloth or mixed-textile-and-sewable-materials item desired, requiring different materials for each project and the presence of appropriate tools. Has a chance of failure.

ANIMATOR SKILLS

ANIMUS
Level 1, Cost 10+ San, Duration: 10 min/level
Turns an object into an animi, capable of movement, combat, and simple tasks as ordered by its creator. Must be in its creator's party to do anything beyond defend itself. The greater the size and mass of the object, the more it costs to animate, and the more hit points, strength, and constitution it begins with. The type of material also factors in, and determines the starting armor rating of the animi.

ANIMUS BLADE
Level: 5, Cost: 15+ Sanity Duration: 10 minutes per animator level
Animates a slashing weapon and grants it minor flight, causing it to move and attack on its own. It cannot venture more than a small distance from you, and will orbit you without taking action unless invited into your party. Its weapon skill is dependent upon your weapon skill, and its equivalent strength is dependent upon your will.

ANIMUS SHIELD
Level: 10, Cost: 20+ San Duration: 10 minutes per level
Animates a shield, that moves as if wielded by an invisible warrior. Must be in a creator's party to do anything beyond defend itself.

ARM CREATION
Level: 5, Cost: 10 San Duration: N/A

Teaches an animi a weapon skill that you know, allowing it to wield and use weapons that are manageable given its size and manipulative appendages. Lasts until the animi deanimates.

COMMAND ANIMUS
Level 1, Cost 5 San, Duration: Instant
Allows the caster to issue one command to an animi that isn't currently in its creator's party. If successfully cast, the animi will follow the command to the best of its ability until it is impossible to do so.

CREATOR'S GUARDIANS
Level 1, Cost N/A, Duration: Passive Constant
Enhances animi in the creator's party, boosting all attributes. The amount buffed is influenced by the animator's will and this skill's level. Has a chance of increasing every time a new animi first joins the animator's party.

DOLLSEYE
Level: 5, Cost: 5 San Duration: 10 minutes per animator level
Allows the animator to see through one of their animi. Lasts until the animi deactivates, or can be shut off at will. Occupies the sight capabilities of one of the Animator's eyes, so perception penalties and confusion may occur if both eyes are open at once. You cannot have more than one dollseye effect active for each functional eye your body possesses.

EYE FOR DETAIL
Level 1, Cost 5 San, Duration: 1 minute
Allows the animator to examine the status of any animi, golem, or other construct he looks upon. Also analyzes any object for animation potential and sanity cost. Can be resisted.

MAGIC MOUTH
Level: 10, Cost: 20 San Duration: 10 minutes per level
Allow the animator to speak through one of the animi currently in their party, regardless of distance. If the animi does not have a mouth, the voice issues forth from the closest approximate place a mouth would be on a living being of similar structure.

MEND
Level 1, Cost 5 San, Duration: Instant
Instantly repairs the target construct or object, restoring a small

amount of HP, influenced by the level of this skill and the animator's will.

DUELIST SKILLS

CHALLENGE
Level 1, Cost 5 Mox, Duration: Instant
Calls out a target to fight you. They suffer combat penalties based on your charisma unless they are actively trying to attack you. Resistible, because some foes are just too cool for you.

DAZZLING ENTRANCE
Level 1, Cost 10 Mox, Duration: Instant
Used before revealing yourself to foes, the more dramatic your appearance the better. Boosts your charisma and cool for a short time.

FANCY FLOURISH
Level 1, Cost 5 Sta, Duration: Instant
Unleash a fancy set of moves that won't hurt your foe but look really cool. Attacks their moxie.

GUARD STANCE
Level 1, Cost 10 Sta, Duration: Until dropped, or the end of the fight
Assume a guard stance, and gain a bonus to your dodge skill and armor, at the cost of lowering your strength and dexterity.

PARRY
Level: 5, Cost: N/A Duration: Passive Constant
While you have your specialized weapon drawn, you have a chance of parrying any melee attack you are aware of.

SWASHBUCKLER'S SPIRIT
Level: 5, Cost: N/A Duration: Passive Constant
Your Charisma buffs your Cool.

SWINGER
Level: 5, Cost: N/A Duration: One minute per skill level
Activate this skill to buff your agility and climb skill while swinging from ropes, chains, chandeliers, etc...

WEAPON SPECIALIST
Level 1, Cost N/A, Duration: Passive Constant

Enhances your weapon skill. Automatically assigned to your highest weapon skill. If you have two or more equal highest weapon skills, you may freely choose which to specialize in at any time.

ENCHANTER SKILLS

APPRAISE
Level 1, Cost 5 San, Duration: 5 minutes
Allows you to see all relevant information about a mundane or magical item.

BOOST +5
Level 5, Cost 25 San, Duration: Permanent
Enchants a magic item to boost an attribute or defense or magical effect by +5. Not cumulative. Consumes three doses of RED Reagents and a level 1 crystal.

BOOST +10
Level 10, Cost 50 San, Duration: Permanent
Enchants a magic item to boost an attribute or defense or magical effect by +10. Not cumulative. Consumes three doses of YELLOW Reagents and a level 2 crystal.

DISENCHANT
Level 10, Cost 30 San, Duration: Instant
Attempts to disenchant a nearby magical item that you have created or that you control or own. Breaks it down into reagents and crystals. Chance of failure based on skill and the complexity of the item, mitigated by intelligence.

ELEMENTAL PROTECTION
Level 5, Cost 50 San, Duration: Permanent
Combine with a dedicated boost to imbue a wielded or worn item with a field that disperses or absorbs elemental energy of the chosen type, sparing you some harm. Consumes one dose of ORANGE Reagents.

GLOWGLEAM
Level 1, Cost 5 San, Duration: 1 hour per level
Infuses any object with a simple light spell. The luminescence is based upon the caster's intelligence.

HARDEN

Level 1, Cost 10 San, Duration: 10 minutes

Increases the toughness of any object or construct temporarily, adding to its armor and/or damage potential.

SOFTEN

Level 1, Cost 10 San, Duration: 10 minutes

Decreases the toughness of any object or construct temporarily, reducing its armor and/or damage potential.

SPELLSTORE I

Level 1, Cost 10 San, Duration: Permanent

Prepares an object that stores a level 1 spell or skill inside of it. Anyone can then read, break, drink, or otherwise use the object in an appropriate manner to activate the spell. Requires and consumes one dose of RED Reagents. The enchanter does not have to be the person storing the spell inside the Spellstore.

SPELLSTORE V

Level 5, Cost 20 San, Duration: Permanent

Prepares an object that stores a level 5 spell or skill inside of it. Anyone can then read, break, drink, or otherwise use the object in an appropriate manner to activate the spell. Requires and consumes one dose of ORANGE Reagents. The enchanter does not have to be the person storing the spell inside the Spellstore.

SPELLSTORE X

Level 10, Cost 40 San, Duration: Permanent

Prepares an object that stores a level 10 spell or skill inside of it. Anyone can then read, break, drink, or otherwise use the object in an appropriate manner to activate the spell. Requires and consumes one dose of YELLOW Reagents. The enchanter does not have to be the person storing the spell inside the Spellstore.

WARDS

Level 5, Cost 50 San, Duration: Permanent until damaged or dispelled

Creates wards within an area against a particular creature type. Creatures of that type within the area are debuffed and affected with a damage-over-time effect based on the skill level. Magical effects created that are tied to that creature type may be suppressed or countered while within the area. Requires and consumes one dose of GREEN Reagents.

GOLEMIST SKILLS

CLAY GOLEM
Level 10, Cost 200 San, Duration: Permanent
Allows the golemist to construct a clay golem shell, which may then be baked or left unfired, as desired. Requires clay, 1 dose of GREEN reagents, and a level 2 Crystal.

COMMAND GOLEM
Level 1, Cost 20 San, Duration: 1 minute per level
Allows the caster to issue one command to a golem that isn't currently in a party. If unresisted, the golem will follow the command to the best of its ability until it is impossible to do so, or until the command wears off.

GOLEM ANIMUS
Level 1, Cost 50 San, Duration: Permanent
Turns a prepared golem shell into a functional lesser golem, that will obey its creator's commands to the best of its ability.

GOLEM GUARDIANS
Level 10, Cost NA, Duration: Passive Constant
Enhances golems in the creator's party, boosting all attributes. The amount buffed is influenced by the Golemist's will.

INVITE GOLEM
Level 1, Cost 10 San, Duration: Instant
Used to invite golems into your party. Automatically affects golems created by the golemist, can be resisted by other golems. Will not affect golems in their creator's party.

MEND GOLEM
Level: 5, Cost: 20 San Duration: Instant
Heals a golem for a moderate amount, dependent upon your intelligence and skill level.

PROGRAM GOLEM
Level: 5, Cost: 50 San Duration: Permanent until changed
Allows the golemist to give conditional instructions to golems under his control. The golems will follow these instructions until it becomes impossible to do so. The higher the skill, the more instructions can be given, and the more complex they can become. Some experimentation is

necessary for best results.

TOY GOLEM
Level 1, Cost 100 San, Duration: Permanent
Allows the golemist to construct a toy golem shell. Requires a toy, one dose of YELLOW reagents, and a level 1 Crystal.

WOOD GOLEM
Level: 5, Cost: 150 San Duration: Permanent
Allows the golemist to construct a wood golem shell. Requires wood, three doses of YELLOW reagents, and a level 2 Crystal.

MODEL SKILLS

CALL OUTFIT
Level: 5, Cost: 20 Mox Duration: Instant
Instantly summons one of your regular equipment sets from wherever it may be. The set must be kept together, and cannot include material heavier than leather.

DIETARY RESTRICTIONS
Level 1, Cost N/A, Duration: Until broken
So long as you have spent the last week without eating anything with the UNHEALTHY identifier you gain a small buff to all pools. This bonus is cumulative, up to twice your rank of this skill. Eating UNHEALTHY designated food immediately removes all versions of the buff.

FASCINATION
Level 1, Cost N/A, Duration: Dependant upon skill
Heal, aid, or otherwise be nice to an enemy in combat. If unresisted by mental fortitude, the foe will become temporarily fascinated with you, for a duration proportionate to this skill's level.

FLEX
Level 1, Cost 10 Sta, Duration: 1 minute per level
Buff your endurance and armor by the level of this skill.

MAKEUP
Level: 5, Cost: 10 Mox Duration: Until smeared or removed
Allows you to apply makeup that buffs any one of your skills. Form follows function, so the makeup must be appropriate to the job that

contains the skill being buffed.

SELF-ESTEEM
Level 1, Cost 10 Mox, Duration: 1 minute per level
Buff your mental fortitude and cool by the level of this skill.

STRONG POSE
Level: 5, Cost: 10 Sta Duration: 1 minute per model level
Buffs your strength. Only one pose may be active at a time.

WORK IT BABY
Level 1, Cost NA, Duration: Passive Constant
Whenever one of your worn or wielded items creates a favorable impression in at least one onlooker, then this skill has a chance of increasing. All worn and wielded items that confer bonuses have their bonuses increased by a small percentage for each level of this skill. Note that the difference is harder to see with lower level gear and lower levels of the skill.

NECROMANCER SKILLS

ASSESS CORPSE
Level 1, Cost 5 San, Duration: 1 minute
Allows the animator to examine the status of any undead creature he looks upon. Also analyzes any corpse for animation potential and sanity cost. Can be resisted.

COMMAND THE DEAD
Level 1, Cost 5 San, Duration: 1 minute per level
Allows the caster to issue a command to a single undead creature. If unresisted, the creature most follow its orders to the best of its ability. Can also be used to invite unintelligent undead into a party, at which point they can be verbally commanded indefinitely by the caster.

DEATHSIGHT
Level: 5, Cost: 10 San Duration: 5 minutes per necromancer level
Automatically tells you the number of hit points any creature you can see has left. May not work on level ???? creatures.

DRAIN LIFE
Level 10, Cost: 20 San Duration: Instant
Drains a small amount of life from a nearby foe and adds it to your hit

points. Will heal regardless of physical form. Does not affect certain monster types.

INVITE UNDEAD
Level: 5 Cost: 10 San Duration: 1 Hour per necromancer level
Invites the targeted undead to your party. Non-sapient undead who are not already in a party will automatically join if this spell is not resisted. Intelligent undead always have the option of refusal.

MANA FOCUS
Level 10 Cost: N/A Duration: Passive Constant
Buffs your sanity pool by a percentage equal to your necromancer level.

SKELETONS
Level: 5 Cost: 15 San Duration: Permanent
Animates one skeleton or skeletal fragment into a skeleton. Requires a spirit.

SOULSTONE
Level 1, Cost: 20 San, Duration: Permanent
Creates a soulstone crystal, which can house a newly-deceased spirit or an existing incorporeal undead. A spirit in a soulstone may be conversed with, used to create a new undead, or simply unleashed upon the world at a time of the caster's choosing.

SPEAK WITH DEAD
Level 1, Cost: 5 San, Duration: 1 minute per level
Allows the necromancer to converse with corpses, spirits, or normally incoherent undead. In places with particularly strong spirits, the caster may be notified of the presence of conversable spirits.

ZOMBIES
Level 1, Cost: 10 San, Duration: Permanent
Turns a corpse into a zombie. Requires a spirit present in the area.

RULER SKILLS

APPOINT OFFICIAL
Level: 5, Cost: 25 Mox Duration: Permanent until changed
You may appoint one official per ruler level. This official, who must be one of your subjects, may accept oaths of fealty, and add them to your

subject pool.

EMBOLDENING SPEECH
Level 1, Cost: 10 Mox, Duration: Instant
Buffs all allies moxie and sanity by an amount related to the ruler's charisma. Only affects allies within earshot.

IDENTIFY SUBJECT
Level 1, Cost: 5 Mox, Duration: 5 minutes
Allows the ruler to examine a sworn subject's status screen. May also be used on people within your party, giving more information than the party status screen.

IT'S GOOD TO BE KING
Level: 10, Cost: N/A Duration: Passive Constant
You gain a tiny fraction of experience whenever one of your subjects does. Experience gained from higher level individuals goes directly to leveling your ruler class. Experience gained from lower level individuals may only be utilized for King's Quest rewards.

KING'S QUEST
Level: 10, Cost: 20 Mox Duration: Permanent until changed
Decree a public quest. All your subjects within earshot may accept. Any who fulfill the quest reap the benefits of the quest immediately.

NOBLESSE OBLIGE
Level 1, Cost: N/A, Duration: Passive Constant
Buffs all sworn subjects and party members a small amount. The stat buffed is dependent upon your highest attribute.

ORGANIZE MINIONS
Level: 5, Cost: 15 Mox Duration: Permanent until changed
You may choose one quest shared among your party members or subjects. While on that quest and working toward that goal, they gain a bonus to all attributes equivalent to your ruler level.

ROYAL AUDIENCE
Level 1, Cost 10 Mox, Duration: 1 Minute per level
Buffs your charisma, but only when dealing with sworn subjects

SIMPLE DECREE
Level 1, Cost 10 Mox, Duration: Permanent until changed

Declare a simple command in twelve words or less. All sworn subjects are notified of the decree. Any who do not comply with this decree take moxie damage influenced by your charisma and wisdom, resisted by cool. Only one simple decree may be in place at a time. Simple commands may not be used to inflict suicidal or self-harmful activities.

SWEAR FEALTY
Level: 5 Cost: Special Duration: Permanent until changed
Any individual may swear fealty to you, spending five moxie while in your presence or the presence of any of your appointed officials. They become one of your subjects and are subject to many of your other ruler skills and effects.

SCOUT SKILLS

ALERTNESS
Level 5 Cost: N/A Duration: Passive Constant
Alertness has a chance to auto-activate all your sensory-enhancing skills for free in the event that you are ambushed or about to encounter unseen danger.

BEST ROUTE
Level 5 Cost: 15 San Duration: One hour per scout level
Activate while examining a visible terrain feature. Examines the best route from your current location to your destination, and marks it visibly. Everyone in your party can see the best route trail. The higher the skill, the better the route found. At high levels it will detect and detour around dangerous monsters and towards treasure and resources.

CAMOUFLAGE
Level 1, Cost 5 San/Min, Duration: Until dismissed or exhausted
Blends the Scout in with his surroundings, buffing their stealth skill. More effective in the wilderness, scales according to skill level.

FIRESTARTER
Level 1, Cost 5 San, Duration: Instant
Creates a fire, burning any flammable material it's used upon. Intensity of the starting flames depends on the skill level.

KEEN EYE
Level 1, Cost 5 Sta, Duration: A minute per scout level

Buffs a scout's perception, effects dependent upon skill level

STURDY BACK
Level 1, Cost NA, Duration: Passive Constant
Lightens the burdens of any heavy load carried, making items literally weigh less. Does not apply to weapons and armor equipped. Higher skill level means more weight reduction

WIND'S WHISPER
Level 1, Cost 5 San, Duration: 1 message
May be activated silently. Sends a message on the wind to any named target within range. Range and amount of words speakable per message increase with skill level.

NOTE: General skills are self-explanatory, and do not have activation costs or require explanation.

Made in the USA
Las Vegas, NV
18 June 2022

50420994R00177